# THE MARK TWAIN PAPERS

# THE MARK TWAIN PAPERS

# MARK TWAIN'S
# SATIRES & BURLESQUES

*Edited with an Introduction by*
*Franklin R. Rogers*

UNIVERSITY OF CALIFORNIA PRESS
*Berkeley and Los Angeles* 1967

University of California Press
Berkeley and Los Angeles, California

Cambridge University Press
London, England



Library of Congress Catalog Card Number: 64–24886

ISBN 0-520-01081-7

Designed by Adrian Wilson

Manufactured in the United States of America

Third Printing, 1988

# *Editor's Preface*

THE AIM of the editor has been to present a readable text which represents as closely as possible Twain's intention as that intention is reflected in his last revision of the various manuscripts. Inserted matter has been run into the text and, except for the more significant passages preserved in the textual notes, deleted matter dropped without overt indication. The editor has also attempted to perform those tasks which Twain expected the printer to perform, principally expanding all ampersands to "and" and in the Simon Wheeler play supplying italics in stage directions. Since it would serve no real purpose to retain them, the occasional misspellings have been corrected without editorial comment. And here and there, omissions in punctuation have been supplied. This is not to say that the text has been normalized or modernized: spellings and punctuation practices which may now seem archaic but which were perfectly proper in the nineteenth century—indeed, punctuation practices which one might call idiosyncratic—have been retained, and the text normalized only in the sense that an attempt has been made to correct obvious spelling errors and slips of the pen. In punctuation, correction has taken the form, generally, of completing the pattern already established by Twain. Almost habitually Twain failed to close parentheses and internal quotations. Frequently he failed to close primary quotations. In such instances the editor has supplied the missing marks without comment. Where there is no such clearly demonstrable error, no correction has been made. Only one substantial alteration in

Twain's punctuation has been made: to avoid confusion, Twain's square brackets have been changed to parentheses; square brackets have been reserved to indicate editorial comments or emendations.

# Acknowledgments

I AM DEEPLY INDEBTED to the late Mrs. Clara Clemens Samossoud and the trustees of the Mark Twain Estate with whose permission this selection from the unpublished manuscripts of Samuel L. Clemens has been assembled. I am indebted as well to Mr. Henry Nash Smith and to Mr. John D. Gordan, curator of the Henry W. and Albert A. Berg Collection of the New York Public Library, not only for their part in the arrangements which made this volume possible but also for their aid during the editorial process. My thanks must also go to Mr. Frederick Anderson, Literary Editor of the Mark Twain Papers, for his assistance with numerous details and to Mr. Hennig Cohen, of the University of Pennsylvania, whose file of Mark Twain's political newsletters, generously offered, greatly facilitated my research.

A substantial amount of the free time devoted to my editorial task was made possible by grants from the Research Committee of the Graduate School, University of Wisconsin. The aid thus given is sincerely appreciated as, too, is the additional financial support, covering a large portion of my expenses, afforded both by the University of Wisconsin and the University of California.

I wish to acknowledge here the kindness of several publishers who have permitted me to quote, sometimes extensively, from their publications: The Belknap Press of Harvard University Press for quotations from *The Mark Twain–Howells Letters,* ed. H. N. Smith and W. M. Gibson; Harper & Row, Publishers, for quotations from *Europe and Elsewhere* and *Mark Twain's Letters,* ed. A. B. Paine, *Mark Twain in Eruption,* ed. B. DeVoto, and *Mark Twain, A Biography* by A. B. Paine; Charles Scribner's Sons for quotations from *The Tocsin of Revolt and Other Essays* by Brander Matthews; and Mrs. Doris Webster for quotations from *Mark Twain, Business Man,* ed. S. C. Webster.

For valuable criticism during the final stages of composition, I am grateful to Mr. Smith and Mr. Walter Blair, both of whom read the introduction and the various headnotes and offered suggestions which proved useful in strengthening these parts. But I cannot, in good conscience, thrust off on them any remaining blameworthy flaws and errors: these must remain mine.

Finally, thanks must go to Mrs. Mary Ann Rogers and Bruce Rogers, who contributed, among other things, a vast amount of patience.

FRANKLIN R. ROGERS

San Jose, California
January, 1966

# Contents

# Abbreviations

| | |
|---|---|
| MT | Mark Twain |
| MTP | The Mark Twain Papers, University of California, Berkeley |
| SLC | Samuel L. Clemens |
| WDH | William Dean Howells |
| | |
| *MTB* | Albert Bigelow Paine, *Mark Twain: A Biography* (New York, 1912) |
| *MTBur* | Franklin R. Rogers, *Mark Twain's Burlesque Patterns* (Dallas, 1960) |
| *MTBus* | *Mark Twain, Business Man,* ed. Samuel C. Webster (Boston, 1946) |
| *MTE* | *Mark Twain in Eruption,* ed. Bernard DeVoto (New York, 1940) |
| *MTF* | *Mark Twain to Mrs. Fairbanks,* ed. Dixon Wecter (San Marino, 1949) |
| *MTHL* | *Mark Twain–Howells Letters,* ed. Henry Nash Smith and William M. Gibson (Cambridge, 1960) |
| *MTL* | *Mark Twain's Letters,* ed. Albert Bigelow Paine (New York, 1917) |
| *MTW* | Bernard DeVoto, *Mark Twain at Work* (Cambridge, 1942) |
| *SCH* | Dixon Wecter, *Sam Clemens of Hannibal* (Boston, 1952) |

# Introduction

It should always be with some misgivings that an editor presents to the public materials which an author has discarded. By returning the materials to his files, the author has voted against publication. By resurrecting them, the editor risks exposing the author to the adverse criticism which he wished to avoid. But, at the same time, the resurrection serves a valuable purpose by making available almost indispensable evidence to be used by those seeking to understand the creative process. It is because they serve such a purpose that the texts published in this volume have been salvaged from Mark Twain's files. Indeed, they are doubly valuable because they aid in dispelling a myth about his own creative process which Twain himself did much to establish.

In several instances Twain gave the impression that for him plotting a novel was a rather simple affair. To Elsie Leslie Lyde he wrote a letter to accompany a gift, a pair of slippers he had embroidered for her. Explaining how he happened upon the design, he said, "I began . . . without ulterior design, or plan of any sort —just as I would begin a Prince and Pauper, or any other tale. And mind you it is the easiest and surest way; because if you invent two or three people and turn them loose in your manuscript, something is bound to happen to them—you can't help it; and then it will take you the rest of the book to get them out of the natural consequences of that occurrence, and so, first thing you know, there's your book all finished up and never cost you an idea." [1] But in actuality, as the

[1] "A Wonderful Pair of Slippers," *Europe and Elsewhere,* ed. Albert B. Paine (New York, 1923), p. 88.

texts published in this volume illustrate, he experienced much more trouble than this statement would suggest in delimiting his fictional world, establishing its nature, and maintaining control over the characters placed therein.

The major difficulty arose the moment he began plotting a new story. The letter to Elsie Lyde is not the only instance in which he gave the impression that his plots developed by a process of autogenesis. The same point is made in a much more frequently quoted passage from the autobiographical dictations of 1906: "I was a faithful and interested amanuensis and my industry did not flag, but the minute that the book tried to shift to *my* head the labor of contriving its situations, inventing its adventures and conducting its conversations, I put it away and dropped it out of my mind. . . . The reason [the book would not go on] was very simple—my tank had run dry; it was empty; the stock of materials in it was exhausted; the story could not go on without materials; it could not be wrought out of nothing." [2] This passage has been interpreted to mean that the only difficulty he experienced in writing a book was in keeping on hand a sufficient supply of episodes and adventures, gleaned from his recollections of his own life, to keep his characters occupied. Such an interpretation implies that the major structural pattern within which the recollections were to be utilized generally gave him no difficulty.

The construction put upon these words would seem to have the highest sort of substantiation, that of Twain himself, who has clearly stated that at least once he put a manuscript aside several times after the tank had run dry and waited until it filled up again with further memories of his own boyhood to be added to the store already accumulated in the manuscript. In the summer of 1890 he described the composition of *Tom Sawyer* to Brander Matthews, who has preserved the substance of his comments:

> He began the composition of 'Tom Sawyer' with certain of his boyish recollections in mind, writing on and on until he had utilized them all, whereupon he put his manuscript aside and ceased to think about it,

[2] *Mark Twain in Eruption,* ed. Bernard DeVoto (New York, 1940), pp. 196–197.

> except in so far as he might recall from time to time, and more or less unconsciously, other recollections of those early days. Sooner or later he would return to his work to make use of memories he had recaptured in the interval. After he had harvested this second crop, he again put his work away, certain that in time he would be able to call back other scenes and other situations. When at last he became convinced that he had made his profit out of every possible reminiscence, he went over what he had written with great care, adjusting the several instalments one to the other, sometimes transposing a chapter or two and sometimes writing into the earlier chapters the necessary preparation for adventures in the later chapters unforeseen when he was engaged on the beginnings of the book. Thus he was enabled to bestow on the completed story a more obvious coherence than his haphazard procedure would otherwise have attained.[3]

To return to the 1906 dictation, what he said there about the composition of *Tom Sawyer* supplements and confirms what he told Matthews: "When the manuscript had lain in a pigeonhole two years I took it out one day and read the last chapter that I had written. It was then that I made the great discovery that when the tank runs dry you've only to leave it alone and it will fill up again in time. . . . There was plenty of material now, and the book went on and finished itself without any trouble." [4] Nothing would seem plainer: the book grew easily as memory after memory was tossed in; when the store of memories was exhausted, he waited two years; then, after reading the last chapter to get his bearings, he pushed on with a replenished stock of memories.

The implication in the various statements about *Tom Sawyer* is that the structural plan remained constant from beginning to end. Further, the emphasis upon memory suggests the structural plan of the biography-novel, what Fielding called the "history," so popular among Victorian novelists. Twain called it the "narrative" novel and once tentatively concluded it was the best form. In his 1886 notebook he wrote, "What is biography? Unadorned romance. What is romance? Adorned biography. Adorn it less and it will be

---

[3] "Memories of Mark Twain," *The Tocsin of Revolt and Other Essays* (New York, 1922), pp. 265–266.

[4] *MTE*, p. 197.

better than it is. A *narrative* novel is the thing, perhaps: where you follow the fortunes of two or three people and have no plot more than real life has." [5]

But recent studies have shown one must be cautious even with such direct testimony as that about the composition of *Tom Sawyer.* The nucleus of the book, as Bernard DeVoto discovered, was "The Boy's Manuscript," a burlesque of the stereotyped courtships found in the Victorian "history," such as David Copperfield's courtship of Dora.[6] As Hamlin Hill has convincingly demonstrated, even the final structural plan underwent a major modification. Twain began with the idea of tracing Tom through his boyhood, youth, and early manhood; depicting his "Battle of Life in many lands"; and finally describing his return to St. Petersburg in middle age. In other words, the book was to be a complete "history" like *David Copperfield* or *Henry Esmond.* Only after he had made substantial progress in pursuit of this plot did he change his mind and decide to restrict himself to Tom's boyhood.[7]

The suggestion of these studies is that the need for modifications in the structure, not the exhaustion of a stock of memories, caused the trouble in the composition of *Tom Sawyer.* And Twain himself, in the 1906 dictation, tended to confirm such a conclusion in a passage which by implication almost directly contradicts his previous assertions about the book:

> There are some books that refuse to be written. They stand their ground year after year and will not be persuaded. It isn't because the book is not there and worth being written—it is only because the right form for the story does not present itself. There is only one right form for a story, and if you fail to find that form the story will not tell itself. You may try a dozen wrong forms but in each case you will not get very far before you discover that you have not found the right one—then that story will always stop and decline to go any further.[8]

---

[5] Typescript Notebook 21, p. 9a, Mark Twain Papers, The General Library, University of California, Berkeley (hereafter MTP).

[6] Franklin R. Rogers, *Mark Twain's Burlesque Patterns* (Dallas, 1960), pp. 101–109.

[7] "The Composition and the Structure of *Tom Sawyer,*" *American Literature,* XXXII (January 1961), 386–387.

[8] *MTE,* p. 199.

Here the writer seems to be talking about the form to which Bernard DeVoto refers when he charges that Twain "could not think and feel [*Huckleberry Finn*] through to its own implicit form." [9] If one is to place any reliance upon Twain's words in this last assertion, one must conclude that he was aware of implicit form and sought to discover it by a sort of trial-and-error method. His routine procedure seems to have been to start a novel with some structural plan which ordinarily soon proved defective, whereupon he would cast about for a new plot which would overcome the difficulty, rewrite what he had already written, and then push on until some new defect forced him to repeat the process once again.

That this conception of the process of composition was not a notion developed late in Twain's career is suggested by at least two additional statements, one written in 1878, the other in 1898. On March 23, 1878, Twain sent a letter to his brother Orion giving advice about the work necessary in the construction of literature. To make his point he enlarged upon his own difficulties with the "Journey in Heaven," which was finally published in 1907 as *Extracts from Captain Stormfield's Visit to Heaven:*

> Nine years ago I mapped out my "Journey in Heaven." I discussed it with literary friends whom I could trust to keep it to themselves.
>
> I gave it a deal of thought, from time to time. After a year or more I wrote it up. It was not a success. Five years ago I wrote it again, altering the plan. That MS is at my elbow now. It was a considerable improvement on the first attempt, but still it wouldn't do—last year and year before I talked frequently with Howells about the subject, and he kept urging me to do it again.
>
> So I thought and thought, at odd moments and at last I struck what I considered to be the right plan! Mind I have never altered the *ideas,* from the first—the plan was the difficulty.[10]

In a letter to Howells from Vienna, August 16, 1898, he described substantially the same process:

> Speaking of that ill luck of starting a piece of literary work wrong—& again—& again; always aware that there *is* a way, if you could only

[9] *Mark Twain at Work* (Cambridge, Mass., 1942), p. 52.

[10] *Mark Twain's Letters,* ed. Albert B. Paine (New York, 1917), I, 323.

think it out, which would make the thing slide effortless from the pen—the one right way, the sole form for *you,* the other forms being for men whose *line* those forms are, or who are capabler than yourself: I've had no end of experience in that (& maybe I am the only one—let us hope so.) Last summer I started 16 things wrong—3 books & 13 mag. articles—& could make only 2 little wee things, 1500 words altogether, succeed;—only that out of piles & stacks of diligently-wrought MS., the labor of 6 weeks' unremitting effort. I could make *all* of those things go if I would take the trouble to re-begin each one half a dozen times on a new plan.[11]

After considering such evidence as this, Sydney J. Krause justifiably came to the conclusion that "Twain was not much bothered by the fact that he could not write from some well-defined plan because, by writing first to acquire his plan, Twain learned to consider creativity as essentially an act of discovery. He discovered his subject, not before, but *as,* he wrote. In the process of composition Twain felt that organization would occur simultaneously with his immersion in his subject and that a unique form would arise from the spontaneous adaptations of his heated imagination." [12]

To a great extent the difficulties which Twain experienced with his plots stem from the fact that more often than not his initial plan depended upon some gaudy, as he would call it, situation or idea which struck him as hilariously funny, as in *A Connecticut Yankee* ("Dream of being a knight errant in armor. . . . No pockets in the armor. Can't scratch. Cold in the head—can't blow—can't get to a handkerchief, can't use iron sleeve. . . .") or upon the plot of a literary burlesque he had previously written, as in *The Prince and the Pauper.*[13] Obviously, if he were at all inclined toward the "serious and instructive vein" in his purpose, a book so begun was bound soon to run into trouble.

In his account of how "Those Extraordinary Twins" grew into *Pudd'nhead Wilson,* Twain described the history of a book begun

---

[11] *Mark Twain–Howells Letters,* ed. Henry Nash Smith and William M. Gibson (Cambridge, Mass., 1960), II, 675.

[12] "Twain's Method and Theory of Composition," *Modern Philology,* LVI (February 1959), 172.

[13] *MTBur,* pp. 114–122.

in this way and the process by which the trouble was overcome. Despite the humorous exaggeration, the prefatory comment with which he introduces "Those Extraordinary Twins" is probably his most candid statement about composition as he practiced it. He started, so he asserted, with a farce, an exploitation of the comic possibilities to be found in the private life or lives "of a youthful Italian 'freak'—or 'freaks' . . . a combination consisting of two heads and four arms joined to a single body and a single pair of legs. . . ." But as he worked from draft to draft, minor characters of the earlier drafts or entirely new characters "got to intruding themselves and taking up more and more room with their talk and their affairs." The intrusion of these characters and their eventual dominance resulted from the discovery in the course of composition of a new, more attractive, and more serious theme or intention: "And I have noticed another thing: that as the short tale grows into the long tale, the original intention (or motif) is apt to get abolished and find itself superseded by a quite different one."

As the history of *Pudd'nhead Wilson* suggests, Twain could not plot in the same way that, say, Henry James could. He needed a starter, either an ingenious and extravagant gimmick such as the Siamese twins or, as the Simon Wheeler and Hellfire Hotchkiss sequences show, a ready-made skeleton provided by a burlesque of some literary work or form. He generally demanded two things of the starter: it must provide a matrix so that he could begin writing with only minimal concern for structure and it must engage his sense of humor, presumably to engender the necessary enthusiasm for composition.

Schooled as he was during his apprentice years in the dominant forms of mid-nineteenth-century humor, and tutored by Bret Harte and Charles Henry Webb, Twain became well acquainted with the condensed burlesque novel, the burlesque form pioneered by Thackeray in "Mr. Punch's Prize Novelists" (reissued in 1856 as "Novels by Eminent Hands"), and wrote a number of them himself. But even while practicing the form he was seeking ways of expanding it and of turning it to serious purposes of his own. His growth in skill in handling the form appears in the contrast between the "Burlesque *Il Trovatore*" and "A Novel: *Who Was*

*He?*" If one assumes that a literary burlesque ridicules or derives humor from the style, characters, conventions, or plot devices of the work on which it is based, the "Burlesque *Il Trovatore*" is not a burlesque at all, since the ridicule focuses upon and the humor derives from the manner of performance and the naïveté of the observer-reporter instead of the techniques and conventions of a Verdi opera. "A Novel: *Who Was He?*" is a typical condensed burlesque novel, in its excellent parody of Hugo's style and mannerisms worthy of ranking with the best. But the form is a restrictive one, and in "The Story of Mamie Grant" and "L'Homme Qui Rit" he explored two methods of escaping its limitations. In "Mamie Grant" he sought expansion by stringing several condensed burlesques upon a central thread furnished by another condensed burlesque. And in "L'Homme Qui Rit" he sought to serve his own purposes by giving allegorical significance to the characters in the burlesque.

The next two works, the "Burlesque *Hamlet*" and the "1,002ᵈ Arabian Night," show Twain moving away from the completely parasitic dependence upon plot, character, and theme of the condensed burlesque. Although both of these works are humorous in tone and are directly dependent upon works by other authors, neither of them is a burlesque as I have defined the term because in neither instance does Twain clearly attempt to capitalize upon the absurdities he may have supposed to be inherent in the originals. Despite the fact that he used the title "Burlesque *Hamlet*," the comic tone of the work results not from a humorous exaggeration of Shakespeare's faults but from the anachronisms resulting from the interpolation of an additional character, a nineteenth-century book agent, into the action at Elsinore. The humor derives, that is, from the incongruity introduced by the additional character, not from any incongruity in Shakespeare's play. The stage of development in the creative process represented by the "Burlesque *Hamlet*" is, of course, that with which *A Connecticut Yankee* began. The "1,002ᵈ Arabian Night" is, as the title indicates, a continuation of the *Thousand and One Nights*. But again, although the tale is written in a near-parody of the style of Edward William Lane's translation (1840) and although it contains a number of devices also used in the burlesques as defined above, the comic focus is not primarily upon the faults of the original (it does ridicule the prolixity), but upon the situation inherent in Twain's addition, the plight of a boy mistaken for and reared as a girl and of a girl mistaken for and reared as a boy. The situation exploited here for its comic possibilities is a stage in that development which leads to the basic plot device of the Hellfire Hotchkiss fragment.

In a sense both the book agent of the "Burlesque *Hamlet*" and Selim and Fatima of the "1,002[d] Arabian Night" are characters in search of a plot. And it is characteristic of Twain that he should attempt first to graft them onto a well-established stock. What he was doing here is quite similar to what he did with his brother Orion in "The Autobiography of a Damned Fool" and with Simon Wheeler in "Cap'n Simon Wheeler, The Amateur Detective." On 9 August 1876, he wrote to William Dean Howells, "So the comedy [Howells' "Out of the Question"] is done, & with a 'fair degree of satisfaction.' That rejoices me, & makes me mad, too—for *I* can't plan a comedy, & what have you done that God should be so good to you? I have racked myself baldheaded trying to plan a comedy-harness for some promising characters of mine to work in, & had to give it up. It is a noble lot of blooded stock & worth no end of money, but they must stand in the stable & be profitless." [14] The blooded stock included Huckleberry Finn, the initial version of whose adventures had just gone into the pigeonhole; Simon Wheeler, whose first plot was being developed at this time; and almost certainly Oscar Carpenter, né Orion Clemens, who would not find a plot until the next summer.

When Orion-Oscar did find a plot in the summer of 1877 in "The Autobiography of a Damned Fool," it was exactly the same sort of plot which Mamie Grant had figured in almost ten years before, a series of condensed burlesques of temperance literature strung on a thread provided by a central character named Bolivar, who to some extent is a fictional representation of Orion but who is predominantly a burlesque of the stereotyped characters of temperance novels. The plot proved unsatisfactory, and the character

---

[14] *MTHL,* I, 144–145.

wandered on to a plot (now lost) outlined in collaboration with Howells in 1878. When Howells withdrew from the project, the character resumed his quest, a long one which this time lasted well over ten years. In 1891 he appeared in scattered notebook references, and at last at the Villa Viviani he took his place with a much more serious purpose in a projected satire on civilization and the colonization of Africa to be called "Affeland (Snivelization)." But this satire was soon abandoned, and the character searched on. Several years later at Weggis he reappeared as Oscar Carpenter, this time moving to a more subordinate role as an effeminate boy paired with the tomboyish Hellfire Hotchkiss in a relationship similar to but much less superficial than the relationship in the "1,002$^{d}$ Arabian Night." Once again the plot proved unsuitable, and the character moved on, this time having gained more direction, to become Oliver Hotchkiss in the "Hannibal version" of *The Mysterious Stranger;* eventually, stripped of almost all traces of his origins in burlesque and in Twain's exasperation with Orion, he became Father Peter in the Eseldorf version.

The movement of the "Damned Fool" from lighthearted—one is tempted to say lightheaded—farce to biting satire and from chief to subordinate role has its counterpart in the history of Simon Wheeler, although here the satire is only partially developed by the time the sequence breaks off. In this instance the plot in which Simon Wheeler first figured has not survived, but we may infer it from the Brummel-Arabella fragment. Undoubtedly farcical, it was probably rather close in tone if not in actual incidents and intent to the play which was constructed in 1877. The play is primarily a burlesque of Allan Pinkerton's detective stories; the other elements, derived from the Brummel-Arabella fragment—the love story, the suicide of the unsuccessful poet-suitor, and the supposed murder—are all subordinate elements, devices to further the central purpose of burlesque. But when Twain undertook to turn the play into a novel, the subordinate characters and interests, as in *Pudd'nhead Wilson,* began to take over the story. In the novel the focus of attention is on Hugh Burnside, Milly Griswold, Hale Dexter, Clara Burnside, and their interrelationships. Simon Wheeler and the burlesque of Pinkerton, although still present, have been pushed into a subordinate role by the new and more serious purpose, the satire on feuding. One has every reason to suspect that, if another start had been made on the story, the trend evident in the contrast between the play and the fragmentary novel eventually would have produced a version much more sharply and exclusively satiric. Indeed, evidence to support such a conjecture appears in the working notes prepared for just such a new start in the late 1890's.

When we measure the distance from the Brummel-Arabella fragment to the Simon Wheeler novel, or from Mamie Grant to the Oscar Carpenter of "Hellfire Hotchkiss," or from Selim and Fatima of the "1,002[d] Arabian Night" to Hellfire Hotchkiss and Oscar Carpenter, another movement becomes evident, a movement which points to the very heart of the creative process in Twain. In each there is a movement from a more or less ill-defined locality or from the remote regions of farcical fantasy into a clearly visualized rural village which is a recognizable derivative of Hannibal.

Very early in his career as a novelist, Twain discovered his predilection for the Mississippi River village as the setting for his novels, and by 1882 he had translated the predilection into a general proposition. In a notebook he wrote, "Human nature cannot be studied in cities except at a disadvantage—a village is the place. There you can know your man inside and out—in a city you but know his crust; and his crust is usually a lie." [15]

Using the Hannibal of his own youth for a foundation, he constructed a fictional world, a village known by various names—St. Petersburg, Guilford, Dawson's Landing. It was more than simply the setting for the adventures of Huck Finn and Tom Sawyer: for him it was a substitute world, and he peopled it with a host of characters who appear in his notebooks, his unpublished manuscripts, and the published works, frequently with different names and sometimes with slight alterations in their characteristics. And for them he constructed a complex of interrelationships only a portion of which appears in the published works or in the Huck Finn–Tom Sawyer material. The texts presented in this volume give us another large portion of that world, and in the fact that the two major sequences presented here declined to go any farther

[15] Typescript Notebook 16, p. 49, MTP.

within that world we can discern the nature of the crisis that Twain the novelist faced in the late 1890's.

In the 1870's and certainly on into the 1880's, he was enthusiastic about the village-world he was constructing. In a letter to Mollie Fairbanks, dated 6 August 1877, he wrote:

> Only Bunyan, Sir Walter Raleigh, the author of Don Quixotte, & a few other people have had the *best* of opportunities for working, in this world. Solitary imprisonment, by compulsion, is the one perfect condition for perfect performance. . . . Then his *work* becomes his pleasure, his recreation, his absorption, his uplifting & all-satisfying enthusiasm. He is miserable only when the work-day closes. And yet a man so circumstanced need never be actually miserable; for he can weave his fancies & continue his work in his head until sleep overtakes him. He lives in a fairer world than any that is outside, he moves in a goodlier company than any that others know, & over them he is king & they obey him.[16]

The "fairer world" and "goodlier company" from which he had recently been distracted, so the previous paragraph of the letter reveals, are those of the play "Cap'n Simon Wheeler, The Amateur Detective." Before the demands of the New York opening of *Ah Sin,* the play written in collaboration with Bret Harte, drew him forth, he had been secluded in his Quarry Farm study, immersed in his fictional world, absorbed in the antics of Captain Wheeler. That the world of Wheeler and the three Pinkerton detectives were at least briefly his "pleasure, his recreation, his absorption" is another illustration of the fact that Twain's critical powers, never very reliable, were at their worst when he was riding on the crest of an "uplifting and all-satisfying enthusiasm" for a gaudy idea. But the passage is of much greater importance for what it reveals about his attitude toward the actuality around him. It is permeated with escapism, a withdrawal from the world of actuality, irksome and frequently unpleasant, into a world where the laws of probability are suspended and only the villains, the Jake Belfords, like the Injun Joes, suffer in any permanent fashion. When one realizes this,

[16] *Mark Twain to Mrs. Fairbanks,* ed. Dixon Wecter (San Marino, 1949), pp. 206–207.

one can readily understand why Simon Wheeler was included in the "goodlier company"—his very improbability qualified him—and why burlesque figured so prominently in the construction of the "fairer world"—it was a readily available means of stepping through the looking-glass into the world of fantasy.

By the mid-1890's the fantasy-world had taken a fairly coherent form in Twain's imagination, but it was already exhibiting an alarming tendency to become not an escapist's retreat but an arena for the satirist's attack on actuality, a tendency already evident in the Dawson's Landing of *Pudd'nhead Wilson* and the river towns of *Huckleberry Finn.* The tendency stems, of course, from a contrary impulse revealed, for example, in the notebook entry quoted above: "Human nature cannot be studied in cities except at a disadvantage—a village is the place." Paradoxically, Mark Twain was seeking refuge in a "fairer world" where he could study human nature, apparently without realizing that to make this fantasy-world into a laboratory for the study of human nature is to transform it into a microcosm, an epitome of the actuality he wished to escape, an admirable and ancient tool of the satirist, but no fairer than the macrocosm and peopled by beings no goodlier. The coherent form and the tendency are both further revealed by two interesting documents of the later 1890's, one a long notebook entry of 1897, the other a sheaf of notes entitled "Villagers of 1840–43."

The notebook entry, a series of notes for a new book, is interesting because scattered here and there in it are suggestions which are developed in the Hellfire Hotchkiss story. There are others which find a place in the unfinished, unpublished "Tom Sawyer's Conspiracy" and the "Hannibal version" of *The Mysterious Stranger.* It is interesting, too, because it contains the intermediate stage of the "Damned Fool's" transmutation into the Oscar Carpenter of "Hellfire Hotchkiss." But for the present purpose the scope of the entry should be particularly noticed: in typescript six pages of brief, suggestive phrases ("Killing the negro man with a chunk of coal. Sheep-nanny tea," "The red-ear and the kiss") with only an occasional suggestion developed in more detail.[17] Twain

[17] Typescript Notebook 32a (II), pp. 56–61, MTP.

could hardly have hoped to include all this material in one book. Instead he jotted down a series of notes providing a rather broad view of the village-world from which he might perhaps later select the best scenes, as he in fact did, not for one story but for several. Despite a disturbing, somber tone in a very few of the entries, for example the one quoted above, in general the world represented here is the escapist's refuge. One entry concerns an episode of Hannibal history which had apparently bothered Clemens for some years, that of a Negro smuggled from Virginia to Missouri because he was in danger of being lynched for raping white women. In Missouri he raped a thirteen-year-old girl and killed her and her brother. Before he was caught, the children's Negro nurse was lynched because of a suspicion that she had poisoned one or both of the children. Immediately after her death, the rapist was captured and he confessed. Twain was not troubled by the subsequent lynching of the rapist—to him that was apparently poetic justice, but he was troubled by the lynching of the nurse. The conclusion to this entry shows the escapist at work: "—or Tom and Huck shall *save* her." Here we see the creator of the village-world fronting a most grim fact indeed of the reality around him and achieving a wish-fulfillment by correcting an injustice of the actual world. But the contrary impulse appears in another note: "If scoundrels needed, there's Webster, Paige, House." This comment is direct evidence that we are watching the growth of a microcosm; if Hannibal does not contain the necessary human types to provide a proper reflection of actuality, the writer supplies the lack by importing the wanting types from the macrocosm.

The second document, written at almost exactly the same time as the notebook entry, affords another broad view of the village, overlapping the other in many respects. Dixon Wecter described it as Twain's "unpublished roster of Hannibal citizens, some cloaked in pseudonyms." [18] But to regard the document as thinly disguised history important only for a reconstruction of the Hannibal of Clemens' youth is to miss its significance. "Villagers of 1840–43" was also apparently intended as a basis for fiction. It includes

---

[18] *Sam Clemens of Hannibal* (Boston, 1952), p. 19.

a detailed and fairly systematic roster of the citizens, and information about dress and popular songs and literature. Several of the characters are given fictitious names, among them the "Damned Fool," né Orion Clemens, who, as in "Hellfire Hotchkiss," is named Oscar Carpenter. The village itself is generally referred to not as Hannibal but as St. Petersburg, usually abbreviated "St. P."

The great interest of the document is in its tone. If somberness is merely a disturbing undercurrent in the notebook entry, it is in "Villagers" an overwhelming force. Dixon Wecter rather correctly reflected its character when he called it Twain's "Spoon River Anthology." We have, that is, in this document a fairly detailed view of the satirist's microcosm. In several interpretative passages in the middle of the manuscript, Twain revealed his awareness of what was happening to his "fairer world" in attempts to recapture the more lightsome tone of the earlier fantasy-village. In these passages he makes generalizations about "St. P." which endow it with idyllic qualities very different from the grim aspects suggested by several of the biographies.[19] Dixon Wecter attributed these passages, especially one headed *"Chastity,"* to Twain's "impulse to idealize Hannibal through the haze of years." [20] But that we are dealing not with an idealization but with a transmutation of Hannibal into the stuff of fiction is revealed by the transformation of the "Chastity" passage into a speech for Aunt Besty in "Hellfire Hotchkiss": "There is one kind of gossip that this town has never dealt in before, in the fifty-two years that I've lived in it—and has never had any occasion to. Not in one single case, if you leave out the town drunkard's girls; and even that turned out to be a lie, and was stopped." Twain was well aware that such a statement could not be truthfully made about the Hannibal of his youth, a fact clearly revealed by other entries in "Villagers." The process is somewhat the reverse of what Wecter assumed: Twain was trying to recapture a once almost unchallenged idyllic quality in his fantasy-world which was now on the verge of obliteration by the truth about Hannibal.

It is no accident that these two documents were written at

[19] DV47, typescript, pp. 10–11, MTP.
[20] *SCH*, p. 174.

precisely the same time when "The Autobiography of a Damned Fool" was becoming "Hellfire Hotchkiss," "Simon Wheeler, Detective" was teetering on the verge of a new transformation, and other episodes from village history were being assembled to make the hopefully begun "Tom Sawyer's Conspiracy." In the notebook entry and "Villagers of 1840–43," Twain was almost desperately surveying his greatest literary treasure, his private world, which like William Faulkner's Yoknapatawpha County belonged in fee simple to the creator and sole proprietor, but which, like the plots for his "Damned Fool" and his amateur detective, was failing him.

He was discovering an unwelcome truth about the village which had so far served him well. Such was his *Weltanschauung* in 1897 that the Mississippi River village appeared the wrong form for his fictional world, for it could no longer serve his needs. The old world was one dependent upon burlesque, farce, and other methods of slipping easily through the looking-glass, and the somber note of the "Villagers" manuscript and portions of the notebook entry provided a violent tonal clash. Farce was on the verge of becoming tragedy: just as "Those Extraordinary Twins" had to be transformed into *Pudd'nhead Wilson,* so the Mississippi River village of 1840–43 had to be transformed into the microcosmic Eseldorf before he could go on.

# BURLESQUE

## *Il Trovatore*

(1866)

Editor's Note: The burlesque *Il Trovatore* was jotted down in Twain's notebook for 1866 following the entries dealing with the trip to the Sandwich Islands (Typescript Notebook 4, pp. 46–52). It begins several pages after the entry for 13 August which announces his arrival in San Francisco. The piece represents the product of a brief respite in what must have been for Twain a rather busy time. After arriving in San Francisco, he had gone at once to Sacramento to conclude his affairs with the editors of the *Union,* for whom he had written the series of humorous and informative letters describing his journey to the Islands. He returned to San Francisco about 20 August and began the rewritten version of his article on the *Hornet* disaster which three months later would appear in *Harper's Magazine.*[1] He also occupied himself with at least the preliminary plans for a book on the Sandwich Islands, and, within two weeks after the return from Sacramento, he was deeply engaged in preparing the lecture he would give at the Academy of Music on 2 October.

According to Albert Bigelow Paine, Clemens "once declared he had

[1] "Forty-three Days in an Open Boat," *Harper's Magazine,* December 1866. The *Hornet,* out of New York with a miscellaneous cargo including a large quantity of kerosene, caught fire and burned early in May 1866, at Lat. 2° North, Long. 135° West. The fifteen survivors finally reached Hawaii in an open boat late in June. The article was based on the diary of Henry Ferguson, one of the survivors, who was a fellow passenger on the *Smyrniote* during the voyage to San Francisco.

been so blue at this period that one morning he put a loaded pistol to his head, but found he lacked courage to pull the trigger." [2] He was not too dejected to accomplish a fair amount of work and to treat himself to an evening of entertainment. On Friday evening, 24 August, Bianchi's Grand Italian Opera Company performed *Il Trovatore* at Maguire's Opera House, the only performance of this work in the 1866–67 season. The performance was something less than magnificent: a brief notice in the *Alta California* on 25 August begins: " 'Il Trovatore' was rendered last evening to a crowded house in an unexceptional manner. . . ." Twain apparently agreed.

The principal device used here is the same as that used in the Thomas Jefferson Snodgrass letters, an unsophisticated observer who is unable to respond to the demands made upon his imagination by the conventions of opera. Like Jonathan in Royal Tyler's *The Contrast,* he cannot distinguish between the make-believe on the stage and the reality in which he lives. But unlike Jonathan, who apparently saw a fairly creditable performance at the theater he visited, the observer-reporter of *Il Trovatore* saw a performance which, according to the *Alta California,* was exceptional only in its weaknesses and lapses. Twain uses the naïveté of his observer-reporter to emphasize the lethargy and lack of skill of Bianchi's Grand Italian Opera Company. The piece exhibits no advance in skill beyond the point already reached in the Snodgrass letters; it may be considered here as the starting point in the development of Twain, the satirist.

---

[2] *Mark Twain, A Biography* (New York, 1912), I, 291 n.

# *Il Trovatore*

## SCENE 1

TROVATORE—25 live shrouds in feathered caps and with sheets around them:—Howl louder than ever when dinner bell rings, and bust through green castle which waves and quakes after them. Never saw hungry crowd in such hurry.

2—Shoved castle aside and exposed a silvery blue moonlight landscape, with a railing in front and 2 steps—Woman came through gate when she could have jumped over the fence easier—

Another woman came from behind some trees that were so matted together that they looked solid.

Without any apparent reason for it, these 2 d—d fools fell to singing.

Principal one sang a long song then straddled around while they applauded and then came back and sang it over again.

3—Fence alone for 3 minutes and impressive music—

Then a queer looking bilk with a gorgeous doublet, plumed smoking cap and white opera cloak hanging to heels came solemnly forward from somewhere till he got to the centre and then began to yell.

But a fellow in the kitchen with a piano crowded him down.

Then the chief woman came back and grabbed the fellow round the neck—Same moment knight in complete armor and with sheet round him rushes in and just saves self from going into orchestra—sensation—hell to pay, in fact.

Knight takes the woman and the other fellow comes forward and just wakes up everything.

Then *they* take up his own tune and beat him at it.

This riles him and he draws his sword.

Free fight—woman trying to stop it—false alarm—after singing and flourishing swords they rush off and the woman falls carefully down on the steps blowing the dust away from the spot where her elbow is going to touch first.

## 2^d ACT.

EXCEEDINGLY gory party of blacksmiths started in to improve a very good sort of a poker and didn't succeed—sung too much and didn't work.

That same knight came into the blacksmith shop with another woman—(you let him alone for always being around when there is a woman to tag after).

The women sang a good while, and then the d—d blacksmiths blasted away and tried to beat her. Then made a fizzle of it and knew enough to curl their tails and leave. Thus the knight and the woman were left in sole possession of the blacksmith shop, but without anything to eat. As usual, with the cheerful spirit this party have manifested from the first as soon as they found there was nothing to eat they fell to singing.

*And* as usual, they hadn't sung five minutes till there was a misunderstanding.

The woman carries on dreadfully and the man stands and leans forward holding his blanket out with outspread hands and looking as if he *would* help, if he could only think of something to do.

Finally she lets down on a bass viol box covered with bearskins and he comes to his milk. They stand up and come to a musical explanation.

This knight looks so stuffed and fat in his silver scale armor that he looked like some sort of a fish.

They have a long explanation and rush off in high glee about something.

2—The boss of the corpses and that plumed fellow came out in the dark before a castle-gate to sing—to practice, likely—the d—d fools—and the blacksmith shop must be close by somewhere.

The Capt soon froze out and left, but the other fellow blasted away by himself.

At 2 oclock by the bell the Capt came back—and of course those hungry ghosts piled in too, the moment they heard that dinner bell. But that plumed fellow fooled them for he kept singing there till they were about starved out—and then they left.

Serenading party heard in the woods—stage vacant—music beautiful—church music and a fine choir—it brought back the feathered chap and the ghosts and the Capt.—and d—n them they went to blatting and interrupted the choir—choked it off and then left.

Five minutes of solemn horn tooting in the orchestra—and then out comes a party of white dressed young women out of the wood (2 ½ AM)—one with a great black cross clasped to her breast—and she stood out and begun to sing.

In comes those fellows and the ghosts and surprises and scares them—but the bold knight rushes in—of course—being so many women—from where the fence corner used to be, and grabbed the X woman and *she* was all right.

Then they stand off in two parties and sing. I thought the knight was in for it once—he didn't know any more than to insult the whole crowd and he unarmed and 20 defenceless women to take care of—had him in the door. Drew sword but didn't kill him.

Arrival of 2 dozen ratty looking soldiers with brass helmets, coats with trunk tacks driven into them and broom stick lances—directly the knight grabbed the X drew his sword and tried to shove—the corpses tried to prevent him, but the soldiers took his part and so they struck a blow apiece and they kept up a desultory sort of hacking here and there till the curtain fell—he holding his sword in a warding position and clasping fainting X.

## ACT. 3

Very handsome silk tent with splendid gold embroidered banner hanging at the door—row of other tents in distance—all those ghosts in a row armed with swords and singing—for hash, *of* course

—I've got them spotted—they are expecting to hear that bell every moment.

They leave and the feathered chap comes out of the tent and goes to swelling around and singing—which disturbs the Capt of the ghosts and *he* comes out of the tent to remonstrate.

Then the ghosts fetch in the fat woman manacled—and yowling as usual—the great overgrown scrubs, to impose on a woman. Sentinels—trunk-button fellows—pacing before the tents.

Sing awhile and the woman tries to break away—d—d fool—they've got her in the door. Then *don't* she throw herself! They argue the case with her but no use—she'll be d—d if she *will* be satisfied, and keeps trying to get away—so they *took* her away—she is evidently breeding trouble for herself the way she is acting.

Scene 2—That knight—with that X woman come into a mighty common looking country hotel and go to making love. She is dressed in white satin trimmed with silver lace and he has got his bulliest opera cloak on over his armor. He sends her off the stage.

He has lost his hat somewhere and he comes down to the footlight and sings about it in a way that shows he set considerable store by it.

He went off finally to hunt for his hat, and in the meantime the curtain came down.

I went down to offer him mine, but they wouldn't let me behind.

## ACT 4—

That old original green castle—night.

Enter a conspirator with red rosettes on his slippers and a black tablecloth on—with a woman in black—(he leaves) she falls to serenading, all by herself.

Opposition serenade in the woods—all men's voices—very solemn stately and impressive—she had the good taste to dry up her screech while they sang, because it stood to reason that she couldn't keep up her end with them.

Then a fellow in the woods went alone on a song about Leonore, and she started in to beat him, thinking she had caught him alone and had an easy thing, but the others broke in at once and helped him out. Grand—that chorus—inexpressibly grand—she wound up the whole thing herself, tho' with a final screech—woman like she *would* have the last word. And then she took up her serenade and blatted away till she had had her sing out, and left.

Then the feathered chap came out of a neighboring house with a soldier—sent him somewhere and went to sloshing around and singing till he came back.

His first blast fetched that same woman back—for she hadn't got far—and they two sang—she appeared to be wanting to make up with him—but he appeared to be telling her how circumstances over which he had no control rendered it entirely out of his power to accede. She even knelt to him.

Finally she happened to sing something he knew or it happened to strike his fancy, and he came right back and made up with her—it *was* a song he knew, for he sailed in and helped her sing it.

2—They shoved the castle aside—and showed the fat woman sitting on that viol box in a dungeon—chained, and only one poor oil lamp over her head while there were hundreds of gas burners all over the theatre—but *hell*—people never help an *unfortunate*—if she was in luck and wanted gas she could get it. The knight was with her—always around where there is a woman—if that fat woman were in *hell* you could look for *him* there shortly.

Then they sang beautifully and feelingly to pathetic accompaniment.

Then she laid down on the viol case and he knelt.

Enter the X woman and a soldier with a torch and threw herself into the knight's arms. He argues with her—evidently don't like to have her there—thinks the fat woman won't like it no doubt—but it appears to be all right—she is asleep—but if they keep up that d—d yelling they are bound to wake her presently.

She sings in her sleep, poor devil—(the fat one,) and they help her out—*beautiful.*

Down comes the X woman to her knees—but it ain't any use—the knight turns his back on her—and so she sets down on the floor and spreads her hand across her breast—ostensibly to feel her heart, but really to make up for the lowness of her low-neck dress—the knight (of course) comes and takes her round the waist and they sing.

Enter the feather chap and soldiers (in red striped breeches and high boots).

And *don't* he and she carry on, and she trying to faint and fall all the time and he holding her—but at last she *does* fall and he and all the soldiers leave—fat woman falls—flames show through cracks.

END

# A NOVEL

# *Who Was He?*

(1867)

Editor's Note: "A Novel: *Who Was He?*" (Typescript Notebook 6, pp. 37–41) is a burlesque of Victor Hugo's *Les Travailleurs de la mer* (1866), or, more precisely, of the English translation, *The Toilers of the Sea* (Harper and Bros., 1866). It was apparently intended as part of the letter to the *Alta California* dated 12 January 1867, which Twain drafted at the end of the notebook detailing the events of his voyage from San Francisco to New York, 15 December 1866, to 12 January 1867 (for a further discussion of dating, see Appendix A). The burlesque was not used in the revised *Alta* letter which he dispatched after his arrival, either because he decided to withhold it, possibly for inclusion in the volume of his sketches which Charles Henry Webb was preparing for publication,[1] or because in the confusion of picking up his affairs in New York he forgot he had inserted it earlier in the notebook.

Hugo was one of Twain's favorite whipping boys, but *The Toilers of the Sea* moved him to more than ordinary derision. Presumably he read

---

[1] After his arrival, Twain first offered the volume to George W. Carleton, who either refused it or insulted Twain so that he withdrew it. The latter possibility is suggested by Twain's comment in a letter to William Dean Howells on 26 April 1876: "Carleton insulted me in Feb, 1867; & so when the day arrives that sees me doing him a civility, I shall feel that I am ready for Paradise, since my list of possible and impossible forgivenesses will then be complete" (*MTHL*, I, 132). After the negotiations with Carleton fell through, Webb published the volume under the title *The Celebrated Jumping Frog of Calaveras County and Other Sketches.*

the novel during his voyage to New York; if so, the burlesque insufficiently vented his feelings, for he was still joking about the book four months later. In his *Alta* letter for 19 April describing his trip to St. Louis and Hannibal, he tells of asking a hotel porter to bring him some reading materials. The porter brought, among other edifying materials, a copy of *The Toilers of the Sea:* "I shall never cease to admire the tact and intelligence of that gifted porter. I moved to the Tepfer House next day." The episode was later used in *Innocents Abroad.*

"A Novel: *Who Was He?*" shows a considerable advance in skill and technique in the art of burlesque beyond the work represented by the burlesque *Il Trovatore.* In form it is a typical condensed burlesque novel, the form pioneered by Thackeray. The parody of Hugo's style may well be considered masterly: the staccato paragraphs, the interpolated disquisitions on scientific phenomena, the irrelevant pontifical utterances, the sudden and frustrating shifts of focus at moments of crisis are all there, carried to the absurd. It should be noticed, however, that the form is a confining one; it allows almost free play for the impulse to ridicule the target work, but all other artistic impulses must be rigidly suppressed: the success of the condensed burlesque novel depends upon its fidelity to its model.

# A NOVEL: *Who Was He?*

AS I PROMISED, I will now write you a novelette.

Gillifat was a man.

All men are men.

No man can be a man who is not a man.

Hence Gillifat was a man.

Such was Gillifat.

Too Many Cooks Spoil the Broth.

At the corner of the beach furthest from the *Tremouille,* which is also between the great rock called Labadois and the Budes du Noir, two men stood talking.

One was a Dutchman.

One wasn't.

Such is life.

Allons.

The Hair of the Dog will Cure the Bite.

The *Enfant* lay at anchor. The *Enfant* was of that style of vessel called by the Guernsey longshoremen a *croupier.*

They always call such vessels *croupiers.*

It is their name.

This is why they call them so.

A storm was rising.

Storms always rise in certain conditions of the atmosphere.

They are caused by certain forces operating against certain other forces which are called by certain names and are well known by persons who are familiar with them. In 1492 Columbus sailed.

There was no storm but he discovered—

What?

A new world!

Oct. 23, 1835, a storm burst upon the coasts of England which drove ships high and dry upon the land—a storm which carried sloops and schooners far inland and perched them upon the tops of hills.

Such is the nature of storms.

Let the Sinless Cast the first Stone.

The house was in flames. From the cellar gratings flames burst upward.

From the ground floor windows, from the doorways, from obscure crevices in the weather boarding flames burst forth.

And black volumes of smoke.

From the second story windows, flames and smoke burst forth—the flames licking the smoke hungrily—the smoke retreating,—from threatened devourment as it were.

The third story was a lashing and hissing world of gloomy smoke, stained with splashes of bloody flame.

At a window of the second story appeared a wild vision of beauty—appeared for a moment, with disheveled hair, with agonized face, with uplifted, imploring hands—appeared for a second, then vanished amid rolling clouds of smoke—appeared again glorified with a rain of fiery cinders from above—and again was swallowed from sight by the remorseless smoke.

It was Demaschette.

In another second Gillifat had seized a ladder and placed it against the house.

In another moment he had ascended half way up.

A thousand anxious eyes were fixed upon him.

The old mother and the distracted father fell upon their knees—looked up at him with streaming eyes—blessed him—prayed for him.

The roof was threatening to fall in.

Not a moment was to be lost.

Gillifat held his breath to keep from inhaling the smoke—then took one, two, six strides and laid his hand upon the window sill.

There are those who believe window sills are sentient beings.

There are those who believe that the moving springs of human action are the Principle of Good and the Principle of Evil—that window may, and they may not, have something to do with these.

It is wonderful.

If they have, where are the labors of our philosophers of a thousand years? If they have not, have we not God? Let us be content. Everything goes.

Time is.

The fatal difference betwixt Tweedledum and Tweedledee.

The two men glared at each other eight minutes—time is terrible in circumstances of danger—men have grown old under the effects of fright while the fleetest horse could canter a mile—eight minutes—eight terrible minutes they glared at each other and then—

Why does the human contract under the influence of joy and dilate under the influence of fear?

It is strange. It is one of the conditions of our being.

The human eye is round. It protrudes from the socket, but it does not fall out. Why? Because certain ligatures, invisible because hidden from sight, chain it to the interior apparatus.

The pupil of the eye is also round. We do not pretend to account for this. We simply accept it as a truth. A man might see as well with a square pupil, perhaps, but what then? The absence of uniformity, of harmony in the species.

The human eye is a beautiful and an expressive feature. In November 1642, John Duke of Sebastiano insulted the Monseigneur de Torbay, Knight of the Cross, Keeper of the Seals, Grand Equerry to the King—insulted him grossly. What did Torbay do?

Split him in the eye.

In 1322 Durande Montesquieu broke a lance with Baron Lonsdale de Lonsdale—drove his weapon through the latter's dexter eye. Hence the injunction, hoary with usage, 'Mind your eye.'

Beautiful?

Without doubt.

Nothing is Hidden, Nothing Lost.

The *Tremouille* lay at anchor. The two men had just finished glaring upon each other, Gillifat was upon the uppermost round of the ladder, the storm was about to burst forth in all its terrible grandeur when—

You remember all these people and things were very close together—grouped in a mass as it were.

The dreadful climax was impending—fearful moment—when

Victor Hugo appeared on the scene and began to read a chapter from one of his books.

All these people and things got interested in his imminently impending climaxes and suspended their several enterprises.

The flames and the smoke stood still.

The girl ceased to fluctuate in the smoke.

Gillifat halted.

The two men about to shed blood, paused.

The *croupier* slacked up on her cable.

But behold!

When after several chapters the climaxes never arrived, but got swallowed up in interminable incomprehensible metaphysical disquisitions, columns of extraneous general information, and chapters of wandering incoherencies, they became disgusted and—

Lo! a miracle!

The *croupier* up anchor and went to sea.

The two disputants left.

The (—girl) disappeared for good.

Gillifat climbed down the ladder and departed.

The fire went out. Voila! They couldn't stand it.

V alone remained—

Victor was Victor still!

THE END

(I pass. I withdraw from my contract. I cannot write the novelette I promised. In an insane moment I ventured to read the opening chapters of the Toilers of the Sea and now I am tangled! My brain is in hopeless disorder. Take back your contract.)

# *The Story of Mamie Grant, the Child-Missionary*

(1868)

Editor's Note: "The Story of Mamie Grant, the Child-Missionary" (Typescript Notebook 10, pp. 1–9) was written during Twain's voyage from San Francisco to New York in 1868, probably during the voyage on the *Montana* from San Francisco to the Isthmus, for the notebook entries following the story deal for the most part with the railroad journey across the Isthmus to Aspinwall (present-day Colón). The entries preceding the story, written on the flyleaf of the notebook, give the date of departure from San Francisco (6 July) and of arrival at Acapulco (13 July).

If Twain's memory can be trusted, "Mamie Grant" was written at about the same time as the first version or partial draft of *Captain Stormfield's Visit to Heaven.* In an autobiographical dictation dated 29 August 1906, Twain stated: "Captain [Edgar] Wakeman had a fine large imagination, and he once told me of a visit which he had made to heaven. I kept it in my mind, and a month or two later I put it on paper—this was in the first quarter of 1868, I think [Wakeman commanded the vessel on which Clemens sailed from the Isthmus to San Francisco in March 1868]. It made a small book of about forty thousand words, and I called it *Captain Stormfield's Visit to Heaven.*" The recollection continues with the assertion that the first version of the Stormfield story was a burlesque of Elizabeth Stuart Phelps' *The Gates Ajar* (1868).[1] But if such were the case, the burlesque intention

[1] *MTE,* pp. 246–247. A conflicting report on the date of the first draft or plan appears in Twain's letter to Orion Clemens, 23 March 1878: "Nine years ago I mapped out my 'Journey to Heaven'" (*MTL,* I, 323). Thus the year would be 1869, not 1868.

was lost in later revisions, for none of the surviving versions is a burlesque of the Phelps book.

"Mamie Grant" is also based upon *The Gates Ajar,* a book composed for the most part of conversations between Mary, familiarly called Mamie, and her "Auntie" Winifred Forceythe on the subjects of death, Christian resignation, and the nature of Heaven (Mary is convulsed with grief because her brother has been killed in the Civil War). Although the roles are reversed (in the novel "Auntie" is the inexhaustible source of religious nostrums) and Mamie Grant is much younger than Phelps' Mamie, the essential structure is the same in both works: Mamie Grant seizes every opportunity to whip out a tract and summarize its contents; Auntie Winifred can scarcely mention a subject without immediately fortifying her position with a passage or a work from an apparently quite complete library of religious and theological works.

The facts concerning "Mamie Grant" suggest either that Twain wrote two burlesques of *The Gates Ajar* in 1868, one of which was in fact the first version of *Captain Stormfield's Visit to Heaven* or that in the 1906 dictation he confused the burlesque story of Mamie with the first version of the Stormfield story.

The technique of "Mamie Grant" is quite interesting. The burlesque escapes the rigid confines of the condensed burlesque novel by means of a relatively simple device which nevertheless produces complex and rich results. Mamie's story is, of course, a condensed burlesque of such temperance literature as that written by Timothy Shay Arthur. By having Mamie summarize the tracts she hands out to the various visitors, Twain is able to work several other condensed burlesques into the major narrative. As simple as this variation may seem when it is described, the result is a dimension and depth, a richness and complexity in ridicule or satire which is rarely found in the burlesque literature of the nineteenth century.

# *The Story of Mamie Grant, the Child-Missionary*

"WILL YOU have cream and sugar in your coffee?"

"Yes, if you please, dear auntie,—would that you could experience a change of heart."

The latter remark came from the sweet young lips of Mamie Grant. She had early come to know the comfort and joy of true religion. She attended church regularly, and looked upon it as a happy privilege, instead of an irksome penance, as is too often the case with children. She was always the first at Sunday School and the last to leave it. To her the Sunday School library was a treasure-house of precious learning. From its volumes she drew those stores of wisdom which made her the wonder of the young and the admiration of the aged. She blessed the gifted theological students who had written those fascinating books, and early resolved to make their heroines her models and turn her whole attention to saving the lost. Thus we find her at breakfast, at nine years of age, seizing upon even so barren an opportunity as a question of milk and sugar in her coffee, to express a prayerful wish in behalf of her aged, unregenerated aunt.

"Batter-cakes?"

"No, auntie, I cannot, I dare not eat batter-cakes while your precious soul is in peril."

"Oh, stuff! eat your breakfast, child, and don't bother. Here is your bowl of milk—break your bread in it and go on with your breakfast."

Pausing, with the uplifted spoonful of milk almost at her lips, Mamie Grant said:

"Auntie, bread and milk are but a vanity of this sinful world; let us take no thought of bread and milk; let us seek first the milk of righteousness, and all these things will be added unto us."

"Oh, don't bother, don't bother, child. There is the door-bell. Run and see who it is."

"Knock and it shall be opened unto you. Oh, auntie, if you would but treasure those words."

Mamie then moved pensively down stairs to open the door. This was her first morning at her aunt's, where she had come to make a week's visit. She opened the door. A quick-stepping, quick-speaking man entered.

"Hurry, my little miss. Sharp's the word. I'm the census-taker. Trot out the old gentleman."

"The census-taker? What is that?"

"I gather all the people together in a book and number them."

"Ah, what a precious opportunity is offered you, for the gathering of souls. If you would but—"

"Oh, blazes! Don't palaver. I'm about my employer's work. Let's have the old man out, quick."

"Mortal, forsake these vanities. Do rather the work of Him who is able to reward you beyond the richest of the lords of earth. Take these tracts. Distribute them far and wide. Wrestle night and day with the lost. It was thus that young Edward Baker became a shining light and a lamp to the feet of the sinner, and acquired deathless fame in the Sunday School books of the whole world. Take these tracts. This one, entitled, 'The Doomed Drunkard, or the Wages of Sin,' teaches how the insidious monster that lurks in the wine-cup, drags souls to perdition. This one, entitled, 'Deuces and, or the Gamester's Last Throw,' tells how the almost ruined gambler, playing at the dreadful game of poker, made a ten strike and a spare, and thus encouraged, drew two cards and pocketed the deep red; urged on by the demon of destruction, he ordered it up and went alone on a double run of eight, with two for his heels, and then, just as fortune seemed at last to have turned in his favor, his opponent coppered the ace and won. The fated gamester blew his brains out and perished. Ah, poker is a dreadful, dreadful game.

You will see in this book how well our theological students are qualified to teach understandingly all classes that come within their reach. Gamblers' souls are worthy to be saved, and so the holy students even acquaint themselves with the science and technicalities of their horrid games, in order to be able to talk to them for the saving of their souls in language which they are accustomed to. This tract, entitled—Why, he is gone! I wonder if my words have sunk into his heart. I wonder if the seeds thus sown will bear fruit. I cannot but believe that he will quit his sinful census-gathering and go to gathering souls. Oh, I *know* he will. It was just in this way that young James Wilson converted the Jew peddlar, and sent him away from his father's house with his boxes full of Bibles and hymn-books—a peddlar no longer, but a blessed colporteur. It is so related in the beautiful Sunday School book entitled 'James Wilson, the Boy Missionary.' "

At this moment the door-bell rang again. She opened it.

"Morning Gazette, Miss—forty cents due, on two weeks."

"Do you carry these papers all about town?"

"To mighty near every house in it—largest daily circulation of any daily paper published in the city—best advertising medium—"

"Oh, to think of your opportunities! This is not a Baptist paper, is it?"

"Well I should think not. She's a Democrat. —"

"Could not you get the editor of it to drop the follies of this world and make the Gazette a messenger of light and hope, a Baptist benediction at every fireside?"

"Oh, I haven't got time to bother about such things. Saving your presence, Miss, Democrats don't care a damn about light and hope —they wouldn't take the paper if she was a Baptist. But hurry, won't you, please—forty cents for two weeks back."

"Ah, well, if they would stop the paper, that would not do. But Oh, you can still labor in the vineyard. When you leave a paper at a house, call all the people of that house together and urge them to turn from the evil of their ways and be saved. Tell them that the meanest and the laziest and the vilest of His creatures is still within the reach of salvation. Fold these tracts inside your papers every day —and when you get out, come for more. This one, entitled 'The Pains of Hell, or the Politician's Fate,' is a beautiful tract, and draws such a frightful picture of perdition, its fires, its monsters, its awful and endless sufferings, that it can never fail to touch even the most hardened sinner, and make him seek the tranquil haven of religion. It would surely have brought Roger Lyman the shoemaker of our village to the fold if he had not become a raving maniac just before he got through. It is an awakening pamphlet for those Democrats who are wasting their time in the vain pursuit of political aggrandizement. Fold in this tract also, entitled—"

"Oh, this won't do. This is all Miss Nancy stuff, you know. Fold them in the papers! I'd like to see myself. Fold tracts in a daily newspa—why I never heard of such a thing. Democrats don't go a cent on tracts. Why, they'd raise more Cain around that office—they'd mob us. Come, Miss—forty cents, you know."

"You are glib with the foolish words of the worldly. Take the tracts; and enter upon the good work. And neglect not your own eternal welfare. Have you ever experienced grace?

"Why *he* is gone, too. But he is gone on a blessed mission. Even this poor creature will be the means of inaugurating a revival in this wicked city that shall sweep far and wide over the domains of sin. I know it, because it was just in this way that young George Berkley converted the itinerant tinker and sent him forth to solder the souls of the ungodly, as is set forth in the Sunday School books, though, still struggling with the thrall of unrighteousness that had so lately bound him, he stole two coffee-pots before he started on his errand of mercy. The door-bell again."

"Good morning, Miss, is Mr. Wagner in? I have come to pay him a thousand dollars which I borrowed last month."

"Alas, all seem busied with the paltry concerns of this world. Oh, beware how you trifle. Think not of the treasures of this perishable sphere. Lay up treasures in that realm where moths do not corrupt nor thieves break through and steal. Have you ever read 'Fire and Brimstone, or the Sinner's Last Gasp?' "

"Well this beats anything I ever heard of—a child preaching before she is weaned. But I am in something of a hurry, Miss. I must pay this money and get about my business. Hurry, please."

"Ah, Sir, it is you that should hurry—hurry to examine into your prospects in the hereafter. In this tract, entitled 'The Slave of Gain or the Dirge of the Damned,' you will learn (pray Heaven it be not too late!) how a thirst for lucre sears the soul and bars it forever from the gentle influences of religion; how it makes of life a cruel curse and in death opens the gates of everlasting woe. It is a precious book. —No sinner can read it and sleep afterward."

"You must excuse me, Miss, but—"

"Turn from the wrath to come! Flee while it is yet time. Your account with sin grows apace. Cash it and open the books anew. Take this tract and read it—'The Blasphemous Sailor Awfully Rebuked.' It tells how, on a stormy night, a wicked sailor was ordered to ascend to the main hatch and reef a gasket in the sheet anchor; from his dizzy height he saw the main-tops'l jib-boom fetch away from the clew-garnets of the booby-hatch; next the lee scuppers of the mizzen-to'-gallant's'l fouled with the peak-halliards of the cat-heads, yet in his uncurbed iniquity, at such a time as this he raised his blasphemous voice and shouted an oath in the teeth of the raging winds. Mark the quick retribution. The weather-brace parted amidships, the mizzen-shrouds fouled the starboard gangway, and the dog-watch whipped clean out of the bolt-ropes quicker than the lightning's flash! Imagine, Oh, imagine that wicked sailor's position! I cannot do it, because I do not know what those dreadful nautical terms mean, for I am not educated and deeply learned in the matters of practical every-day life like the gifted theological students, who have learned all about practical life from the writings of other theological students who went before them, but O, it must have been frightful, *so* frightful. Pilgrim, let this be a warning to you—let this—

"*He* is gone. Well, to the longest day he lives he cannot forget that it was *I* that brought peace to his troubled spirit, it was *I* that poured balm upon his bruised heart, it was *I* that pointed him the way to happiness. Ah, the good I am doing fills me with bliss. I am but an humble instrument, yet I feel that I am like, very like, some of the infant prodigies in the Sunday School books. I know that I use as fine language as they do. Oh that *I* might be an example to the young—a beacon light flashing its cheering rays far over the tossing waves of iniquity from the watch-tower of a Sunday School book with a marbled back. Door-bell again. Truly my ways are ways of pleasantness this day. Good morning, Sir. Come in, please."

"Miss, will you tell Mr. Wagner that I am come to foreclose the mortgage unless he pays the thousand dollars he owes me at once—will you tell him that, please?"

Mamie Grant's sweet face grew troubled. It was easy to see that a painful thought was in her mind.—She looked earnestly into the face of the stranger, and said with emotion:

"Have you ever experienced a change of heart?"

"Heavens, what a question!"

"You know not what you do. You stand upon a volcano. You may perish at any moment. Mortal, beware. Leave worldly concerns, and go to doing good. Give your property to the poor and go off somewhere for a missionary. You are not lost, if you will but move quickly. Shun the intoxicating bowl. Oh, take this tract, and read it night and morning and treasure up its lessons. Read it—'William Baxter, the Reformed Inebriate, or, Saved as by fire.' This poor sinner, in a fit of drunken madness, slew his entire family with a junk bottle—see the picture of it. Remorse brought its tortures and he signed the temperance pledge. He married again and raised a pious, interesting family. The tempter led him astray again, and when wild with liquor again he brained his family with the fell junk bottle. He heard Gough [2] lecture, and reformed once more. Once more he reared a family of bright and beautiful children. But alas, in an evil hour his wicked companions placed the intoxicating bowl to his lips and that very day his babes fell victims to the junk bottle and he threw the wife of his bosom from the third story window. He woke from his drunken stupor to find himself alone in the world, a homeless, friendless outcast. Be warned, be warned by his experience. But see what perseverance may accomplish. Thor-

---

[2] John Ballantine Gough, a noted Anglo-American orator and temperance lecturer, was born at Sandgate, England, 22 August 1817, and died at Philadelphia, 18 February 1886. He came to the United States in 1829 and, after taking a temperance pledge and reforming from alcoholism, began lecturing for the temperance cause in 1843. Among his publications are an *Autobiography* (1846) and *Sunshine and Shadow* (1881). He is the subject of a fictional biography, *Tiger! Tiger!* (1930), by Honoré Morrow. A comment in a letter dated 4 June 1869, implies that Twain had met and talked with Gough (and other lecturers) a number of times prior to that date: "In all conversations with Gough, and Anna Dickinson, Nasby, Oliver Wendell Holmes, Wendell Phillips and the other old stagers, I could not observe that *they* ever expected or hoped to get out of the business" (*MTL*, I, 159). But these meetings probably took place during the lecture tour in the fall of 1868, a few months after the composition of "Mamie Grant."

oughly reformed at last, he now traverses the land a brand plucked from the burning, and delivers temperance lectures and organizes Sunday Schools. Go thou and do likewise. It is never too late. Hasten, while yet the spirit is upon you.

"But *he* is gone, too, and took his mortgage with him. He will reform, I know he will. And then the good he will do can never be estimated. Truly this has been to me a blessed day."

So saying, Mamie Grant put on her little bonnet and went forth into the city to carry tracts to the naked and hungry poor, to the banker in his busy office, to the rumseller dealing out his soul-destroying abominations.

That night when she returned, her uncle Wagner was in deep distress. He said:

"Alas, we are ruined. My newspaper is stopped, and I am posted on its bulletin board as a delinquent. The tax-collecting census-taker has set his black mark opposite my name. Martin, who should have returned the thousand dollars he borrowed has not come, and Phillips, in consequence, has foreclosed the mortgage, and we are homeless!"

"Be not cast down, dear uncle," Mamie said, "for I have sent all these men into the vineyard. They shall sow the fields far and wide and reap a rich harvest. Cease to repine at worldly ills, and attend only to the behests of the great hereafter."

Mr. Wagner only groaned, for he was an unregenerated man.

Mamie placed a happy head upon her pillow that night. She said:

"I have saved a paper carrier, a census bureau, a creditor and a debtor, and they will bless me forever. I have done a noble work to-day. I may yet see my poor little name in a beautiful Sunday School book, and maybe T. S. Arthur [3] may write it. Oh, joy!"

Such is the history of "Mamie Grant, the Child-Missionary."

---

[3] Timothy Shay Arthur (1809–1885) was the most widely known nineteenth-century American writer for the temperance cause, and certainly the most prolific. During his lifetime he wrote over 100 tales, tracts, essays, and novels. He also founded, edited, and published *Arthur's Home Magazine.* His most popular and famous work is the novel *Ten Nights in a Bar-Room, and What I Saw There* (1854). The work also achieved great popularity in a dramatic version (1858) prepared by William W. Pratt for which Henry Clay Work composed his most popular song, "Father, Dear Father, Come Home with Me Now."

# *L'Homme Qui Rit*

(Translated from Victor Hugo)

(1869)

Editor's Note: As Twain notes at the end, his burlesque of Victor Hugo's *L'Homme qui rit* is based upon William Young's translation of *The Man Who Laughs* (New York: D. Appleton and Co., 1869). The burlesque was written in the fall of 1869 and, after revision, partially prepared for publication in the Buffalo *Express.* Its importance derives not from the fact that it is a burlesque of Hugo's novel but from the fact that in the revision Twain turned it into an allegorical depiction of Andrew Johnson's political career, particularly of Johnson's fortunes after he succeeded Lincoln in the presidency. It is an attempt to mold burlesque to his own satiric theme. As a political allegory, the burlesque throws considerable light upon Clemens' political affiliations in 1869 and upon his shifting allegiance from 1867 to 1869.

The date of the piece is indicated not only by the publication date of the translation upon which it is based but also by the use in the burlesque of a jibe used in another squib, "Last Words of Great Men," published in the Buffalo *Express,* 11 September 1869. In the squib, Twain suggests that Johnson should say, "I have been an Alderman, Member of Congress, Governor, Senator, Pres—adieu, you know the rest." [1] In the burlesque he summarizes Gwynplaine's farewell speech: "He told how he had played all the characters known to the profession —Alderman, Mayor, Legislator, Congressman, Senator, Vice President, President!" The use in the two works of the same jibe, a hit at Johnson's frequent public references to his political experience and his pride in himself as a self-made man, suggests a conjunction in time—sug-

[1] Reprinted in Mark Twain, *Life as I Find It,* ed. Charles Neider (Garden City, 1961), p. 32.

gests that 'L'Homme Qui Rit" was also written about September 1869.

"L'Homme Qui Rit" apparently grew out of an animus not only against Johnson but also against the Democrats in general. Certainly, turning Johnson into a burlesque Gwynplaine, "the most popular clown in all Southwark," is highly unflattering to Johnson (a Democrat would have found greater point in doing such an honor to "Smiler" Colfax, Speaker of the House). The reference to the "Ark" as the Confederate ship of state is as thoroughly Radical Republican as one could be in this period: the "Ark" was a derisive Republican epithet for the convention hall in Philadelphia used by the Johnson Democrats in 1866. The term itself in the burlesque continues the Republican derision, and its allegorical significance adds the Radical Republican charge that the Democrats were still the party of treason and secession. Finally, the assertion that Johnson became the heir of Lord Clancharlie hides another Radical Republican charge and suggests the event which caused Twain to write the piece. At first glance, one might assume that Lord Clancharlie represents Lincoln, but the description of Clancharlie as one "who exiled himself . . . in a foreign land" rather clearly identifies him as Jefferson Davis. The charge buried in the allegory reflects the one made by Senator Charles Sumner in his opinion on the acquittal of Johnson: "Andrew Johnson is the impersonation of the tyrannical slave power. In him it lives again. He is the lineal successor of John C. Calhoun and Jefferson Davis; and he gathers about him the same supporters." [2] The echo of Sumner's charge not only reinforces the impression of Radical Republican sympathies, but also suggests that Twain turned to the burlesque-allegory after reading the official record of the impeachment proceedings (in which Sumner's opinion first appeared) published by the Government Printing Office in 1868.

The conclusion suggested by the evidence of "L'Homme Qui Rit," then, is that, if Clemens were sympathetic to the Southern cause in 1861, he had changed allegiance completely by mid-1869 and, further, had become a Radical Republican. For a detailed discussion of Clemens' political activities and affiliations in Washington and after and the bearing of these upon "L'Homme Qui Rit," see Appendix B.

---

[2] U. S. Senate, *Trial of Andrew Johnson, President of the United States, before the Senate of the United States on Impeachment by the House of Representatives for High Crimes and Misdemeanors* (Washington, 1868), III, 247.

# *L'Homme Qui Rit.*

(Translated from Victor Hugo)

## Chap. I.

## The Boy, Gwynplaine

The boy started up the hill!

Only a poor tailor boy.[3]

It was night.

Midnight.

It was black—awful.

Ice covered ground, rocks—everything. It was snowing.

Far up the hill, steeped in solitude, reeking with silence, he—hark!

Something creaked!

Something moaned!

The boy listened—held his breath and listened, in the storm.

The storm is always itself—the storm. It comes whence it emanates, and proceeds whither it listeth.—Hence it is mysterious.—Mists upon the ocean hold the electricity—in solution and counterbalance the disintegrated oxydes in the flying spume of the sea. Drooping clouds, over the land, dispensing oxygen and absorbing hydrogen, impart phosphorescent light to the falling snow. Hence it is darker upon the sea than upon the land while a storm lasts.

[3] This sentence, a later insertion and a departure from the facts of Hugo's novel, is the first indication that Gwynplaine is an allegorical representation of Andrew Johnson. One may see in it simply a reference to Johnson's humble beginning as a tailor in Greeneville, Tennessee, but there is a strong likelihood that it reflects a popular jibe used by the Radical Republicans during the election campaign of 1864 when the prospective Lincoln-Johnson administration was ridiculed as "the age of rail splitters and tailors."

The storm cares for nothing. It lashes the waves—sweeps the coasts—splits the rocks—rushes, roars, crashes, thunders above the sea! It tears up trees—rends the solid earth—topples buildings to the ground—whoops, howls, screams over moors,—mows its way through forests, thrashes its terrific road along the hillsides! Such is the storm. You cannot modify it. You cannot account for it.

Very well.

The boy peered through the thick snow—and listened.

Snow never falls otherwise than in flakes. When it falls in icy pellets it is hail—in homeopathic pills, it is sleet—in globules of water, it is rain. Such is snow. You never see it otherwise. Never otherwise than in flakes. It is the nature of snow. Eternity is the end of all things. Immutability incomprehensible—unintelligibility profound. Time is eternity. Eternity is time. This is the supreme unity of the Soul. *Allons!*

The boy heard a creak. Not a creak with water in it, but a creak to make a sound—*chupā,* in the Pawnee tongue, *chipper* in the Bengalese, *cheep* in the Hottentot.

He crept closer.

He peered through the darkness, the falling snow.

He saw something—a post. Touched it. It was greasy. He looked up.

It was a gallows!

Suspended to it was a shapeless mass. A shapeless mass, hung in chains. A putrid carcass—with obscene ravens flapping their heavy wings about the eyeless face. A horrible, ghastly, decaying party, this boy saw—a party labeled "AFRICAN SLAVE TRADE," on the mutilated rear of his trowsers.[4]

He did not want the corpse.

He left.

An hour after—still plodding barefoot, nearly naked, uncomplainingly through the snow—the driving, cruel snow—the malignant, thrashing snow—whistling, this lone boy, for company, on this bleak moor—thermometer ten below—he heard a groan.

He treed the groan.

He found a corpse.

---

[4] Before revision, Gwynplaine, as in Hugo's novel, discovers a criminal's corpse.

It was not the corpse that groaned. It was a baby at the dead woman's breast.

The boy dug out the baby.

Adopted it.

He desired an heir—to leave his misfortunes to.

He called the baby Dea. (Dea for short and Democracy was the full name.) He was too cold to say Dear.

He tramped to the next town, and put up with a gentleman and a wolf.[5] They were theatre actors in a small itinerant way.—He and Dea grew up in the profession. They played in many places, some great, some greater—played for years. And all the time, he was in love with her, and she with him. Just then—

## Chap. II.
## The Ork.

The ork "African Slavery" (otherwise the ark) was out in the storm that awful night.[6]

Carrying no signals.

They were afraid of discovery.

The storm increased. The wind shrieked through the cordage—ripped the sails—sent the sea flying in sprays over the deck. The vessel labored. She sprang a leak!

[5] This and the preceding paragraph were deleted in the MS; they have been restored because they are necessary for continuity and for greater clarity in the allegory which follows. One should not attempt to find allegorical consistency in a passage which has been deleted (the deletion may have been necessitated by a lack of consistency), but the tramp "to the next town" may refer to Johnson's removal to Washington either to join the Senate in December 1857, or to join Lincoln as Vice-President in 1865.

[6] The word "ark" hides a reference to the convention of Johnson supporters at Philadelphia, 14–16 August 1866. To dramatize the new brotherhood of northern and southern citizens, the delegates entered the convention hall in pairs, arm in arm, a northerner paired with a southerner. The gesture furnished ammunition for the Radical Republicans, who dubbed the convention hall "Noah's Ark" and likened the grand march into the hall to the biblical pairing *"of clean beasts, and of beasts that are not clean, and of fowls, and of everything that creepeth upon the earth."* See James G. Blaine, *Twenty Years of Congress* (Norwich, 1884–86), II, 223. The allegorical identification of the ark was added during revision.

Overboard with the freight! Overboard with the express packages! Overboard with the mails!

A pause.

Overboard with the baggage! [7]

Too late. The leak gains.

The Stranger Confederacy called for a bottle of brandy. It was brought. He emptied it—not into the ocean—that was overflowing already. He drew from his pocket the parchment about that boy—wrote in the margin the particulars of leaving him behind when he wanted to go [8] —wrote it in Greek so it would be easier understood —signed it with the names of all the passengers who could not write—the whole ship's crew, in fact.—

The rudder was gone, the ship was sinking.

He called for twine.

The water was up to their knees—all hands stood about the Stranger on the deck, in the awful darkness, under the storm.

He called for leather.

The water was up to their middles—and gaining.

He tied the leather over the neck of the bottle.

Up to their chins!

He threw the bottle into the sea.

The ork shuddered, and—down she went. No insurance.

Never a soul lived to tell the tale of that fearful night.

Except Victor Hugo.

How he found it out is—

Too many for me.

## Chap. III.

### The Rocket Ascends

Twenty years after. Heir wanted for Lord Clancharlie. For Lord Clancharlie, who exiled himself and made himself uncom-

---

[7] Above "baggage" in light pencil Twain wrote, "Means slaves."

[8] The reference is to Johnson's refusal in 1861, while senator from Tennessee, to follow his fellow congressmen from Tennessee and the other southern states into secession.

fortable because it was pleasanter to be uncomfortable and morbidly virtuous in a foreign land than live at home in comfort and see the way the vile sycophants of the government do go on.

Nobody can supply that want.

The agonized solicitors advertise in the "Personals" in vain.

Gwynplaine and troupe are playing an engagement of six nights only, behind a barn in Southwark. The old man, and Dea, and the wolf, are of the troupe yet. Gwynplaine is "The Man Who Laughs," and he is an excellent hand at it, for his mouth was improved by art for it when he was young.

He was the most popular clown in all Southwark.

He played so well that they put him in jail. Now he suffered! He still loved Dea, but he could not see her, because they would not let him. Dea loved him, but she could not see him because she was as blind as a bat.

About this time, that jug came ashore—that brandy bottle with the ork's manifest in it—and that paper about the boy, telling who he was, and why?

The boy was Gwynplaine!

Gwynplaine the miserable, the wretched, the unhappy!

They snatched him out of jail and made him an earl!

He could not comprehend it. It surely was a dream. It *must* be a dream!

He had a vertigo.[9]

A double vertigo.

The vertigo of an ascent, and the vertigo of a fall.

Fatal compound.

He had felt himself to be mounting up, and had not felt himself to be falling down.

There is something formidable in the aspect of a new horizon.

A vista suggests counsel. Not always good.

He had had before him the fairy opening—snare, perhaps—of a cloud that breaks away, and that shows the deep azure.

So deep, that it is dark.

---

[9] The remainder of this chapter is composed of three clippings from William Young's translation of Hugo's novel, *The Man Who Laughs* (New York, 1869).

He was on the mountain, whence are visible the kingdoms of the earth.

Mountain all the more terrible, that it has no existence. They are in a dream, who are on this summit.

A man going to sleep in a mole's hole, and awaking on the highest point of Strasburg Cathedral spire—such was Gwynplaine.

Vertigo is a kind of fearful lucidity. That vertigo especially, which, carrying you at once toward day and toward night, is made up of two wheelings in contrary directions.

You see too much—and not enough.

You see all—and nothing.

Suddenly he stopped, his hands behind his back, looking up at the ceiling—or heaven, it matters not which—at what was up above.

—Vengeance! said he.

## Chap. IV.
## The Rocket Descends.

He forsook Dea, his beloved. He forsook Democracy.[10]

Vengeance!

That was what he wanted. Vengeance upon the class that had once abused him—that had now lifted him to the clouds. At last he compassed it.

He went before the greatest tribunal in the land—before the mighty People.

He made a speech.

He mounted the wind—he rode upon the whirlwind.

He swung round the circle.[11]

---

[10] I.e., the Democratic Party. The reference is, of course, to Johnson's candidacy as Vice-President on the Union-Republican ticket with Lincoln.

[11] Johnson called his speech-making tour, 28 August to 15 September 1866, his "Swing around the Circle." The tour covered the strongholds of Radical Republicanism in an effort to strengthen the Democratic hand in Congress.

He told how he had played all the characters known to the profession—Alderman, Mayor, Legislator, Congressman, Senator, Vice President, President! He told them what they were coming to, and left the Constitution with them. Also the flag, with thirty-six stars on it.[12]

That speech finished *him.*[13]

Then he deserted.

He rushed madly away and joined his beloved Dea again. Hand in hand they sailed away.

Up Salt River.

And when she sickened and died, he threw himself overboard.

He is there yet.

Such is life.

Mark Twain

P.S.—I do not wish to be accused of stealing, and therefore I will remark that in one place in this article I have sandwiched in some thirty or forty lines of the Appletons' translation of Victor Hugo's *"L'Homme Qui Rit,"* without altering a line or a syllable. M.T.

---

[12] Johnson's habitual whistle-stop benediction during his "Swing around the Circle" was "I leave in your hands the Constitution and the Union, and the glorious flag of your country not with twenty-five but with thirty-six stars" (Lloyd P. Stryker, *Andrew Johnson, A Study in Courage* [New York, 1929], p. 349).

[13] A reference to either the Cleveland speech of 3 September 1866, or the St. Louis speech of 8 September. In both speeches, Johnson spoke intemperately of the Radical Republican plot to usurp the powers of the Executive. These speeches became the basis for Article Ten in the Bill of Impeachment. See U.S. Senate, *Trial of Andrew Johnson,* I, 6–10.

# BURLESQUE

## *Hamlet*

(1881)

Editor's Note: The fragmentary burlesque *Hamlet* which survives in the Mark Twain Papers was written in three days of enthusiastic work at Quarry Farm, Elmira, following Clemens' visit to Boston, 25–26 August 1881. After his return to Elmira, Clemens wrote William Dean Howells on 3 September 1881:

> At your house (I think it was) an old idea came again into my head which I had missed from that treasury during seven or eight years or more: that of adding a character to Hamlet. I did the thing once—nine years ago; the addition was a country cousin of Hamlet's. But it did not suit me, & I burnt it. A cousin wouldn't answer; the family could not consistently ignore him; one couldn't rationally explain a *cousin's* standing around the stage during 5 acts & never being spoken to: yet of course the added character must *not* be spoken to; for the sacrilegious scribbler who ventured to put words into Shakspeare's mouth would probably be hanged. But I've got a character, now, who is all right. He goes & comes as he pleases; yet he does not need to be spoken to. I've done the first & second Acts; but this was too much work for three days; so I am in bed.[1]

As Clemens told Howells, the text was written in 1881, but the comic possibilities of adding a character to *Hamlet* had fascinated him for a number of years. The difficulty was to find the right character. Later in the letter he announced his belief that the visit

[1] *MTHL,* I, 369.

had solved his difficulty: "Take it all around, it was a pretty fat visit that I made to Boston & Belmont. Among other things, that visit . . . gave me the right character for my Hamlet." But the aid which he received must have been indirect and unwitting, either the result of a chance remark during the discussion of an unrelated topic or the result of an encounter with a person whose characteristics furnished the clue, for Howells' reply of 11 September 1881, suggests that Twain's letter was the first he had heard of the project: "That is a famous idea about the Hamlet, and I should like ever so much to see your play when it's done. Of course you'll put it on the stage, and I prophesy a great triumph for it." [2]

According to Albert Bigelow Paine, Twain first mentioned his idea for the improvement of *Hamlet* in a backstage conversation with Edwin Booth during one of Booth's appearances as the Dane. To document his statement Paine quotes Orion Clemens: "[Sam and Livy] went to see Booth in *Hamlet,* and Booth sent for Sam to come behind the scenes, and when Sam proposed to add a part to *Hamlet,* the part of a bystander who makes humorous modern comment on the situations in the play, Booth laughed immoderately." [3] (Walter Blair suggests that for "immoderately" one should read "hysterically.") I have been unable to find the document from which Paine quotes, but the occasion must have been Clemens' and Livy's visit to the theater in New York on 3 November 1873, the day after their return from England, for on that date Orion wrote to his wife, Mollie, that the two returned travelers had seen Booth in *Hamlet* that evening. But Orion's letter makes no mention of the visit backstage or of the proposal to Booth.[4]

Never one to let a gaudy idea, no matter how bizarre, languish long in the realms of the untried, Twain probably plunged into composition as soon as possible after the idea occurred to him. His enthusiasm cooled, and work on the project ground to a halt when, as he indicated to Howells, the introduction of the new character threatened to force him into taking liberties with Shakespeare's words. Although his dissatisfaction with the result of his labors led

---

[2] *Ibid.,* I, 373.
[3] *MTB,* I, 495.
[4] Original in MTP.

him, according to the statement to Howells, to burn the manuscript, the idea continued to attract him. Early in 1879 he became bold enough to defy his scruples concerning Shakespeare's words and jotted in his notebook, "Try Hamlet again, and make free with Shakspere—let Hamlet and everybody else talk with the fellow and wish he was in Hölle as the G's say." [5] If his recollection of 1881 is correct, he did not act upon this suggestion; at least no clear evidence exists to show that he attemped either in 1879 or 1880 to translate the new conception into manuscript. In mid-1880 he jotted in his notebook an idea which he evidently considered comic and later worked into the 1881 "Hamlet" manuscript: "Tight man who had swallowed a small ball of thread and stood pulling it out, yard after yard and swearing to himself." [6] But the appearance of the idea both in the 1880 notebook and later in the 1881 "Hamlet" does not, of course, necessarily mean that Twain was working on a version of the burlesque in 1880. He seems, however, to have outlined his new idea to Joseph T. Goodman, who had been the editor during his days as a reporter for the Virginia City *Territorial Enterprise*. Responding to a now-lost letter from Clemens mentioning the renewed interest of September 1881, Goodman wrote on 24 October 1881, "It was singular that I should have been thinking of your 'Hamlet' scheme just before your letter came. I still believe it would make an immense hit if you chanced to get the brother sandwiched in happily." [7] Clearly at some time prior to September 1881, Twain had mentioned the *Hamlet* idea to Goodman, an idea which involved the addition of Hamlet's brother. Since the 1873 plan revolved around a country cousin and the 1881 text uses a foster-brother, the blood-brother mentioned to Goodman probably came from a further development connected with the 1879 notebook entry.

---

[5] Typescript Notebook 13, p. 38 (following the entry for 14 January 1879), MTP. I must confess my inability to understand Twain's scruples. Apparently Twain did not object to a disruption of the total fabric of *Hamlet* with the introduction of a new character, but he did object violently to the disruption or alteration of individual speeches or lines. The effects of the scruples are easily perceived, but the scale of values behind them defies analysis.

[6] Typescript Notebook 15, p. 7 (following the entry for 1 August 1880), MTP.

[7] Original in MTP.

Twain was apparently already brimming with enthusiasm when he entrained for his return from Boston to Elmira on 26 August 1881. Stopping in New York, he left instructions with his nephew, Charles Webster, to purchase and forward to him four copies of *Hamlet* from Samuel French. Five days later, still anxious to get to work and curious about the fate of the copies of *Hamlet,* which had failed to follow him to Elmira as promptly as he had expected, he wrote Webster, "If anything happened to the 4 acting copies of Hamlet, buy them again, of Samuel French, Nassau St., (see Directory,) and mail them to me." [8] The original four copies must have arrived on the same day as his query to Webster, for by 3 September he had already put in three days' work on the play. He worked fast, scribbling lines for his new character and clipping portions from the acting copies to be pasted in the manuscript, but he apparently did not work as fast as he claimed in the letter to Howells. To Howells he boasted that he had completed the first two acts, but the surviving manuscript breaks off with Polonius' speech "Still harping on my daughter!" early in Act II, scene ii.

Twain abandoned the project at this point and seems to have lost all enthusiasm for the idea during the next fifteen years, although his friends continued to encourage him. On 31 January 1882, Howells inquired, "What did you ever do with your amended Hamlet? That was a famous idea." [9] If Twain answered the query, the answer has not survived. Early in 1883 Goodman prodded him even more sharply by sending him a complete draft of an amended *Hamlet* based on the blood-brother idea of 1879. Ever since learning in 1881 of Goodman's financial misfortunes and his retirement as a farmer in Fresno, California, Clemens had urged him to repair his finances with literary endeavors. To Clemens' various suggestions Goodman replied apathetically, but in March 1883, he completed on his own initiative and for his own amusement a version of the *Hamlet* idea and forwarded it with a letter gently hinting at Twain's own apathy: "Here is your 'Hamlet's Brother,' roughly blocked out. I thought you would never get about it in earnest, and did it to amuse myself. . . . You will have to re-

[8] SLC to Charles Webster, Elmira, 31 August 1881.

[9] *MTHL,* I, 391.

write his part [Bill, Hamlet's brother] throughout. I started to cut the acts that are rather too long, but came to the conclusion it would be better to leave it until you had altered it, then you can prune the longer acts so as to make the whole symmetrical." [10]

Twain failed to rise to Goodman's bait; "Hamlet's Brother" was packaged and filed away among Twain's papers, where it still rests today, untouched anywhere by Twain's revising hand. A possible reason for the cool reception of Goodman's effort appears in another sentence of Goodman's covering letter: "I was speaking to Barrett once about your idea, and he thought it would be a sort of sacrilege." Goodman went on to scoff at such an attitude, but perhaps the damage had been done: he may have evoked unwittingly those scruples which Twain had so bravely flouted in his 1879 notebook. The apathy lasted for almost a decade and a half, until some time early in 1897, when the idea and the enthusiasm suddenly but briefly flickered back to life. In his notebook, shortly after the entry for 23 February 1897, Twain wrote:

> Hamlet's country cousin. H to be *real,* not a play. H and the others to be allowed to speak to him now and then in stately form.
>
> Could *he* bring about any of the situations?
>
> 25 years ago Edwin Booth told me to *do* this. I tried and couldn't succeed.[11]

But the flicker died as soon as it appeared and left nothing but a small spark that winked briefly in a later notebook entry, after 28 June 1897, repeating what to Twain was apparently the most convulsing joke in the whole idea: "Drunken man who has swallowed a ball of thread." [12] After this, not even a wisp of smoke.

In "L'Homme Qui Rit" Twain attempted to impose his own purpose, a satirical attack upon Andrew Johnson, on Hugo's novel without making any major alterations in or additions to Hugo's plot, characters, and setting. He still, that is, accepted for the most part the restrictions which the writer of condensed burlesque novels was

---

[10] J. T. Goodman to SLC, Fresno, Calif., 18 March 1883 (original in MTP).
[11] Typescript Notebook 32a (I), pp. 14–15, MTP.
[12] Typescript Notebook 32a (II), p. 38, MTP.

obliged to regard as the price to be paid for his fun. In the burlesque *Hamlet* we see Twain taking a greater measure of freedom with his materials. Although still exhibiting the parasitism of the writer of condensed burlesque novels in his retention of Shakespeare's text, he asserts his independence by adding a character of his own. The result is something quite different from, say, "A Novel: *Who Was He?*" or "Mamie Grant." In these two works the fun derives from the reflection of idiosyncracies and absurdities in the original works. But in the burlesque *Hamlet* Twain hoped to derive fun from the character which he himself had added. One cannot heap much praise upon the result of his effort, but one should recognize that the device used here is precisely the device used to much greater effect in *A Connecticut Yankee.*

The readings, punctuation, and spellings peculiar to the Samuel French version of *Hamlet* which Twain used have been preserved in the following text.

# *Hamlet.*

## To Precede Act. I.

(Slide a scene across, to hide the Palace.)

ENTER Basil Stockmar, book agent (with a canvassing copy), weary with tramping.—with old satchel and old umbrella.

*Basil, (solus,) sitting down.* Ten days tramp, over Denmark roads, in this weather, is a wearisome business; but that is no matter, for this is a business trip, not a pleasure excursion. One doesn't walk these frosty roads ten days for recreation when he could stay at home and do it up a ladder, with a hod, and get five times the recreation out of it, and wages to boot. But I judge I am about to the end of my journey; for the dim pile of buildings yonder must be the palace. The old king is dead; that's a pity; and his brother is king in his place—which is another pity, I take it; though none but an ass would betray his own confidence sufficiently to say it in public; but the queen is alive, yet, and young Hamlet—maybe these will still remember Basil Stockmar, the farmer's humble baby who was foster-brother to Hamlet, and milked the same plebeian breast along with him at a time when he wasn't as particular about the style of his company as he is now, perhaps. It is only twenty-three years since they saw me last. I was fifteen months old, then, and so was Hamlet. I reckon we can't either of us be much changed. However, one can't tell, as to that. But if I could see him biting at a rattle, once, I know I could recognize him in a minute. He was a very nice baby indeed; and would have been perfectly agreeable in a deaf and dumb asylum—everybody said that. Now if either of them *will* remember poor Basil, my fortune is made and I am done with grinding poverty; for they will subscribe for the book I've started out to canvass for; and with *their* names to head my list, I reckon the general public will be in more or less of a hurry to alter their form of salutation to me. And I shall be glad of that. Yes, I shall. (*Pensively*)—For sometimes I do get mighty tired of hearing that same old welcome, always in the same old words, "O, here's another dam *book* agent!" Now let me see—maybe I better practice my new canvassing lesson a little, and see if I've got it by heart [13]—for such a thing wants to glide off the tongue pretty glib and oily and natural-like, you know, to get the best effect and convert the candidate. (*Rising and addressing the seat, at the same time opening and fluttering the leaves of the book.*) "Sir, the book which I have the honor to offer for your worship's consideration, is a work which—which—which—O, yes!—is a work which is—is a work which has been commended by the highest authorities as an achievement of transcendent and hitherto unparalleled merit." O, yes—that's all right—I can rattle it off like a furniture auction. "Sir, it is a work which the family circle cannot afford to be without. Let me call your worship's particular attention to this admirable chapter upon 'The Mythological Era of Denmark';—and to this one upon 'Denmark's High Place Among the Historical Empires of Antiquity'; and *most* particularly to this noble, and beautiful, and convincing dissertation upon the old, old vexed question, 'Inasmuch as Methuselah lived to the very building of the Ark and the very day of the flood, how was it he got left?' And also to this exquisite satirical description of old men: 'Old men have gray beards; their faces are wrinkled; their eyes purging thick amber and plum-tree gum,' etcetera, etcetera and so on"—O, it's just tip-top—lays over anything you ever saw. "Let me also call your worship's worshipful attention to"—(*Closing book*)—O, it's all right—no use to study it any more—I can say it as glib as a highwayman can say his neck-verse. And after I leave *here,* don't you know, the common herd won't interrupt me the way they've been doing for a week past. *No,* sir; they'll swarm around and say, "No, but *did* 'er majesty look at this very picture, with 'er very own eyes?—how nice! And *did* sweet

[13] A marginal note reads, "This canvassing lesson is on fly-leaf of his book."

prince Hamlet say, with his very own mouth, that if he had his choice between this book and a barrel of di'monds, he wouldn't hesitate a minute to say 'O, rot the di'monds, gimme the book?'—*O, how nice!*" Whereas those very same clod-hoppers used to break right in on me in the rudest way, and spread the door open and say, "Now my friend, just you take a *walk!*" (*Going.*) But it's all right, it's all right; every dog has his day. They've had theirs, and mine's a-coming. (*Tapping his book.*) Just you let me get old mammy Hamlet's little old signature scratched down on this-here list of mine, and if I don't . . . . well, *you'll* see! (*Exit.*

Scene changes to "Platform near Palace. FRANCISCO at his post, R.

*Enter* BERNARDO, L.

*Ber.* (L.) Who's there?

*Fran.* Nay, answer me:—stand, and unfold yourself.

*Ber.* Long live the king!

*Fran.* Bernardo?

*Ber.* He.

*Fran.* You come most carefully upon your hour.

*Ber.* (L.C.) 'Tis now struck twelve; get thee to bed, Francisco.

*Fran.* (R.C.) For this relief, much thanks:—'tis bitter cold,
And I am sick at heart.

*Ber.* Have you had quiet guard?

*Fran.* (L.C.) Not a mouse stirring.

*Ber.* (R.) Well, good night.
If you do meet Horatio and Marcellus,
The rivals of my watch, bid them make haste.

*Fran.* I think I hear them. Stand, ho! (L.) Who is there?

*Enter* HORATIO *and* MARCELLUS, L.

*Hor.* (L.) Friends to this ground.

*Mar.* (R.) And liegemen to the Dane.

*Fran.* Give you good night.

*Mar.* Oh, farewell, honest soldier!
Who hath relieved you?

*Fran.* Bernardo hath my place.
Give you good night. (*Exit,* L.

*Mar.* Holloa! Bernardo!

*Ber.* Say,

What, is Horatio there?

*Hor.* A piece of him. (*Giving his hand*

*Ber.* Welcome, Horatio; welcome, good Marcellus.

*Hor.* What, has this thing appeared again to-night?

*Ber.* I have seen nothing.

*Mar.* (L.C.) Horatio says, 'tis but our fantasy:
And will not let belief take hold of him,
Touching this dreaded sight, twice seen of us:
Therefore I have entreated him along
With us to watch the minutes of this night:
That, if again this apparition come,
He may approve our eyes, and speak to it.

*Hor.* (R.C.) Tush! tush! 'twill not appear.

*Ber.* Come, let us once again assail your ears,
That are so fortified against our story,
What we two nights have seen.

*Hor.* (C.) Well, let us hear Bernardo speak of this.

*Ber.* Last night of all,
When yon same star, that's westward from the pole,
Had made his course to illume that part of heaven
Where now it burns, Marcellus, and myself,
The bell then beating one,—

*Mar.* (C.) Peace, break thee off; look, where it comes again!

*Enter* GHOST, L., *and* BASIL, R.

*Basil.* Say—can any of you fellows tell me—(*perceives Ghost*)—
O, my God! (*Exit with precipitation.*)

*Ber.* In the same figure, like the king that's dead.

*Hor.* (R.C.) Most like:—it harrows me with fear and wonder.

*Ber.* It would be spoke to.

*Mar.* Speak to it, Horatio.

*Hor.* What art thou, that usurp'st this time of night,
Together with that fair and warlike form,
In which the majesty of buried Denmark
Did sometimes march? By heaven, I charge thee, speak.

(*Ghost crosses to R.*

*Mar.* It is offended.

*Ber.* See! it stalks away.

*Hor.* Stay; speak; speak, I charge thee, speak!

(*Exit Ghost,* R.

*Mar.* 'Tis gone, and will not answer.

*Ber.* How now, Horatio? you tremble and look pale:
Is not this something more than fantasy?
What think you of it?

*Hor.* (R.) I might not this believe,
Without the sensible and true avouch
Of mine own eyes.

*Mar.* (C.) Is it not like the king?

*Hor.* As thou art to thyself:
Such was the very armour he had on,
When he the ambitious Norway combated.

*Mar.* Thus, twice before, and jump at this dead hour,
With martial stalk he hath gone by our watch.

*Hor.* In what particular thought to work, I know not
But, in the gross and scope of mine opinion,
This bodes some strange eruption to our state.

*Re-enter* GHOST, L. *and* BASIL, R.

*Basil.* (*Advancing, stooping, brushing dust from his knees, and laughing.*) Well, that's mighty funny! To think that I, a full grown lout—but at the same time I wish I may die if I didn't think I saw —(*Stops, with his hands on his knees, trying to control his consuming laughter, under the Ghost's nose. Follows the Ghost's form up to its face with his eyes and then sneaks trembling away without a word. Or, looks suddenly up and says,* "God bless me!" and EXIT *precipitately.*) (*Silent pantomime is best, no doubt.*)

*Hor.* But, soft; behold! lo, where it comes again!
I'll cross it, though it blast me (*Ghost crosses to* R.) Stay illusion!
If thou hast any sound or use of voice,
Speak to me: (*Ghost stops at* R.
If there be any good thing to be done,
That may to thee do ease, and grace to me,
Speak to me. (L.C.)
If thou art privy to thy country's fate,
Which, happily, fore-knowing may avoid
Oh, speak!

Or, if thou hast uphoarded in thy life
Extorted treasure in the womb of the earth,
For which, they say, you spirits oft walk in death,
Speak of it—(*Exit Ghost,* L.)—stay, and speak.

*Mar.* 'Tis gone!
We do it wrong, being so majestical,
To offer it the show of violence.

*Ber.* It was about to speak, when the cock crew.

*Hor.* (R.) And then it started like a guilty thing
Upon a fearful summons. I have heard,
The cock, that is the trumpet of the morn,
Doth, with his lofty and shrill-sounding throat,
Awake the god of day; and, at his warning,
Whether in sea or fire, in earth or air,
The extravagant and erring spirit hies
To his confine.
But, look, the morn in russet mantle clad,
Walks o'er the dew of yon high eastern hill:
Break we our watch up; (*Crosses,* L.) and, by my advice
Let (L.C.) us impart what we have seen to-night
Unto young Hamlet; for, upon my life,
This spirit, dumb to us, will speak to him. (*Exeunt,* L.

*Re-enter* BASIL.

*Basil.* (*Sweaty and panting, and glancing uneasily about.*) O, he was a sure-'nough ghost, there ain't any question about *that,* don't you know. . . . I wonder if he's really gone, or only hanging around here somewheres, laying for a fellow? . . . I don't think much of that kind of conduct; I don't just exactly like that sort of thing—with parties I'm not acquainted with. Why, *I* don't know that old spectre; and what does he mean by . . . well I consider it a little too blamed familiar. 'Mf! By—*George!* what a club he had; and what a helmet. I don't think much of a country where they let a dead policeman go swelling around that way, nights. You bet you you wouldn't see him around so free if he was alive. 'Tain't their style, don't you know. . . . Sho! come to think, I reckon I begin to see what he was chasing me around like that, for. Why of course that's it—he wanted to *subscribe.* I'll just set him down for a couple of copies, anyway (*doing it*) and I'll find out who he is and collect from the heirs or there'll be trouble. A man can't subscribe for *my* books, and then slide out of paying simply because he . . . Well, I reckon I'll just put him down for *six* copies, (*doing it*) while I'm at it;—if he runs short of brimstone they'll come handy to him. My soul, but he did look ghastly! It was as much as I could do to keep calm. I wasn't *afraid* of him; I ain't afraid of *any* ghost that subscribes as liberally as what he has done. No, he didn't scare me, but by *George*, I don't think I've been as surprised, before, in seventeen years. (*Enter* GHOST, *behind.*) But I was a little off my guard, you see. I wasn't expecting anything. But if he was to come, *now*, I should just turn calmly on him and say, (*turning and discovering Ghost,*) "O, *don't* hurt a poor devil! Upon my sacred word and honor I wish I may die if I didn't come just only to fetch your worship a presentation copy! (*Kneels, quaking, before Ghost, and holds out his book.*) (*Or, let him simply exclaim* "Gee-whillikins!" *and skip out.*)

## SCENE II. THE PALACE.

BASIL discovered in shirt sleeves, coat lying by, sitting at ease in the king's throne, one foot resting on the other knee, smoking—in a brown study. After a pause—

*Basil.*—(*Examining cigar.*) But this is an anachronism—the art of smoking hasn't been discovered yet. (*Throws away cigar.*) There is a good deal of a muddle going on here. Deep down in their secret hearts, everybody in this gang is in more or less trouble. I don't know whether it's right, or not, for me to mix in; and yet, as a friend of the family, it seemed a kind of duty.—I hope I've done right—I certainly meant for the best, anyway. If my little private endeavors succeed, Hamlet will be made to stay right where he is—no trips to Wittenberg; and that chuckleheaded Laertes will ask leave to go to France, and will *get* it, too. Ham was just bound to go, and tother fellow was just bound to stay; and I do hope I have done some real good by reversing that program. Now the next job on my hands is to break up this love match of Hamlet's and Ophelia Polonius's. It can't ever do for that gentle little dove to marry the prince. He would break her heart in six months. Then I should feel myself to blame. I wonder how I'm going to manage that thing?—that is, so that I shan't appear too prominently in it. Got to work through other people, of course. Got to rig some purchase to persuade Polonius and Laertes [to] disapprove the match—I'll go to work on them right away. I'll ask them to take a drink, and-ah——(*going*) ——or if they should ask me to take a drink. . . . . . But the *neatest* thing—yes, and the necessary thing, too, will be to invent some scheme to get Hamlet *himself* to break off the match. I was afraid it was going to be dull, here, but I judge I've got business enough on hand to keep me on the jump for a while. I hear somebody out yonder. Maybe it's Polonius—I'll go see. (*Exit.*

*Flourish of Trumpets*

*Enter* POLONIUS, *the* KING, QUEEN, HAMLET, *Ladies and Attendants,* L., LAERTES, R., *and stand thus:*

R. LAERTES. POLON. KING. QUEEN. HAMLET.

*King.* (C.) Though yet of Hamlet, our dear brother's death,
The memory be green; and that it us befitted
To bear our hearts in grief, and our whole kingdom
To be contracted in one brow of woe;
Yet so far hath discretion fought with nature,
That we, with wisest sorrow, think on him,
Together with remembrance of ourselves.
Therefore, our sometime sister, now our queen,
The imperial jointress of this warlike state,
Have we, as 'twere with a defeated joy,
Taken to wife; nor have we herein barred
Your better wisdoms, which have freely gone
With this affair along: for all, our thanks.—
And now, Laertes, what's the news with you?
You told us of some suit.—What is't, Laertes?

*Laer.* My dread Lord,
Your leave and favour to return to France;
From whence, though willingly, I came to Denmark
To show my duty in your coronation;

Yet now, I must confess, that duty done,
My thoughts and wishes bend again toward France,
And bow them to your gracious leave and pardon.
*King.* Have you your father's leave? What says Polonius?
*Pol.* He hath, my Lord;
I do beseech you, give him leave to go.
*King.* Take thy fair hour, Laertes; time be thine,
And thy best graces; spend it at thy will.
But now, my cousin Hamlet, and my son—
*Ham.* A little more than kin, and less than kind. (*Aside.*
*King.* How is it that the clouds still hang on you?
*Ham.* Not so my Lord; I am too much i'the sun.
*Queen.* Good Hamlet, cast thy nighted colour off,
And let thine eye look like a friend on Denmark.
Do not, forever, with thy vailéd lids,
Seek for thy noble father in the dust:
Thou know'st 'tis common; all that live must die,
Passing through nature to eternity.
*Ham.* Ay, madam, it is common.
*Queen.* If it be,
Why seems it so particular with thee?
*Ham.* Seems, madam! nay, it is; I know not seems.
'Tis not alone my inky cloak, good mother,
Nor the dejected 'haviour of the visage,
No, nor the fruitful river in the eye,
Together with all forms, modes, shows of grief,
That can denote me truly: these, indeed, seem,
For they are actions that a man might play;
But I have that within, which passeth show;
These but the trappings and the suits of woe.
*King.* 'Tis sweet and commendable in your nature Hamlet,
To give these mourning duties to your father:
But, you must know, your father lost a father;
That father lost, lost his; and the survivor bound
In filial obligation for some term,
To do obsequious sorrow: but to persevere
In obstinate condolement, is a course

Of impious stubbornness; 'tis unmanly grief,
It shows a will most incorrect to heaven.
We pray you, throw to earth
This unprevailing woe, and think of us
As of a father: for let the world take note,
You are the most immediate to our throne,
Our chiefest courtier, cousin, and our son.

*Queen.* Let not thy mother lose her prayers, Hamlet.
I pray thee, stay with us, go not to Wittenberg.

*Ham.* I shall, in all my best, obey you, madam.

*King.* Why, 'tis a loving and a fair reply;
Be as ourself in Denmark. Madam, come;
This gentle and unforced accord of Hamlet
Sits smiling to my heart: in grace whereof,
No jocund health, that Denmark drinks to-day,
But the great cannon to the clouds shall tell,
Re-speaking earthly thunder.

*(Flourish of Trumpets*

*(Exeunt in the following order, viz. 1st, Polonius, with a White Rod, formally leading the way; 2d, the King and Queen; 3d, Laertes; 4th, male and female Attendants.*

*Ham.* *(Standing alone,* L.) Oh, that this too, too solid flesh would melt,
Thaw, and resolve itself into a dew!
Or that the Everlasting had not fixed
His canon 'gainst self-slaughter! God! O God!
How weary, stale, flat, and unprofitable,
Seem to me all the uses of this world!
Fie on't! O fie! (C.) 'Tis an unweeded garden,
That grows to seed; things rank and gross in nature
Possess it merely. That it should come to this!
But two months dead!—nay, not so much, not two—
So excellent a king; that was, to this,
Hyperion to a satyr; so loving to my mother,
That he might not beteem the winds of heaven
Visit her face too roughly. Heaven and earth!
Must I remember? Why, she would hang on him,

As if increase of appetite had grown
By what it fed on—and yet, within a month—
Let me not think on't;—Frailty, thy name is woman!—
A little month; or ere those shoes were old,
With which she followed my poor father's body,
Like Niobe, all tears;—
She married with my uncle,
My father's brother; but no more like my father,
Than I to Hercules.
It is not, nor it cannot come to, good;—
But break my heart: (L.) for I must hold my tongue!

*Enter* HORATIO, MARCELLUS, *and* BERNARDO, R.

*Hor.* (R.) Hail to your Lordship!

*Ham.* I am glad to see you well:
Horatio—or I do forget myself?

*Hor.* The same, my Lord, and your poor servant ever.

*Ham.* (R.) Sir, my good friend; I'll change that name with you.
And what make you from Wittenberg, Horatio?—
Marcellus?

*Mar.* (R.) My good Lord—

*Ham.* (C.) I am very glad to see you—Good even, sir—
But what, in faith, make you from Wittenberg?

*Hor.* (L.C.) A truant disposition, good my lord.

(*Marcellus and Bernardo stand,* R.

*Ham.* I would not hear your enemy say so;
Nor shall you do mine ear that violence,
To make it truster of your own report
Against yourself: I know you are no truant.
But, what is your affair in Elsinore?
We'll teach you to drink deep, ere you depart.

*Hor.* My lord, I came to see your father's funeral.

*Ham.* I pray thee, do not mock me, fellow-student;
I think it was to see my mother's wedding.

*Hor.* Indeed, my lord, it followed hard upon.

*Ham.* Thrift, thrift, Horatio! the funeral baked meats
Did coldly furnish forth the marriage tables.
Would I had met my dearest foe in heaven,

Or ever I had seen that day, Horatio! (*Enter* BASIL.)
My father—methinks, I see my father.

*Basil.* (*Aside.*) His father! Well, I *like* that! I resemble his grandmother as much. (*Much affected.*) I didn't expect him to recognize me right off, but this is *too* much.

*Hor.* Where, my lord?

*Ham.* In my mind's eye, Horatio!

*Basil.* (*Aside.*) Well, that's *one* way to get out of it. Pretty thin. . . . Seems to me these are the boys that were out cooling themselves when I struck the late policeman.

*Hor.* I saw him once: he was a goodly king.

*Ham.* He was a man, take him for all in all,
I shall not look upon his like again. (L.C.)

*Hor.* (R.C.) My lord, I think I saw him yesternight.

*Ham.* (L.) Saw! who?

*Hor.* My lord, the king, your father.

*Ham.* The king, my father!

*Hor.* Season your admiration for awhile
With an attent ear: till I may deliver
Upon the witness of these gentlemen,
This marvel to you.

*Ham.* (C.) For heaven's love, let me hear.

*Hor.* (C.) Two nights together had these gentlemen,
Marcellus and Bernardo, on their watch,
In the dead waste and middle of the night,
Been thus encountered;—a figure like your father,
Armèd at point, exactly cap-à-pé,
Appears before them, and, with solemn march,
Goes slow and stately by them: thrice he walked,
By their oppressed and fear surprisèd eyes,
Within his truncheon's length; whilst they, distilled
Almost to jelly with the act of fear,
Stand dumb and speak not to him. This to me
In dreadful secresy impart they did;
And I with them, the third night, kept the watch:
Where, as they had delivered, both in time,
Form of the thing, each word made true and good,

The apparition comes.

*(Basil listens with awed wonder, but the closing sentence takes the grandeur out of the thing for him.)*

*Basil.* (*Aside.*) Shucks, it was only the policeman.

*Ham.* (*To Bernardo and Marcellus,* R.) But where was this?

*Mar.* My lord, upon the platform where we watched.

*Ham.* Did you not speak to it?

*Hor.* (L.) My lord, I did;
But answer made it none; yet once, methought,
It lifted up its head, and did address
Itself to motion, like as it would speak;
But, even then, the morning cock crew loud;—
And, at the sound, it shrunk in haste away,
And vanished from our sight.

*Ham.* 'Tis very strange.

*Hor.* As I do live, my honoured lord, 'tis true;
And we did think it writ down in our duty,
To let you know of it.

*Ham.* (R.C.) Indeed, indeed, sirs: but this troubles me.—
Hold you the watch to-night?

*Mar.* We do, my lord.

*Ham.* Armed, say you?

*Mar.* Armed, my lord.

*Ham.* From top to toe?

*Mar.* My lord, from head to foot.

*Ham.* Then saw you not his face!

*Hor.* Oh, yes, my lord, he wore his beaver up.

*Ham.* What, looked he frowningly?

*Hor.* A countenance more
In sorrow than in anger.

*Ham.* Pale, or red?

*Hor.* Nay, very pale.

*Basil.* (*Aside.*) Ugh! it ain't no *name* for it!

*Ham.* And fixed his eyes upon you?

*Hor.* Most constantly.

*Ham.* I would I had been there.

*Basil.* (*Aside.*) There was *one* front seat he could 'a got cheap.

*Hor.* It would have much amazed you.

*Basil.* (*Aside.*) *Amazed* him, would it?—simply *amazed* him, says this duck. Well you better *bet* it would. It would 'a made him climb the highest tree in *this* school deestrict. And don't you *forget* it.

*Ham.* Very like,
Very like:—stayed it long?

*Hor.* While one, with moderate haste,
Might tell a hundred.

*Mar.* Longer, longer.

*Hor.* Not when I saw it.

*Basil.* (*Aside.*) I don't know which of 'em's right—let them settle it themselves. May 'a been shorter, may 'a been longer; *I* don't know —I went outside to count.

*Ham.* His beard was grizzled?—no?

*Hor.* It was, as I have seen it in his life,
A sable, silvered.

*Basil.* (*Aside.*) That's *him*—no two ways about that; they've got him down to a spot. So, as sure as guns, it *wasn't* a policeman, after all. No *sir,* it was the king—it was the late Grand Turk himself. Let *him* off with six copies? (*Getting out his book.*) I think I *see* myself! I'll just chalk him up for a level *hundred,* easy enough—and sue the estate!

*Ham.* I will watch to-night;
Perchance 'twill walk again.

*Hor.* I warrant 'twill.

*Ham.* If it assume my noble father's person,
I'll speak to it, though hell itself should gape,
And bid me hold my peace.

*Basil.* (*Aside.*) O, yes—*he*'ll speak to it! Of *course* he will!—I think I *see* him at it! Maybe he wouldn't mind getting it to subscribe for *another* hundred.[14]

*Ham.* (*Crosses* L.) I pray you all, (*Returns to* R.)
If you have hitherto concealed this sight,

---

[14] Two notes inserted in the MS following p. 26 read:

"Maybe let him exit with his speech on 26, and say he will go to old Polonius and strike him for a subscription."

"B. I will be there myself and see that Ghost again."

Let it be tenable in your silence still;
And whatsoever else shall hap to-night,
Give it an understanding, but no tongue.
I will requite your loves: so, fare you well:
Upon the platform, 'twixt eleven and twelve,
I'll visit you.

*Hor.* (R.) Our duty to your honour.

*Ham.* (R.) Your loves, as mine to you:

(*Exeunt all but Hamlet,* R., *and Basil*

My father's spirit! (C.)—in arms!—all is not well;
I doubt some foul play: 'would the night were come!
Till then, sit still, my soul: (L.) foul deeds will rise,
Though all the earth o'erwhelm them, to men's eyes. (*Going.*)

*Basil.* (*Following.*) Sir, the book which I have the honor to offer for your worship's consideration, is a work which—

(*Exit together.*)

### SC. III. AN APARTMENT IN POLONIUS'S HOUSE. BASIL DISCOVERED.

*Basil* (*solus.*) Well, I never saw anything just like this state of things before. They're the oddest lot of lunatics outside the asylum. Take 'em in the parlor—take 'em ANYwhere in the front part of the house—and they won't any more notice me than if I was the cat. If I speak to them, they give me the cold shake every time—don't even let on to *see* me. They're on the high horse all the time, then: they swell around, and talk the grandest kind of book-talk, and look just as if they were on exhibition. It's the most unnatural stuff! why, it ain't *human* talk; nobody that ever lived, ever talked the way they do. Even the flunkies can't say the simplest thing the way a human being would say it. (*Striding, stage-fashion, and imitating them.*) "Me lord hath given commandment, sirrah, that the vehicle wherein he doth, of ancient custom, his daily recreation take, shall unto the portal of the palace be straight conveyed; the which commandment, mark ye well, admitteth not of wasteful dalliance, like to the tranquil march of yon gilded moon athwart the dappled fields of space, but, even as the molten meteor cleaves the skies, or the red-tongued bolts of heaven, charged with death, to their dread office speed, let this, me lord's commandment, have instant consummation!" Now what d—d rot that is! Why, a man in his right mind would simply say, "Fetch the carriage, you duffer, and *hump* yourself!" Lord, I get mighty tired of this everlasting speechifying. —But just as soon as these people get out in the hall or in the back entry, they are just as natural as anybody, and plenty sociable enough. Hamlet talks to me in a perfectly rational way; asks after my old mother, that used to nurse him; promises to subscribe as soon as he ain't so busy; and once he scratched his chin with his other foot, just as simple and unaffected as an angel would. The old lady's good to me; feeds me and beds me with the flunkeys, and makes me feel at home and comfortable, but *she* won't notice me in the parlor. And Ophelia!—Ophelia Polonius!—ah, there's a nice girl—that's a daisy! She's just as good to me as she can be—anywhere but in the parlor.—They all say that when they're in the parlor, it's always an occasion of state, and common people must take rank with the furniture, then. I don't amount to a split-bottom chair. All right, I ain't complaining; I can stand it if *they* can. Meantime my little benevolent game glides along first-rate. I have persuaded Laertes and Polonius that that match won't do at all. Reasons of state, you know!—and all that fol-de-rol—political incompatibility. I've secured a lower berth amidships for Laertes, and he'll sail to-day. I think I'll go and send the customary wagon load of farewell bouquets and champagne aboard, now, from the customary host of imaginary friends.

(*Exit.*

*Enter* LAERTES *and* OPHELIA, R.

*Laer.* (R.) My necessaries are embarked: farewell!
And, sister, as the winds give benefit,
Pray, let me hear from you.

*Oph.* (R.) Do you doubt that?

*Laer.* For Hamlet, and the trifling of his favour,
Hold it a fashion, and a toy in blood;
He may not, as unvalued persons do,

Carve for himself; for on his choice depends
The safety and the health of the whole state;
Then weigh what loss your honour may sustain,
If with too credent ear you list his songs.
Fear it, Ophelia, fear it, my dear sister;
And keep you in the rear of your affection,
Out of the shot and danger of desire;
The chariest maid is prodigal enough,
If she unmask her beauty to the moon.

*Oph.* (R.C.) I shall the effect of this good lesson keep
As watchman to my heart. But, good my brother,
Do not, as some ungracious pastors do,
Show me the steep and thorny way to heaven:
Whilst, like a reckless libertine,
Himself the primrose path of dalliance treads,
And recks not his own rede.

*Laer.* (C.) Oh, fear me not!
I stay too long;—But here my father comes.

*Enter* POLONIUS, L.

*Pol.* (L.C.) Yet here, Laertes! aboard, aboard, for shame;
The wind sits in the shoulder of your sail,
And you are staid for.

*Laer.* Most humbly do I take my leave, my lord.
Farewell, Ophelia, and remember well
What I have said to you.

*Oph.* 'Tis in my memory locked,
And you yourself shall keep the key of it.

*Laer.* Farewell.

(*Exit*, L.

*Pol.* What is't, Ophelia, he hath said to you?

*Oph.* So please you, something touching the lord Hamlet.

*Pol.* (C.) Marry, well bethought;
'Tis told to me, he hath very oft of late,
Given private time to you; and you yourself
Have of your audience been most free and bounteous.
If it be so, (as so 'tis put on me,
And that in way of caution,) I must tell you,

You do not understand yourself so clearly,
As it behoves my daughter, and your honour.
What is between you? give me up the truth.
*Oph.* (C.) He hath, my lord, of late made many tenders
Of his affection to me.
*Pol.* Affection! puh! you speak like a green girl,
Unsifted in such perilous circumstance.
Do you believe his tenders, as you call them?
*Oph.* I do not know, my lord, what I should think.
*Pol.* Marry, I'll teach you: think yourself a baby;
That you have ta'en these tenders for true pay,
Which are not sterling. Tender yourself more dearly;
Or you'll tender me a fool.
*Oph.* My lord, he hath importuned me with love,
In honourable fashion.
*Pol.* Ay, fashion you may call it; go to, go to.
*Oph.* And hath given countenance to his speech, my lord,
With almost all the holy vows of heaven.
*Pol.* Ay, springes to catch woodcocks. I do know,
When the blood burns, how prodigal the soul
Lends the tongue vows.
This is for all,—
I would not, in plain terms, from this time forth,
Have you so slander any moment's leisure,
As to give words or talk with the lord Hamlet.
Look to't, I charge you; (*Crosses*, R.) come your ways.
*Oph.* (R.) I shall obey, my lord. (*Exeunt*, R.

## SCENE IV.—THE PLATFORM

*Enter* HAMLET, HORATIO, *and* MARCELLUS, R. U. E.
*Ham.* (R.) The air bites shrewdly; it is very cold. (C.)
*Hor.* (R.) It is a nipping and an eager air.
*Ham.* What hour now?

*Hor*. (C.) I think it lacks of twelve.

*Mar*. (R.C.) No, it is struck.

*Hor*. I heard it not; it then draws near the season,
Wherein the spirit held his wont to walk.

*(Flourish of Trumpets and Drums, and Ordnance shot off, within.*

What does this mean, my lord?

*Ham*. (L.) The king doth wake to-night, and takes his rouse;
And as he drains his draughts of Rhenish down
The kettle-drum and trumpet thus bray out
The triumph of his pledge.

*Hor*. Is it a custom?

*Ham*. Ay, marry, is't;
But to my mind—though I am native here,
And to the manner born—it is a custom
More honoured in the breach, than the observance.

*Enter* GHOST, L.

*Hor*. (R.) Look, my lord, it comes!

*Ham*. (R.C.) (*Horatio stands about two yards from the back of Hamlet; Marcellus about the same distance from Hamlet, up the Stage.*) Angels and ministers of grace defend us!

(*Ghost stops* L.C.

Be thou a spirit of health, or goblin damned,
Bring with thee airs from heaven, or blasts from hell,
Be thy intents wicked, or charitable,
Thou com'st in such a questionable shape,
That I will speak to thee: I'll call thee Hamlet,
King, father!—Royal Dane: Oh, answer me!
Let me not burst in ignorance! but tell,
Why thy canonized bones, hearsed in death,
Have burst their cerements! why the sepulchre,
Wherein we saw thee quietly in-urned,
Hath op'd his ponderous and marble jaws,
To cast thee up again! What may this mean,
That thou, dead corse, again, in complete steel,
Revisit'st thus the glimpses of the moon,

Making night hideous; and we fools of nature,
So horridly to shake our disposition,
With thoughts beyond the reaches of our souls?
Say, why is this? wherefore? what should we do?
*(Ghost beckons*

*Hor.* It beckons you to go away with it,
As if it some impartment did desire
To you alone.

*Mar.* Look with what courteous action
It waves you to a more removéd ground;
But do not go with it.

*Hor.* No, by no means.

*Ham.* It will not speak; then I will follow it.

*Hor. (Taking Hamlet's arm.)* Do not, my lord.

*Ham.* Why, what should be the fear?
I do not set my life at a pin's fee;
And, for my soul, what can it do to that,
Being a thing immortal as itself?—
It waves me forth again;—I'll follow it.

*Hor.* What, if it tempt you toward the flood, my lord?
Or to the dreadful summit of the cliff,
And there assume some other horrible form,
And draw you into madness?

*Ham.* (C.) It waves me still;
Go on, I'll follow thee. *(Breaks away, and crosses,* L.C.

*Mar.* You shall not go, my lord. *(Both hold him again.*

*Ham.* (C.) Hold off your hands.

*Hor.* (C.) Be ruled, you shall not go.

*Ham.* My fate cries out,
And makes each petty artery in this body
As hardy as the Neméan lion's nerve. *(Ghost beckons.*
Still am I called—unhand me, gentlemen;—
By heaven, I'll make a ghost of him that lets me.
*(Breaks away from them.*
I say away:—Go on—I'll follow thee.

*(Exeunt Ghost and Hamlet,* L.—*Horatio and Marcellus slowly follow.*

## SCENE V.—A REMOTE PART OF THE PLATFORM

*Re-enter* GHOST *and* HAMLET, *from* L.U.E. *to* L.C.

*Ham.* (C.) Whither wilt thou lead me? speak
I'll go no further.

*Ghost.* (L.C.) Mark me.

*Ham.* (R.C.) I will.

*Ghost.* My hour is almost come
When I to sulph'rous and tormenting flames
Must render up myself.

*Ham.* Alas poor ghost!

*Ghost.* Pity me not, but lend thy serious hearing
To what I shall unfold.

*Ham.* Speak, I am bound to hear.

*Ghost.* So art thou to revenge, when thou shalt hear.

*Ham.* What?

*Ghost.* I am thy father's spirit;
Doomed for a certain term to walk the night;
And, for the day, confined to fast in fires,
Till the foul crimes, done in my days of nature,
Are burnt and purged away. But that I am forbid
To tell the secrets of my prison-house,
I could a tale unfold, whose lightest word
Would harrow up thy soul; freeze thy young blood;
Make thy two eyes, like stars, start from their spheres,
Thy knotted and combined locks to part,
And each particular hair to stand on end,
Like quills upon the fretful porcupine:
But this eternal blazon must not be
To ears of flesh and blood:—List, list, Oh, list!—
If thou didst ever thy dear father love—

*Ham.* Oh, heaven!

*Ghost.* Revenge his foul and most unnatural murder.

*Ham.* Murder!

*Ghost*. Murder most foul, as in the best it is;
But this most foul, strange, and unnatural.
*Ham*. Haste me to know it, that I with wings as swift
As meditation, or the thoughts of love,
May sweep to my revenge.
*Ghost*. I find thee apt.—
Now, Hamlet, hear:
'Tis given out, that, sleeping in my orchard,
A serpent stung me; so the whole ear of Denmark
Is by a forgéd process of my death
Rankly abused: but know, thou noble youth,
The serpent that did sting thy father's life,
Now wears his crown.
*Ham*. Oh, my prophetic soul! my uncle?
*Ghost*. Ay, that incestuous, that adulterate beast.
With witchcraft of his wit, with traitorous gifts,
Won to his shameful lust
The will of my most seeming-virtuous queen:
Oh, Hamlet, what a falling off was there!
From me, whose love was of that dignity,
That it went hand in hand, even with the vow
I made to her in marriage; and to decline
Upon a wretch, whose natural gifts were poor
To those of mine!—
But, soft, methinks I scent the morning air—
Brief let me be:—sleeping within mine orchard
My custom always of the afternoon,
Upon my secure hour thy uncle stole,
With juice of curséd hebenon in a phial,
And in the porches of mine ears did pour
The leperous distilment: whose effect
Holds such an enmity with blood of man,
That swift as quicksilver it courses through
The natural gates and alleys of the body;
So it did mine.
Thus was I, sleeping, by a brother's hand,
Of life, of crown, of queen, at once despatched!

Cut off, even in the blossoms of my sin,
No reck'ning made, but sent to my account
With all my imperfections on my head.

*Ham.* Oh, horrible! Oh, horrible! most horrible!

*Ghost.* If thou has nature in thee, bear it not;
Let not the royal bed of Denmark be
A couch for luxury and damnéd incest
But, howsoever thou pursu'st this act,
Taint not thy mind, nor let thy soul contrive
Against thy mother aught; leave her to Heaven,
And to those thorns that in her bosom lodge,
To goad and sting her. Fare thee well at once!
The glow-worm shows the matin to be near,
And 'gins to pale his uneffectual fire.—
Adieu, adieu, adieu! remember me. (*Vanishes,* L.

*Ham.* (R.) Hold, hold, my heart;
And you, my sinews, grow not instant old,
But bear me stiffly up;—(C.)—Remember thee?
Ay, thou poor ghost, while memory holds a seat
In this distracted globe. Remember thee?
Yea, from the table of my memory
I'll wipe away all forms, all pressures past,
And thy commandment all alone shall live
Within the book and volume of my brain,
Unmix'd with baser matter; yes, by heaven,
I have sworn it.

*Hor.* (*Within,* L.) My lord, my lord.—

*Mar.* (*Within.*) Lord Hamlet,—

*Hor.* (*Within.*) Heaven secure him!

*Ham.* So be it!

*Hor.* (*Within.*) Hillo, ho, ho, my lord!

*Ham.* Hillo, ho, ho, boy! come, bird, come!

*Enter* HORATIO *and* MARCELLUS, L.U.E.

*Mar.* (R.C.) How is't, my noble lord?

*Hor.* (L.C.) What news, my lord?

*Ham.* (C.) Oh, wonderful!

*Hor.* Good, my lord, tell it?

*Ham.* No; you will reveal it.

*Hor.* Not I, my lord, by heaven.

*Ham.* How say you, then; would heart of man once think it?—
But you'll be secret?

*Hor.* Ay, by heaven, my lord.

*Ham.* There's ne'er a villain, dwelling in all Denmark
But he's an arrant knave.

*Hor.* There needs no ghost, my lord, come from the grave,
To tell us this.

*Ham.* Why, right; you are in the right;
And so, without more circumstance at all,
I hold it fit, that we shake hands and part;
You, as your business and desire shall point you;—
For every man hath business and desire,
Such as it is—and, for my own poor part,
I will go pray.

*Hor.* These are but wild and whirling words, my lord.

*Ham.* I am sorry they offend you, heartily.

*Hor.* There's no offence, my lord.

*Ham.* Yes, by Saint Patrick, but there is, Horatio,
And much offence, too. (*Takes his hand.*) Touching this vision here—
It is an honest ghost, that let me tell you.
For your desire to know what is between us,
O'er-master it as you may. (*Part.*) And now, good friends, (*Crosses,* L.
As you are friends, scholars, and soldiers,
Give me one poor request.

*Hor.* What is't, my lord?
We will.

*Ham.* (C.) Never make known what you have seen to-night.

*Hor. & Mar.* My lord, we will not.

*Ham.* Nay, but swear it.

(*Dumb show of arguing, between them.*)

*Enter* BASIL, *pretty tight.*

*Basil.* (*Aside.*) Rattling blow-out in the palace to-night. Everybody drinking Hamlet's health. But I swallowed a dam spool of thread. (*He has the end of the thread*[15] *in his fingers, and talks along disjointedly while he pulls out a couple of hundred yards of it.*) Pretty good times, I tell you. I clean forgot about the ghost business. Too late, now, I reckon. Hope not. Wouldn't miss the ghost for anything. Yes, indeedy, mighty good times in the palace. I got off a conundrum on 'is majesty the king—(*maudlin laughter at the thought of it*)—bes' conundrum I ever heard—all out o' my own head, too—wish I may die if tain't so. I got it off on 'is majesty —THERE! (*finishing the thread*)—now 'f I had the spool out, I wouldn't give a continental whether school keeps or not. Bes' conundrum ever I struck. I got it off on 'is majesty the king. Says I, "Boss" (*perceives the others and approaches them unsteadily*)—why here's those fellows, *now*. P'raps I ain't too late. How'r ye, boys —what luck? Seen him, yet? Got him treed? (*Joins the party.*)

*Hor.* Have then your way. Propose the oath, my lord.

*Ham.* Never to speak of this that you have seen; (R.)
Swear by my sword.

*Ghost.* (*Beneath.*) Swear! (*Business for Basil.*

*Hor.* Oh, day and night, but this is wond'rous strange.

*Ham.* And therefore as a stranger give it welcome.
There are more things in heav'n and earth, Horatio,
Than are dreamt of in your philosophy.
But come:—
Here, (*All three stand,* R.) as before, never, so help you mercy!
How strange or odd soe'er I bear myself—
As I, perchance, hereafter shall think meet
To put an antic disposition on—
That you, at such times seeing me, never shall,
With arms encumbered thus, or this head-shake,
Or by pronouncing of some doubtful phrase,
As, "Well, well, we know:"—or, "We could, an if we would:"
or, "If we list to speak;" or, "There be, an if they might;"
Or such ambiguous giving out, to note
That you know aught of me:—this do ye swear,
So grace and mercy at your most need help you!

---

[15] Between the lines Twain wrote, "(imaginary?)."

*Ghost.* (*Beneath.*) Swear! (*Business for Basil.*

*Ham.* Rest, rest, perturbéd spirit! (*All at* C.)—So, gentlemen,
With all my love I do commend me to you:
And what so poor a man as Hamlet is, (*Takes a hand of each.*
May do to express his love and friending to you,
Heaven willing shall not lack. Let us go in together;
(*Crosses,* L.
And still your fingers on your lips, I pray.
The time is out of joint;—Oh, curséd spite!
That ever I was born to set it right! (*Ex. all but Basil.*

*Basil.* (*Suffering on the ground.*) Why, they're going! Boys, you ain't going, are you? *Don't* go away and leave a fellow, that way, in this awful place. I'm all played out, and gone in, and used up. *I* can't walk. Hang it, they *are* gone. . . . (*Chuckling.*) 'Twas a *mighty* good conundrum—awful good. I got it off on 'is majesty the king. Says I, "BOSS!"—(*A groan from beneath*) (*Exit in a drunken hurry, falling down a few times.*

END OF ACT I.

## ACT II

### SCENE I.

HERE BASIL discovers a mare's nest. He has been misjudging these people all along, but he sees clearly, now. There is a plot to massacre Hamlet, and certain of them are in it—Ophelia, that artful, malignant little devil, is at the bottom of it? The match *must* be broken off. Yes, and all these people are lunatics—every one—Hamlet is plainly the only one in his right mind. He must be *got away,* out of danger—but he must not know why he is gotten away.[16]

Scene 1.—*An Apartment in Polonius's House*

*Enter* POLONIUS, L., *and* OPHELIA, R.

---

[16] On the following page of the MS (p. 44), a marginal note reads, "Stop players to beguile H from going mad."

*Pol.* (L.) How now, Ophelia? what's the matter?
*Oph.* (R.) Oh, my lord, my lord, I have been so affrighted!
*Pol.* With what, in the name of heaven?
*Oph.* My lord, as I was sewing in my closet,
Lord Hamlet—with his doublet all unbraced,
No hat upon his head,
Pale as his shirt, his knees knocking each other,
He comes before me.
*Pol.* (C.) Mad for thy love?
*Oph.* (C.) My lord, I do not know;
But, truly, I do fear it.
*Pol.* What said he?
*Oph.* He took me by the wrist, and held me hard;
Then goes he to the length of all his arm,
And with his other hand thus o'er his brow,
He falls to such perusal of my face,
As he would draw it. Long stayed he so;
At last, a little shaking of mine arm,
And thrice his head thus waving up and down—
He raised a sigh so piteous and profound,
As it did seem to shatter all his bulk,
And end his being: that done, he lets me go;
And, with his head over his shoulder turned,
He seemed to find his way without his eyes;
For out o'doors he went without their helps,
And, to the last, bended their light on me.
*Pol.* Come, go with me; I will go seek the king.
This is the very ecstasy of love.
What, have you given him any hard words of late?
*Oph.* No, my good lord; but, as you did command,
I did repel his letters, and denied
His access to me.
*Pol.* That hath made him mad.
Come, go we to the king:
This must be known; which, being kept close, might move
More grief to hide, than hate to utter love. (*Exeunt*, L.

### SCENE II.—THE PALACE

*Enter the* KING, QUEEN, ROSENCRANTZ, GUILDENSTERN, L., FRANCISCO *and* BERNARDO, R.

*King.* (C.) Welcome, dear Rosencrantz and Guildenstern!
Moreover that we did much long to see you,
The need we have to use you, did provide
Our hasty sending. Something have you heard
Of Hamlet's transformation:
What it should be,
More than his father's death, that thus hath put him
So much from the understanding of himself,
I cannot dream of; I entreat you both,
That you vouchsafe your rest here in our court
Some little time; so by your companies,
To draw him on to pleasures, and to gather,
Whether aught, to us unknown, afflicts him thus,
That, opened, lies within our remedy.

*Queen.* (C.) Good gentlemen, he hath much talked of you;
And, sure I am, two men there are not living
To whom he more adheres. If it will please you
So to expend your time with us a while,
Your visitation shall receive such thanks
As fits a king's remembrance.

*Ros.* (L.) Both your majesties
Might, by the sovereign power you have of us,
Put your dread pleasures more into command
Than to entreaty.

*Guil.* (L.) But we both obey;
And here give up ourselves, in the full bent,
To lay our service freely at your feet.

*King.* Thanks, Rosencrantz and gentle Guildenstern.

*Queen.* I do beseech you instantly to visit
My too much changéd son. Go, some of you,

And bring these gentlemen where Hamlet is.

(*Exeunt all but King and Queen*, R.

*Enter* POLONIUS, L.

*Pol.* (L.C.) I now do think (or else this brain of mine
Hunts not the trail of policy so sure
As it hath used to do), that I have found
The very cause of Hamlet's lunacy.

*King.* (C.) Oh, speak of that; that do I long to hear.

*Pol.* My liege and madam, to expostulate
What majesty should be, what duty is,
Why day is day, night, night, and time is time,
Were nothing but to waste night, day, and time.
Therefore—since brevity is the soul of wit,
And tediousness the limbs and outward flourishes—
I will be brief: your noble son is mad:
Mad call I it; for, to define true madness,
What is't, but to be nothing else but mad?
But let that go.

*Queen.* (R.C.) More matter, with less art.

*Pol.* Madam, I swear, I use no art at all.
That he is mad, 'tis true; 'tis true, 'tis pity;
And pity 'tis, 'tis true; a foolish figure;
But farewell it; for I will use no art.
Mad let us grant him, then: and now remains,
That we find out the cause of this effect;
Or, rather say, the cause of this defect;
For this effect, defective, comes by cause:
Thus it remains, and the remainder thus.
Perpend—
I have a daughter: have, while she is mine;
Who, in her duty and obedience, mark,
Hath given me this: (*Shews a paper.*) now gather, and surmise.
(*Reads.*)—"To the celestial, and my soul's idol, the most beautified Ophelia,"—That's an ill phrase, a vile phrase; beautified is a vile phrase; but you shall hear:—(*Reads.*)—"In her excellent white bosom, these," &c.

*Queen.* Came this from Hamlet to her?

*Pol.* Good madam, stay awhile; I will be faithful:—
(*Reads.*)—"Doubt thou, the stars are fire;
Doubt, that the sun doth move;
Doubt truth to be a liar;
But never doubt, I love.

"Oh, dear Ophelia, I am ill at these numbers; I have no art to reckon my groans; but, that I love thee best, oh most best, believe it! Adieu

"Thine evermore, most dear lady, whilst this
machine is to him, HAMLET."

This, in obedience, hath my daughter shown me;
And more above, hath his solicitings,
As they fell out by time, by means and place,
All given to mine ear.

*King.* How hath she
Received his love?

*Pol.* What do you think of me?

*King.* As of a man faithful and honourable.

*Pol.* I would fain prove so. But what might you think,
When I had seen this hot love on the wing
(As I perceived it, I must tell you that,
Before my daughter told me), what might you,
Or my dear majesty, your queen here, think,
If I had played the desk or table-book;
Or looked upon this love with idle sight;
What might you think? No, I went round to work,
And my young mistress thus did I bespeak:
Lord Hamlet is a prince; out of thy sphere;
This must not be: and then I precepts gave her
That she should lock herself from his resort,
Admit no messengers, receive no tokens;
Which done, she took the fruits of my advice:
And he, repulsed, (a short tale to make),
Fell into a sadness;
Thence into a weakness;
Thence to a lightness; and by this declension,
Into the madness wherein now he raves,

And all we mourn for.

*King.* Do you think 'tis this?

*Queen.* It may be, very likely.

*Pol.* Hath there been such a time, (I'd fain know that),
That I have positively said, 'Tis so,
When it proved otherwise?

*King.* Not that I know.

*Pol.* Take this from this, if this be otherwise.

(*Pointing to his head and shoulders.*

If circumstances lead me, I will find
Where truth is hid, though it were hid indeed
Within the centre.

*King.* How may we try it further?

*Pol.* You know, sometimes he walks for hours together
Here in the lobby.

*Queen.* So he does, indeed.

*Pol.* At such a time, I'll loose my daughter to him;
Mark the encounter: if he love her not,
And be not from his reason fallen thereon,
Let me be no assistant for a state,
But keep a farm, and carters. (*Crosses,* L.

*King.* (R.) We will try it.

*Queen.* (R.) But, look, where sadly the poor wretch comes reading!

*Pol.* Away, I do beseech you; both away!
I'll board him presently. (*Exeunt King and Queen,* R.S.E.

*Enter* HAMLET, M.D., *reading.*

(R.C.) How does my good Lord Hamlet?

*Ham.* (L.C.) Excellent well.

*Pol.* (C.) Do you know me, my lord?

*Ham.* (R.C.) Excellent well: you are a fishmonger.

*Pol.* Not I, my lord.

*Ham.* Then I would you were so honest a man.

*Pol.* Honest, my lord?

*Ham.* Ay, sir! to be honest as this world goes, is to be one man picked out of ten thousand.

*Pol.* That's very true, my lord.

*Ham.* For, if the sun breed maggots in a dead dog, being a god, kissing carrion—Have you a daughter?

*Pol.* I have, my lord.

*Ham.* Let her not walk i' the sun: conception is a blessing; but as your daughter may conceive—friend, look to't.

(*Turns to the* R. *and reads.*

*Pol.* (C.) Still harping on my daughter!—yet he knew

[The text breaks off at this point.]

# *Working Notes for*
# the Burlesque Hamlet

[The following notes were written on three unnumbered sheets and filed at the end of the fragment.]

Sheet 1:

This fellow always trying to sneeze and never succeeds. In places where he has nothing to say, he can appear and disappear trying to sneeze. ("I wouldn't take £1,000,000 for that sneeze—when I get it")

Sheet 2:

give him away

Put description of old man in Sc. 1. Quote half of it.

Appears with umbrella, in royal procession.—

Comes on stage, feverishly—finds umbrella (joy) takes it up with look at king as much as to say "Blame you, I had my eye on you." (Exit.) (Perhaps he takes it *from* the king who has picked it up unconsciously.)

Sheet 3:

Before page 18 [i.e., before opening of actual scene ii, Act I], Basil persuades Laertes to apply for leave to go to France—"tell king you only came to attend the cornation—fill him up with pleasant phrases—he'll let you go."

Persuades Polonius to give Laertes leave.

Persuades king and queen to not let Hamlet go to Wittenberg.

# *1,002*[d] ARABIAN NIGHT

(1883)

Editor's Note: Samuel Clemens left Hartford on Thursday, 14 June 1883, to spend the summer at Quarry Farm, Elmira. This was the summer during which he would complete his greatest work, *Huckleberry Finn,* but the first order of business was to write the "1,002[d] Arabian Night," which, in the fashion of his *Burlesque Autobiography,* was to be illustrated, this time with grotesque drawings of his own composition. On 20 July he reported to Howells, "I have finished one small book, & am away along in a big one that I half-finished two or three years ago." [1] The big one, of course was *Huckleberry Finn;* the small one, "1,002." From the date of the letter it is apparent that he finished his burlesque addition to the tales of Scheherazade in slightly over a month of what must have been enthusiastic and intense work, since the typescript surviving in the Mark Twain Papers runs to over 20,000 words and the key to the illustrations (arabic numerals within parentheses) shows he drew 131 pictures to accompany the text.

The speed with which he worked suggests that the idea had been in his mind for some time; one might even suspect that he had made one or two previous attempts to develop the idea into manuscript. But there is no clear evidence in the surviving documents bearing on the point. A comment which may have set him off on his imaginative flight appears in a letter from Howells written in Venice, 22 April 1883. Referring to a possible collaboration on a Colonel Sellers play, Howells wrote, "There is the making of a good comedy in it without any doubt—something that would run like Scheherazade, for A Thousand and One Nights." [2] The comment may have set him off hot on the trail of a new

[1] *MTHL,* I, 435.

[2] *Ibid.,* I, 429–430.

and, to him at any rate, brilliant idea: "Ah, but suppose it runs like Scheherazade for A Thousand and *Two* Nights . . . !" Or it may have recalled an idea already lurking in his mind—we have no way of knowing. Certainly, sometime prior to 10 December 1880, he was struck sufficiently by a notion connected with one incident in the Arabian Nights to make the cryptic comment in his notebook, "The Talkative barber in Arabian Nights." [3] Since the note emphasizes the prolixity which became the major point in "1,002," it may well mark the beginning of the idea.

Probably still chortling with glee, he sent a typescript to James R. Osgood, the Boston publisher. In mid-September, Osgood passed it on to Howells for a critical appraisal. On 18 September Howells wrote a letter to Twain in which, in the words of the editors of the Twain-Howells correspondence, "Howells's tact as a friend and his taste as a critic are particularly clear." In part, Howells said:

> Osgood gave me your MS. to read last night, and I understood from him that you wanted my opinion of it. The opening passages are the funniest you have ever done; but when I got into the story itself, it seemed to me that I was made a fellow-sufferer with the Sultan from Sheherazade's prolixity. The effect was like that of a play in which the audience is surprised along with the characters by some turn in the plot. I don't mean to say that there were not extremely killing things in it; but on the whole it was not your best or your second-best; and all the way it skirts a certain kind of fun which you can't afford to indulge in: it's a little too broad, as well as exquisitely ludicrous, at times. . . . At any rate I feel bound to say that I think this burlesque falls short of being amusing.[4]

By the time Howells' letter reached him, Twain was deeply involved in plans to perfect and market his history game, preparations for the publication of *Huckleberry Finn,* attempts to write a Colonel Sellers play in collaboration with Howells, and the dramatization of *Tom Sawyer*. But by 14 April 1884, his attention returned to his *jeu d'esprit*. On that date he wrote his nephew, Charles Webster, "I think we'll publish '1002,' anonymously, in a 15 or 20 cent form, right after Huck." [5] He was still enthusiastic enough to undertake publication himself if Osgood would not have anything to do with it, although the "anonymously" suggests that he was partially daunted by Howells' reaction.

---

[3] Typescript Notebook 15, p. 50, MTP.

[4] *MTHL*, I, 441–442.

[5] *Mark Twain, Business Man,* ed. Samuel C. Webster (Boston, 1946), p. 249.

The publication plans apparently were frustrated by the loss of the illustrations. On 2 July 1884, he wrote to Webster, "The Osgoods gave you the type-writered tale, '1,002,' & you handed it to me; but I don't remember that you gave me the 113 (or 121) *pictures* that belong with it. I don't remember seeing a single one of the pictures. If they didn't give them to you, you may apply to them again." [6] A week later, Webster replied, "In regard to that tale '1,002,' I never saw it. Osgood's people must have sent it to you, they promised to. Neither did I ever see any pictures belonging to it." [7] If Webster applied again for the pictures, it must have been in vain, for the pictures are still missing, and the surviving Webster-Osgood-Twain correspondence contains no further reference to them. Despite the loss, I have retained in parentheses the numbers keying the illustrations to the text.

"1,002" is a good illustration of the unlikely sort of thing which could fire Twain's enthusiasm and get him started on the task of composition. The idea behind the piece had two distinct advantages in his eyes: the intention to base the story directly on the *Thousand and One Nights,* a manifestation of the impulse to burlesque, freed Twain from the chore of creating many details of the fictional world in which the characters were to move; and the plight of the two chief characters, a boy mistaken for a girl and a girl mistaken for a boy, was precisely the sort of gimmick that would send Twain to his desk itching to pile up manuscript. "1,002" is a "starter" analogous to "Those Extraordinary Twins," "The Autobiography of a Damned Fool," and the Simon Wheeler play. But in this one, nothing appeared during the course of composition or in later ruminations to provoke a renewed and more serious purpose. After the initial enthusiasm died, the piece went into the pigeonhole and there it stayed.

The tale survives in an incomplete holograph manuscript and in a typescript revised by Mark Twain. The text followed here is that of the revised typescript.

---

[6] *Ibid.,* pp. 263–264.

[7] Webster to SLC, New York, July 9, 1884, original in MTP.

# 1,002

## Chap. 1

"It was a very good tale," said King Shahriyar, stretching, and preparing to turn over upon his sleeping-side, "a very good one indeed; one of the best of the series, I think. Kiss me good-bye. Now, if you will be so good as to let the headsman know you are ready—and shut the door after you, please."

The beautiful Scherezade kissed him tenderly, then arose, and began to dress, with a sorrowing heart. Taking a stocking in her hand, she contemplated it sadly, and said, as one who thinks aloud,—

"Alas, in the old, old times, in Persia, there was a lovely princess whose strange and wonderful—"

"Is that another one?" inquired the king, raising his head from the pillow.

"It is, O Commander of the Faithful, King of Kings, Lord of the Universe, Dread of Nations, Dispenser of Dignities, Source of Blessings, the Mighty One, the Gracious One, the Powerful, the Splendid! whose name be magnified! It is Number One Thousand and Two."

"Is it good?"

"It surpasseth all the rest, O Light of the Earth, Ornament of Creation, Hope of the Hopeless, Refuge of the Forsaken, Shelter of the Desolate, Glory of the World, the High, the Beneficent, the All-Beautiful—on whom be peace!"

"The execution is postponed till the morrow. Come back to bed, and proceed."

"I hear and obey."

So saying, the lovely Scherezade returned to bed and began as follows:

(Private)

(The figures inserted thus, (1) (2) (3), etc., refer to corresponding numbers on the illustrations.)

## Chap. 2

THE SULTAN of the Indies was at that time holding the Ramadan, or Feast of the Tabernacles, at the imperial palace in his noble city of Bagdad. (1)

*"What business had the Sultan of the Indies in Bagdad?"*

It was the will of God, sire, against which the preferences of man are powerless to contend.

*"Extolled be his perfection! Proceed."*

The aspect of the city was charming, for the straightness of its streets, the uniformity of its architecture, the sublimity of its principal palaces and public buildings, the ease and variety of their attitudes, the—(2)

"Omit the rest of the catalogue."

I hear and obey. Now the sultan had long desired to have a son. He had prayed; he had fasted; he had sent nine of his favorite nephews on pilgrimage to Mecca and the other holy places; (3) but all in vain. During years, the wise men had scanned the heavens nightly for a favorable sign, but to no purpose. They were troubled; for they and all men knew of a prophecy which presaged the downfall of the dynasty; and were aware, also, that by the terms of this prophecy nothing could avert the disaster except—1. *The Sultan have an heir;* 2. *that this heir have also an heir; and* 3. *that this latter be born in a miraculous way.*

The Sultan's sorrow was great; his heart was contracted. One day, as usual, he was on his way to his bath, in deep dejection. (4). All at once his spirits began to lighten strangely. He recognized the mysterious message of the All-Merciful, (whose perfection be extolled!) and said, "May he let this new hope live and fructify, who reigneth forever and who is able to do whatsoever he will." Whereupon, with a glad spirit, he spread his prayer carpet upon the ground (5) and lifted up his petition for a son yet once again. While he was still praying, a great darkness overspread the heavens, and upon looking up he saw a roc descending upon the city, and this it was which had veiled the sun and caused the darkness. The roc came slowly down, upon wide extended wings, (6) and hovered in the air immediately over the city during the space of half an hour, exerting itself meanwhile. At length it dropped an egg, marked with mysterious unknown characters, in the street behind the Sultan. (7) The Sultan would have returned immediately to consult his astrologers, but this he could not do, because the vast egg blocked up the street. Wherefore he sent orders to the astrologers to come and examine it; and also commanded that a new street be opened against his return. He then resumed his way, fatigued by excitement but hopeful and tranquil in mind.

As he proceeded, steeped in thought, he became aware of a sound as of a violent stamping, which approached rapidly; whereupon, commending himself to Allah, he sat up and looked forward, and presently beheld a thing which caused him to turn white with fear and confusion of mind. (8) This was an enchanted horse which was without body or head, and consisted of legs alone, and these not complete, nor yet rights and lefts, but also deformed by disproportionate lengths. (9) Not any part of the rider could be seen; and by this the Sultan knew that he was clothed with an enchanted robe which caused his person to be invisible. The Sultan was filled with bodings; and wondered who the invisible horseman might be, and what his apparition portended. Reventl uncovering, exposing the sacred head of the nation to the lances of the sun and the arrows of the wind, the Sultan of the Indies said, whilst streams of bitter tears flowed down his cheeks—(10)

*"Omit what he said. Proceed."*

I hear and obey. Arrived at the imperial bath, he halted in the empty and spacious marble court, and listened; for his heart was contracted and his spirit a prey to painful solicitudes, by reason of the strange things which God had set before him to warn him. Thus he stood, for a time, and ceased presently to listen; and so standing, he became unconscious of all things, and was sunk in abysses of reflection. (11) Long, long remained he thus, and the time magnified itself, and he knew it not, for profound was his thought, and wide the area which it traversed. First, he recalled how, in the rosy dawn of life's young dream—

*"Leave out the reflections. Proceed."*

I hear and obey. Suddenly all his being was congealed by the horror of a strange and awful sound. (12) Chill shudders came and went through all his frame, and he murmured, "He, only, is great, He only is mighty; He is able to do whatsoever He will." But the sound repeating itself no more, he smiled, and was comforted, and said, "Lo, I did but dream; verily it was but a fancy, clothed on with my fears." (13) Yet nevertheless in his heart was he still not tranquil; wherefore, as he trod the great corridor that led to the bath, he went not as one without fear, but picked his way with soft and stealthy steps, and with hand upon his weapon. (14)

Yea, and even when he stripped to his trade-mark, he got him not immediately into the bath, but set his ear in attitude for sharp attention, and tarried to listen yet again. (15)

But the beating of his own heart was all the sound he heard. Perceiving that this was so, his spirit was glad, his liver was rejoiced. And so, praising God, he removed his talisman with care, for it had come down from Solomon the son of David, (on whom be peace!) and got into his bath and stretched him out, and—

*"So he has actually arrived at last, praise be to him unto whom alone are all things possible, and who only is great, Kings being but as dust beneath his feet! Verily it is the most intolerable tale for tediousness and undue attention to particulars, wherewith in my life mine ears have been assailed. Lend it a grain more of activity, slave, lest age overtake me ere I hear the end—if, in the beneficent providence of God it have an end."*

I hear and obey. Whilst the Sultan lay at rest, reflecting upon the shortness of life, the unstable nature of earthly things, the proneness of man to evil, the—

*"Put it in the appendix. Proceed, proceed!"*

I hear and obey. Whilst these musings were weltering softly through his mind, as dimming rags of cloud welter in noiseless procession athwart the moon's silver disk by night, a wild fierce clamor broke suddenly upon the Sultan's ear, and he rose to a sitting posture, with all his senses appalled. (16)

The clamor continued. At first it seemed to come from somewhere toward the Sultan's front; then from the rearward; then from one side, then the other—and always it grew nearer. Now it came from below; and finally from above. The Sultan raised his eyes, and behold, straight down the wall came raging a most strange and peculiar dog, of evil aspect and violent expression, whose red jaws stood wide and fish-like, emitting thunderous barkings, and whose eyes shot baleful fires and whose body discharged angular lightnings which enclosed the creature like to a dazzling fence. (17)

The Sultan trembling said, "There is no strength nor power but in God, the High, the Great—extolled be his perfection!"

The creature of unholy magic, offspring of jinnee and devils, approached with frantic bounds, purposing to devour the Sultan. Commending himself to the Prophet, the Sultan drew his dagger. But its sheath shrank to nothing in his left hand, (18) and he knew by this sign that a spell had been cast upon the weapon by the invisible spirts with which the place was now swarming and that in consequence of this misfortune it was become useless. He threw it away, and drew his enchanted death-promoter, a wondrous thing made by the genii, in the days of antiquity, for Suleiman Ben Daoud, and named Mother-of-a-Million-Deaths; but lo, upon it also the evil spirits had cast a spell, and it acted in a most strange and ineffectual way. (19)

The raging beast came on. The Sultan shouted for help, and also clapped his hands; but those who should have heard, heard not, by reason that the spell of the evil spirits was upon their ears and upon their limbs, and they were as men that be dead. Now, then, the Sultan experiencing a great access of courage through the very desperateness of his situation, sprang out of the bath, girded on his talisman, and confronted the furious messenger of Sathanas with a high and dauntless mien. (20)

The beast paused, and gathered its infernal powers for a deadly spring. Pallid was the Sultan's face, but great was his heart at this supreme moment; for he was reduced, now to his last resource—a resource forbidden by the protecting shades of his house except as a last resource—and he knew that if it failed, the circle of his mortality was completed. He placed his right hand upon his left hip—paused one pregnant moment, then drew the magic scymitar of the kings of the East, upon which is engraved the Secret Word which dissolves the awfullest enchantments, and waved its glittering blade in the air! (21)

With a fierce cry of agony and disappointed malice, the evil beast discharged from its mouth a silver plate bearing a mysterious symbol, (22) and fled howling away, while all the air resounded with the wailing clamors of the defeated minions of darkness.

Almost overcome with joy and gratitude, in view of his so great and miraculous deliverance, the Sultan threw himself into reverent attitude, and spreading his arms abroad, gave thanks out of the fulness of his heart. (23)

All the way, as he wended homeward, unconscious of the rain which was now falling, he reflected, pensively, with his hand pressed to his throbbing brow, (24) upon the prodigies which had been assailing him in such surprising number and significance. But he could not penetrate their meaning. Plainly he perceived that they contained prophecies and purposes too profound for any but the most learned children of science to resolve. When he presently reached the palace, he lost no time in sending for the chief of the soothsayers, Bahram Bahadoor, the most illustrious of all the brotherhood of wise men then inhabiting the earth. The doors being closed and the servants sent without, the great magician stood in grave and reverent attitude whilst the Sultan excitedly poured into his ear the amazing history of the morning. (25)

Bahram Bahadoor pondered these things deeply, during some time. Then he said:

"Sire, these are matters of mighty import. They portend events which will be charged with weal and woe to unborn generations of men. It will be well to bring to bear upon them the combined wisdom of the world, for nothing less will be equal to the needs of so high and weighty an occasion. Will it please your Sublimity to command that all the doctors of magic, all men of repute in occult learning that be in these realms, shall gather here with dispatch to consider these omens and marvels?"

The Sultan clapped his hands. In response to the signal, the chief eunuch appeared, and said—(26)

"Lo, it is thine to command, it is mine to obey. Thy slave waits."

The Sultan gave the order, and the chief eunuch flew to execute it. Bowing three times to the earth, and kissing the ground each time, Bahram Bahadoor then took his leave.

Being now alone, the Sultan fell to brooding over the strange and dreadful things which had been happening to him; and under the oppression of these thoughts his heart was contracted and he became a prey to grief and melancholy so poignant that the expression of what he was feeling reflected its heart-break in his face as upon the sensitive surface of a Bogodalian mirror. (27)

Whilst he sat thus brooding, the lady Alida, sister of the favorite Sultana, entered, intent upon affairs of the household, and saw him not. (28) But as she moved hither and thither about the apartment, softly singing to herself the song that telleth of the sweet sympathy of her species for all that languish under the ailments wherewith the children of men are afflicted, her eye chanced to fall upon the agonized form of her suffering master. As swiftly as the evanescent color cometh and goeth in the cheek of youth, so swiftly turned she deadly pale. (29)

Casting herself at the feet of the Sultan, she exclaimed—

"There is no strength nor power but in God, the High, the great, whose lances are the lightnings, whose clarion is the thunder! Will my lord acquaint his slave with the sorrow that contracteth his heart?"

The Sultan smiled sadly, and patted the fair young head with gracious gentleness, but answered not, save with a sigh. Long the distressed maid wrought to comfort him with her brave good words, but without avail. At last she said in her secret heart, "He must weep or he will die; may not the sight of his loved ones break his iron apathy, melt this frozen grief?" So saying, she took him by the hand and gently led him into the bosom of one of his families. (30)

The stratagem was effectual. At sight of the innocent labors and pastimes of his precious ones, the fountains of the stricken Sultan's heart were broken up, and the saving tears welled from his eyes and streamed adown his happy cheeks. One of the Sultanas flew to his side, and her affectionate endearments, added to the lady Alida's winning solicitudes, presently restored their master to a condition of hopefulness and tranquility which filled their bosoms with gratitude, and his own with a sense of the healing service done him. He placed his beautiful guardian angels side by side, (31) and gazed long and earnestly into their comely faces, speaking not a word, for he was too full for utterance.

At last, having acquired some command of his voice, he placed his hand tenderly upon their heads, and then, in accents broken by emotion, he said—(32)

"Bless you—bless you, my children."

So saying, he turned slowly away, amid a solemn hush, and disappeared through the door of the adjoining chamber. The two princesses stood spellbound, in this holy calm, during many moments, neither of them being able to speak or move, so profoundly were they affected by what had occurred.

At last the lady Alida recovered some slight command over herself, though not over her voice; and so, turning away, she, with an infinitely touching grace, delivered a gesture over her shoulder whose prayer needed no words, but carried its own sufficient meaning—"Follow him, sweet lady, and save, oh save him from any return of his all too cruel hurt."

*"Verily, if this be not the most tedious lie the invention of man hath yet conceived, may Islam perish, and the children of the infidel defile with shodden feet the high places of the faith. Move it along—move it along!"*

## Chap. 3

I HEAR and obey. On the morrow the most illustrious of the wise men of the East, the children of science, and masters of the occult arts, gathered themselves together in a secret chamber of the palace to consider the signs which had been vouchsafed to the Sultan, and determine their import. (34)

They decided that the roc's egg signified that in the fulness of time the favorite Sultana, the peerless Shakahgah, would give birth to a son whose face would transcend the moon's, for beauty, whose form and eyes would outrival the stag's, and whose dispositions would be like to the dispositions of the warrior sons of Malachite.

Whereupon, according to ancient custom, they sent for the slipper of the peerless Shakahgah, and blessed it. (35)

The Sultan was mad for joy, and did naught, for hours, but go up and down the public ways of the city smiling a smile of ineffable content upon all whom he met. (36) He also set all prisoners and all accused persons free, beheaded the accusers, cancelled all debts owed by his subjects to foreigners, decreed a national holiday for the space of a year; and in many other ways testified his gratitude to Him from whom alone emanate grace, and peace, and blessing.

When the favorite Sultana learned the happiness which was in store for her, her beautiful face was irradiated, for a single moment, with a smile of unutterable tenderness and hope, (37) and she then swooned softly away, overcome by excess of grateful emotion. Had not the eunuchs flown quickly to her aid with reviving cordials, her joy might have wrought her destruction. (38)

Great was the rejoicing, all over the land; and the Sultan, in order that he might gladden his heart with the sight of it without his presence being suspected, bought of a magician, for a thousand pieces of gold, an enchanted garment which rendered the extremities of its wearer entirely invisible. (39) Concealed in this, he went hither and thither, marveling much and being much marvelled at.

The soothsayers decided that the mysterious characters upon the roc's egg signified that the Grand Vizier, Bashi Bazouk, would presently become the father of a lovely and gifted daughter, whose destinies would be closely linked, from the cradle, with those of the imperial house.

When the Grand Vizier heard this intoxicating news, his gratitude exceeded the power of speech. Desiring to testify his thankfulness to the wise men in a manner regardless of cost, and consonant with the greatness of his rank and the dignity of his office, he clothed certain of his servants in rich robes of ceremony, and caused them to carry to Bahram Bahadoor a present of rare fruits of more worth than diamonds of Binderpoor or emeralds of Djalmak, these being two oranges, three watermelons, and a bunch of Ghoorza grapes, (40) all from the renowned Garden named and called the

Ineffable Glory of Paradise; and at the same time he sent to the other soothsayers a freezer-full of the delicious ice which was sacred to the Sultan's house-hold and was made from snow of Mount Dahrheem, refined sugar from Oman-Bopal, and tears shed in moments of joy by princesses of the royal house of Persia. (41)

It was ardently hoped that the wise men would be able to resolve all the omens in one or two days, or at most a week. But they had been put on salary; high salary. Men labor carefully, and take exceeding pains, in such cases. This work waxed not with dispatch. Presently the soothsayers recommended that inquiries concerning the symbol left by the enchanted dog be addressed to the wise men of distant lands, this symbol being foreign in appearance and seemingly impossible of translation. They also recommended that these inquiries be written by experts in the great and abstruse art of spelling, who should be educated in that science for that especial purpose, to the end that the crown's dignity might be preserved, and no shame brought upon it abroad through the handiwork of the ignorant and unmasterly.

In consequence, it was decreed that certain gifted youths be devoted to this matter. Wherefore, they were selected, and sent to the imperial College of Orthography, (42) where they would be taught by a special method. Their portraits were taken, and preserved; together with a specimen of their spelling; and at the time of their perfection and graduation, new portraits would be taken, and new specimens of their spelling, in order that a royal commission might determine the improvement wrought in the person and orthography of each pupil by the said special method of teaching, to the end that he who should have attained to the highest advancement in these regards might be chosen to write the letters of inquiry; and for this high service be rewarded by having his two portraits exposed to public admiration.

Two hundred and ten of the most beautiful and gifted among the youth of the empire were selected by competitive examination and placed in the college; and there they remained, and wrought; (43) and afterward, in the fulness of time, the survivors were called together by the imperial commission to undergo the graduating inquisition. And behold, far in advance of his fellows stood Ali

Mohammed ben Mahound ibn ben Ali, son of the humblest marabout of the mosque of Shah Safet ibn Jan; and with a loud voice was his triumph proclaimed in the market place and from the steps of the palace; and unto him was command given to write the letters unto the wise of the far lands; and as reward his portraits (44–44½–45–45½) were exposed for public applause; and from that day forth was he no longer obscure, but famous in the land; and the ignorant bowed down before him and praised him, giving thanks to God in his behalf—in whom alone is power and majesty.

Also, in the fulness of time, the great day foretold by the soothsayers approached, and the Persian world ceased from its affairs and stood waiting, breathless, for the announcement of the mighty tidings. It came, at last, and the nation rose up as one man, and rejoiced with their sovereign, and said, "Blessed forever be this newborn child, and may Allah whiten its face, and give it honor and virtue to its portion." And in the self-same hour was the Grand Vizier's child born, also; and the Vizier and the Sultan came forth, radiant with joy and pride, and stood back to back in the balcony, clothed in their robes of state; and thus standing, received the clamorous congratulations of the people, and acknowledged the same with gracious bows. (46)

This was all premature. For, meantime, a dark and hateful deed was being done—a deed which was to change the imperial and ministerial complacency to consternation. Observe, neither of the babes had yet been seen by their parents, or indeed by anyone. The Sultan and the Vizier merely knew of the births, and had gone to the balcony without waiting to learn particulars. *Now at the very moment of the births a wicked witch had come, invisible, and by parting the hair of the Sultan's boy-babe in the middle had made it seem to be a girl, and by parting the hair of the grand Vizier's girl-babe on the side, had thus caused it to seem to be a boy.* In this manner had the inscrutable fates ordained that the boy should be named and reared as a girl, and the girl be named and reared as a boy, whilst the world and the two families moved on unto the goal of their several destinies, unsuspicious of the error.

"This is indeed marvelous!"

Truth, sire, is ever stranger than fiction.

"Why did the wicked witch wish to make this trouble?"

She desired to bring shame and confusion upon the Juree—the gathering of wise men was called, in the Persian tongue, a Juree. She despised a Juree; she could not think of a Juree without loathing. She said a Juree was always composed of idiots. She meant to bring this one to shame by placing this mystery under their very chins, and leaving them to struggle helplessly with it, she being confident that they would never be able to solve it.

*"Verily it was a bold and admirable idea."*

Truth hast thou spoken, and luminous is thy mind and limitless thine understanding, O Prince of Islam, from whose penetration nothing can be hid. At the end of half an hour the jubilant Sultan and Vizier made their farewell bows to the populace and came, upon flying feet, to look upon their just-born treasures. They little imagined what was in store for them.

The Sultana Shakahgah was standing upon a pearl-embattled gonfalon which elevated her a little above the common level of the apartment—in accordance with the requirements of her rank—and she was reading in the Koran and weeping bitterly. As soon as the Sultan beheld her, he cried out:

"Oh, mine idol, my life, where is my son?—show me my son!"

Without attempting to speak, his stricken queen simply raised her hand and pointed. (47)

The Sultan glanced in the direction thus indicated, and there, sitting with its back against a crystal cake-basket, and with one innocent limb crossed upon the other, his eyes perceived, and his heart recognized, his child. (48) Staggering a few steps, he leaned his elbow upon the peristyle of a richly carved Egyptian Odalisque which was embossed with gold and inlaid with precious stones, and exclaimed in broken accents:

"Alas, it is a girl!"

Near the coffee urn, which stood, as was customary in Persia, upon a small ornamental halidome, sat the beautiful lady of the Vizier, steeped in grief, and bedewing her costly raiment with still more precious tears. (49) The Vizier flew toward her, crying:

"Joy of my heart, set forth our treasure—let me see my girl!"

Without speaking she raised to her lap a tiny babe, upon whose innocent countenance the rudiments of a smile had already begun to appear. (50)

Murmuring "Alas, alas, it is a boy!" the sorrowing Vizier sank unconscious to the floor. One by one the others swooned also, and lay in a deadly torpor. But in accordance with the will of the Dispensor of Destinies, a passing stranger entered, with his brush and a bucket of paint, and after (51) limning a beautiful picture of himself upon the palace wall, rescued them from their perilous lethargy by administering to them a mysterious and powerful medicine for which he solely was the licensed agent in that part of the empire.

During many minutes the Sultan brooded over his trouble, and would not be comforted. Unto all who would console him he said, mournfully:

"Plague me not with hollow words, for the doom of my house is sealed. The sceptre must pass from my line with my daughter; for, although the law permits her to reign, it also requires that *if an heir be born of her body, it and herself also must be beheaded,* and a new monarch elected from among the great nobles. *No birth, however miraculous,* can save my dynasty, in these circumstances. I am old; no son will be born to me; my line must perish. It is written!" He was silent during some moments, meanwhile gazing steadfastly toward his child with that far-away look in the eyes which tells of burdened thought and a boding spirit; then he said, slowly, and as if thinking aloud: "It is but a little body—a tiny, tiny obstruction amid the wastes of the wide sea of human history; yet upon it, tiny as it is, will one day split a majestic ship, and about it will lie the broken fortunes of a dynasty and the wreck of an empire!"

When the poor Sultana heard these heavy words, she smiled a haggard smile and said, "My heart is broken!" (52)

The mad rompings and gambolings of the innocent little babes only cast a deeper gloom upon the brooding hearts about them, their guileless gaiety only gave pain where at a happier time it would have brought peace and gladness.

But time reconciles all things, soothes all sorrows. It was not long before the Sultan's little helpless child had won his heart. From being unwelcome in the beginning, it was now become the light of his eyes, the breath of his nostrils, his comfort, his rest, his joy. When the nobles and the people learned this, they were touched, and rejoiced with him. And even as the Sultan now felt toward his child, so also felt the Grand Vizier toward his. That this new feeling was shared by the two illustrious mothers, any will know who has ever been a mother himself.

## Chap. 4

A DAY was by and by appointed for the naming of the babes; and at that time the great mosque was crowded with the Sultan's nobles to witness and do honor to the ceremony. Standing at the altar, the high priest, with solemn and impressive ceremonial, took the Sultan's babe in his hands, and held it aloft, amid a profound hush, that all might look upon it. So awful was this moment, that the Sultan, weakened by excitement, was obliged to place himself in the Grand Vizier's lap for support; and whilst he thus sat, weeping, yet rejoicing, the chief Sultana bowed her head against the altar and communed with her overwrought soul. And now, amid a deep and brooding silence, which was broken only by smothered sobs of the vast assemblage, the venerable high priest, lifting his tear-stained face toward heaven, gently lowered the imperial babe into the urn of holy water with his right hand, and murmured, in a trembling voice,—(53)

"Unto fortune and power, and the grace of life and the reverence of men, baptize I thee, Fatima-Nooreddin-Sitt el-Hosn-Bab-en-Nasr-el-Jawalee—and abide thou in love and peace under the shelter of thy sire's sceptre and in the shadow of his throne! Allah Akbar, Alla il Alla, allaku!"

And after this, he put down his hand and lifted the Grand Vizier's child out of the altar wherein it sat sleeping and baptized it, also, giving it the name of Suleyman-Mohammed-Akbar-ben-Selim-ben-Ali-ibn-Noormahal-ben-Saladin-Badoorah-el-Shazaman-Aladdin-ben-Yusuf-ibn-Kismet-el-Emir-Abdallah-ben—

*"O* DAM*—ascene liverwort,*[8] *rotten apples of Beni-Hassan, weariness of sick souls, incarnate spirit of hope deferred,* LEAVE *the rest of it to the imagination, consider the brevity of life! Condense, slave, condense! Cut the details, get thee swiftly to the vital facts!"*

I hear and obey. Now began a gentle and beautiful domestic life which was idyllic. The babes were kept in each other's society day and night, and their mutual love grew with the growth of their bodies. The Grand Vizier was never absent from his little Selim, the Sultana Shakahgah was never absent from her little Fatima. When the babes took their bath, nothing pleased the doting Vizier and the loving Sultana so much as to be themselves near by, and witness their healthful pastime. (54)

The loves and sympathies of the babes continued to wax in strength and breadth and depth day by day. In the process of teething, if the little Fatima succumbed to the pain, and wept, the little Selim would try to comfort him; and would rub her small gums with her ivory teething instrument, and try to encourage him to do the same, and all the while would smile so tenderly and so benignantly upon him that none could behold it without being softened and made better and holier. (55)

Upon such occasions the happy Grand Vizier would sit entranced with a dreamy delight, a smile of almost feminine grace and sweetness illumining his face the while. (56)

While the precious ones were still babes as yet, they began to develop talents of several kinds, and of a high degree of excellence. Among their gifts was that of music. They sang all the day long; and so marvelously, withal, that the very birds would cease, discouraged, when they began. To the Sultana and the Grand Vizier there was not in all the world such music as the singing of these two little creatures. Often, when out for an airing, the children would begin to sing; whereupon straightway the Grand Vizier and the mistress of the mightiest of the empires of earth

[8] Another version of this joke, *"Dam*—mascus blades," appears in the top margin of p. 116 of the Simon Wheeler novel manuscript (1877–78).

would instantly cease from conversation, bend their heads in listening attitude, and forget this world and its griefs and troubles; and so, without motion or utterance, stand there as in a divine rapture, and let the immortal harmony sweep in upon their spirits and inundate all their being with its golden tides of melody. (57)

So the children grew along; and by and by the results of the unsolved mystery began little by little to appear. That is to say, people came to observe that Selim-Mahomet-Abdallah, the ostensible *boy,* always interested herself in feminine matters; and that Fatima, the ostensible *girl,* always interested himself in masculine things. It was noticed that every Saturday morning little Fatima would throw aside all his sports in order to run and see the Sultan pay off the Court. The Sultan would glance at him and then drop his chin reflectively in his hand (58) and mutter,—

"It is strange, it is passing strange—she takes as much interest in finance as a male person might."

Fatima cared nothing for dolls; he scorned them, and would not play with them. Neither cared he for singing-birds or for cats. To the astonishment of all, he took for a pet a fierce young tiger-cub, and made it his constant companion. And there was another strange thing: whenever the Sultana sat down to tell the little Fatima a fairy tale, he would listen patiently a while, then drop his elbow wearily upon the ferocious tiger-cub's head, and look appealingly up into his mother's face and say,—(59)

"Prithee, peace; I care not for fairies—tell me of massacres and harems!"

Then would the startled Sultana gaze upon him and murmur,—

"Surely she is the strangest child that ever the hand of the Most High hath fashioned—by whose compassion we exist, and unto whose name be praise!"

At the same time, the little ostensible boy, Selim-Abdallah, was distressing her parents similarly. They were grieved and amazed, daily, at her strange ways. They said, "Verily his heart is all with dolls—how despicable is this, in a boy!" And wherever Selim went, she always had a little pet kitten whining at her heels; (60) and this kitten she loved above all other creatures. This gave her parents great sorrow; and they often contemplated her mournfully and said,

"Would God he would renounce the cat."

They tried to teach Selim to act like other boys, but she responded with a reluctance which showed that she had no heart in the matter. Once they persuaded her to swing on the palace gate, after the fashion of the boy kind; but when they observed the pitiful terror that expressed itself in her pallid face, (61) their compassion was moved, and they said,

"Take him down, poor thing, his anguish is dreadful to look upon."

In time, the children arrived at the age that is proper for the separation of the sexes; so they embraced and took farewell of each other, Selim weeping bitterly and voicing her grief in lamentations, while Fatima wore a mournful countenance but withheld all other manifestation of the emotions that were ebbing and flowing in his breast.

## Chap. 5

YEARS went by, the separation continued, as required by the holy Koran, and in time they forgot each other. And so, eventually, they arrived at the age of maturity. That is to say, they were now thirteen years old. Yet, to the amazement of all, Fatima still showed interest in none but matters proper to the manly sex, and Selim cared for nothing but matters proper to the womanly sex. Instead of exercising the sword and lance, Selim would steal away privately to the garden and amuse herself with wheeling a baby carriage up and down the walks. (62) Wherefore the people would look upon her scornfully and say,—

"Verily he is a milksop."

On the other hand, whensoever Fatima observed that none was looking he would throw down his embroidery-work, elevate his hands, (63) count one—two—three—and then fling himself high in the air and turn a handspring. At other times he would stand on his head, making of himself a rude spectacle. Insomuch that if any discovered him in this attitude, they cursed and swore under their breath, and muttered, "Of a truth she is defective, in that she hath no sufficient modesty."

Yet four years more added themselves to the unreturning past. Selim-Abdallah was seventeen years old, the glory of her young womanhood was perfect, yea, matchless. In the book of fate it was written that her long-forgotten cradle-mate should now at last look upon her again. In a remote part of the palace park there was a pretty garden, situated in a retired and shady glade; and in the midst of this fragrant spot was a beautiful shekinah. It was Selim's favorite resort and refuge when her spirit was low and her heart contracted. Thither would she go, and dream away the hours, and so solace herself. We will return to her presently.

Now the prince Fatima, during all his life, had detested his feminine costume, without knowing why. So it was his habit to steal away, when opportunity offered, and seek out unfrequented places, and there rid himself of most of the hated garments; and then, being unencumbered, he would comfort himself with the forbidden exercises of the manly sex. (64)

One day he found himself in regions that were new to him; and whilst he was gliding swiftly and silently along, he thought he heard an angel singing. He checked his progress and leaned his shoulder against a tree. The singing ceased. He waited, but the silence continued. Then he pushed a branch aside, and exclaimed in delighted astonishment,—

"Surely Allah hath created this place for one who is divine!"

This is what he saw: at a little distance was a gate; and it was arched, and over it were vines with grapes of different colors; the red, like rubies, and the black like ebony. And there was a bower; within it fruits were growing in clusters and singly, and the birds were warbling their various notes upon the branches: the nightingale was pouring forth its melodious sounds, and the turtle dove filled the place with its cooing; and the blackbird in its singing resembled a human being; and the ring-dove a person exhilarated with wine. The fruits upon the trees, comprising every description that was good to eat, had ripened; and there were two of each kind; there were the camphor-apricot, and the almond-apricot, and the apricot of Khurasan; the plum of a color like the complexion of beauties; the cherry delighting the senses of every man; the red, the white, and the green fig, of the most beautiful colors; and flowers like pearls and coral; the rose, whose redness put to shame the cheeks of the lovely; the pansy, like sulphur in contact with fire; the myrtle, the gillyflower, the lavender and the anemone; and their leaves were bespangled with the tears of the clouds; the chamomile smiled, displaying its teeth, and the narcissus looked at the rose with its negroes' eyes; the citrons resembled round cups, the limes were like bullets of gold; the ground was carpeted with flowers of every color, and the place beamed with the charms of spring; the river murmured by while the bees droned and the birds sang and the winds sighed among the trees; the season was temperate and the zephyr was languishing; the grapes, the citrons, the—sire, thou snorest! (65)

*"O, Hel—"*

Sire!

*"—en's Babies,*[9] *art thou still driveling out thy weary statistics? Get thee to the marrow of thine immortal lie—bestir thyself, slave!"*

I hear and obey. Near the bower stood an exquisite shekinah, which—

*"What in the name of the portals of perdition and the red-hot hinges of Gehennum, is a* SHEKINAH?"

Verily, they that know, know; they that know not, know not, and unto them it is hidden; such is fate; and God, who createth all things, ordaineth that which he will, and annulleth that which he will not, neither asking counsel of any, nor abiding it, yet visiting the iniquities of the fathers upon the children even to the third and fourth generation of them that go not according to the law and the prophets, but are stiff-necked and of evil disposition, tarrying not with the pure in heart, but going astray after the Urim and Thummum of unrighteousness, the wages of which is death, the

---

[9] The same joke also appears in the top margin of p. 116 of the Simon Wheeler novel manuscript (1877–78).

sustenance of the same being the bowels of wrath and the gall of bitterness whereunto—

*"Peace, peace, my curiosity is assuaged whilst as yet the explanation is but scarce begun: Have thy will with thy shekinah, do with it as thou desirest; but in the hour that thou shalt attempt to explain it again, thou shalt surely die. Proceed."*

I hear and obey. Upon the pedestal of the shekinah lay a handful of those delicious lozenges of Balsora (66) whereof the Prophet (upon whom be peace!) hath said, in the fourteenth sura of the book entitled the Cow, "Neither in Yemen the Happy, nor yet in the mansions of Skanderbeg the Blest is their like to be found for the savoriness which inciteth to godliness, and that fragrance which moveth to charitable deeds."

And now, while Fatima observed and took note of these things, behold, the divine Selim, lovely as Ayesha, radiant as Khadijah, stepped forth from the bower, leaned her elbow upon the pedestal of the shekinah, crossed her dainty feet, took up a lozenge in her fingers, and in this ravishing attitude paused for a time in melancholy reflection, ere proceeding to eat the precious comfit. (67)

All unseen, his presence unsuspected, Fatima gazed in rapture upon this charming vision, and murmured,—

"Can it be that ever a man lived before, who was so beautiful as is this knightly young stranger! Lo, he hath all the perfections, he lacketh none. He is of elegant stature, high-bosomed, with black eyelashes, and smooth cheek, and slender waist, and large hips, and is clad in the handsomest apparel; his figure puts to shame the Oriental willow; his voice is more soft than the zephyr passing over the flowers of the garden; his skin is like silk; his eyes affect the heart with the potency of wine; the locks on his brow are dark as night, while his forehead shines like the gleam of morning. Ah, my heart, my heart! O, divine one, I love thee, I love thee; and thee only will I love whilst the red blood flows in these veins and the breath of life abides in these nostrils!"

With these words yet trembling on his lips he hied him sadly away, lest Selim might come upon him and discover him; "for," said he, within himself, "it would not be meet or modest that I, being a girl, should be seen and accosted by a man."

When he had proceeded to a safe distance, he dismounted and

hid himself near the path, hoping he might be blessed with another glimpse of Selim, and yet be more secure from detection than he had been before. In no long time his devotion was rewarded. Selim, wending homeward, passed by that very spot, and so closely that Fatima was enabled to reach out his hand and touch her garments; which so intoxicated him with joy that he swooned away.

Upon recovering, he found himself sick at heart and disconsolate for the loss of that divine presence. He wandered mournfully back, and viewed again the garden; but he wept, and said, "Alas, it is no longer beautiful, now that *he* is gone." After a little, he murmured, "I will enter, and kiss the sod which his sacred feet have pressed—it cannot bring back the banished cheer of life, but it will yet ease somewhat of my pain to be where he has been, and breathe the air which his breath has made fragrant."

So saying, he passed within the garden, and kneeling reverently down, kissed the ground where Selim had stood; then, still kneeling, whilst tender tears streamed adown his cheeks, he gathered two or three humble violets; (68) and pressing these to his breast, he resolved that he would wear them next his heart whilst that heart continued to beat, and so bear them to the grave when that heart, broken by its sorrows, should find rest and peace in death.

## Chap. 6

THE DAYS went lagging by, but Fatima saw them come and go without interest, for his spirit was in that far garden—a spot which he might not visit again; "for," said he, "where a man is, there it is not proper that a damsel should go."

He fell gradually into a decline; he scarcely ate or slept; he was restless; he forsook all his ordinary occupations; he but sighed, dreamed day-dreams, and nursed his unspoken griefs. His only solace was found in taking long solitary walks, thus removing himself from prying eyes and curious questionings. He wished to muse and brood undisturbed. But secretly he had also another object. He always went to a certain remote piece of high ground, which commanded a distant view of Selim's glade; and with him he took his telescope; and there he would set it up on its supports and peer through it by the hour, (69) patiently hoping that in some fortunate season Allah might grant him one more glimpse of his lost love.

Now it was Selim's custom to go to that very region, on certain days, to practice some of her hated masculine exercises. Among these was marksmanship. The master of the ordnance had erected for her a huge image of the head of a man, and she used to take her gun to that spot and shoot at that thing. She could not hit the figure at long range and offhand; but when she placed her gun against the mark and supported it with a rest, she was often able to hit it very well. (70)

One day she arrived with her gun, and was standing leaning against her mark, musing and smelling at a beautiful bouquet of flowers which she had secretly brought along (for she was forbidden to have such feminine things), when she happened to turn her head, and there, in plain view, stood Fatima, absorbed in gazing through his telescope. With parted lip and leaping pulse the entranced Selim looked and worshipped; (71) then she murmured fervently,—

"O exile from Paradise, daughter of the angels, houri of loveliness unspeakable!—how came she here, and lo, how empty and forlorn must the heavens be without her! My heart is stricken to the core with love—I must possess her, or I die!" She continued to stand spellbound for a while; then she muttered, "It is not proper that I, a young man, should accost a maiden and bring her modesty to shame; yet must I indeed do it, for love is stronger than law, passion derideth custom. I will speak to her, I will throw myself in adoration at her feet, I will give voice to my love though it cost my blood and life to cancel the outrage!"

Then she sprang quickly forward, cast herself upon her knees, and laying her bouquet at Selim's feet, lifted her imploring eyes toward his face, and exclaimed,—

"O, lady, deign to take this humble offering, and spurn not a suffering wretch whose heart is breaking for love of thee!"

The startled youth cast one astonished glance upon the fair

upturned countenance; then exclaiming, "Allah preserve me, it is a man!" veiled his dishonored face with a fold of his garment and fled like lightning away. Far, far he sped; and when at last his strength was exhausted and he could no further go, he sank down in the shady and secure depths of the forest and gave free reign to blissful reflections; saying to himself, over and over again, in an ecstasy of joy,—

"It was he!—it was he!—now let me die, if die I must, for I have seen his face again, I have tasted earth's supremest joy; and I would die, if die I must, now while I may bear to Paradise a memory able to double the bliss of heaven and make the eternal happiness of the angels seem touched with sadness by comparison!"

Long, long he sat there, indulging these raptures; then, as the day drew toward its close, he wended stealthily back, in the hope that, unseen, he might seek for that bouquet, and perchance find it. Arrived at the target-ground, he peered cautiously out from among the trees, and perceived that the place was deserted. Then stepped he forth, searching the ground with eager eye, yet with a sickening dread of possible disappointment stealing over his heart. But the next moment his quick vision discovered the precious keepsake, and with a wild cry of delight he seized it, and then, during many unconscious moments, stood gazing gratefully upon it, his countenance radiant as the sun with joy, and his whole frame trembling with emotion. (72)

Wonderful is requited love! It made of Fatima a new person. It drove him so mad with happiness that he could not express himself in temperate ways but was obliged to seek an outlet for his feelings in the most violent and extravagant actions. So astonished were his parents, observing the things he did, that they moved about, from morn till night, in a state of dazed and pathetic stupefaction. Twenty times in an hour the one would seek out the other and say, concerning him:

"As God liveth, she is standing on her head again, in presence of the entire (73) harem!"

Then the two would visit Fatima to remonstrate, and find him throwing handsprings with such dizzying and incredible velocity that his bones shone through his skin, whilst his head and his legs were actually invisible, no eye being swift enough to perceive them as they whirled round and round through the intoxicated air. (74)

Then would the parents contemplate him mournfully and say: "Her conduct is indeed scandalous."

Between ebullitions of this nature, Fatima would fall into dreamy and sentimental moods again. At such times he would play plaintive airs upon his accordion, and sing. (75) Anon would come the Sultan, sad at heart, and say to his queen:

"Behold she hath got out that aged bouquet and is smelling at it again. (76) It is withered, and is fallen to colorless rags; yet doth she cling to it, and care for it alone, albeit at her command are limitless supplies of fresh flowers; and of such breeds, indeed, as none other in this realm may by love or purchase procure."

How fared it with Selim, meanwhile? Even as it ever does with the perfect ones of her sex and age. The arrow of love—first love—had pierced to the core of her virgin heart, and had left its sweet poison there, there to remain forever. All in one little moment Selim had been changed from a girl, with a girl's small interests, to a woman, with a woman's ocean-deep feelings and all-embracing sympathies. Life had seemed paltry, before; now it seemed sublime. Before, she had lived in the earth, among dull earthly things; now she abode in a celestial realm, whose forms were spiritual, radiant, whose atmosphere was love, and whose sun, forever present and riding in intolerable splendor among the painted clouds, was Fatima.

All her dream was Fatima. In her memory of her one vision of Fatima she lived, and moved, and had her being. Hour after hour would she lie, with closed eyes, in her gently swinging holocaust, communing in spirit with her loved one, and enriching the fragrant air with her yet more fragrant sighs. (77)

Daily she haunted the now hallowed target-ground, in the hope of once more finding Fatima there; but she ever suffered disappointment, for the shy youth dared not venture again to a neighborhood where he might once more be exposed to the forbidden gaze of a masculine eye.

Gradually she extended her wanderings to remoter regions. The same, also, was Fatima doing. Thus they were often near each other, though they never knew it or suspected it. One day Fatima, having stolen away, according to his custom, to enjoy an hour's freedom from his hated feminine garments, and to secretly practice exercises denied to his ostensible sex, was riding pensively through a deep wood, when a wild scream broke suddenly upon the stillness. The next moment he emerged into a grassy opening, and there in the midst of it, transfixed with fright, stood the beautiful Selim gazing at some object near by, and shrieking piteously for help. (78)

Fatima, following the direction of her eye, was thrilled with horror to perceive a prodigious serpent, of hideous form, moving stealthily along the ground, with its vast oval eye riveted with malignant purpose upon the almost fainting Selim. (79)

Even in this fateful moment the creature suddenly coiled itself in a maze of intricate folds, hung down its horrid pear-shaped head and prepared to spring. (80)

But quicker than the forked lightning, plunged the brave Fatima among those writhing coils, neither waiting to put on his jacket nor cast it from his arm, and fierce was the conflict which followed. The thunderous hoof-beats of the hero's noble steed resounded from the monster's rhadamanthine scales, and his wild neighings were mingled with its hoarse roarings and the booming lashings and thrashings of its mighty tail, each sweep of which mowed down wide swathes of forest oaks and filled all the air with clouds of hurtling leaves and branches. Sublimely the daring Fatima bore himself, and marvelous was the gory work wrought by his javelin; for he knew that those eyes which he loved best in all the world were upon him, and the thought filled his heart with a courage more than human, and nerved his arm with the strength of a hundred men. Long and uncertain was the battle; but at last, with one fell stroke the hero drove his lance down through the dragon's yawning jaws, and down, down its poison-exhaling throat, and deep into its vitals—and the historic conflict was over. (81)

Now was Fatima mad with eagerness to fly to his loved one's side; but his ostensible sex forbade such unmaidenly conduct. So, with a sigh, he turned sadly away—first, with infinite delicacy, putting on his polonaise—and disappeared in the wood. Immediately the adoring Selim followed after him upon flying feet. Presently she came upon him leaning upon his reeking spear and absorbed in tender musings. (82) Flinging herself at his feet, she exclaimed:

"O loveliest of earth's creatures, behold thy redeemed slave, whose life is at thy disposal; and, despicable as he is, deign to give him some sign whereby he may know that he has found somewhat of favor in thy sight!"

For answer—and oh how eloquent it was and how sufficient!—the vanquished and yielding Fatima drooped his countenance toward her, and parted his lips in a smile of such infinite grace and sweetness that she sank to the ground overwhelmed with gratitude, while her soul swam in seas of intoxicating bliss.

Now were their loves confessed; and when they parted, it was with mutual promises to meet in some secret place as often as opportunity would permit. As Fatima was turning to go, he held out his hand, and Selim rapturously seized it and kissed it again and again, exclaiming, "O dainty hand, oh incomparable hand!" (84) Then she observed that something was concealed in its palm. It was a most rich and costly breastpin. (85) Whilst her heart was bursting with mingled hopes and fears, the princely youth murmured, "Wear it, for my sake!" and, blushing crimson, fled lightly away, leaving the poor young damsel's cup of happiness full to the very brim. From that day forth she ever wore the pretty bauble next her heart.

## Chap. 7

How sweetly, now, and how swiftly, did the joyous days wing their flight! When the Grand Vizier sought his Selim, mornings, he would find her, deep in reverie, thinking out a sonnet to her Fatima's eyes. (86) Prose was her speech no longer. Her heart was filled with spondees, hectagons and pterodactyls, now, and only in the rhythm and measure of poesy did she utter herself.

Yes, mornings would the Vizier find her thinking out a poem; and evenings, with rapt uplifted countenance, would he find her getting it by heart. (87) She no longer fed herself with coarse food, but only with sherbets and the most exquisite and unsubstantial dainties. Often the lady of the Grand Vizier would gaze long and wondering upon her, and then say to her lord:

"Of a truth is that boy an enigma to me. Lo, there he is with his wearisome spoon and his monotonous sherbet yet again." (88)

On the other hand, the glad new sense of being some beloved one's idol, wrought in Fatima a desire to adorn and beautify his person and so make himself the worthier of love's sweet and exalting homage. He would busy himself by the hour in binding one elegantly wrought scarf after another around his head, and in noting with giddy ecstasy the effect in the glass. (89) Also, hour after hour would he brush and dress his hair—at least seem to do so, though in truth he spent most of the time in gazing adoringly upon the brush, or kissing it, for it had been given him by Selim, at one of their meetings, and was of majestic proportions, full jewelled, chronometer movement, compensation balance, and was the work of an Afreet, who, by enchantment, had stored it with many healing virtues. (90) So went he about, hour after hour, employed as just described; insomuch that the Sultan looking at him with troubled eyes, would often mutter:

"Alas, her life is wholly absorbed in the contemplation of that curry-comb." (91)

The palace buildings were very numerous and grand. They formed an oblong square of great extent, and about them, on every hand, the luxuriant grove of the Sultanic park stretched, dim with the mellowing effects of perspective, to the horizon. (92) The southern length of the square, stretching from west to east, was occupied by four clusters of edifices, and in these was compressed the Sultan's harem. Along the whole western frontage of the great square stretched a single rank of colossal terra cottas, whose stupendous agglomerations of foliage cast wide firmaments of grateful shade abroad over the neighboring portions of the empire, during the heats of summer, and whose opulent tribute of golden fruit caused each returning autumn to be longed for in the time of its approach and welcomed in the day of its arrival. In truth, it was said of these trees that—

*"Truce to thy weary statistics, thy tedious biographies of inconsequential things, remember that man is but mortal, and may not tarry here alway!"*

I hear and obey. At the south-west corner of the square stood a cluster of five buildings; of these, one was taller than the rest, and in the top of this one abode the prince Fatima; and he had dormers toward the north, and an oriel toward the west. Separating this edifice from the next one northwards—which was occupied by a detachment of the Grand Vizier's harem—was a courtyard-outlet or lane of little more than a quadrilateral rhomboid in width.

*"A which?"*

Quadrilateral rhomboid.

*"By the tables of stone that brake in the hands of Musa on the declivities of Sinai, they vex my soul, these intricate technicalities. Now what in the name of the seven kidneys and forty-seven gallbladders of Joshua the son of Nun, is a quadrilateral rhomboid?"*

God is the contriver of all things, oh Scourge of the Infidel, Refuge of the Faithful! and he also is the creator of the same; upon such as He will confer life He conferreth it, and unto such as He will deny it He denieth it; and he that will comment, even he that goeth about to murmur, verily he hath his reward; for though he hide himself under mountains he shall be found; though he cover his limbs with a talmud and conceal his body in a sackbut, yet shall the folds be loosed, the fabrics rent, and his nakedness be brought to the light; yea, though he take wings unto himself and fly to the uttermost parts of the morning, the bands of Orion shall encompass him, the stars in their courses shall fight against him, and a still small voice shall point him out; for man that is born of woman is of few days and full of trouble, his life is but a logarithm, his momentary being is but the occultation of a differential calculus, his——

*"Forbear! Leave me to mine ignorance; for better is ignorance, with peace, than knowledge acquired through suffering. Thy*

*definitions weary my spirit, thine explanations fatigue mine understanding; I care not to know the meaning of the rest of that thing, being content with that portion which I have already learned. Proceed with thine interminable lie, and be thou brief."*

I hear and obey. Separating the abode of the prince Fatima from the next edifice northwards—which was occupied by a detachment of the Grand Vizier's harem, part regulars and part militia—was a lane, of a width already described. Through the roof of this harem projected a considerable row of chimneys, and behind these chimneys, and extending along the comb of the roof, was a rank of skylight apartments. (93)

Now, at a certain time, and all unknown to Fatima, the Vizier brought Selim from one of his harems which lay a mile to the eastward, and domiciled her in one of those skylight rooms—the one nearest to the lane. As soon as she was alone she ran and peeped eagerly through the slats of the blinds, and there, sure enough, she saw what she had expected to see—Fatima sitting within his dormer window. His attitude was pensive, (94) for he was being delivered of another poem—a lambent and vitreous little holograph, of extraordinary depth of feeling, grace of expression, and decency, entitled "Thee! ah, Thee Only, only Thee! Thee, Mine Own!" All the long afternoon she watched him, adored him, devoured him with her eyes; but she gave no sign whereby he might suspect her presence, for although she proposed giving him a delightful surprise, she had another plan.

How she longed for the night to come! and when at last it came, how she longed for the later hours, when all should be still! In time, even these came; all the world lay steeped in tranquil sleep, no sound disturbing the mighty quiet but the occasional deep baying of a distant dog, the soft sighing of the night breeze, the subdued rasping of the moon against the clouds.

Now arose the happy Selim, and, adjusting the crank of her harpsichord, she stood close by her window, and sent a rich flood of murmurous melody weltering abroad over the dreaming land. (95) Her countenance shining with the fires of inspiration, her lithe form swaying to the measure of the music, her fair head graciously poised, the volcanic splendors of her deep eyes glinting fitfully from out the shadows cast by her silken cap—ah, she was a fitting subject for the pencil of earth's master artist!

Fatima listened, (96) and his soul was entranced with an unearthly rapture; but he did not know the tune, he did not divine the performer. When the music was ended, and its closing notes had died away upon the night wind and become silent, he took out his flute, and placing it to his lips, answered the invisible serenader with the mournful opening bars of a tender and plaintive cathartic, and then ceasing, waited in listening attitude. (97)

Again the harpsichord poured forth its melodious strain, and straightway the listener's reason well nigh forsook him for joy; for this time he knew the air; it was one which he himself had composed, and none but he was acquainted with it save Selim, to whom he had taught it. He seized his flute and responded, charming the silences with soulful ecstasies of passion; and again the witching harpsichord replied. Thus, during two long hours, the lovers communed together; then sought their couches to dream of each other and the happy promises of the morrow.

From this time forth their days were indeed filled with joy. They were able to see each other a hundred times a day; by means of air-guns (98) they fired loving messages into each other's windows; by the same method they made appointments to meet. By signals they guarded carefully against discovery. When Fatima was not alone, he signified this fact by hanging his fan out of the window. (99) When Selim was encumbered with a visitor, she gave warning by hanging her handkerchief out of her window. (100)

The lovers had their clandestine meetings in one of that sort of intricate gardens which is called a maze. (101) It was situated in a retired part of the Grand Vizier's private park, and was seldom visited by any one. Selim taught the secret of its intricate ways to Fatima, and thither they used to repair, with frequency, to enjoy a stolen interview. Their favorite retreat was a cozy little oval nook, called *El Mich,* which was situated far away eastward among the tangled solitudes of the labyrinth. In this place they met, undisturbed, during many, many months; and there Fatima read his poems, while Selim listened and testified her pleasure in them.

## Chap. 8

But in the year that the lovers were eighteen, a day at last came wherein this soft security was to suffer a rude interruption. Fatima, sitting at his careless ease, was synopsizing to Selim the argument of a poem which he proposed to presently read, when he thought he detected a sound as of a footstep. Starting violently, he rose to his feet, placing his fan to his lips as a warning to his companion to preserve silence, whilst Selim, trembling in every limb, seized one of Fatima's hands, and sat listening, a prey to the cruelest apprehensions. (102) As soon as she could command the use of her limbs, she rose, and turning a pallid visage toward the choice of her heart, (103) whispered, in accents of terror:

"Alas, what is it?"

"I thought I heard a footprint. But be not disturbed, love; for about thee is the protecting arm of one who fears no footprint that was ever uttered."

She could have worshipped him for those brave words. They calmed her terrors, even as oil calms the troubled waters when the storm-wind is abroad on the sea; and smiling at her fears she said:

"I will tarry here; go thou and see."

Kissing her brow, in mute thanks for her trustfulness, he did as he was bid. For a while after he was gone, Selim was content; but as the moments lengthened and he returned not, she grew afraid once more, and resolved to follow after him—die with him, if need be. So she arose and went stealthily tip-toeing through the mazy paths, (104) expecting, every moment, to overtake her lover; but in this she was disappointed.

Now it so happened that the Vizier, being oppressed with cares of state, was visiting the maze-garden that day, to rest his mind with the healing tranquility of its solitudes, and had ordered the chief hammam or duenna of his harem to bring after him a cup of Burmese *cho.* (105) It was this woman's footstep that had been overheard by the lovers; and hardly had Selim quitted El Mich when the hammam appeared there. A glance told her that the place had been recently occupied; for on the ground lay Fatima's crochet-work, (106) which he had not thought to conceal. Greatly agitated, the hammam fled swiftly away, to bear to the Vizier the news of her strange discovery.

Poor Selim, not being able to find her lover, presently turned back toward El Mich, sadly distressed, and stopping every little while to listen, with bursting heart, for the sound of that footstep which was dearer to her ear than song of bulbul or voice of holy minaret calling the faithful to prayer. (107)

At last, in the course of one of these intervals of standing, what was her joy to see Fatima come suddenly in sight, unscathed, not even wounded. Overcome with gratitude, she fell fainting upon his breast, and they returned at once to El Mich, too overjoyed in finding each other again to give a further thought to danger.

Fatima now arranged his poems in two tiers, and selecting the one which he had written latest, proceeded to unfurl it, whilst his beloved bent over it in deep admiration of its orthography. Hardly, however, had he recited the opening verse when he was aware of the presence of a third party. (108)

It was the hammam. Coldly she stood there, rigid, pitiless, an incarnate besom of fate impending over these friendless young forms, a cloud laden with destructive thunders, a palladium freighted with humiliation, woe, and death. No words spake she; but coldly she stood there, and turned upon them the countenance of a sardonyx—malignant, salacious, bituminous, fit reflection of a heart in whose dark recesses reposed no bowels of pity, flowed no tear of compassion, sparkled no aureate sands of sympathy.

"What wouldst thou?" demanded Fatima, endeavoring to master his emotion.

For answer she coldly pointed rearward with her palanquin, as if to indicate that from that direction might presently come—

Fatima shuddered.

"Woman!" he cried, "thou holdest in thy hand the lives of two young unfriended beings, whose only crime is that they love, whose only trespass is that they have concealed it. Save us, or ere thou canst! Speak—is it greatness thou desirest? Thou shalt be exalted above the headship of the nobility; thou shalt take precedence of the tributary queens, men shall make the seven prostrations and two genuflexions before thee; and from Samarcand to the Ghauts of Guicowar, from the sterile plains of El Medineh to the fruitful hills of Ceylon, all the Oriental world shall bare the head when thy great name is spoken!"

She but uttered a scornful smile.

"Say, is it wealth thou cravest? Thou shalt be mistress of thirty palaces and a thousand slaves; thy meanest raiment shall be of the fabric called 'woven dreams,' whose warp is the viewless films of the sacred spider, and whose woof is opal dust; thou shalt sup from a service of precious stones, each piece wrought from a single gem; thy bed shall be of down of the phenix, whereof each flake is the slow product of a century and exceedeth in value the revenues of a principality; thy highways shall be paved with silver, thy rivers bridged with gold, thy treasure house shall be the bottomless abyss of Bhunderpoor, and it shall be stored to the brim with dinars of Cashmere and shekels of Daghestan!"

With these words, he placed a coin in her hand, (109) as earnest of what he had promised. But coldly she flung it away. The heart of Fatima congealed to curds within him. Now heard they a great noise, and in that moment the Grand Vizier, insane with wrath, appeared and hovered over his child, his baton of office uplifted to strike. (110)

Pallid with terror, Selim fell upon her knees, and clasping her beautiful hands, exclaimed:

"Strike, but hear me! When I stood at death's door, and but for instant help thou hadst been childless, behold this damsel saved my life."

Turning to see who was indicated, the Grand Vizier for the first time perceived Fatima. Then his own cheek blanched, and, sinking to his knees he bowed his head to the ground and said:

"My life is forfeit, it is the Sultan's daughter! Do with thy slave as thou wilt, O princess, for heavy is his transgression. I have lifted weapon in the sacred presence of the imperial blood, and only my death, and the death of all my house, and the confiscation of my goods, can obliterate the offense and cancel the crime—yet in my heart am I innocent, for as the Prophet liveth, lady, I saw thee not."

With a noble pity the prince Fatima raised up the trembling minister and said:

"Unto the Sultan my father thou hast been a good servant, faithful and true; banish thy fears, for though thy transgression is grave, yet will I harm thee not."

The poor Vizier, hearing these gracious, life-restoring words, was so transported with joy that he was scarce able to conceal it; and when Fatima further astounded him by saying it was his actual and serious desire to take his loved Selim as husband in holy marriage, the ecstatic minister in spite of all he could do, was no longer able to wholly control his emotion; and so, struggling through all barriers of restraint, a dim, grateful smile welled up and flickered vaguely in his countenance for a moment, (111) and then disappeared under an inundation of thankful tears.

"Now," said Fatima, "seeing I have spared thy life, thou shalt in return be of our party; thou shalt help us to win my father's consent."

"It shall be even as thou commandest," said the happy Vizier.

Then, consulting a one-eyed calendar to learn if the day might haply be auspicious, he presently proclaimed that it undoubtedly was, by reason that Saturn and Jupiter being in conjunction in the sign of the Ram, the occultation of Taurus must follow in the house of the Twins; wherefore, enterprises assayed at such a time must in the end be fortunate. This gladdened all hearts.

## Chap. 9

Now sought they the Sultan in a body, in the Great Hall of Audience, and prostrated themselves upon their faces before him, and in this posture stated their errand, and implored his merciful attention to the prayer of their petition. (112)

The monarch paled, and was visibly moved, yet manifestly not with anger—which unhoped for grace was indeed a pleasant sign, and caused the hearts of the suppliants to expand with gratitude.

Long the Sultan sat silent, absorbed in melancholy thought. But at last he said, with sorrow in his tones:

"I will reveal that which is in my mind. It is this. My desire is not against this marriage—not against this marriage in particular; but it is against any marriage wherein my daughter shall be a party, for that it must imperil her life. Ye know the law: if a child be born of her body, it must die, and herself also. How can I be a willing accessory to thy destruction, O Fatima, joy of mine eyes, daughter of my heart! How canst thou thyself endure to contemplate so dread a fate?"

Rising to his knees, and stretching forward his appealing hands, Fatima responded:

"Upon my head be it, O my father! For what is life to me without Selim; and what, to me, would death be, having possessed him? As for life without him, I value it not; it is but as ashes in the mouth of him that famisheth. Behold I would pay down a hundred of its empty years for one rich love-freighted month of life with my Selim, with usury of fifty deaths at the end! Speak the gracious word, O my liege and father; and so, with future death redeem and vitalize this present death in life!"

Proud was the Sultan's heart to behold this lofty spirit and hear these high and dauntless words. Fervidly he exclaimed:

"Right princely hast thou spoken, child after mine own heart, worthy of thy great line, daughter of a thousand kings, last and noblest of thy race,—thou shouldst have been born a man! By the beard of the Prophet, thou deservest to have thy wish; and but for yet another barrier, the existence whereof I do regret, I would surely grant it thee."

"What is it, sire? O name it, and by thy regal might, which hath nor bound nor limit in all this far-stretching empire, the traversing whereof doth fatigue the sun in his course, remove it!"

Sadly shaking his head, the Sultan said:

"It may not be, my child. Alas, it may not be, as thou wilt see. Listen, then. Thou knowest of the mighty monster, the great dragon that hath ravaged the realm this hundred years, laying waste the harvests, devouring nations, depopulating principalities, and annihilating the eight-score armies which in these three generations I and my fathers have sent against him? Sooth, then, know that once in an evil hour I swore a great oath that none but he who should rid my realm of that fell monster should wed my daughter—and woe is me that I said those words, for not even my puissance can break the chain they have welded, or throw down the barrier they have raised between thee and marriage."

Joyfully Fatima looked up and exclaimed:

"Lo, is that all?" at the same time delivering to Selim, by a furtive glance, a mute command which she understood and immediately obeyed. Rising, and standing reverently before the Sultan, (113) she veiled her modest head from view and murmured:

"Sword of God, Glory of Islam, Marvel of the Nations, Dimmer of the Sun, I—being supported by the Most High, and protected by His angels—I slew that dragon!"

The Sultan, his noble countenance distorted with surprise and aflame with excitement, (114) gazed with deep and emotionless stupefaction upon the slender figure before him, ever and anon clasping and unclasping his hands, pounding upon the throne with his sceptre, and shouting:

"What, *thou!* And dids't *thou* do it?—*thou!* It is marvelous, it is amazing, it passeth comprehension! What, *thou!*—even *thou?* If it be true, the renown of it can never perish from the memory and the applause of men! But *is* it true? can it *be* true? Prove it, and my daughter is thine, thou heart of gold, glory of the age, in whom is the soul of Rustam and the arm of Khaled jointed to the visage of Azrael, Angel of Compassion!"

With a sweet and engaging shyness, Selim supplicated the monarch to give her the opportunity to prove the truth of her assertions by allowing her to conduct him to the remote place in the forest where lay the decaying remains of the dragon. He willingly consented; and, guarded by a brigade of the imperial cavalry, (115) the party immediately set out. As the mighty cavalcade wound its glittering length along, vast multitudes of citizens massed themselves together along the sidewalks (116) to view the gorgeous spectacle and give it God-speed with the thunder of their acclamations.

Arrived at the ground, there, stretched out league on league in diminishing perspective, lay the bleaching skeleton of the hideous colossus, a spectacle which caused the Sultan to shudder and give thanks. Somewhat of the trunk had gone to decay, but a cluster of the prodigious heads (118) was still perfect, and these the Sultan contemplated with mingled shame and ecstasy. Riding adown the far-reaching shibboleth of arching bones, the company found here and there fragments of the viscera which were still but little touched by decay; and at last they discovered also one fin which was measurably perfect. (119)

The Sultan was convinced; and there, in the presence of the dread ravisher of the realm, he joined the hands of Selim and Fatima in holy betrothal, and commanded that ambassadors be dispatched to the several courts of the world with official notice of the fact.

Freighted with the recovered specimens of the late monster for the Sultan's cabinet of strange curiosities, the party now returned to the palace in the same order in which they had come, but moving difficultly through wide seas of massed and jubilant people; for these had learned of the death of their great enemy, and of the betrothal, and were come to testify their gratitude and joy. Removing his crown, (120) the happy Sultan bowed right and left to his salaaming subjects, who, frantic with delight at this condescension, rent the air with the thunder of their shoutings.

*"I wish to God he had died: then mayhap might this weary tale end with time, and so not drag beyond, vexing the tranquil aeons of eternity!"*

Patience, sire, the history draweth near to its close. In due season the marriage day came round, and the friends and neighbors sent wedding presents; and those that contributed not were cut. (121)

The day that the lovers attained to the age of nineteen, they were married, with the utmost pomp, the resources of the realm being taxed nigh to exhaustion to give splendor to the occasion.

As the moment for the ceremony approached, Fatima, with happiness too deep for words, retired to his chamber, attended by his maidens, to array his person in his bridal apparel.

First he clothed himself in that wonder of wonders, her loose-flowing Samovar, whose embroideries and minor adornments were wrought wholly by hand, and whose material was a curious and ingenious combination of sackcloth and ashes of roses, through whose lambent meshes frisked and shimmered, myriad-glinting, the evasive and eluding counterfeits of those brief-lived sparks which spray hither and thither athwart the crisping texture of a flake of burnt paper.

Next he put on his blue and old gold Cyclone, with low neck and short sleeves, trimmed with algonquins and alguazils of varied forms, some cylindrical, some celluloid, others flatulent.[10] Over his head he threw a filmy and spectral cloud called Visible Atmosphere, which was so sensitive that each breath from a neighboring nostril set it in a panic of fluttering motion. From his shoulders drooped the imperial Banshee, of a rich crimson, shading off into scarlatina, then into a tint less redolent, and then dreamily on down through the softening gamut of color, a dimming strain of painted music, and going out at last in a swoon of glimmering purples melting into faintest blues, and the blues into vanishing vague radiances of gangrene.

Then he donned his nuptial Lambrequins, which were crusted with precious stones of every hue, laid on in mottled patterns which caught the light at every turn and every movement, and imitated the tides of colored splendor cast from a prism and washed to and fro upon the surface of some unrestful object.

Next added he his Bridal Veil, which fell in glittering ripples to the floor, a cobweb of flossy glass which had come compacted in the shell of a filbert.

Last of all, he placed a single modest Gloria-in-Excelsis in his hair, and staked it out with a simple hairpin.

Now was he complete, now was he perfect; and thus he burst upon a waiting world like a vision out of Paradise.

---

[10] In revising the typescript, Twain underscored this word and put a question mark in the margin.

And now, when, amid the hush of the vast conclave, the tender young couple stood up (120½) before the venerable archimandrite, with his attendant archipelagoes and theodolites, the spectacle was indeed sublime and impressive. Here knelt a group of mitred acolytes; there a croziered band of holy parasites; in this place a reverend body of aged stalactites; in that, crimson-robed anchorites and purple-surpliced troglodytes; while at intervals, all down the converging lines of the spacious chancel, and conspicuous in their gorgeous ecclesiastical panoply, appeared imposing platoons of hoary patriarchs, interspersed with batteries of bishops.

The Sultan, arrayed in his sumptuous imperial regalia, looked abroad over the mighty assemblage massed in the naves and transepts, with proud heart and stern and majestic mien; for he was very happy. (121)

The lovers stood side by side: Fatima erect and interested, with the hand containing the license flung carelessly behind him; (122) Selim, with the diffidence proper to her sex and age, drooping her graceful body slightly, and bending her modest eyes earthward. (123)

The stately service dragged its slow length along; anthems were sung, sermons were droned, advice was given, admonitions lavished. At last the fateful question was asked; and though Selim's frightened answer was hardly heard, such was not the case with Fatima's reply. Stretching himself to his full height, he turned proudly toward the vast multitude, and, placing his hand upon his heart, proclaimed in deep organ tones these words:

"YES!" (124)

Whereupon the whole great concourse rose as one man and burst into salvos of artillery, while the national anthem pealed from ten thousand throats, and in turn was taken up by the waiting multitudes outside, who passed it from mouth to mouth, from city to city, from nation to nation, till all the limitless empire was joined together in the triumphant song and its uttermost horizons quaked to the roar and crash thereof.

During the extended and delightful wedding excursion, which was made in the most splendid of all the state coaches, (125) and which began with an exciting thirty-day jaunt across the—

*"Call me when they—"*

I pray thee go not to sleep, sire; I will forbear to describe the journey, since it is not to thy liking.

*"Proceed then; and harkye, mend thy gait."*

## Chap. 10

I HEAR and obey. Months sped; and now did the waiting empire hold its breath, expectant, and oppressed with bodings. Men shook their heads and said:

"The day of sorrow approacheth, the dynasty is doomed; for albeit according to the prophecy a miracle could save it, it so happeneth, in this case, that no miracle is conceivable that could by any possibility meet the requirements of the emergency. Therefore let us set our houses in order and prepare for the political convulsions which must accompany the going down of the old dynasty and the elevation of the new."

Steadily and surely died the cheer out of the Sultan's countenance in these heavy days; and at last he ceased to smile. All the day long he walked the floor, moaning in his trouble, and saying:

"Alas, I shall lose her, I shall lose my sweet child; there is no hope!"

And every hour would he drag his worn body before the Juree of Magicians to learn if there was yet any sign of the vouchsafing of the saving miracle. But always they shook their heads sorrowfully, and turned them to their difficult labors. Then would the Sultan retire to the privacy of his closet and there weep, saying:

"Lo, hope is indeed vain; for by the terms of the prophecy none but a miracle that can neither be devised nor imagined can meet this case."

Many hours did Fatima spend with him daily, for both desired to be with each other as much as they might during the little time that remained. And often he tried to hearten his father saying:

"Grieve not, for thou art old and frail, and wilt soon join me beyond the grave, and there shall we never more be separated. My heart is not troubled for my case; I go to my death without repining, for I have possessed my Selim, and that compensates me. Daily I watch the sorrowing workmen building the scaffold for my execution, and I shudder not, but say comforting words to them, bidding them mourn not for me."

At last the Sultan took to his bed, all his strength being gone. Then, on a day, went there a dread report through the city, and all men ceased from their labors, and stared dazed and miserable into each other's blanched faces, saying:

"The doom is come—the child is born!"

The Sultan heard, and turned his face to the wall, with a great sigh, and said:

"Let me die. Alas, my sweet daughter, now will it soon be over with thee."

At this moment burst Fatima into the presence, wild with excitement, crying:

"Come back to life, O my father, for the miracle of miracles has come to pass, and thy daughter and thy dynasty are redeemed; for lo, *not I but my husband is the child's mother!*"

And straightway unwinding a blanket, he showed him the babe, a wee little red-haired thing, and the transported Sultan kissed it and blessed it and named it Ethelred.

And now at this instant flew *Selim* into the presence, crying:

"Lo, it is twins, for I am mother to yet another, and our happiness is complete!"

Then she showed the sweet hairless little creature, and the hosannahing Sultan embraced it and blessed it, and named it Ethelbald; and then, placing the two babes side by side, Ethelred on the right, Ethelbald on the left, (126) he lifted up his streaming eyes, and spread abroad his emaciated hands, and blessed them both again, and yet again, exclaiming:

"Now will I never doubt again; for in the contemplation of this miracle I perceive and shall henceforth know and realize, that no miracle which the imagination can conceive, is impossible. My dynasty is saved, my daughter is redeemed; glorious is this day!"

Then he gave commandment that the babes go forth and show

themselves to the people. Whereupon, arrayed in dainty and costly raiment, as became their princely rank, the little innocents hied them to the great balcony and prettily danced and sang before the huzzaing world of rejoicing subjects, (127) who flung their turbans into the air and caused the welkin to ring with their shouts; and well they might; for they knew that but for the interposition of that stupendous miracle the throne would have gone down in blood, and they and their children become the prey of wars and misery all their days. And still amazed, and filled with wonder by the greatness of the event, they communed together, saying, one to another:

"To think that the father, and not the mother, should be the mother of the babes! Now of a truth are all things possible with God—whose name be exalted, whose perfections be extolled!"

*"Verily it was indeed a most strange and unusual miracle."*

It was so regarded, sire, by many.

*"What became of those other prophetic signs and marvels? What was it decided that their meaning was?"*

That, indeed, was never determined; the Juree disagreed.

*"So? After all that tedious time and expense? What did the Sultan with the Juree?"*

He applied to them the remedy, according to the dictates of wisdom. Wherefore, they announced the two professions of the faith, uttered a sigh, and were recorded among the company of the blest.

*"It were well that this might happen unto all such. In this thing the Sultan acted commendably, as concerned them; soothly, he did as well as he might, seeing he could not also damn them. But I die of weariness, I perish with exhaustion: make thou an end, quickly."*

Lo, the noble history, O Prince of the Faithful, Lord of the Earth, Joy of the Seven Kingdoms, Shadow of the Most High, seemeth to be finished; yea, except my memory deceive me, it *is* finished!

*"Praise and thanksgiving, now and forever, that I have endured to see this hour! Headsman! Rouse thee, slave—hither, I say!* HEADSMAN!*—dost hear? Alas, he hath not survived!"*

Now, therefore, did the monarch make a great clamor, which brought another headsman; unto whom he cried:

"Take thou this tedious woman hence, and cut off thirty yards of her tongue, and hang her with it!"

The which would of a certainty have been done; but just as the sobbing and struggling Scherezade was being dragged out of the door, she chanced to recall a circumstance of very great moment connected with her late tale. This additional particular the king could in no wise resist the temptation to listen to; wherefore he called the Queen to bed, and bade her tell it with all possible dispatch, at the same time commanding the new headsman to seat himself and wait for her.

But now, indeed, a most sad thing happened. It took longer to tell the circumstance than any had supposed it would; and so, in the course of the narration the new headsman ceased from sorrow, joining his predecessor in the vale of imperishable delights; and in time King Shahriar expired also.

But the beautiful Scherezade remained as fresh as in the beginning, and straightway ordered up another king; and another, and still another; and so continued until all the people were alarmed for the perpetuity of their royal line, its material being by this time very greatly reduced. So all the nation knelt before the beautiful Scherezade and implored her to desist from her desolating narrations. But she said no—not until she had sent as many kings to the tomb as the late king had sent poor unoffending Queens, would she stay her hand. She called it hand, and it is meet and respectful that her words be preserved unamended.

She nobly stood to her purpose, until one thousand and ninety-five new tombs had been added to the royal cemetery; (128) then she said her poor slaughtered predecessors were avenged and she was satisfied. Whereupon she coiled her weapon away, and from that time forth gave it and the royal stock a rest.

THE END

# THE HELLFIRE HOTCHKISS SEQUENCE

(1877–1897)

# I

# *Autobiography of a Damned Fool*

(1877)

Editor's Note: Although the title I have used for this fragment is one supplied by Albert Bigelow Paine, I have retained it here to avoid confusion because it is the title by which the fragment has been known in the critical literature on Mark Twain. Twain himself never gave it a formal title, but he referred to it once in a letter to Howells as "Orion's autobiography," a description in itself capable of confusing the unwary because in 1880 Orion undertook to write an autobiography and corresponded to some extent with Twain on the project.

Twain began the "Autobiography of a Damned Fool" late in March 1877. In a letter to Howells at that time he wrote, "I began Orion's autobiography yesterday & am charmed with the work. I have started him at 18, printer's apprentice, soft & sappy, full of fine intentions & shifting religions & not aware that he is a shining ass. Like Tom Sawyer he will stop where I start him, no doubt—20, 21 or along there; can't tell; am driving along without plot, plan, or purpose—& enjoying it." [1]

He probably worked on it only two or three weeks, for by late April he was in Baltimore for rehearsals and last-minute revisions of *Ah Sin,* the play written in collaboration with Bret Harte. He may have found time for an additional touch or two on the manuscript in early May, but by 16 May he was off to Bermuda with Joseph H. Twichell. When he returned, he was engrossed with "Some Rambling Notes of an Idle Excursion," his account of the Bermuda trip, and, after his removal to Quarry Farm on 6 June, with a new literary enthusiasm, his play about Captain Simon Wheeler. The manuscript contains no revisions or additions subsequent to the work of March and April; the "autobiography" had gone to the pigeonhole to make way for the new projects.

Although the phrase "Orion's autobiography" suggests that the conception of the central character owes much to Twain's exasperation with his brother, the exaggerations in the depiction turn the "Damned Fool" into a character quite similar to Mamie Grant, and the story so far as it was developed before it was pigeonholed, is quite similar in structure to the story of the child-missionary.

---

[1] *MTHL,* I, 173. The letter is headed simply "Friday, AM," but the approximate date of the letter is fairly clear from the reference in the opening paragraph to finishing Howells' *Out of the Question,* the last installment of which appeared in the April *Atlantic.* This issue of the magazine would have reached Hartford shortly after 15 March.

# *Autobiography of a Damned Fool*

MY FATHER was a man of considerable consequence in the Southern village in which I was born. He was greatly respected, for he was a man of very high principle. His father was Scotch and his mother Irish; so he was as saving and thrifty as a Scot, sometimes, and as lavish and careless as an Irishman at others; he was full of Scotch gravity at times, and at other times he was as full of Irish vivacity and eloquence. Sometimes he was firm, sometimes the opposite—nobody could tell which characteristic would come uppermost in any given emergency. In religion he was a Presbyterian, with a vague, haunting leaning toward papacy. But he was at all times a good man—in this he was consistent and unvarying. His benevolences ate up a good share of his profits; so when he followed my mother to the grave, his orphans had not a great substance to divide between them.

I was eighteen, then, and a printer's apprentice. My father's funeral brought me suddenly and violently face to face with the great concerns of the hereafter. During many nights I could not sleep for thinking of my perilous situation. I resolved at last upon an immediate and thorough reform of all my ways. I was a smoker. I began my reform there. I took my stock of penny cigars, and addressed them thus: "Pernicious things, you shall defile me no more; we part this hour, and forever; and observe, I will not do as some do, give you away, and defile others whilst I cleanse myself; you shall be destroyed." So saying, I made a little fire on the public sidewalk and burned them.

Many elderly people admired this spectacle, as one by one they gathered about me and learned my resolve. The Methodist minister said he wished all the youth of Christendom might see this thing, for it could not fail of good effect. He took me home with him and we had a long talk upon sacred matters, which ended in my taking a class in his Sunday school and promising to attend his services with the purpose of joining his church.

This was on Friday. As I walked homeward I suddenly remembered that there was an important job at the office which had been promised for that day. It was now too late to finish it, but when I reflected upon the manner in which I had been employed I said to myself, "Better a thousand jobs fail, so that the time be devoted as I have devoted it."

When I reached the office I found the boss in a frenzy of rage. He said he had had several persons hunting for me to no purpose and felt now in a fit humor to break every bone in my body. I listened calmly, and let him finish his vituperation without interruption, saying to myself, "Little does he know what remorse he is storing up for himself."

When he came at last to an end with the demand that I tell him what idle business I had been upon, I spoke with a forgiving gentleness and serenity that must have seemed in notable contrast with his unrefined loudness and passion, and told my story. To my astonishment it threw him into a more frantic rage than he was in before. He cursed me, he called me a sentimental ass, a Miss Nancy, and all the harsh names he could think of. I was petrified with surprise, but still I was not hurt nor cast down, for I was supported and made strong by the graciousness of my late conduct. When he had again concluded, I regarded him with compassion and said, "I forgive you for this, in spirit and in truth; and if the prayers of one so humble as myself can avail, He also shall forgive you."

One would have supposed that this magnanimity would humble him and fill him with contrition; but to my surprise it had exactly the opposite effect. He raged up and down like a demented person; he pulled out handfuls of his hair, he struck inanimate things with his cane, he kicked the coal-scuttle across the house, cursing it for being always in the way, though in truth it was in its usual place and not in the way at all; and as he hopped about with his hurt foot in his hand, he swore that if he caught me praying for him he would take me by the scruff of the neck and heave me through the third-story window. Then he ordered me to get out of his sight, lest he do me a violence. As I went, I said, "Do with me as seems best, for in this cold world a friendless orphan has none to—"

In the providence of God I was not to finish, for a small job-roller, delivered from my master's hand, whizzed past my head and crashed through a window; and I, observing that he sought another, took my leave.

I went to the Methodist minister and related my victory over my passions, and he said Would God there were more youths like me. At his instance we prayed for Mr. Sprague, my master, supplicating that he might have a change of heart.

I turned that night to advantage with devotional readings, though tormented by fleshly desire to return to my late habit of smoking. This desire grew upon me hour by hour the next day, but nothing could conquer my purpose. I would not yield, further than to buy a plug of tobacco and chew a little of it from time to time. I presently found that by taking a chew whenever the desire to smoke came on, I was at once relieved of my longing and amply strengthened to go on in my good resolve.

Saturday night I set myself to work to prepare for my work in the Sunday school. In the course of my reading I conceived the idea that the account of the deluge could not have been written from sacred inspiration, but must have been interlarded by some person of a light mind during the early ages of the world. The more I reasoned over the matter, and the more I prayed over it for light and help, the more I was convinced; so it seemed imperative that I correct any erroneous impressions concerning this thing which my Sabbath scholars might have gathered from other teachers.

I found them eager to learn, the next morning; so I showed them that it would not be possible for the earth to be submerged with only a forty-days' rain; that a vessel the size of the ark could not contain a pair of each and every sort of animal in the earth; that eight persons, the youngest of them a hundred years old, could not accomplish the enormous task of daily feeding and watering all those beasts and birds; and finally, that it would be better for us to reject the entire chapter as being spurious than to attempt to pick out and preserve the few minor details that had a plausible look. I was greatly encouraged by my success, for not a pupil in the class hesitated to pronounce the deluge a fiction; and not only that, but some of the elder ones proposed to look into the matter of the creation and see if there might not be questionable statements there also—a work in which I engaged to assist, to the best of my powers.

That day the minister brought my Friday's conduct into his sermon so praisefully and so happily that it seemed even higher and nobler than before—insomuch that I found myself surcharged with happiness and with grateful wonderings if it was really I that had done this thing. Everybody was moved—I even to tears. And when at last an aged deacon took me by the hand, pressed it with emotion and led me forward in a solemn hush to the mourner's bench, sobs could be heard all about, mingled with muffled ejaculations of "Bless God!" "Precious soul!" etc.

I joined the church on a six months' probation; and after the benediction, crowds came up to shake hands and welcome me. I made a solemn resolution that from that moment my fellow-beings should profit by my sojourn in the earth, though the time might be short, since one elderly lady said, with tears in her eyes, "You are not long for this world—your place is up there"—and she cast her eyes up to the ceiling with the holiest expression I had ever seen in the face of a mortal.

## Chap. 2

MY MASTER, Mr. Bangs,[2] was a small, wiry, red-headed man of forty, a relative of my father's. He was very honest, sincere and matter-of-fact, and at bottom good-hearted, but excessively impatient and irascible. He was void of sentiment; this was his chief

---

[2] Above this name, Twain wrote "Sprague?" the name used in Chapter 1.

blemish. My father had saved him from financial ruin more than once, and he was grateful for it. He did not love me, he only tolerated me; he could not appreciate me; very few could, in that poor ignorant little village. I was his indentured apprentice—bound to him until I should be twenty-one. My emoluments were the customary "board and clothes" of that era and locality. I boarded and lodged in his house—I and the other apprentice, Hank Flanders, and also Tom Rogers, the only regular journeyman.

It was a frame house, and an unusually large one for that day. Hank and Tom had rooms in the third story, and I had a room on the second floor, immediately over Mr. and Mrs. Bangs's chamber.

Mrs. Bangs was three years older than her husband. She was a very thin, tall, Yankee person, who came west when she was thirty, taught school nine years in our town, and then married Mr. Bangs. They had been man and wife four years, now. She had ringlets, and a long sharp nose, and thin, colorless lips, and you could not tell her breast from her back if she had her head up a stove-pipe hole looking for something in the attic. She had the only set of false teeth that had ever been in the town, and simple country people often came to the house and asked to see them. The upper ones did not fit closely, and so they always dropped down with a little click when she opened her mouth to speak. She was a Calvinist and devotedly pious, but otherwise she was a most disagreeable woman. She had her share of vinegar.

But I wander from my narrative. Sunday night I lay awake, hour after hour, thinking over Mr. Bangs's lost condition, and especially over the sin of his conduct toward me in the late episode. It seemed my plain duty to reason with him and endeavor to reclaim him. I canvassed several different modes of procedure. At last I said to myself, "If I could only get him to read a tract!" He was a man who loathed tracts; therefore, since conversions are usually made in mysterious and unexpected ways, doubtless a tract was to be the appointed means of grace for him. This thought calmed all my misgivings and filled me with confidence. I made a selection from the little store of pamphlets which I had brought home, and then fell contentedly asleep.

I was late to breakfast. Everybody had finished and gone. My food was cold, but I did not mind it; my soul was engaged with higher things. I frequently forgot myself, forgot where I was, forgot everything but the saving work which was before me. I was so moved, at times, by the thought of my generous mission that I could not keep back my tears, and they dropped one by one into my plate, thus making precious a gravy which had not a merit before. I had an impulse to put some of this in a phial, to give to my master some day as a memento of the hour the seed was planted which was to bear the blessed fruit of his redeemed and purified life.

I walked to the office in a dream of ecstasy, and entered it like one in a trance. Mr. Bangs began to storm at me for being late; and as usual, the further he went the more violent he grew. I let him finish, and then said:

"Dear sir and brother, there are things of higher moment than the saving of what you call wasted time. I implore you, for your own good, to cease from worrying over the sordid interests of this life, and give your mind to that which is to come. Read this little tract, thoughtfully, prayerfully, and then come to me and I will give you more."

It was a tract entitled "The Pit Yawns for You." He took it, and tore it into small fragments and danced upon them. He tried to speak, but there was a power upon him and he could not. He turned red, and then white, and then red again, and swallowed and strained like a person that was choking. At last he found his tongue and commanded me to go, and not show my face again that day lest he lose his reason and kill me. Then he made the air thick with profanity, mingled with self-upbraidings and regrets that he had neglected his chances for an education and could only curse in one language.

I went away well satisfied with my work, for I believed that this paroxysm would clear his moral atmosphere and leave him mellowed and meet for the reception of the truth.

On the street I met the Rev. Mr. Soper the Methodist minister, and found him in a state of great distress. He said he was just on his way to the office to talk with me. So I went to his study with him, and learned that the trouble was about my Sunday-school teachings concerning the deluge. He said that the parents of my pupils were well nigh beside themselves with anguish because of the havoc I had wrought with their children's beliefs. Mr. Soper begged me to explain my extraordinary conduct. I did so, and gave him my grounds for rejecting the Biblical account of the deluge. He saw that I was earnest and sincere, and his manner changed at once and all his impatience and vexation passed away.

He argued the matter with me and thoroughly conquered my objections in a few minutes. He did this so completely that I wondered how I could ever have viewed the history of the deluge differently from his way of looking at it. I was enthusiastic in my new belief, now, and eager to undo my mis-teachings. Mr. Soper praised my pliability, and said that there were no fears for me. He said that the only dangerous people were those who embraced an error and would never afterward relax their stubbornness and give it up. He said a body must keep constant watch upon his own foolish thoughts and reasonings, and also upon the innumerable pitfalls of a like kind that wicked men were always placing in the way of the unwary.

"Now here is a book," said he, "which has been the ruin of many a soul. It is the work of an abandoned infidel and is packed with specious reasonings. Take it and read it, observe its manner, and thus learn to know the ways of these wretches so that you may be always armed and fortified against their seductions."

That night I was harried with remorse for my unfortunate work with those poor children, and thought, "What if one of them should die!" I longed for the Sabbath to come, so that I could undo the wrong I had done them. I could get no peace. I was blue and miserable past help.

At last I picked up the infidel book and soon lost myself in its smoothly flowing argument. As I read on, my sufferings diminished gradually, my despondency fled away, a great sense of restfulness and peace descended upon me. It seemed strange that I should gather such a result from such a source; but no matter, I was content, I was grateful.

During several days I avoided the master, for he looked dangerous, and my mind was not now concerned about his rescue, anyway. I continued to read that book, and presently was filled with enthusiasm over the conviction that there was no God, and no salvation. And now it began to seem selfish in me to be keeping to myself the new blessing which had come upon me, and I presently resolved to give others the benefit of it and shed upon them the peace that had been so richly lavished upon me.

One morning, at breakfast, Mr. Bangs said—

"Look here, my lad, I have waited to cool down, and I believe I am calm enough at last. Go and fetch me every tract you have got on the premises."

Mrs. Bangs's eyes and lips flew open and her upper teeth dropped to the half-cock with a click:

"Milton! What is it you are going to do?"

"Burn them!"

"You'll do nothing of the kind in this house, I can tell you. Bolivar, keep your tracts—I will protect you." She turned upon her husband. "Have you anything to say to that, sir?"

Mr. Bangs fidgeted a moment and then said:

"Very well, let him keep them, since you desire it. But he will keep them to himself, you mark that. If he sticks another one under my nose it will make trouble for him."

"No, it won't make trouble for him, either. You will see the day when you will be glad to have a tract stuck under your nose—but it will be too late, then."

"When is that going to be?"

"When you are with Dives—where you surely will be if you go on in your unrighteous course."

"Pardon me; the thing that will go farthest toward making Dives's home tolerable will be the absence of tracts and the sort of people that I usually see aiming for the other place."

"Milton! Do you forget that *I* am aiming for the other place, as you call it?"

"It had not slipped my mind. I figured you heading the procession—and this cherub gracing the tail of it."

"Mr. Bangs, you are not fit to live in decent society. Your example is odious. It is incredible that you should be capable of holding such language in the presence of this lad who is struggling to keep his feet in the new path wherein grace has set them. His noble course is an example which it would be well for you to emulate, not discourage. He shall not stick tracts under your nose, forsooth! We shall see. Bolivar, go and get a tract—and read it aloud, here!"

"Bolivar shall not stir!"

"Indeed he shall! Bolivar, do as I bid you."

"Bolivar will stay where he is. I am not usually master in my own house, but I propose to make a stand this once."

I tried hard to get in a word, whilst the quarrel waxed hotter and hotter, but to no purpose. But at last I succeeded. I said that the tracts were all burned up, and I had done it myself, for I had found out the error of my ways and become an infidel.

I will not try to describe the scene that ensued, further than to say that Mrs. Bangs abused me while her breath lasted, and Tom and Hank and the master laughed as if it were the most amusing occasion in the world. To me it was not amusing, for nothing that concerned religion was ever matter of levity to me, at any period of my life.

## Chap. 3

I PRESENTLY got hold of a copy of Benjamin Franklin's autobiography, and was charmed with it. I saw that here was a man after my own heart. I think it is not immodest in me to say this, for it is the simple truth. I drew a parallel between myself and this great man, and was delighted and heartened to perceive how close the resemblance was. Franklin had the welfare of his fellow beings far more at heart than his own; I could sincerely say that in this I was his counterpart. Franklin had an unquenchable thirst for knowledge; it was the same with myself. Franklin had grand progressive ideas, and plans of reform, looking to the advancement of the whole human race; the same was my own case. Franklin was imbued with a profound and reverent religious spirit; in this I was again his counterpart. Franklin had no sympathy with the small vanities and frivolities of life; to him life was a solemn thing and weighted with responsibilities; this was my own feeling. Franklin was a tireless seeker after truth for its own sake; in this we were alike. Franklin was broad, liberal, catholic; he could reject without a pang an error which had become dear to him, the moment its fallacy was discovered to him; in this respect I was worthy to call him brother. The moving impulse of Franklin's every act was a principle; the man was built up of great and noble principles; in its humble way my nature was the same. The twinship between us was perfect in every detail save one: Franklin had a disposition to accumulate money for his own selfish uses; there was no instinct of this sort in me.

I read Franklin with avidity, and took him for my model. I determined to become everything that he had been. He had educated himself: I would do the same. He had studied by the light of the embers; I proceeded to do that, myself, though there was a plenty of candles. Like Franklin, I began to put in the noon dinner hour at the office, with a piece of dry bread in one hand and an arithmetic in the other. Franklin practiced oratory in private. I followed this example in my chamber, at a late hour, but only once. It brought the whole household to my door in their night clothes, with the idea that I was struggling with burglars. I explained, and Mrs. Bangs said she would have no more oratory on the premises.

I began to get up at three o'clock in the morning, like Franklin, and take a cold plunge bath in a neighboring creek in the dark, after breaking the ice; but on the second morning a thief stole off with my clothes; the journey home, naked, produced an illness which brought me near to death's door. I lay abed three weeks, and during this calm season of reflection I reached the conclusion that Franklin was in error about those baths, so I resolved to discard them.

Meantime my church heard that I had been teaching my Sunday school class the principles of infidelity with a success which had made converts of the whole class; wherefore my name had been stricken from the roll of membership in the church and another person appointed to my place in the Sunday school.

These things did not disturb me, because I had diligently and thoughtfully read the Koran during my sickness and was now a firm and restful believer in the religion of Mahomet.

It seemed a plain religious duty, now, that I should have a harem.

The thing was repugnant to my feelings, but I knew that I ought never to allow a prejudice to stand in the way of a principle; so, with a stern effort I drove away all rebellious reflections and reconciled myself to the burden of a harem. I was resolved that this assemblage of women should be made up of material in character with its religious nature; wherefore I would have no giddy and frivolous younglings in it, but only ladies of mature years and exceptional gravity. I wrote letters to Miss Hatcher, Miss Rankin, Miss Tunstall, Miss Watson, and Miss Dunlap, offering them positions in the harem and explaining the Mohammedan form of religion and begging them to embrace it and be saved. These were all spare ladies, of a rigid uprightness of character, and good extraction, and therefore well calculated to compel the respect and esteem of the public for the new institution. The youngest of them was 38, the eldest 44. I sent the letters around by hand, and then sought an interview with Mrs. Bangs in order to arrange for this considerable addition to her family. I was much surprised at the reception I got. This unreasonable woman would listen to nothing. She poured out upon me every vile epithet she could think of during half an hour; and then the harem arrived on the scene and completed my misfortunes. These elderly persons took up the business of vituperation—not one at a time, but in deafening chorus—and to hear them one would suppose I had been committing some great crime or other. They ended by belaboring me with parasols, umbrellas and slippers until I was black and blue and scarcely able to move hand or foot for pain and lameness.

I did not get out of the house for a week, and then I was assailed everywhere with such a clamor of ridicule, laughter and insult that I was almost sorry I had not died of my injuries.

## Chap. [4]

ONE OF these insulters was a youth named Simpson, who was a year or two younger than I and not very strong. He took advantage of my religious character, in making his venture; he knew me well, and would have been careful not to speculate in this way in the days when I was a worldling. Being applauded by other youths who stood around, he grew bolder and bolder and more and more offensive; but his conduct only awoke my compassion. I could not dignify a person of so mean a spirit by hating him.

Presently, in the midst of his revilings, he threw a handful of black mud and it struck full upon my shirt bosom. I felt a hot impulse for a moment, but banished it and began to scrape off the mud with a chip. There was great laughter at this, which so charmed Simpson, who was not used to being a hero, that he at once gathered up another handful of mud and threw it; but a pebble under his foot rolled, and disordered his aim; the mud went splashing into the face of Jim Frisbie, a big hulking bully who lorded it over all the youth of the town. It was time to beg, now, and Simpson fell to it, most abjectly, though he had meant no offense to Frisbie and loudly iterated and reiterated it. But it was of no use; the big brute brought him a slap on the cheek with the flat of his hand that laid him sprawling. He was going to strike him again, but I said—

"Stop—he is no match for you; let him alone."

Frisbie turned on me with a scowl and said—

"What have you got to say about it?"

"This. The poor cur never meant you any harm. He has neither pluck nor strength and I won't let you impose on him."

"*You* won't! I like that. What do you think you'll do if I impose on him?"

Simpson was sneaking off, now. Frisbie sprang after him but I put out my foot and tripped him up. He had always seemed to avoid trouble with me, but he could not decently avoid it now. So I gave him a sound good thrashing, which so injured his reputation that he never amounted to much as a bully afterward.

I had very active times for a day or two, now. The ladies who had scorned my seraglio had a number of brothers of various ages and sizes, and they gave me no rest. I could not seem to turn a corner without finding one or two of these people. Then there was a fight. Sometimes I got the worst of it, sometimes I got the best of it; but on the whole I averaged pretty well, and was satisfied. Hank Flanders helped me with several of these fights, just for love of the excitement. To me, however, it was distasteful to have to go around with a purple face gridironed with court-plaster, and therefore I was glad when the last brother had been served and peace ensued.

About this time we had a great temperance revival in the village. Everybody got interested in the matter. A clerical looking man in spectacles came along and lectured in a church, and the whole town was there, both the friends and the foes of the movement. I was entirely carried away with this lecturer's arguments, and threw myself heart and soul into the new cause. The second night this man handled the liquor dealers without gloves, calling them by name and applying all sorts of harsh epithets to them. The town was all alive the next day, but little business was done, and all the talk was about the new excitement. The liquor men warned the lecturer not to attempt to speak again, and the reformers warned the said dealers to carry themselves circumspectly or expect trouble.

So there was a fine time the third night. The lecturer began to call names, and then the spoiled eggs began to fly. Within five minutes the lecturer was a sight to behold; he was reeking with the results of the bombardment and the odor was nearly insupportable. Then a dead cat came sailing through the air and hit him full in the face and knocked him down. There was a wonderful scramble, now; the men roared and the women shrieked; the masses surged, this way and that, some trying to get at the lecturer and some trying to reach the doors. In the midst of it all, the lights went out. The lecturer was snatched out at the back door and hurried away by his friends, else it might have gone hard with him.

Day after day the turmoil kept up, but it presently became apparent that the reformers were winning the fight. Now they received great help from an unexpected quarter. Lawson, the principal liquor dealer, got up one night at a temperance meeting and said he had tried to hold out against this reform, but day by day his conscience tortured him more and more; he would struggle no more; it was a hard matter to throw away his business because he had a new stock of twenty barrels of whisky and could ill afford to empty it into the street; in fact the act might bring his family to want; but no matter, he would never allow one drop of that whisky to defile a fellow-being's lips; his whole heart was in this reform, now, and that whisky should be poured into the gutter. He begged that his fellow-reformers would march in a body to his place and stave in the heads of his barrels themselves.

This speech was received with tremendous applause. This man became a glittering hero, an idol, in an instant. Everybody wanted to embrace him. Then there was a movement to form procession and march forth to the destruction of the whisky; but an enthusiast jumped up and shouted:

"Wait! Shall this generous hero make this great sacrifice to a noble cause unassisted? Never! I contribute twenty-five dollars toward reimbursing him! Who joins me!" [3]

"I! and I! and I!" from all over the house. So within ten minutes that hero had pocketed about double the value of his whisky. Then away went the procession with a drum and fife and torches and knocked in the heads of the barrels and emptied the contents into the gutter, amid vast shoutings and rejoicings; and it was as much as two months afterward, when the temperance frenzy was dead again, before those reformers found out that they had paid that rascal about two hundred and twenty-five dollars for ten barrels of water! He had seen what things were coming to, and had put his whisky in safe hiding and replaced it with the cheaper fluid. He made temperance speeches and was a great pet, until the last dealer was broken up and the public interest drifting into other channels, and then he got out his hidden whisky and went into business once more, and very prosperously, too.

During the temperance epidemic several societies were formed, in aid of the good cause. One of these I joined—the Paladins of Purity. It was composed of men and women; also the advanced youth of both sexes. It had a great array of officers, and these were all aggrandized with the most imposing titles—you give an American a hand in creating a title which he may bear himself some day, and you may let him alone to make that title pompous [4] enough. One of our head chiefs was a shoemaker, and another a milliner;

---

[3] Following MS p. 61 Twain inserted a page on which he wrote, "Oughtn't Bolivar to make this gaudy proposition, and get into trouble about it afterward?"

[4] "Gaudy" was written interlinearly as an alternative.

but if you heard these people addressed officially in the dark you would think you had stumbled among a lot of stray kings or such. My zeal gave me prominence at once in the society and I was elected Most Puissant, Mighty and Illustrious Warder of the Inner Door. It was a position of great dignity and responsibility. I stood by the door of entrance, within, armed with a very tall and picturesque battle-axe, of painted wood and of ancient pattern, and it was my duty to split any person who intruded without the pass-words. I was clothed like a conflagration. I have never enjoyed any dress so much as I enjoyed that "regalia." Nothing has ever made so pleasant a sound in my ears as that title which I bore then. There was a charm about the pomp, the ceremony, and the solemn mystery of those nights which satisfied the ancient cravings in my soul for the romantic. I seemed to live among princes and paladins indeed, and to hear the speech and feel the spirit of the old martial age. I loved to stand at my post, with my trusty battle-axe, and answer to the summons of the faithful. This was the routine:

First a challenge outside:

*Paladin*—Most Faithful, Dauntless and Renowned Seneschal of the Castle-keep, hail, all hail!

*Seneschal*—What ho! who cometh there!

*Paladin*—A paladin of ancient lineage and high degree.

*Seneschal*—Advance, most noble, potent and thrice-illustrious prince, and give the countersign.

*Paladin*—Death to the tyrant Alcohol!

*Seneschal*—Enter, battle-scarred and peerless champion and salute the Inner Door.

Three knocks upon the door; three from me in answer. Then one sharp, quick knock; two of the same sort from me in reply.

*Myself*—By what sign may I know thy worthiness, exalted guest?

*Paladin*—By that dread secret word which none may speak aloud and live.

*Myself*—Approach the wicket, be wary, and deliver it into mine ear.

This wicket was a square hole in the middle of the door, which closed with a sliding panel. So I would lift this panel and place my ear there.

*Paladin*—(in a solemn whisper)—DOOM!

*Myself*—'Tis well. Enter illustrious one of princely blood, clothed in the raiment of thy degree and in the intolerable splendor of thy fame and worth, and take thy place among thy peers.

Then, arrayed in the spectacular regalia of our order, would enter Molly Sims the tavern chambermaid, or Sam Jenkins the butcher's apprentice, or some other villager of high or low estate, and take her or his place among her or his peers, adorned with the intolerable splendor of her or his fame and worth.

The "Imperial Hall of Audience" being at length full, the assemblage would be called to order with a sounding formula, a series of fantastic signs and grips would be exchanged, and then we were ready for business. The Most Noble Grand Secretary, assisted by the Most Noble Grand Deputy Scribe, would read the minutes of the last meeting, and then would our stately work proceed in due order to the end. These toy grandeurs had an indescribable charm for me.

For a time my office and its fine title were sufficient for my pride, and I wanted nothing more in this world; but presently my ambition began to grow. I longed to be Lord High Constable of the Lodge. It seemed a dizzy height to strive for, but nothing could keep my hungry ambition down, now, and I strove for it with might and main. I triumphed. But in a little while I lifted my eyes still higher —I would be Hereditary Lord Grand Marshal; ("hereditary" meant nothing with us—all we required was that a title should have bulk). I won again. When I looked back to my humble beginnings, and then contemplated my present glittering exaltation I felt that I was entirely satisfied at last.

But was I?—No. I soon found that out. I looked higher still. I would be the very head of the Lodge. I would be Doge! and hear the command, when I entered the Imperial Hall of Audience, "Way for the high and mighty, the illustrious prince, the most glorious and beneficent Grand Duke—whom God preserve!"

To be Grand Duke, and head the public processions, by virtue of my office—this was an ambition worthy a soul like mine. I set myself to thinking. The conclusion I arrived at was that I must do a shining work of some sort that would attract to me the attention and the talk of the whole town. I turned over many and many a suggestion of my mind, but none seemed to promise a big enough sensation. But at last the right thing struck me like lightning—I would reform old Si Higgins the town drunkard! Si's case had long been given up. He was considered to be clear beyond redemption. He was a monument of rags and dirt; he was the profanest man in town; he had bleary eyes, and a nose like a mildewed cauliflower; he slept with the hogs in an abandoned tan-yard.

I went to him and made a contract. I agreed to support him six months in plenty and comfort if he would reform. We had a small wooden box of a house down in the corner of our yard which was not used. I asked Mr. Bangs to let me have it awhile to reform Si Higgins in. Mr. Bangs was practical, as usual, and said go to grass with my idiot projects. That was just such a speech as I wanted from him; I then went to his wife, and as soon as she found that Bangs was opposed, she came over to my flag and told me to take the shanty and do as I pleased with it.

So I furnished the shanty in a cheap way and put Higgins in there. I dressed him in clean, cheap clothes and gave him books to read. I spent all my spare time with him, in order to keep him steadfast to his promises, and often had him in my own room until bedtime. Mrs. Bangs kept his table well supplied and his shanty in neat order. We prospered handsomely, and I felt perfectly sure that I should compass a thorough and lasting reform in this poor vagabond and show the world at last that no human creature is ever too far gone to be saved from ruin.

I was soon the talk of the town, and the pet of the Paladins. Everybody flocked to see Higgins daily and marvel over him. He had to hold receptions, like a governor or a president. The old ladies brought tracts and testaments to him and had elevating talks with him about his soul; the middle-aged matrons brought sweetmeats and dainties of various kinds and made their little children sit on his knees and repeat beautiful moral maxims which they had been crammed with for the occasion; bands of sweet young ladies came daily and clothed Si and his shanty with an odorous lavishness of fresh flowers; and they sang hymns to him and with him, and some of them wrote poems about him and printed them in our paper.

Si was oathless, now, and talked a saintly language that charmed the ears of all who listened. He was the happiest creature in the village except me. I swam in seas of bliss.

My reward came; when my name was put up for Grand Duke I was elected with a burst of acclamation, no candidate venturing to oppose me.

A proud day approached. The Paladins were to turn out in grand procession and march to our house. They were to receive me there and place me in the van with grand ceremonies; Tim [5] was to take his place at my side, and then the procession was to march through the principal streets and go finally to the court room over the market house, where I was to stand up in the judge's place with Tim at my side and tell the touching story of this poor vagabond's reform. At night Tim was to become a Paladin.

I could eat no breakfast that day, I was so excited. I flitted to and fro between my room and Tim's shanty and could not keep still a moment. Tim was all ready in a new suit of clothes, topped with a stove-pipe hat.

About nine o'clock Hank Flanders came to my room and said—

"Say, Bolivar, it's a great day, and you'll need something to help you keep up the strain; here's my contribution to it."

He put something on the bureau and went out. I hardly heard him, for my thoughts were far away at the moment. Hank was always doing innocent, stupid things, with the best intentions, and I never paid any attention to him when my mind was busy with weighty matters.

My eye wandered about the room, presently, and fell upon Hank's "contribution." It was a tall black bottle, labeled "Best Old Rye." I smiled at the absurdity of such a contribution as this, and was about to throw the bottle out of the window when a thought struck me and soon I was absorbed in following the train thus suggested.

My thinking took somewhat this form. What am I doing? Whither am I rushing? Do I know of my own knowledge what I am about, or am I acting merely from hearsay testimony? Ah, I fear my

[5] From this point on, Si Higgins becomes Tim Higgins.

feelings have been running away with my brains. Here, all this time, have I been warring with all my might against whisky. Why? Do I know anything about whisky? Nothing whatever. I have never even tasted it. Is it right to war against a thing which one knows nothing about? It certainly is not. It is unjust. It is wholly wrong. It is inexcusable, and I begin to be ashamed of myself. But it is not too late to right myself. If whisky is pernicious, I will know it of my own knowledge before I weakly proceed further in this frantic crusade.

* * * * * * * * * *

I roused up from the sofa and tried to collect my faculties. Everything was swimming before me confusedly, in a room that was slowly revolving as upon a pivot. A faint sound of martial music came murmuring to my ear, and I remembered the procession. The sound came near and nearer, but instead of being thrilled by it, I was drowsily indifferent to it. I could not account for this state of feeling. While I was dimly struggling with the problem the sounds reached the house and three rousing cheers were delivered before the doors.

This brought me to myself after a fashion, and I got on my legs to go to my great post and begin my grand work. I found I was very dizzy. I fell over a chair, but gathered myself up and started down stairs assisting myself by the balusters. I was vaguely conscious of a footstep behind me, but not interested in it.

I reached and opened the front door and stood in it leaning against the door-post, dreamily admiring the long line of gaudy male and female costumes and the fluttering banners. A committee approached and delivered a fine little set speech to me, and then I found my tongue, and said, thickly:

"Th (ic!) Thanks—you're we (ic!) welcome, lays and gents!"

Then a reeling figure plunged past me out of the door, its right hand snatching my coat as it went, and the next moment I and the figure sprawled into the arms of the committee. The figure recovered its perpendicular, flourished a black bottle in its left hand and shouted:

"Hoo (uc!)—hooray f'r Plaladdilins of Poo (huc!) poohoority! Moo (huc!) move on wiz procesh! We're wi' you, by dam sight!"

This figure was Tim Higgins—with the new plug hat jammed down on his nose and his whole person in a most fantastic and disreputable condition.

I tried in a dull, groping way to travel to my place in the van, and the shouting and blasphemous Higgins came roaring in my wake. But the Paladins took me up gently, bore me to my room, put me to bed, and began a lecture over me, but I was sound asleep before it was much more than begun; so they left me.

The Paladins broke ranks, discharged the band, gave Higgins a pains-taking and detailed kicking, and retired to their homes by way of back streets and alleys wherever these were available. A new Grand Duke was elected that night, and I was expelled from the order. Mr. Bangs threw all of Higgins's furniture, flowers, tracts and other rubbish into the street and the reformed vagabond retired to his ancient quarters in the tan-yard, never to shine in society or breathe a sober breath or utter a clean word any more forever.

So much for Hank Flanders's "contribution."

## Chap. [5]

HANK WAS a kindly and simple good youth of nineteen, with a prodigious frame, and legs like a derrick. He lacked stability of character; therefore he was given to taking up with new things and new fancies, all the time, and deserting the old. This was his only serious fault. It did little or no good to try to make him understand that success in life depends upon steadfast fidelity to one's enterprises. One might as well talk to the wind as to one of these fickle fly-up-the-creeks. Hank was one of the most giddy and thoughtless persons I have ever known—but then one must remember that he was very young. He put a wasp's nest in my chair one night and forgot all about it. I had use for the chair, presently, but only for a little while, as it turned out—it seemed as if I had sat down in the fire.

Persons who did not know him well, accused him of being a practical joker, but this was an error. I studied him, secretly and thoroughly, and became entirely convinced that there was nothing of the practical joker in him. I am never mistaken in my estimate of a character. I will not judge of a character upon insufficient evidence; but, let me have all the evidence that is needful, let me study it at my leisure and by my own methods, and my verdict upon that character shall defy all assaults.

Hank was sorry that I was stung; he was always sorry when his thoughtlessness inflicted pain or got people into trouble. No practical joker has this trait; indeed the joker enjoys the pain his witless performances inflict.

Hank was one of the kindest hearted persons I have ever met. His charity for dumb brutes was so large and generous that it compelled my admiration and made me often wish I could be like him in that matter. Indeed I tried to emulate him, but it was up-hill work, for in truth I could not abide the companionship of dumb pets. Knowing how I felt, Hank did everything his simple mind could suggest to help me; and with a diligence, in fact, that sometimes made his assistance irksome, though I would not confess that to him, of course. He used to populate my room with starveling one-eyed cats and damaged animals of various kinds; and although I tried hard to love and fondle them, they were a sore offense to my eyes, and their untidy ways and nightly wailings a source of profound discomfort. They were unpopular with Mrs. Bangs, too, and kept me in hot water with her.

One cold night after I had gone to bed, Hank came in, in his night clothes, and woke me up. He had a long-legged, mangy looking, half-grown yellow dog in his arms, and asked me if I would take the creature to bed with me. It seemed a loathsome suggestion, and I could not keep from demurring a little; but the next instant I would have given anything to recal the words; for a grieved look came into Hank's face that smote me to the heart, as, turning away, he said, gently—

"I am sorry I proposed it, and will not do so any more; but I found it so impossible to get the poor sick thing warm in my bed, that I thought that rather than see it suffer so I would risk—"

"Give it here!" I cried; "and try to forgive my heartlessness, Hank. Being roused out of sleep, I really did not know what I was saying."

Hank put the dog in the bed and went away forgiving me freely.

I spent a most restless and in every way uncomfortable night. It was exceedingly distasteful to have the dog's body next to mine, yet would he be satisfied with nothing else, but snuggled close in my arms and rooted under my chin with his clammy nose. If I dozed a moment, he chose that moment to stir and yawn and stretch himself, and this woke me again. I never knew a dog to stretch himself so much; but the bed was warm, and he did it from excess of comfort, doubtless. One great trouble was, that as often as he did it he dug into my legs with his sharp claws and caused me great pain. Most flesh-eating brutes have bad breaths, and this one's was peculiarly disagreeable. If I fell partly asleep, he was sure to spread his mouth and yawn and gape in my face, and then I was like to suffocate, and woke up gasping. At last I turned my back to him, thinking to mend matters, but such was not the result. He slept awhile, snoring softly, then woke up and began to stretch, bracing all four of his feet against my back and pushing with such vigor as to threaten to shove me out of bed. Occasionally he woke me up with a sort of whining or half barking, for he had evidently been dreaming and was frightened. At other times I came dimly up out of a drowse, and found him gnawing at my hair behind, or burrowing his nose into it for pastime. Twenty times he waked me with his frantic struggles to capture fleas. Finally, very late at night, I awoke and found him chewing my night-shirt, just as a calf might do. I struck a light and rummaged around till I found an old sock and gave him that, and went to sleep again; but soon he heard something outside and delivered a fierce bark in my ear that nearly froze me with fright. I found, then, that he had discarded the sock and been chewing my shirt again.

My legs were scratched to pieces, my hair was gnawed and beslavered, my shirt was in a curious state, and I was well nigh worn out with harassment and loss of sleep. So I got up, lit my candle and sat down on the sofa, disheartened, with my overcoat on and a dressing-gown wrapped around my legs. The pup was bright-eyed and wide awake, now, and seemed thoroughly refreshed by the activities which I have described. He had burrowed into the pillow and was taking out feathers by the mouthful, which he mouthed and snapped at and snorted into the air when they obstructed his nostrils, and then jumped at them as they fell, and pawed them on the sheet after he had captured them. I was too worn and weary to interfere, and presently dropped asleep where I sat. Naturally I overslept myself; and when Mrs. Bangs came up to see what the matter was, the dog was still hard at his performance and the room was snowed over with feathers from one end to the other. Mrs. Bangs threw the dog out of the window, and then woke me up, and abused me soundly and warned me not to make a foundling hospital of her house again.

When Hank heard what I had gone through, and the climax of it all, he was very sorry, and insisted on going and telling Mrs. Bangs that he and he alone was to blame for the whole matter; but I would not let him; his impulse had been good and noble, and he was not to blame that it had miscarried. He could not foresee how much discomfort the dog would give me, neither could he foreknow that Mrs. Bangs would be so greatly and unnecessarily disturbed about the matter.

## Chap. [6]

I MET with one or two trifling misfortunes, about this time which caused me deep mortification.[6] It so happened that I was engaged, once more; I had been engaged several times before, but without result. One night, in an absent frame of mind, I called on my intended, and knocked at the door. After some delay her father

---

[6] At the top of MS p. 104, Twain jotted the following notes:
Funeral axident.
Parable.
Purchase Han. Journal
Join Fire Co.
cats on roof
These notes were written in the same ink as the text.

opened the door, and stood there, in his long night-shirt, with a candle in his hand, staring at me. Then he invited me into the parlor. I sat down, and he did so also. There was silence and a pause. He was an austere person, and I felt considerable embarrassment, for I was expecting his daughter, not himself, to receive me. In fact I was not popular with him. Presently he excused himself and left the room. When he returned, he was enveloped from head to heel in a green blanket, and was a most fantastic spectacle.

He sat down and began a conversation about politics; then he drifted into religion; then into matters of education; next into ancient history, and so on. It was horribly cold. I bore this ordeal an hour, execrating the tedious old creature in my heart all the while, and wondering if he seriously imagined that I had come to call on *him*. At last, when I was nearly frozen, I gave the daughter up and rose to go. He looked greatly surprised, and said—

"My dear young friend, why do you go so early? Won't you stop to breakfast?"

I was too outraged to reply, and so took my leave. When the door closed behind me I was astounded to observe that the day was breaking. I was cordially ashamed of myself, and blushed crimson to think of that malicious old man telling this adventure on me. And then the girl. She was a giddy thing, and it fretted me to imagine how much enjoyment she would get out of my blunder.

During the forenoon she sent me a note filled with good-natured chaff that burned like caustic, and closed her remarks with ever so many regrets that she had "overslept herself" and missed my visit.[7] Then there was a postscript in which she intimated that my coming at such an hour had been matter of surprise, but she would endeavor to accommodate herself to my peculiarities, and not be found napping again when I called.

I sent a cold reply, and clinched it with the remark that when I called again she would be more "surprised" than ever—as much so, indeed, as if I "descended out of the clouds."

That was an unfortunate remark, as events finally proved.

I sent off my missive and then gave myself up to an hour's

---

[7] At the top of MS p. 108, Twain wrote, "J. H. Iscariott."

injured pouting. By and by I read her note again, turned the sheet and found a second postscript—to this effect:

"The great Alexander Campbell will be here Sunday and preach his celebrated sermon about the false disciple. I thought maybe you would go with me."

All the giddiness of the girl's nature shone out in that apparently harmless sentence. I resolved that from that moment I would never hold communication with her again. I wanted nothing more to do with one who could find pleasure in dragging old sore remembrances out of the past to shame a friend with. However, the reader cannot understand how that postscript cut me unless I go back and explain.

When I was seventeen years old and miserably ignorant, the great preacher, Alexander Campbell, came to our town and preached the sermon referred to. Nothing was talked of for days afterward but this wonderful sermon. It must be printed; so we set it up in pamphlet form and sent him the proofs. He was a very grim, frozen, unapproachable man, and very particular about every little thing, though I did not know this at the time.

By and by, the great man walked slowly in, with a countenance as black as a thunder cloud. He approached Hank Flanders and held the proofs before him; (it was Saturday and everybody [except] Hank and me were taking holiday.) Said he:

"Who set this up?"

Hank indicated me. Mr. Campbell held a page up and pointed with his finger at a particular place on it, looking me steadily and accusingly in the eyes meanwhile, until I dropped my countenance. Said he:

"I am astounded—and shocked. Read that."

Tremblingly I read:

"This disciple's name was J. Iscariot."

The old man said:

"Why did you make that blasphemous abbreviation?"

I could hardly speak for fright. But I stammered out:

"I didn't know it was any harm, sir. I left out the word 'name,' and I abbreviated Judas to get it in without overrunning. We always do that, sir."

The preacher gazed upon me some time without a word. Then he said:

"I can hardly restrain my desire to punish you, young sir. Now remember this, while you live—always put Scripture names in full—put them always in full. Do you hear?"

Then he strode out and I was unspeakably glad to see him go. I was in a state of wonderment; all that fuss about such a little thing. I had only abbreviated the name twice.

# *Working Notes for*
# "Autobiography of a Damned Fool"

[The following notes were written in pencil at the bottom of the last page of the manuscript, p. 114.]

Diary

---

Old darkey and darkey talk
Mrs. Holliday proverbs and damaged Scripture

[The following notes were written on the same paper (Crystal Lake Mills) and in the same purple ink as the text on half-sheets numbered 2–9.]

"I yield your indentures."
"I will never leave you."

---

Gives his inheritance to a pompous benevolent concern.

---

Borrows of his uncle Talmud.
*Reads Franklin.* Tal
Tries studying arithmetic while eating dry bread and water while other hands gone to noon meal.—a la Franklin.
Always bent on "improving his mind." "D—n you, you haven't got any."
Sprague his cousin—been helped by his father.
Studies by light of a chunk, tho' got plenty candles.
Gets up before daylight to study—twice is enough.

---

Get in all the Belfords.

---

Miss Newcomb[8] is Bangs' wife and henpecks him, but doesn't get much the advantage. Spit curls.

Revivals.
*Cadets*
4th July.
One-legged Higgins.
Trying to reform Henry Beebe

Every reform includes a sacrifice for himself.

---

Argues with whisky sellers and slave-owners and dealers on immorality of their trades and they take away their printing and advertising.

Frees his only slave—which makes the slave friendless at once and hated of all. Poor slave pleads not to be freed.

---

Thinks it his duty to marry a wench. This is carrying abolitionism too far. Is notified to draw the line or will be tarred.

---

Makes a convert or so to anti-slavery and then becomes pro-slavery himself again.

---

Hell and brimstone

---

Tries law—goes over to the enemy in his first case and loses suit he should have won.

Tries hermit life.

---

Always borrowing of uncle.

---

Turns other cheek to boy to strike, then whales a big fellow for abusing the boy.

---

Always had an intensely practical mind, with just enough sentiment to keep from being hard.

---

I have not spoken "rather harshly" of you around. Who says so, lies! No—I have spoken G D harshly of you. Every vile name I could think of to describe a thief, beggar, sneak, traitor, liar, and coward, I have applied to you in a feeble and bootless effort to make the hearer comprehend what a loathsome thing you are! But language could not do it. I stand uncovered and look up to you, and as I contemplate your

[8] Mary Ann Newcomb, Twain's schoolteacher in Hannibal and a close friend of the Clemens family.

majestic proportions I realize that you are the monumentalest ass of the world!

Write a letter in anger, fill it with raging profanity. Have a friend plead for pity upon this victim. Then with generous zeal and impetuosity erase and interline in ink of a different color until all the profanity is turned into sweet and kindly phrases. Have letter as at first —repeat with alterations—all in facsimile.

Have Mrs. B.'s sister paying court, assisted by Mrs. B. and he not perceiving it.

On the contrary trying to help on somebody else's suit.

Minister's salary unpaid. Donation party in which every trivial gift is charged against the salary. Bolivar rips out against it and raises a fine stink.

Listens to the printer-tramp and is charmed. Goes on a month's expedition in summer with him, delivering temperance lectures and sermons and spreeing on the proceeds.

"BURNING SHAME."

---

Let the practical joker get off in S S a rigmarole somewhat like the Oxford student's religious treatise.
(Lecture)

---

[The following notes were written on an unnumbered half-sheet of Crystal Lake Mills paper in the same purple ink as the text and other notes.]

Present Bible
Indentured prentice
Reform Jimmy Finn (secretly)
Go after the cats.
Print and pass around and stick up godly mottoes.
Hand tracts in at a low den and get into trouble.
After each adventure deep despondency
—blues for 2 to 4 hours
—number increases.
*Suicide.*
Helen H.
Cold bath every morning.
—break ice.
Long walk in place of bath.
Elaborate gymnastic apparatus in place of walk.

# II

# *Affeland (Snivelization)*

(1892)

EDITOR'S NOTE: Despite the abandonment of the "Autobiography of a Damned Fool" manuscript and the temporary shelving of the idea, Twain remained fascinated by the literary possibilities inherent in a character similar to his brother Orion. The next step in the development of his idea was a play which he sketched out in collaboration with Howells and then left for Howells to complete. This plan developed during Howells' visit to Hartford, 6–7 March 1878, just prior to Clemens' departure for Europe. By 21 January 1879, the play idea had been abandoned, and Twain was regretting the fact, for on that date he wrote Howells:

> I have always been sorry we threw up that play embodying Orion which you began. It was a mistake to do that. Do keep that MS & tackle it again. It will work out all right, you will see. I don't believe that that character exists in literature in so well developed a condition as it exists in Orion's person. Now won't you put Orion in a *story*? Then he will go handsomely into a play afterwards. How deliciously you could paint him —it would make fascinating reading,—the sort that makes a reader laugh & cry at the same time, for Orion is as good & ridiculous a soul as ever was.[1]

The notion of writing a story which later could be dramatized may have struck Twain as something within his own capabilities, for, two

---

[1] *MTHL,* I, 246.

days after the letter to Howells, he jotted in his notebook a memorandum of three notable adventures in Orion's career, one of which he had already used in the "Autobiography," either as further material for his own imaginative flights or as further ammunition to be supplied to Howells:

> Orion's 3 famous adventures—
> 1. Getting into bed between 2 old maids when he was 21.
> 2. Calling on a young lady at 3. AM and being received by her father in long night shirt entertained an hour in a freezing parlor by the old man, then invited to stop to breakfast. 3. Taking bath in Hartford boarding house without locking door.[2]

A week or so later he was apparently still fondling his literary treasure: This time he jotted in his notebook the cryptic comment "The Burning Shame," a reference to a projected escapade for his "Damned Fool" according to the notes appended to the "Autobiography of a Damned Fool." [3]

If he had had any notions of doing the story himself, his review of the materials convinced him of his inability to do justice to them. On 9 February he wrote to Howells from Munich, "You *must* put him in a book or a play right away. You are the only man capable of doing it. You might die at any moment, & your very greatest work would be lost to the world. *I* could write Orion's simple biography, & make it effective, too, by merely stating the bald facts—& this I will do if he dies before I do; but *you* must put him into romance. This was the understanding you & I had the day I sailed." [4] He continued the letter with a long summary of Orion's career which in its exaggerations more nearly resembles the humorous fictions of the "Autobiography of a Damned Fool" than it does the pathetic realities of Orion's life. With his letter, he forwarded one of Orion's letters and a partial draft of an unsent response.

Until the fall of 1879 he was engrossed in the struggle to produce *A Tramp Abroad,* but, after his return to the Quarry Farm study at Elmira and after the solution of his major difficulties with his travel book, he turned his attention once again to Orion as literary material. By this time he had lost sight of the story idea and now thought of Orion primarily as the central character of a play. On 15 September he wrote to Howells proposing collaboration in a play and commenting:

---

[2] Typescript Notebook 13, p. 50 (entry for 23 January 1879), MTP.
[3] Typescript Notebook 13, p. 54 (following entry for 30 January 1879), MTP.
[4] *MTHL,* I, 253.

> Orion is a field which grows richer & richer the more he matures it with each new top-dressing of religion or other guano. . . . I imagine I see Orion on the stage, always gentle, always melancholy, always changing his politics & religion, & trying to reform the world, always inventing something, & losing a limb by a new kind of explosion at the end of each of the four acts. Poor old chap, he is good material. I can imagine his wife or his sweetheart reluctantly adopting each of his new religions in turn, just in time to see him waltz into the next one & leave her isolated once more.—(*Mem.* Orion's wife *has* followed him into outer darkness, after 30 years' rabid membership in the Presbyterian church.) [5]

As far as the surviving correspondence reveals, Howells had remained silent for some time in the face of Twain's enthusiasm. The collaboration proposal, a return to the original scheme, at last moved him to phrase as tactfully as he could—and Howells could be most tactful when the occasion demanded—a compunction he had been feeling strongly for the last eight months. On 17 September he replied to Twain's proposal:

> More than once I've taken out the skeleton of that comedy of ours, and viewed it with tears. You know I hate to say or do anything definitive; but I really have a compunction or two about helping to put your brother into drama. You can say that he is your brother, to do what you like with him; but the alien hand might inflict an incurable hurt to his tender heart. That's the way I have felt since your enclosure of his letter to me. I might think differently,—and probably should, as soon as the chance of cooperating with you was gone. I would prefer to talk with you about the matter.[6]

The surviving evidence does not indicate whether or not the talk took place. If it did, Howells failed to convince Twain of the impropriety involved, for Twain continued to dispatch bulletins concerning Orion's activities.[7] Howells was saved from the necessity of a more definite refusal by Orion himself, who, with Twain's enthusiastic blessings, had begun his own autobiography in March.[8] By June 9, Twain had received at least the first hundred pages of Orion's manuscript, and in a letter to Howells of that date he proceeded to crowd Howells into another close place. After describing briefly his original advice to Orion on how to succeed with the project, Twain wrote: "I think the result is killingly entertaining; in parts absolutely

---

[5] *Ibid.*, I, 269.

[6] *Ibid.*, I, 270.

[7] See SLC to Howells, 9 October 1879, and 1 April 1880 (*MTHL*, I, 273–275 and 296–297).

[8] Orion Clemens to SLC, 3 and 26 March 1880, originals in MTP.

delicious. I'm going to mail you 100 pages or so of the MS. Read it; keep his secret; & tell me, if, after surplusage has been weeded out, & I ring into the MS here & there a characteristic letter of his, you'll buy the stuff for the Atlantic at the ordinary rates for anonymous matter from unknown writers." [9] Once again Howells' tact was put to trial. On 14 June he replied:

> I have read the autobiography with close and painful interest. It wrung my heart, and I felt haggard after I had finished it. There is no doubt about its interest to *me;* but I got to questioning whether this interest was not mostly from my knowledge of you and your brother—whether the reader would not need some sort of "inside track" for its appreciation. The best touches in it are those which make us acquainted with *you;* and they will be valuable material hereafter. But the writer's soul is laid *too* bare: it is shocking. I can't risk the paper in the Atlantic; and if you print it anywhere, I hope you wont let your love of the naked truth prevent you from striking out some of the most intimate pages. Don't let any one else even see those passages about the autopsy. The light on your father's character is most pathetic.[10]

Until early in 1883, Orion continued to send Twain the manuscript of his autobiography and portions of other literary projects. But Twain found his brother's literature less and less "killingly entertaining," and finally, on 22 February 1883, he blew up and wrote a blistering letter to Orion: "Let this thing stop here; for if your time is not valuable, mine is; and I cannot waste it in combating your projects, which are *always* wild, and not worth combating. Submit no more projects to me, and no more MS. I have not an iota of faith in either." [11] With the letter he enclosed an oath to be signed and returned, an oath to refrain from literary and lecture projects during the remainder of 1883 and all of 1884. Orion signed the oath and returned it with an abjectly apologetic letter.

Whether it was because of the exasperations provoked by Orion's endeavors or the dampening effects of Howells' compunctions, Twain's enthusiasm remained cooled during most of the next decade. It revived early in 1891, and he jotted in his notebook an idea for a character in a

---

[9] *MTHL,* I, 313. Although Orion eventually wrote well over a thousand pages of his autobiography, only seven survive in MTP: two alternative openings for chapter 1 (5 pages), one page numbered 341, and one numbered 1027½.

[10] *Ibid.,* I, 315. The autopsy reference is probably to the post-mortem examination of Twain's father (see *SCH,* pp. 116–117).

[11] SLC to Orion, 22 February 1883, original in MTP.

story: "One called popularly the Changeling or the Weather Vane, because like Orion he is always trying new things, religions, politics, etc. and sticks to nothing." [12] A year or so later, probably at the Villa Viviani, Florence, in 1892, he was working this character into an elaborate satire on civilization to be called "Affeland (Snivelization)." Only a sheaf of notes, including a map of Affeland, and twenty-two pages of manuscript (pp. 2–6, 14b–14d, and 70–83) survive, but there is enough to furnish a glimpse of the major idea. Albert, who in his youth displays the characteristics of Orion or rather of the "Damned Fool," discovers in Affeland a tribe of monkeys apparently already sporting the grandiose titles of an aristocracy. The source of the aristocratic structure of the monkey society is not clear from the fragment, but possibly it is the villain, Skidmore, who, according to one note, was to be modeled after Cecil Rhodes. Like Hank Morgan in sixth-century England, or Anatole France's good priest among the penguins, Albert undertakes to bring the democratic civilization of the nineteenth century to the monkeys. Some of the monkeys rebel against the loss of their former happiness, against the encumbrance of clothes, and are suppressed by the military; most resign themselves, saying that some sacrifice is necessary to gain the blessings of civilization. Reproduced below are pages 2–6 of the fragment, all that remains characterizing the hero, Albert.

---

[12] Typescript Notebook 25, p. 40 (following entry for 2 May 1891), MTP.

# FROM *"Affeland (Snivelization)"*

a grave mien and big earnest eyes that seemed to be always searching, seeking, weighing, considering. He had a precocious intellect, and a voracious appetite for books and study. He had no playmates, of course; he had nothing to offer them, they had nothing to offer him.[13]

Much is expected of such a boy, and much was expected of this one—at first. Then it was discovered that he was fatally discursive in his interests and ambitions, and didn't stick to any one thing long at a time. His stock went down. The village gave up its high hopes of him with sorrow and with sighs, and thenceforth its interest in him deteriorated to the uneasy interest which conservative people take in an erratic machine whose performances compel attention by their oddity and inspire alarm by their variety and the suddenness with which the changes of program are made.

When the little boy gave his heart to a thing, he gave the whole of it. The first Sunday school he gave it to was the Methodist, and his zeal and capacity easily and quickly made him its most prized scholar. Then his Methodism presently cooled and he flitted to the Presbyterian camp; next to the Baptist, and so on. He furnished reasons for flitting. He was seeking the right one, he said, the satisfying one, the one that should perfectly content his spirit. Not finding it, he continued to flit.

At nine, he began to study for the ministry. It made great talk in the village; but at the end of two months he was tired of the matter and began to take a fiery interest in something else. At twelve he read the life of Franklin, and at once set about making a Franklin of himself. For a month he lived scantly on bread and vegetables, did his studying

[13] On the reverse of 1st page of MS, Twain wrote the word "Snivelization." Note that in "Hellfire Hotchkiss," Oscar Carpenter is nicknamed "Parson Snivel."

at night by the light of a single candle, rose before dawn, bathed in deadly cold water, practiced gymnastic exercises in his room, took stated walks, framed a set of austere rules of conduct, listened sharply to the sermon, Sundays, and from memory bored the family with it at dinner. In fact he faithfully did all the things that go to the making of a Franklin; then at the end of the month he retired [from] the contest, unhindered by the grateful family, and plunged into some new ambition or other.

He went on diligently flitting and flitting, constantly conferring new surprises upon the village, and becoming more and more a puzzle to it and an anxiety. It was evident that he was seeking truth, and seeking earnestly, but finding it a troublesome business and disappointing. At fifteen he began the study of law, but presently gave it up and decided to study

# III

# *Hellfire Hotchkiss*

(1897)

Editor's Note: Precisely why Twain abandoned the Affeland story must remain a matter of speculation. Certainly the basic idea is a good one, and he devoted a fair amount of energy to a rather detailed plan of characters and events. From the materials remaining in the Mark Twain Papers, it would seem the stage was well set for the production of another literary success. But for some reason the props were suddenly packed and stowed away. All one can do now is to assume that the abandonment of the story was in some way connected with Clemens' increasing concern for the state of his finances and the pending collapse of Charles L. Webster & Company, his publishing firm.

For the ensuing five years the "Damned Fool" remains hidden from sight. Then in 1897 at Weggis, Switzerland, he suddenly reappears again in a story which, as Twain frequently put it, promises to "go." Visible in the fragment is the verve and the skill of Twain at his best. In his notebook entry for 4 August 1897, Twain wrote, "Began ⟨Hellfire⟩ Hotchkiss," and then, after an intervening note about a joke which he had dreamed the previous night, he began a list of characters for the novel:

<Hellfire> Hotchkiss (Rachel)<br>
Rev. Caleb " (Perennial Slush)<br>
Oscar Carpenter (<Thug>)<br>
Her Royal Shyness.<br>
Sally, <Thugs> negro.<br>
Reuben, the Judge's.

After another intervening note, this one about Tillou, the model for the Partingtonian-Malapropian character Ballou in *Roughing It,* the list continues:

> <Bully> Hal Stover (Henry Hyde)
> <Shagbark> Shad " (Ed " )
> The tavern gang—at Pavey's.
> Jim Quarles, Dr. Rayley, Ed Buchanan
> Stimson, Benny
> The boys' friend and loafer
> Bence Blankenship.
> Leona Loretta etc. Hinkley (?) [1]

Pleased with the initial progress on the novel, he commented in a letter to Henry H. Rogers, dated "August the something or other, 1897," "I am writing a novel, and am getting along very well with it." [2] The evidence of paper and ink indicates that, except for revisions and inserts, the entire surviving text was written at Weggis before the Clemenses moved to Vienna in September. After arriving in Vienna, Twain apparently tried to pick up the threads of the story. He revised the manuscript written at Weggis, and between chapters 1 and 2 tried to restore what he thought was a lost portion. But he did not proceed beyond the point reached at Weggis. His failure to proceed and a comment in a letter to Frank Bliss of 4 November 1897, indicate that once again he had lost interest. To Bliss he wrote, "It has been reported that I am writing books—for publication; I am not doing anything of the kind. It would surprise (and gratify) me if I should be able to get another book ready for the press within the next three years." [3] On 16 August 1898, from Kaltenleutgeben, he wrote Howells a letter which reveals the causes of his dissatisfaction. He had concluded that his plan for the book was wrong, and, in comparison with another work, "Hellfire Hotchkiss" did not seem important enough to warrant the expenditure of further effort:

> Last summer I started 16 things wrong—3 books & 13 mag. articles—& could make only 2 little wee things, 1500 words altogether, succeed; —only that out of piles & stacks of diligently-wrought MS., the labor of 6 weeks' unremitting effort. I could make *all* of those things go if I would

---

[1] Typescript Notebook 32b (I), p. 24, MTP (deleted words have been restored in brackets). To a great extent the list is based upon Twain's "master list" of characters, "Villagers of 1840–43." See Introduction for a discussion of this point.

[2] *MTL,* II, 644.

[3] *Ibid.,* II, 650.

> take the trouble to re-begin each one half a dozen times on a new plan. But none of them was important enough except one: the story I (in the wrong form) mapped out in Paris three or four years ago & told you about in New York under seal of confidence . . . the story to be called "*Which* was the Dream?"[4]

But he still could not abandon his character. Defeated at least four times in his attempt to weave a story around a central character such as his "Damned Fool," he shifted his ground slightly and, shortly after abandoning "Hellfire Hotchkiss," planned secondary roles both for the "Damned Fool" and Hellfire in a new story the central character of which was to be a mysterious stranger named Forty-Four whose miraculous powers were to astonish Huck Finn, Tom Sawyer, and all the other inhabitants of St. Petersburg. In this, the "Hannibal" version of *The Mysterious Stranger,* Forty-Four, the forerunner of Satan, rooms with Oliver Hotchkiss, a kindly man but one who is so constantly changing his religious and other convictions that he reminds one of a weathervane. On page 9 of the packet of notes supplemental to the "Hannibal" version appears a notation to the effect that Oliver Hotchkiss has a daughter nicknamed "Hellfire" with whom Forty-Four is to fall in love. Thus the "Damned Fool" merges into the character which eventually became the Father Peter of Eseldorf, and Hellfire Hotchkiss points toward Marget.

---

[4] *MTHL,* II, 675.

# *Hellfire Hotchkiss*[5]

## [Chapter 1]

"BUT JAMES, he is our son, and we must bear with him. If we cannot bear with him, how can we expect others to do it?"

"I have not said I expected it, Sarah. I am very far from expecting it. He is the most trying ass that was ever born."

"James! You forget that he is our son."

"That does not save him from being an ass. It does not even take the sting out of it."

"I do not see how you can be so hard toward your own flesh and blood. Mr. Rucker does not think of him as you do."

"And why should he? Mr. Rucker is an ass himself."

"James—do think what you are saying. Do you think it becoming to speak so of a minister—a person called of God?"

"Who said he was?"

"Who *said* he was? Now you are becoming blasphemous. His office is proof that he was called."

"Very well, then, perhaps he was. But it was an error of judgment."

"James, I might have known you would say some awful thing like that. Some day a judgment will overtake you when you least expect it. And after saying what you have said about Mr. Rucker, perhaps you will feel some natural shame when you learn what he has been saying to me about our Oscar."

---

[5] According to Twain's notation on the envelope containing the MS, an alternate title was "Sugar-Rag Hotchkiss." On the envelope he wrote, "Hellfire Hotchkiss, or Sugar-Rag ditto and (25 to 33) rejected MS that may come good."

"What was it? What did he say?"

"He said there was not another youth of seventeen in the Sunday School that was so bright."

"Bright. What of that? He is bright enough, but what is brightness worth when it is allied to constitutional and indestructible instability of character? Oscar's a fool."

"For pity's sake! And he your own son."

"It's what he is. He is a fool. And *I* can't help his being my son. It is one of those judgments that overtake a person when he is least expecting it."

"James, I wonder how you can say such things. The idea of calling your own son a judgment."

"Oh, call him a benefaction if you like."

"I do call him one, James; and I bless the day that God in his loving thoughtfulness gave him to us."

"That is pure flattery."

"James Carpenter!"

"That is what it is, and you know it. What is there about it to suggest loving thoughtfulness—or any kind of thoughtfulness? It was an inadvertence."

"James, such language is perfectly shocking. It is profanity."

"Profanity is better than flattery. The trouble with you Presbyterians and other church-people is that you exercise no discrimination. Whatever comes, you praise; you call it praise, and you think it praise; yet in the majority of cases it is flattery. Flattery, and undignified; undignified and unworthy. Your singular idea that Oscar was a result of thoughtfulness—"

"James, I won't listen to such talk! If you would go to church yourself, instead of finding fault with people who do, it would be better."

"But I don't find fault with people who do."

"Didn't you just say that they exercise no discrimination, and all that?"

"Certainly, but I did not say that that was an *effect* of going to church. It probably is; and now that you press me, I think it *is;* but I didn't quite say it."

"Well, James, you as good as said it; and now it comes out that at bottom you thought it. It shows how staying away from church makes a person uncharitable in his judgments and opinions."

"Oh, come!"

"But it does."

"I dissent—distinctly."

"Now James, how can you know? In the nineteen years that we have been married, you have been to church only once, and that was nearly nineteen years ago. You have been uncharitable in your judgments ever since—more or less so."

"I do not quite catch your argument. Do you mean that going to church only once made me uncharitable for life?"

"James, you know very well that I meant nothing of the kind. You just said that to provoke me. You know perfectly well that I meant—I meant—now you have got me all confused, and I don't know what I did mean."

"Don't trouble about it, Sarah. It's not like having a new experience, you know. For—"

"That will do, James. I do not wish to hear anything more about it. And as for Oscar—"

"Good—let us have some more Oscar for a change. Is it true that he has resigned from the Cadets of Temperance?"

"Ye-s."

"I thought he would."

"Indeed? And what made you think it?"

"Because he has been a member three months."

"What has that to do with it?"

"It's his limit."

"What do you mean by that, James?"

"Three months is his limit—in most things. When it isn't three weeks or three days or three hours. You must have noticed that. He revolves in threes—it is his make. He is a creature of enthusiasms. Burning enthusiasms. They flare up, and light all the region round. For three months, or weeks, or days. Then they go out and he catches fire in another place. You remember he was the joy of the Methodist Sunday school at 7—for three months. Then he was the joy of the Campbellite Sunday school—for three months. Then of the Baptist—for three months. Then of the Presbyterian—for three months. Then he started over again with the Methodist contingent, and went through the list again; and yet again; and still again; and so on. He has been the hope and joy of each of those sources of spiritual supply nine times in nine years; and from Mr. Rucker's remark I gather that he is now booming the Presbyterian interest once more. As concerns the Cadets of Temperance, I was just thinking that his quarterly period—"

"James, it makes me sick to hear you talk like that. You have never loved your boy. And you never encourage him. You know how sensitive he is to slights and neglect, yet you have always neglected him. You know how quickly he responds to praise, and how necessary praise and commendation and encouragement are to him—indeed they are his very life—yet he gets none of these helps from you. How can you expect him to be steadfast; how can you expect him to keep up his heart in his little affairs and plans when you never show any interest in them and never applaud anything he does?"

"Applaud? What is there to applaud? It is just as you say: praise is his meat and bread—it is his life. And there never was such an unappeasable appetite. So long as you feed him praise, he gorges, gorges, gorges, and is obscenely happy; the moment you stop he is famished—famished and wretched; utterly miserable, despondent, despairing. You ought to know all about it. You have tried to keep him fed-up, all his life, and you know what a job it is. I detest that word—encouragement—where the male sex is concerned. The boy that needs much of it is a girl in disguise. He ought to put on petticoats. Praise has a value—when it is earned. When it isn't earned, the male creature receiving it ought to despise it; and will, when there is a proper degree of manliness in him. Sarah, if it is possible to make anything creditable out of the boy, only a strong hand can do it. Not yours, and not mine. You are all indulgence, I all indifference. The earlier the strong hand takes him in charge, the better. And not here in Dawson's Landing, where he can be always running home for sympathy and pettings, but in some other place—as far off as St. Louis, say. You gasp!"

"Oh, James, James, you can't mean what you say! Oh, I never could bear it; oh, I know I never could."

"Now come, don't cry, Sarah. Be reasonable. *You* don't want the boy ruined. Now do you?"

"But oh, to have him away off there, and I not by if anything should happen."

"Nothing's going to happen. He—"

"James—he might get sick. And if I were not there—"

"But you can go there, if he gets sick. Let us not borrow trouble —there is time enough. Other boys go from home—it is nothing new—and if Oscar doesn't, he will be ruined. Now you know Underwood—a good man, and an old and trusty friend of mine."

"The printer?"

"Yes. I have been corresponding with him. He is willing to take Oscar as an apprentice. Now doesn't that strike you pleasantly?"

"Why—yes. If he *must* go away from home—oh, dear, dear, dear!—why of course I would rather have him with Mr. Underwood than with anyone else. I want to see Oscar succeed in the world; I desire it as much as you can. But surely there are other ways than the one proposed; and ways more soothing to one's pride, too. Why should our son be a common mechanic—a printer? As far back as we can go there have been no mechanics in your family, and none in mine. In Virginia, for more than two centuries they have been as good as anybody about them; they have been slaveholding planters, professional men, politicians—now and then a merchant, but never a mechanic. They have always been gentlemen. And they were that in England before they came over. Isn't it so?"

"I am not denying it. Go on."

"Don't speak in that tired way, James. You always act annoyed when I speak of our ancestors, and once you said 'Damn the ancestors.' I remember it very well. I wonder you could say such a horrid thing about them, knowing, as you do, how brief this life is, and how soon you must be an ancestor yourself."

"God forgive me, I never thought of that."

"I *heard* that, James—heard every word of it; and you said it ironically, too, which is not good taste—no better taste than muttering it was—muttering to yourself like that when your wife is talking to you."

"Well, I'm sorry; go on, I won't do it again. But if the irony was the thing that pinched, that was a quite unnecessary unkindness; I could have said it seriously, and so saved you the hurt."

"Seriously? How do you mean?"

"Oh, sometimes I feel as if I could give anything to give it all up and lie down in the peace and the quiet and be an ancestor, I do get so tired of being posterity. It is when things go wrong and I am low spirited that I feel like that. At such times—peculiarly dark times, times of deep depression, when the heart is bruised and sore and the light of life is veiled in shadows—it has seemed to me that I would rather be a dog's ancestor than a lieutenant governor's posterity."

"For shame! James, it is the same as saying I am a disappointment to you, and that you would be happier without me than with me. Oh, James, how could you say such a thing?"

"I didn't say it."

"What *did* you say?"

"I said that sometimes I would rather be an ancestor than posterity."

"Well, isn't that separating us?"

"No—for I included you."

"That is different. But James you didn't *say* so. It sounded as if you only wanted to be an ancestor by yourself, and of course that hurt me. Did you *always* think of me, James? Did you always include me? Did you wish I was an ancestor as often as you wished you were one?"

"Yes. Oftener. Twice as often."

"How good you are, James—when you *want* to be. But you are not always good; I wish you were. Still, I am satisfied with you, just as you are; I don't want you changed. You don't want me changed, do you, James?"

"No, I don't think of any change that I would want to risk."

"How lovely of you!"

"Don't mention it. Now, as I remember it, your argument had reached the point where—well, I think you had about finished with the ancestry, and—"

"Yes—and was coming to you. You are county judge—the position of highest dignity in the gift of the ballot—and yet you would see your son become a mechanic."

"I would see him become a *man*. He needn't *remain* a mechanic, if you think it would damage his chances for the peerage."

"The peerage! I never said anything about the peerage. He would never get rid of the stain. It would always be remembered that he had been a mechanic."

"To his discredit? Nonsense. Who would remember it as a smirch?"

"Well, I would, for one. And so would the widow Buckner—"

"Grand-daughter of a Hessian corporal, whom she has painted up in a breastpin as an English general. *She* despise mechanics! Why, her ancestors were bought and sold in shoals in Cassel, at the price of a pound of candles apiece. And it was an overcharge."

"Well, there's Miss Rector—"

"Bosh!"

"It isn't bosh! She—"

"Oh, I know all about that old Tabby. She claims to be descended in an illegal and indelicate way from Charles II. That is no distinction; we are all that. Come, she is no aristocracy. Her opinion is of no consequence. That poor scraggy old thing—why, she is the descendant of an interminable line of Presbyterian Scotch fishermen, and is built, from the ground up, out of hereditary holiness and herring-bones."

"James, it is scandalous to talk so. She—"

"Get back on your course, Sarah. We can discuss the Hessian and the osteological remains another time. You were coming to some more reasons why Oscar should not be a printer."

"Yes. It is not a necessity—either moneywise or otherwise. You are comfortably off and need no help from earnings of his. By grace of his grandfather he has a permanent income of four hundred dollars [6] a year, which makes him rich—at least for this town and region."

"Yes; and fortunately for him it is but a life-interest and he can never touch the principal; otherwise I would rather have a hatful of smoke than that property."

---

[6] In the margin opposite this sum, Twain wrote "6" and beneath that, "nigger Sally."

"Well, that is neither here nor there. He has that income; and has six hundred dollars saved from it and laid up."

"Don't let him find it out, Sarah."

"I—I—he already knows it, James. I did not mean to tell him; it escaped me when I wasn't thinking. I'm sorry."

"I am, too. But it is no matter—yet awhile. It is out of his reach until he is of age."

Sarah said nothing, but she was a little troubled. She had lent trifles of money to Oscar from time to time, against the day of his financial independence.[7]

Judge Carpenter mused a while, then said—

"Sarah, I think your objections to my project are not very strong. I believe we must let it stand, unless you can suggest something better. What is your idea about the boy?"

"I think he ought to be trained to one of the professions, James."

"Um-m. Medicine and surgery?"

"Oh, dear no! not surgery. He is too kind-hearted to give pain, and the sight of blood distresses him. A physician has to turn out of his bed at all hours and expose himself to all weathers. I should be afraid of that—for his health, I mean. I should prefer the law. There is opportunity for advancement in that; such a long and grand line of promotions open to one who is diligent and has talent. James, only think of it—he could become Chief Justice of the Supreme Court of the United States!"

"*Could? Would,* you mean."

"Oh, James, do you think he would?"

"Undoubtedly."

"Oh, James, what makes you think so?"

"I don't know."

"You don't *know?*"

"No."

"Then what made you say so?"

---

[7] The three paragraphs which follow are an insertion written on the back of MS p. 25. They were apparently intended to replace two paragraphs of the original text which, however, were not deleted. The original passage reads:

"Well, he is to stay at home—that is settled. My idea has been exploited and found wanting; what is your own, Sarah?"

"I should think he ought to be trained to one of the professions, James."

"I don't know."

"James, I think you are the most provoking man that ever— James, are you trifling with me? But I know you are—I can see it. I don't see how you can act so. *I* think he would be a great lawyer. If you have doubts—"

"Well, Sarah, I have. He has a fair education; good enough for the business—here in a region where lawyers are hardly ever college-bred men; he has a brighter mind than the average, hereabouts—very much brighter than the average, indeed; he is honest, upright, honorable, his impulses are always high, never otherwise—but he would make a poor lawyer. He has no firmness, no steadfastness, he is as changeable as the wind. He will stick at a thing no longer than the novelty of it lasts, and the praises—then he is off again. When his whole heart is in something and all his fires blazing, anybody can squirt a discouraging word on them and put them out; and any wordy, half-clever person can talk him out of his dearest opinion and make him abandon it. This is not the stuff that good lawyers are made of."

"James, you *cannot* be right. It cannot be as bad as you think; you are prejudiced. You never would consent to see any but the most unfavorable side of Oscar. Do you believe he is unfitted for *all* the professions?"

"All but one."

"Which one?"

"The pulpit."

"James, I could hug you for that! It was the secret wish of my heart—my day-dream all these years; but I never dared to speak of it to *you,* of all creatures. Oh, James, do you think, do you really and seriously think that he would make a name for himself in the pulpit—be spoken of, written about?"

"I *know* it."

"Oh, it is *too* good, too lovely! Think of it—our Oscar famous! You really believe he would be famous!"

"No. Notorious."

"Well—what is the difference?"

"There is a good deal."

"Well, what *is* it?"

"Why, fame is a great and noble thing—and permanent. Notoriety is a noise—just a noise, and doesn't last."

"So *that* is what you think our Oscar would reach. Then pray, why do you think him suited for the pulpit?"

"The law is a narrow field, Sarah; in fact it is merely a groove. Or, you may call it a house with only one room in it. But in religion there are a hundred sects. It is a hotel. Oscar could move from room to room, you know."

"James!"

"Yes, he could. He could move every quarter, and take a fresh start. And every time he moved, there would be a grand to-do about it. The newspapers would be full of it. That would make him happy. It is my opinion that he ought to be dedicated to this career of sparkling holiness, usefulness and health-giving theological travel."

Sarah's face flushed and all her frame quivered with anger. Her breath came in gasps; for the moment she could not get her voice. Then she got it, but before she could use it the thin pipe of a boy calling to a mate pierced to her ear through the still and murky air—

"Thug Carpenter's got drownded!"

"Oh, James, our Oscar—drowned!" She sank into a chair, pallid and faint, and muttered, "The judgment—I warned you."

[During revision in Vienna, Twain discarded three pages of manuscript and composed the following material as a conclusion to the chapter. The new material, although it continues the pagination without a break, was apparently to be inserted in the third paragraph above, after the words "get her voice." The remaining material above presumably was to be deleted.]

Her husband noticed the signs, and said to himself, "The worm has turned." He sat patiently, and said no word, intruded no interruption, while she delivered her wounded spirit. Then he conceded that what she had been saying about him was true; that she had said it well; that it could not have been better said by anyone; and he would say again what he had more than once said before: that whenever by chance she wandered into a subject which she was acquainted with, she was the ablest talker in the town.

This handsome compliment took all the soreness out of the wife's heart, and made her a proud and happy woman. If husbands could realize what large returns of profit may be gotten out of a wife by a small word of praise paid over the counter when the market is just right, they would bring matters around the way they wish them much oftener than they usually do. Arguments are unsafe with wives, because they examine them; but they do not examine compliments. One can pass upon a wife a compliment that is three-fourths base metal; she will not even bite it to see if it is good; all she notices is the size of it, not the quality.

The present compliment put Mrs. Carpenter into an impressionable mood, and before she was out of it again she had consented to let her son go to St. Louis.

[Having trouble reorienting himself in the story, Twain concluded this revision with a note to himself:

(Something lost out.)

Think a boy is heard shouting to another one—

"Say, Ed, Thug Carpenter's drownded!"]

## Chapter [2]

"DROWNDED, you say?" This from another boy.

"Well, not just entirely, but he's goin' to be. The ice is breaking up, and he's got caught all by himself on 'tother side of the split, about a half a mile from shore. He's a goner!"

Sarah Carpenter was on her feet in a moment, and fumbling with bonnet and shawl with quaking hands. "Quick, James, there's hope yet!" The Judge was getting into his overcoat with all haste. Outside, the patter of hurrying footsteps was heard, and a confusion of excited voices; through the window one could see the village population pouring out upon the white surface of the vast Mississippi in a ragged long stream, the further end of it, away toward the middle of the river, reduced by distance to a creeping swarm of black ants.

Now arose the ringing sound of flying hoofs, and a trim and fair young girl, bareheaded and riding bareback and astride, went thundering by on a great black horse.

"There goes Hellfire Hotchkiss! Oh, James, he's saved, if anybody can save him!"

"You've said the truth, Sarah. She has saved him before, and she will do it again. Keep up your heart, it will all come right."

By this time the couple had crossed the river road and were starting down the ice-paved slope of the bank. Ahead, on the level white plain, the black horse was speeding past detachment after detachment of plodding citizens; and all along the route hats and handkerchiefs went up in welcome as the young girl swept by, and burst after burst of cheers rose and floated back, fainter and fainter, as the distance grew.

Far out toward the middle of the river the early arrivals were massed together on the border of a wide rift of indeterminable length. They could get no further. In front of them was the water; beyond it, clear to the Illinois shore, a moaning and grinding drift and turmoil of monster ice-cakes, which wandered apart at times, by compulsion of the swirling currents, then crashed thunderously together again, piling one upon another and rising for a moment into rugged hillocks, then falling to ruin and sagging apart once more. It was an impressive spectacle, and the people were awed by the sight and by the brooding spirit of danger and death that was in the air, and they spoke but little, and then in low voices. Most of them said nothing at all, but gazed fixedly out over the drifting plain, searching it for the missing boy. Now and then, through the vague steam that rose from the thawing ice they caught sight of a black speck away out among the recurrent up-bursting hillocks under the lowering sky, and then there would be a stir among the crowd, and eager questions of "Where? which is it? where do you see it?" and answers of "There—more to the right—still more—look where I am pointing—further out—away out—just a black speck—don't you see it now?" But the speck would turn out to be a log or some such thing, and the crowd would fall silent again.

By and by distant cheering was heard, and all turned to listen. The sound grew and grew, approached nearer and nearer, the black horse was sighted, the people fell apart, and down the lane the young girl came flying, with her welcome roaring about her. Evidently she was a favorite. All along, from the beginning of her flight, as soon as she was recognized the cry went up—

"It's Hellfire Hotchkiss—stand back and give her the road!" and then the cheers broke out.

She reined up, now, and spoke—

"Where is he?"

"Nobody knows. Him and the other boys were skating, along about yonder, somewheres, and they heard a rip, and the first they knew their side of the river begun to break up. They made a rush, and got through all right; but he was behind, and by the time he got here the split was too wide for him—for *him,* you understand—so they flew home to tell, and get help, and he broke for up the river to hunt a better place, and—"

The girl did not wait for the rest, but rode off up stream, peering across the chasm as she went, the people following her with their eyes, and commenting.

"She's the only person that had enough presence of mind to come fixed to *do* something in case there was a chance. She's got a life-preserver along." It was Miss Hepworth, the milliner, that said that. Peter Jones, the blacksmith, said—

"It ought to do some good, seeing she took the trouble and had the thoughtfulness to fetch it, but there's never any telling which way Thug Carpenter is going to act. Take him as a rule, he is afraid of his shadow; and then again, after a mighty long spell, he'll up and do a thing which is brave enough for most anybody to be proud of. If he is just his ordinary natural self to-day, the life-preserver ain't going to be any good; he won't dare use it when Hellfire throws it to him."

"That's about the size of it," said Jake Thompson, the baker. "There's considerable difference betwixt them two—Thug and her. Pudd'nhead Wilson says Hellfire Hotchkiss is the only genuwyne male man in this town and Thug Carpenter's the only genuwyne female girl, if you leave out sex and just consider the business facts; and says her pap used to—hey, she's stopped."

"So she has. Maybe she's found him."

"No, only thought she had. She's moving on, again. Pudd'nhead

Wilson says Thug's got the rightest heart and the best disposition of any person in this town, and pretty near the quickest brains, too, but is a most noble derned fool just the same. And *he* says Hellfire's a long sight the prettiest human creature that ever lived, and the trimmest built, too, and as graceful as a fish; and says he'd druther see her eyes snap when she's mad, or water up when she's touched than—'y George, she's stopped again. Say—she's faced around; she's coming this way."

"It's so. Stopped again. She's found him, sure. Seems to be talking across the rift—don't you see? Got her hand up to her mouth for a trumpet. Ain't it so?"

"Oh, yes, there ain't any doubt. She's got off of her horse. Hi!—come along, everybody. Hellfire's found him!"

The crowd set out at a pace which soon brought them to the girl; then they faced about and walked along with her. Oscar was abreast, prisoner on a detached and independent great square of ice, with a couple of hundred yards of water and scattered ice-cakes between him and the people. His case had a bad look. Oscar's parents arrived, now, and when his mother realized the situation she put out her hands toward him and began to wail and sob, and call him by endearing names, and implore him not to leave her, not to take away the light of her life and make it desolate; and then she looked beseechingly into the faces about her, and said, "Oh, will nobody save him? he is all the world to me; oh, I cannot give him up." She caught sight of the young girl, now, and ran to her and said, "Oh, Rachel, dear, dear Rachel, you saved him before, you'll not let him die now, *will* you?"

"No."

"Oh, you precious child! if ever—"

" 'Sh! What is he saying? Listen."

Oscar was shouting something, but the words could not be made out with certainty.

"Wasn't it something about snags?" asked the girl. "Are there snags down yonder?"

"Snags? Yes," said the baker, "there's a whole rack-heap of them. That is what he's talking about, sure. He knows they are there, and he knows they'll wreck him."

"Then it won't do to wait any longer for the rift to get narrower," said Rachel. "He must be helped now or it will be too late."

She threw off her winter wrap, and began to take off her shoes.

"What are you going to do?" said old Uncle Benny Stimson, Indian doctor and tavern keeper.

"Take him the preserver. He isn't much of a swimmer, and couldn't ever make the trip without it."

"You little fool, you'll freeze to death."

"Freeze to death—the idea!"

"Well, you will. You let some of these young fellows do it."

"When I want anybody's help, I'll ask for it, Uncle Benny. I am one of the young fellows myself, I'll let you know."

"Right you are. The pig-headedest little devil for a parson's daughter, I ever saw. But a brick just the same; I'll say that for you, Hellfire Hotchkiss,—every time."

"Thank you, dear. Please lead my horse and carry my things, and go along down yonder and stand by. Thug is pretty well chilled by this time; somebody please lend me a whisky-flask."

Thirty-five were offered. She took one, and put it in her bosom. Uncle Benny said—

"No use in that, he's teetotal—he won't touch it, girly."

"That was last week. He has reformed by this time."

She plunged in and struck out. Somebody said "Let us pray," but no one heard; all were absorbed in watching. The girl made good progress both ways—forward, by her own strength, and down-stream by the force of the current. She made her goal, and got a cheer when she climbed out of the water. Oscar had been in a state of exhausting fright for an hour and more, and he said he was weak and chilled and helpless and unmanned, and would rather die where he was than chance the desperate swim—he knew he couldn't make it.

"Yes you can. I'll help you, Thug, and the presérver will keep you up. Here, take some of this—it will hearten you."

"What is it?"

"Milk."

He took a drain.

"Good milk, too," he said. "It is so comforting, and I was so cold.

I will take some more. How thoughtful it was of you to bring the flask; but you always think of everything."

"Hurry. Get off your overcoat, Thug."

But he glanced at the water and the wide distance, and said, "Oh, I don't dare to venture it. I never could make it."

"Yes you can. Trust to me. I'll help you with the coat. There, it's off. Now the boots. Sit down—I'll help. Now the preserver; hold still, I'll strap it around you. We are ready, now. Come—you are not afraid to trust to me, Thug?"

"I am going to do it, if I die—but I wouldn't risk it with any other person. You'll go through safe, I know that; and you'll fetch me through if anybody can." He added, tearfully, "But it may be that I'll never get across; I don't feel that I shall. And if these are my last words, I want to say this. If I go down, you must tell my mother that I loved her and thought of her to the last; and I want you to remember always that I was grateful to you. I think you are the best, best girl that ever lived; and if I pass from this troubled life this day, I shall enter heaven with a prayer on my lips for you, Hellfire. I am ready."

"You are a dear good boy, Thug, but it is not wise to be thinking about death at such a time as this. Come along, and don't be afraid; your mother is yonder, and you will be with her in a very little while. Quick, here are the snags."

They were away in time: in a few moments more their late refuge went to wreck and ruin with a crash.

"Rest your right hand on my shoulder, Thug, and keep the same stroke with me. And no matter what happens, don't get rattled. Slack up a little—we mustn't hurry." After a little she said, "We are half way, now—are you getting tired?"

"Yes, and oh, so cold! I can't hold out, Rachel."

"Yes you can. You *must*. We are doing well; we are going to make it. Turn on your back and float a little—two minutes. There, that will do; you mustn't get cramps."

"Rachel, they are cheering us. How that warms a person up! If they'll keep that up, I believe I can make it."

"They'll do it—hear that!"

"Rachel—"

"What?"

"I'm afraid there's a cramp coming."

"Hush—put it out of your mind!"

"I can't, Rachel—it's coming."

"Thug, you *must* put it out of your mind. Brace up—we are almost there. It is no distance at all, now. Two minutes more. Brace up. Don't give in—I know we are safe."

Both were well spent when they were hauled out on the ice, and also fairly well frozen; but a warm welcome and good whisky refreshed them and made them comfortable; and the attentions and congratulations and interest and sympathy and admiration lavished upon them deeply gratified Oscar's love of distinction and made him glad the catastrophe had happened to him.

## Chapter [3]

VESUVIUS, isolated, conspicuous, graceful of contour, is lovely when it is at peace, with the sunshine pouring upon its rich vineyards and its embowered homes and hamlets drowsing in the drift of the cloud-shadows; but it is subject to irruptions. Rachel was a Vesuvius, seen through the butt-end of the telescope. She was largely made up of feelings. She had a tropically warm heart, a right spirit and a good disposition; but under resentment her weather could change with remarkable promptness, and break into tempests of a surprising sort. Still, while the bulk of her was heart and impulse, the rest of her was mental, and good in quality. She had a business head, and practical sense, and it had been believed from the first, by Judge Carpenter and other thoughtful people, that she would be a valuable person when she got tame.

Part of what she was was born to her, the rest was due to environment and to her up-bringing. She had had neither brothers nor sisters; there was no young society for her in the house. Her mother was an invalid and kept her room the most of the time. She could not endure noise, nor tempers, nor restless activities; and from the cradle her child was a master hand in these matters. So, in her first years she was deprived of the society of her mother. The young slave woman, Martha, was superstitious about her, thinking at first that she was possessed of a devil, and later that he had found accommodations to his mind and had brought his family. She petted and spoiled the child, partly out of her race's natural fondness for children of any sort or kind, and partly to placate and pacify the devils; but she had a world of work to do and could give but little time to play, so the child would soon find the kitchen a dull place and seek elsewhere for amusement.

The father was sweetness and amiability itself, and greatly loved the child, but he was no company for the volatile creature, nor she for him. He was always musing, dreaming, absorbing himself in his books, or grinding out sermons, and while the child was present these industries suffered considerable interruption. There was conversation—abundance of it—but it was of a wearing and nerve-racking kind.

"Can I have this, fa'r?" (father.)

"No, dear, that is not for lit—"

"Could I have that?"

"No, dear, please don't handle it. It is very frail and you might—"

"What is *this* for, fa'r? Can Wildcat have it?" This was Martha's love-name for Rachel.

"Oh, *dear* no! My child, you must *not* put your hands on things without asking *beforehand* whether you may or—"

"Ain't there anything for me to play with?—and it's so lonesome; and there isn't any place to go."

"Ah, poor child, I wish—there! Oh, I knew you would; the whole inkstand emptied onto your nice clean clothes. Run along, dear, and tell Martha to attend to you—quick, before you smear it over everything."

There was no one to govern Rachel, no one to train her, so she drifted along without these aids; and such rearing as she got was her own handiwork and was not according to any familiar pattern. She was never still when awake, she was stored to the eyelids with energies and enthusiasms, her mind, her hands, her feet, her body, were in a state of constant and tireless activity, and her weather was about equally divided between brilliant and happy sunshine and devastating tempests of wrath. Martha said she was a "sudden" child—the suddenest she had ever seen; that when anything went wrong with her there was no time to provide against consequences: she had smashed every breakable thing she could get her hands on before a body could say a word; and then as suddenly her fury was over and she was gathering up the wreckage and mourning over it remorsefully.

By the law of her nature she had to have society; and as she could not get it in the house she forsook that desert early and found it outside. And so while she was as yet a toddling little thing it became a peaceful house—a home of deep and slumberous tranquillity, and for a good while perhaps forgot that it had ever been harassed and harried and terrorised by her family of uneasy devils.

She was a stranger outside, but that was nothing; she soon had a reputation there. She laid its foundations in her first week at Miss Roper's school, when she was six years old and a little past. At first she took up with the little girls, but they were a disappointment; she found their society a weariness. They played with dolls; she found that dull. They cried for a pin-scratch: she did not like that. When they quarreled, they took it out in calling each other names; according to her ideas, this was inadequate. They would not jump from high places; they would not climb high trees; they were afraid of the thunder; and of the water; and of cows; and would take no perilous risks; and had no love of danger for its own sake. She tried to reform them, but it failed. So she went over to the boys.

They would have none of her, and told her so. They said they were not going to play with girls—they despised them. Shad Stover threatened her with a stout hickory, and told her to move along or she would catch it. She perceived, now, that she could be happy, here, and was sorry she had wasted so much time with the little girls. She did not say anything to the boy, but snatched his switch away and wore it out on him. She made him beg. He was nearly twice her own age and size, and as he was the bully of the small-fry side of the school, she had established her ability to whip the whole of his following by whipping him—and if she had been a boy this would have been conceded and she would have succeeded to the bully's captainship without further balloting; but she was a girl, and boys have no manly sense of fairness and justice where girls are concerned; so she had to whip two or three of the others before opposition was quenched and her wish to play with the gang granted. Shad Stover withdrew and took a minor place in a group of somewhat larger boys.

Thenceforth Rachel trained with the boys altogether, and found in their rough play and tough combats and dangerous enterprises the contentment and joy for which she long had hungered. She took her full share in all their sports, and was a happy child. All through the summer she was encountering perils, but she had luck, and disappointed all the prophets. They all said she would get herself killed, but in no instance did her damages reach quite to that, though several times there were good hopes. She was a hardy and determined fighter, and attacked anything that came along, if it offended. By and by when the cool October came and the news went about that the circus was coming, on its way to the South, she was on hand outside the village with many others, at sunrise, to get a look at the elephant free of charge. With a cake in her hand for the animal, she sat with the crowd on the grass by the country road. When he elephant was passing by, he scooped up a snoutful of dust and flung it over his back, then scooped up another and discharged it into the faces of the audience. They were astonished and frightened, and all except Rachel flitted promptly over the rail fence with a rush, gasping and coughing; but the child was not moved to run away. The little creature was in a towering rage; for she had come to offer hospitality, and this was the thanks she got. She sprang into the road with the first stick that came handy and began to fiercely bang and hammer the elephant's hind legs and scream at him all the injurious epithets she could think of. But the elephant swayed along, and was not aware of what was happening. This offensive indifference set fire to all the child's reserves of temper, and she ran forward to see if she could get any attention at that end. She gave the trunk a cordial bang, saying, "Now let *that* learn you!" and raised her stick for another stroke; but before she could deliver it the elephant, without changing his gait, gathered her gently up and tossed her over the fence among the crowd. She was beside herself at this new affront, and was for clearing out after him again; and struggled to get free, but the people held her. They reasoned with her, and said it was no use to fight the elephant, for he didn't mind a stick. "I know it," she said, "but I've got a pin, now, and if I can get to him I will stick it in him."

A few months later her mother died. Rachel was then seven years old. During the next three years she went on playing with the boys, and gradually building up a perfect conflagration of a reputation, as far as unusual enterprises and unsafe exploits went. Then at last arguments and reasonings began to have an effect upon her, and she presently stopped training with the boys.

She played with the girls six months, and tried to get used to it and fond of it, but finally had to give it up. The amusements were not rugged enough; they were much too tame, not to say drowsy. Kissing parties and candy pullings in the winter, and picnics in the summer: these were good romps and lively, but they did not happen often enough, and the intermediate dissipations seemed wholly colorless to Rachel.

She withdrew. She did not go back to the boys at once, but tried to get along by herself. But nature was too strong for her; she had to have company; within two months she was a tomboy again, and her life was once more a satisfaction to her, a worry to her friends, and a marvel to the rest of the community.

Before the next four and a half years were out she had learned many masculine arts, and was more competent in them than any boy of her age in the town. All alone she learned how to swim, and with the boys she learned to skate. She was the only person of her sex in the county who had these accomplishments—they were taboo. She fished, boated, hunted, trapped, played "shinny" on the ice and ball on the land, and ran foot races. She broke horses for pastime, and for the risk there was in it. At fifteen she ranked as the strongest "boy" in the town, the smartest boxer, a willing and fearless fighter, and good to win any fight that her heart was in. The firemen conferred an honorary membership upon her, and allowed her to scale the roofs of burning houses and help handle the hose; for she liked that sort of employment. She had good judgment and coolness in danger, she was spry and active, and she attended strictly to business when on the roof. Whenever there was a fire she and her official belt and helmet were a part of the spectacle—sometimes lit up with the red flush of the flames, sometimes dimly glimpsed through the tumbling volumes of smoke, sometimes helping to get out the inmates, sometimes being helped out herself in a suffocated condition. Several times she saved lives, several times her own life was saved by her mates; and once when she was overcome by the smoke they penetrated to her and rescued her when the chance of success was so slender that they would not have taken the risk for another.

She kept the community in an unrestful state; it could settle to no permanent conclusion about her. She was always rousing its resentment by her wild unfeminine ways, and always winning back its forgiveness again by some act or other of an undeniably creditable sort.

By the time she was ten she had begun to help about the house, and before she was thirteen she was become in effect its mistress—mistress and assistant housekeeper. She kept the accounts, checked wastage, and was useful in other ways. But she had earned her picturesque nickname, and it stayed by her. It was a country where nicknames were common; and once acquired they were a life-property, and inalienable. Rachel might develop into a saint, but that would not matter: the village would acknowledge the saintship and revere the saint, but it would still call her Hellfire Hotchkiss. Old use and habit would take care of that.

Along in her sixteenth year she accidentally crossed the orbit of her early antagonist, Shad Stover, and this had good results for her; or rather it led up to something which did her that service. Shad Stover was now twenty, and had gone to the dogs, along with his brother Hal, who was twenty-one. They were dissipated young loafers, and had gotten the reputation of being desperadoes, also. They were as vain of this dark name as if they had legitimately earned it—which they hadn't. They went armed—which was not the custom of the town—and every now and then they pulled their pepper-box revolvers and made someone beg for his life. They traveled in a pair—two on one—and they always selected their man with good discretion, and no bloodshed followed. It was a cheap way to build up a reputation, but it was effective. About once a month they added something to it in an inexpensive way: they got drunk and rode the streets firing their revolvers in the air and scaring the people out of their wits. They had become the terror of the town. There was a sheriff, and there was also a constable, but they could never be found when these things were going on. Warrants were not sued out by witnesses, for no one wanted to get into trouble with the Stovers.

One day there was a commotion in the streets, and the cry went about that the Stovers had picked a quarrel with a stranger and were killing him. Rachel was on her way home from a ball-game, and had her bat in her hand. She turned a corner, and came upon the three men struggling together; at a little distance was gathered a crowd of citizens, gazing spell-bound and paralyzed. The Stovers had the stranger down, and he had a grip upon each of them and was shouting wildly for help. Just as Rachel arrived Shad snatched himself free and drew his revolver and bent over and thrust it in the man's face and pulled the trigger. It missed fire, and Rachel's bat fell before he could pull again. Then she struck the other brother senseless, and the stranger jumped up and ran away, grateful but not stopping to say so.

A few days later old aunt Betsy Davis paid Rachel a visit. She was no one's aunt in particular, but just the town's. The title indicated that she was kind and good and wise, well beloved, and in age. She said—

"I want to have a little talk with you, dear. I was your mother's friend, and I am yours, although you are so headstrong and have never done as I've tried to get you to do. But I've got to try again, and you must let me; for at last the thing has happened that I was afraid might happen: you are being talked about."

Rachel's expression had been hardening for battle; but she broke into a little laugh, now, and said—

"Talked about? Why, aunt Betsy, I was always talked about."

"Yes, dear, but not in this new way."

"New way?"

"Yes. There is one kind of gossip that this town has never dealt in before, in the fifty-two years that I've lived in it—and has never had any occasion to. Not in one single case, if you leave out the town drunkard's girls; and even that turned out to be a lie, and was stopped."

"Aunt Betsy!" Rachel's face was crimson, and an angry light rose in her eyes.

"There—now don't lose your temper, child. Keep calm, and let us have a good sensible talk, and talk it out. Take it all around, this is a fair town, and a just town, and has been good to you—very good to you, everything considered, for you *have* led it a dance, and you know it. Now ain't that so?"

"Ye-s, but—"

"Never mind the buts. Leave it just so. The town has been quite reasonably good to you, everything considered. Partly it was on account of your poor mother, partly on your father's account and your own, and partly because it's its natural and honorable disposition to stand by all its old families the best it can. Now then, haven't you got your share to do by *it?* Of course you have. Have you done it? In some ways you haven't, and I'm going to tell you about it. You've always preferred to play with the boys. Well, that's all right, up to a certain limit; but you've gone away beyond the limit. You ought to have stopped long ago—oh, long ago. And stopped being fireman, too. Then there's another thing. It's all right for you to break all the wild horses in the county, as long as you like it and are the best hand at it; and it's all right for you to keep a wild horse of your own and tear around the country everywhere on it all alone; but you are fifteen years old, now, and in many ways you are seventeen and could pass for a woman, and so the time has gone by for you to be riding astraddle."

"Why, I've not done it once since I was twelve, aunt Betsy."

"Is that so? Well, I'm glad of it; I hadn't noticed. I'll set that down to your credit. Now there's another thing. If you *must* go boating, and shooting, and skating, and all that—however, let that go. I reckon you couldn't break yourself. But anyway, you don't need the boys' company—you can go alone. You see, if you had let the boys alone, why then these reports wouldn't ever—"

"Aunt Betsy, does anybody *believe* those reports?"

"Believe them? Why, how you talk! Of course they don't. Our people don't believe such things about our old families so easy as all that. They don't believe it *now,* but if a thing goes on, and on, and on, being talked about, why that's another matter. The thing to do is to stop it in time, and that is what I've come to plead with you to do, child, for your own sake and your father's and for the sake of your mother who is in her grave—a good friend to me she was, and I'm trying to be hers, now."

She closed with a trembling lip and an unsteady voice. Rachel was not hearing; she was lost in a reverie. Presently a flush crept into her face, and she muttered—

"And they are talking about me—like that!" After a little she glanced up suddenly and said, "You spoke of it as new talk; how new is it?"

"Two or three days old."

"Two or three days. Who started it?"

"Can't you guess?"

"I think I can. The Stovers."

"Yes."

"I'll horsewhip them both."

The old lady said with simplicity—

"I was afraid you would. You are a dear good child, and your heart is always in the right place. And so like your grandfather. Dear me but he was a topper! And just as splendid as he could be."

After aunt Betsy took her leave, Rachel sat a long time silent and thinking. In the end, she arrived at a conclusion, apparently.

"And they are talking about me—like that. Who would ever have dreamed it? Aunt Betsy is right. It *is* time to call a halt. It is a pity, too. The boys are such good company, and it is going to be so dull without them. Oh, everything seems to be made wrong, nothing seems to [be] the way it ought to be. Thug Carpenter is out of his sphere, I am out of mine. Neither of us can arrive at any success in life, we shall always be hampered and fretted and kept back by our misplaced sexes, and in the end defeated by them, whereas if we could change we should stand as good a chance as any of the young people in the town. I wonder which case is the hardest. I am sorry for him, and yet I do not see that he is any more entitled to pity than I am."

She went on thinking at random for a while longer, then her thoughts began to settle and take form and shape, and she ended by making a definite plan.

"I will change my way of life. I will begin now, and stick to it. I will not train with the boys any more, nor do ungirlish things except when it is a duty and I ought to do them. I mean, I will not do them for mere pleasure. Before this I would have horsewhipped the Stovers just as a pleasure; but now it will be for a higher motive —a higher motive, and in every way a worthier one.

"That is for Monday. Tomorrow I will go to church. I will go every Sunday. I do not want to, but it must be done. It is a duty.

"Withdraw from the boys. The Stovers. Church. That makes three. Three in three days. It is enough to begin with; I suppose I have never done three in three weeks before—just *as* duties."

And being refreshed and contented by this wholesale purification, she went to bed.

[On the envelope containing the "Hellfire Hotchkiss" manuscript, Twain noted the inclusion of the following material as "rejected manuscript that may come good." A fragment of a story in which the "Damned Fool" was presumably to be the chief character, this manuscript only slightly precedes the "Hellfire Hotchkiss" manuscript, a fact established by the use of the same paper (a graphlike paper peculiar to the months at Weggis, mid-July to mid-September 1897), and the same pen and ink as in the Hotchkiss manuscript.]

to persuade the other young boarders and Ustick's other cubs, to eschew beer. They called him Parson Snivel and gave him frank and admirable cursings, and urged him to mind his own business. All of which pleased him, and made him a hero to himself: for he was turning his other cheek, as commanded, he was being reviled and persecuted for righteousness' sake, and all that. Privately his little Presbyterian mother was not pleased with this too-literal loyalty to the theoretical Bible-teachings which he had acquired through her agency, for, slender and delicately moulded as she was, she had a dauntless courage and a high spirit, and was not of the cheek-turning sort. She believed fervently in her religion and strenuously believed it was a person's duty to turn the cheek, but she was quite open and aboveboard in saying that she wouldn't turn her own cheek nor respect anybody that did. "Why, how do you reconcile that with—" "I don't reconcile it with anything. I am the way I am made. Religion is a jugful; I hold a dipperful. You can't crowd a jugful of *any*thing into a dipper—there's no way. I'm holding what I can, and I'm not going to cry because I can't crowd the rest in. I know that a person that can turn his cheek is higher and holier than I am, and better every way. And of course I reverence him; but I despise him, too, and I wouldn't have him for a doormat."

We know what she meant. Her attitude is easily understandable, but we get our comprehension of it not through her explanation of it but in spite of it. Her language won't scan, but its meaning is clear, all the same.

She did not show Oscar's letter to his father; the Judge would have taken no great interest in it. There were few points of contact between him and his son; there were few or no openings for sympathy between the two. The father was as steady as a church-tower, the son as capricious as the weather-vane on its top. Steady people do not admire the weather-vane sort.

But the mother answered the letter; and she poured out her affection upon her boy, and her praises, too; praises of his resolution to be a Franklin and become great and good and renowned; for she always said that he was distrustful of himself and a prey to despondencies, and that no opportunity to praise him and encourage him must be lost, or he would lose heart and be defeated in his struggles to gain the front in the race of life. She had to do all the encouraging herself; the rest of the family were indifferent, and this wounded her, and brought gentle reproaches out of her that were strangely eloquent and moving, considering how simple and unaffected her language was, and how effortless and unconscious. But there was a subtle something in her voice and her manner that was irresistibly pathetic, and perhaps that was where a great part of the power lay; in that and in her moist eyes and trembling lip. I know now that she was the most eloquent person whom I have met in all my days, but I did not know it then, and I suppose that no one in all the village suspected that she was a marvel, or indeed that she was in any degree above the common. I had been abroad in the world for twenty years and known and listened to many of its best talkers before it at last dawned upon me that in the matter of moving and pathetic eloquence none of them was the equal of that untrained and artless talker out there in the western village, that obscure little woman with the beautiful spirit and the great heart and the enchanted tongue.

Oscar's mother praised in her letter what she was able to praise; and she praised forcefully and generously and heartily, too. There was no uncertain ring about her words. But her gorge rose at the cheek-turning heroisms, and since she could not commend them and be honest, she skipped them wholly, and made no reference to them.

Oscar's next week's letter showed further progress. He was now getting up at four in the morning, because that was Franklin's way; he had divided his day on the Franklin plan—eight hours for labor, eight for sleep, eight for study, meditation and exercise; he had pinned Franklin's rules up in a handy place, and divided the hours into minutes, and distributed the minutes among the rules, each minute sacred to its appointed duty: so many minutes for the morning prayer; so many for the Bible chapter; so many for the dumb-bells; so many for the bath; so many for What did I do yesterday that was morally and mentally profitable? What did I do which should have been left undone? What opportunity did I neglect of doing good? Whom did I injure, whom did I help, whose burden did I lighten? How shall I order this day to the approval of God, my own spiritual elevation, and the betterment of my fellow beings? And so on, and so on, all the way through: sixteen waking hours cut up into minutes, and each minute labeled with its own particular duty-tag.

He wrote it all home to his mother; and added that he found that life was a noble and beautiful thing when reduced to order and system; that he was astonished to see what briskness, mentally and physically, early rising gave him, and what a difference he could already notice between himself and the late-rising boarders—the greatest difference in the world, and all in four days.

But he said he had taken to his lamp again, for he had found that he could not read his fine-print books by the Franklin tallow candle. Also, he had been to a lecture, and was now a vegetarian, and an enthusiastic one. He had discarded bread, and also water; vegetables, pure and simple, made the most effective and inspiring diet in the world, and the most thoroughly satisfying; he wondered how his intellect had ever survived the gross food with which he had formerly burdened it; but he sometimes almost feared that it had suffered impairment. He had mentioned this fear to the foreman of the office, but the foreman had said, almost with enthusiasm, considering what a lifeless and indifferent man he usually was, "Don't worry—nothing can impair your intellect."

The mother's face flushed when she read that, and the foreman was better off where he was than he would have been, here, in reach of her tongue.

# THE SIMON WHEELER SEQUENCE

(1870–1898?)

# I

## *The Brummel-Arabella Fragment*

(?–1870)

EDITOR'S NOTE: In his Buffalo study in 1870, Mark Twain dug into his file of unfinished manuscripts and drew forth thirteen and a half pages of a play he had begun some time earlier. He read over what he had written, made a few corrections, and then continued the story on the bottom half of page 14, writing now with the gorgeous purple ink of the Buffalo period. The spirit seemed to be upon him, and sheet after sheet of the Minerva Crest paper which he now affected as husband of the former Miss Olivia Langdon was added to the previous fourteen sheets. Before he stopped, he added at least thirteen pages of manuscript, actually less than half the number of words previously written because the Minerva Crest paper is a note paper which Twain tore into half-sheets, and the first fourteen sheets are legal size, a semi-onionskin.

The dating of the last thirteen pages of the fragment is fairly easy because of the distinctive ink and paper. But all one can do is to speculate about the first portion: the ink is of a nondescript variety, the paper seems to be unique, no other samples of it appearing in the surviving manuscripts, and the text offers no clues. The legal size of the paper may indicate that Twain began the play during his days in Washington as a private secretary for William M. Stewart, senator from Nevada and a former lawyer who probably still retained the habit of using such paper. But the same grounds can be used to argue for composition in Nevada, where Twain was working with his brother Orion, Territorial Secretary, who with equal probability could have used such paper. And, of course, the assumption that a legal-size paper indicates an association with the legal fraternity is of questionable validity. All one can say with a degree of certainty is that Twain began the play before he transferred his private literary endeavors to the study of his Buffalo home after his marriage.

# *The Brummel-Arabella Fragment*

ENTER *Brummel, soliloquising.*

*B.*—Arabella! Beautiful name! No—damnable name—execrable name! Damnable name, abstractly considered *as* a name, but lovely—surpassingly lovely as the medium through which one indicates *her*. Well, there's no question about it—I can't live without her. I can't do it—I *must* have her, and I'll ask the tremendous question within the hour. I'm thinking about her all the time—and I don't care what I'm writing—whether the item's about pigs, or poultry, or conflagrations or steamboat disasters, I manage to get her mixed into it somehow or other. How humiliating it was last night when the chief editor looked over my proof and wanted to know what Arabella Webster it was who was going to fight the prize fight with Rough Scotty the Kentucky Infant. And the day before I had her in three financial notices and drat it, for a week past they haven't sent a pack of old blisters to the county jail for getting on a bender and breaking things but what I've written up the item in a state of semi-consciousness and entire absent-mindedness and added my Arabella's name to the list. This sort of thing won't do, you know. Some day I'll make a mistake and publish her as arrested for arson, or manslaughter, or shoplifting, or infanticide, or some other little eccentricity of the kind, and she'll notify me to inflict my company and my extraordinary attentions on somebody else. I'll go and see her now. I'll go and fall down on my knees and say "O, my own—"

(*Cries of Murder! without.*)

Hi-yi! here's an item! (*Exit.*)

(*Arabella in her parlor.*)

*Arabella*—Well, well, well—shall I *ever* know my fate! George Sherman loves me and is always trying to get an opportunity of asking me to marry him, and it requires all my woman's wit to prevent the opportunity from occurring. It never *shall* occur, though, until I know whether John Brummel is going to propose or not. I think he has been on the point of proposing five or six times, but at the critical moment that wretched firebell always strikes an alarm and Brummel's off in an instant to get the "item," as he calls it. I know he loves me, though—I know he loves me better than anything in the world, except a sensation item. I can tell it by his manner. When he sees me his countenance glows with animation, and his eye lights up and he seems all suffused with pleasurable emotion—just the same, for the world, as when he hears of an unusually atrocious murder, or of a family being burned to death, or of any kind of dreadful disaster to life or property. "Lucky disaster," *he* calls it—what fearful language! (*Knock.*) He's at the door—that's his knock.

(*Enter Brummel.*)

*B.*—Good morning, Miss Arabella.

*A.*—Good morning, Mr. Brummel—draw up a chair and sit down.

*B.*—(*Aside.*) Bless my soul, see that smile!—it does me more good than a mysterious murder! (*Aloud.*) Fine day, Miss Arabella.

*A.*—Yes, very. (*Aside.*) He's confused—I know what he's here for—it's coming now. (*Aloud.*) But why don't you sit down—John?

*B.*—(*Aside.*) The suffering Moses, listen to that! Calls me John! To think there could be *music* in the name of John! I'd rather hear it than a steamboat explosion. (*Aloud.*) Yes—you—you, are sound—that is, I mean, your remark is very just—it *is* an uncommonly fine day.

*A.*—(*Aside.*) O this is encouraging—he don't know his own remarks from mine—I *know* he's going to propose—he's coming to the point—but very slowly, and in something of a roundabout way.

(*Aloud.*) O, yes, we've settled the weather—that is, we have decided as to the character of the day. But come, John, why don't you sit down?

*B.*—(*Aside.*) Rapture! It's better than an earthquake! (*Aloud.*) Well, Air—(*sitting down*) Air—a—bella (*Aside.*) The dear, delightful damned name sticks in my throat like a sugar-coated pill that'll neither go down nor come up. (*Aloud.*) As I was saying—or rather, as I was going to say, I am glad to find you alone because I have got something particular to say to you—(*Aside.*) O Lord, *now* what'll I say? (*Searches desperately for his note-book.*)

*A.*—(*Aside.*) Oh, the happy day!—it's coming at last! (*Hanging her head and seeming confused.*) (*Aloud.*) Something particular to say to me? Why what can you have to say that—

*B.*—Arabella! *Dear* Arabella! (*Aside.*) Oh, fire and brimstone, I can't do it! (*Aloud.*) As I came along, I—I—heard somebody shout "Murder!"—

*A.*—(*Aside.*) Oh, *bother* the murder!

*B.*—And I ran up Cherokee alley; and—well, I've got it all here in my note-book—two Frenchmen killed, dead as Judas Iscariott—and mangled!—Oh, mutilated in the most interesting manner!—and another one so perforated with bullet-holes that if you were to fill him up with water he'd leak in a dozen places—can't live—there's no use in talking—he *can't* live—confound those meddling surgeons, if they'd left him alone he'd been dead before *this* time—and a middle-aged woman with her arms full of twins fell down three flights of stairs and broke herself all to pieces same as if she'd been made out of plaster of Paris, and—

*A.*—(*Aside.*) Oh, aggravation! (*Aloud.*) Mr. Brummel, is this the matter which was so excessively private and confidential that it could only be imparted to me in secrecy and seclusion?

*B.*—(*Aside.*) Oh, *this* won't do! I'll put on a bold front, and speak out—(*Aloud.*) Ah, I beg your pardon, Miss Arabella, I had forgotten myself. (*Aside.*) Now for it! (*Aloud.*) Miss Arabella—dear Miss Arabella—I—I—have known you a good while! (*Aside.*) By George, that villainous anvil chorus has been running in my head all day, and now it has got down to my heart.

*A.*—Ah!—yes, you have known me a good while, and I hope the acquaintance has not been unpleasant—it has not been so to me, certainly. (*Aside.*) Oh, he is doing better, now—if he follows the groove he is in, it will bring him to a proposal sure.

*B.*—Unpleasant! No! Far from it. It has been the pleasantest of my life. I have known you long, and always liked you. I liked you even from the first—and now, for weeks and months this simple liking has been gradually growing into a stronger passion. From thinking of you casually, I have got to thinking of you constantly—and from dreaming of you occasionally I have finally got to dreaming of you unceasingly. Oh, Arabella (*seizing her hand*).

*A.*—Oh, John! Oh, Mr. Brummel!—This is so unexpected! Oh dear!

*B.*—Ah, my Arabella! do not say that the words I have spoken are unpleasant to your ear. Give me leave to hope! Do not say that my faithful eternal thoughts and my confiding everlasting dreams have been for naught. Do not say—

*A.*—My salts, my salts, please! Ah, I am overwhelmed with conflicting emotions—but—but—they are not—not—altogether unpleasant!

*B.*—Blessed words! Then you are *not* indifferent to your Brummel!—and I *may* hope! Arabella, here (*Enter Sherman unperceived.*) on my bended knees I swear that—(*seizing and kissing her hand*). (*Cries without of "Stop him! lynch him! hang him!"*)—*Here's* a gorgeous item! (*Exit running.*)

*Sherman*—You love him, Arabella. No—do not deny it—I saw it in your whole manner—I saw it in your blushing cheeks and in your beaming eyes.—There's nothing left for me to live for now. Farewell, and may God bless you. (*Exit.*)

*A.*—Oh, clear out, and commit suicide if you want to—I suppose that is what you mean—I've half a mind to go and take a dose of arsenic myself, I feel so aggravated and desperate. Plague take that numscull and his infatuated items. This is the *fourth* time. (*Sobs awhile.*) Well, he comes nearer it every time, anyway,—though of course, just as usual, something had to go and happen, to interfere. The first time he tried to propose, there was fire; the next time, there was a riot; the third time there was a bloody murder; this time there was a mob, and next time he tries it I suppose there'll be an earthquake. Well, let it come!—I don't care, so that he gets through before the roof falls in! (*Exit, angrily.*)

Scene—A dark, lonely street.
Time 2.30 A.M.

*Enter Sherman.*

*Sherman.*—So—The poison works. Welcome, Death, thou peerless leech, whose medicine alone hath power to heal a broken heart! And welcome, Grave! Thou only Home, in all the world, where Grief and Care can ne'er intrude! Here, in this gloomy spot, on these unfeeling stones, I'll yield my weary spirit up and pass into forgetfulness. (*Dies, after several discouraging attempts.*)

*Enter B. Drunk and Singing.*

*B.*—There was a woman in our town—
In our town did dwell—
She loved her husband dearilee,
But another man twyste as well!

Hic! I'm not very drunk, but I'm drunk *enough*. I said a good thing at that re-reception dinner—I said a very good thing—I said it in reply to the old regular toast to the Press. I said—said—"Eternal Vil-vilijance is price of Lib—lib—erality!" It was dam good. *They* thought 'twas original—*they* didn' know any better—humph! Gennel Washnton said same thing once. Say!

*Enter old Webster.*

*W.*—Good evening—did you speak to me, Sir?

*B.*—Speak to you? Why cert'nly. Where you goin'?

*W.*—Well, if the news can be of any use to you, I was going home.

*B.*—What you goin' home for?

*W.*—Why, I don't know of any particular reason, only I was just going home.

*B.*—*Only* you was just goin' home. Look me in 'e eye—and don't slobber round so—stan' up!—so. What you goin' home for?

*W.*—Well, I don't understand you, Sir. What do you mean by—

*B.*—You don't understand me! You don't understand anything.

Because you're drunk. You don't know what you're talking about. You say Good-night—I say it ain't good-night—it's good-morning. And it ain't *good* morning neither, because it's too hot.

*W.*—Hot! I wish you could have seen it in Mexico when I was there. I was with Taylor at Buena Vista, and—

*B.*—Hold on, there! (*Getting out his note-book and scribbling*). With Taylor at Buena Vista—go on—Taylor *who? What* Taylor? —Bayard Taylor? What was you doin' there?—What was goin' on?

*W.*—Fighting, like smoke!

*B.*—Fighting! Splennid!—go on! No other paper got this item, hey? Well—go on—who started it?

*W.*—I was with Taylor, and I had been pelting away with my battery—

*B.*—'Sault and battery—go on.

*W.*—When all at once a large body of Mexican lancers dashed down upon us from the left—

*B.*—Aw-right—go on—large body Mexican dancers dashed down, and you and Taylor left—

*W.*—No! They dashed down on us *from* the left, and Taylor laid his hand on my shoulder—just this way—and said, "My brave Colonel—"

*B.*—(*Aside.*) Oh, the devil—that's that same old everlasting yarn, and this is old Webster. (*Aloud.*) Good morning, old gentleman—good morning—I've got the small-pox bad, and you must excuse me for not thinking to mention it sooner—you'll make allowances, though, considering—

*W.*—Bless my soul—what an adventure! (*Exit.*)

*B.*—(*Discovering dead body of Sherman and out with his note-book.*) Oh, ge-('ic)-ge-whillikins ain't this splennid! Suicide or murder or 'sassination or ap'plexy or heart disease or sum-('ic)-sum'n 'ruther. (*Feeling him, and smiling with tranquil gratification.*) Oh, no *he* ain't dead—a-ha!—Oh, no course not—on'y jes' layin' 'roun' pass'n away the time. (*Oracularly, to audience.*) Now *this* fel'r ain't a fraud. Man can depend on him. He's so permanent! But some of these 'sass'nation's so un-unreliable. See 'em git up right in the middle of the cor'ner's jury and jes' gap and stretch once or twice and tilt their hat on the side of their head and walk off as comfortable as if swindling a poor hard-worked reporter out of an item was a perfectly gentlemanly thing to do—'gra-'graded ruffians! Those kind of 'sass'nations ain't dead, ye see—ain't dead in a reliable and trustworthy way, but only dead *drunk*. Dis-('ic)-dis'pation's an awful thing—awful. Robs wife of peace mind, robs chil'n of schoolin', an' food, an' good family name, which is better'n ever'thing else. ('c!) Dang a dis'pated man! Ain't good to 'sociate with—ain't got any money, as gen'l thing—don't smell good. *Never* smell good. Never see one in my life that smelt good. (*Sniffs.*) I've fetched away the smell from that gang in the gin-mill—jes' 'spected it. Nev-('ic) never get rid of that in *this* world. Man might 's well dis'pate 's *own* self as be smelling so, and goin' 'roun' representin' people 't *does* dis'pate. Well it's just a perfect luxury (*sitting down on the body*) to have this feller all to myself—all to myself and nary a soul in the neighborhood. Take him every way, he's one of the very bulliest items that ever has happened. First place, because he's all mine, and the evening papers 'll have to get him from me 8 hours late, and the other morning papers 'll have to do the same 24 hours after me. Gorgis! Second place, there's mystery here! There's awful mystery! A man's more free to expatiate where there's a wide margin of mystery to slosh around in. Facts hamper a body so—many's the item they've ruined for *me*. Mystery!—dark and bloody mystery's the ticket! I wish this feller was gashed up, some. I'd really ruther have one big rattlin' murder with a mystery clouding it—or with a lot of oyster-headed detectives (as they call themselves) to *make* a mystery out of it by walking right over clues as big as a cow and never seeing them—I say I'd ruther have one rattlin' murder with a mystery to it than have the cholera come or see a norphan 'sylum burn down with all its contents—no insurance. ('ic!) I would—I wish I may die if I wouldn't. This party is warm yet. It's a mighty, mighty long way back to the office, but I s'pose I've got to go—it ain't likely that I'm going to fool away *this* item, I don't reckon. (*Clock strikes* 3.) Jings, it's too late!—paper's gone to press! Now *here's* a go! MagNIficent mysterious dead man, and got to leave him for the evening papers. Ah, what have I done to merit a fate like—NO, sir! I have it! I'll take him *home* with me and keep him for tomorrow's paper! By George, and I'll gash him up and make him a spectacle! He's no slouch of an item, just the way he is —but when I get him gashed up he'll be a perfect luxury to contemplate! (*With infinite trouble and many failures, manages to get the still limp body back to back and arms over his shoulders, and so drags him off and exit.*)

Scene—a cheap lodging room. B. staggers in singing, and heaves himself and corpse across his sleeping roommate (Rogers). The latter wakes up angry, jumps out of bed and a fight ensues, in which they handle each other pretty roughly and some blood from a nose spatters on the bed, floor and dead body. Their racket rouses the whole boarding house and certain boarders are heard to shout "Murder! police!" etcetera. This brings the sober one to a comprehension of the very peculiar situation.

*Rogers.*—Heavens and earth, Brummel, snatch some of my clothes, I'll snatch the rest and the quicker we get out of this the better. Did you kill this man? However—don't answer—Lord bless me it don't make a particle of difference *who* killed him, both of us 'll have to answer for it. The police will be here in two minutes, for the racket these fools are making will wake even *them*. Hurry up!—hurry, hurry, hurry! Snatch that little carpet-sack. (*Exit.*)

Scene—a wood—time, dawn. Enter Brummel and Rogers out of breath. They throw themselves down to rest.

*Rogers.*—Oh, my poor mother!

*B.*—Poor Arabella!—Poor me!

*R.*—This is *such* a curious, such a strange, such an unheard-of circumstance! What a weird romance! And O God, how awful! To be thought a murderer! Think of it! What a dreadful, dreadful thing this whole business is!

*B.*—But it's a noble item—noble! (*Gets out his note-book hurriedly and proceeds to write.*)

*R.*—(*Knocking note-book out of his hand.*) Fool, can't they detect us fast enough without your infernal notes!

*B.*—Didn't think of that. (*Sighs.*) Noble item—noble. And the other papers 'll get it.

*R.*—Now here. Desperate as the case is, it won't do any good to sit here and wail. We two must hang together. And to begin, we must hatch some sort of a plan—some sort of an idea of what is best to do. The essential foundation of any plan is, knowledge of existing circumstances. Right there is the rub. We know all we want to know about circumstances as they existed an hour or two ago, but what we want is to know how they exist *now*. I haven't a doubt but that the entire police force is roused by this time, or at least enough of it to make trouble for *us*—but what are they *doing?*—that is the thing. What measures are they taking?—If we only knew *their* plan, ours would be so easy! (*Thinks a bit,—then jumps up excitedly.*) I have it! I have it! By George, I *tell* you I've got it! Give me the carpet-sack—quick, quick! All right—here she is!—it was the luckiest thing that we brought the old carpet-sack. (*Gets out a little pocket-telegraphic machine as big as his fist.*) I haven't been a telegraph-operator all my life for nothing. I'll have the news now, pretty quick. (*Climbs telegraph pole, or borrows ladder from neighboring orchard: cuts the wire, attaches one end of it to his instrument and holds it to his ear, while B. stands guard at the foot of the pole.*)

R. — (*Reading messages.*) *Corn — closed — heavy — let — it — alone — buy — all — the — early — wheat — You — can — get. George — B. — Howard.* (That don't concern *us*, DOES it?) *Mary — died — 8 — 30 — P. — M. — Mother — ar-rived — five — min-utes — too — late — to — see — her. Henry.* (Poor Mary! — poor mother!) *Four — two — nine — nine, — ten, nine — fifteen — one G. — L. — W. — fourteen, W. — thirteen — B. — nine. Gridley.* (Plagued cipher — all Greek, — and *may* refer to us, for all we know. I hate people who telegraph in cipher.) *The — baby — was — born — at — exactly — fifteen — min-utes — after nine; — eight — pounds — and — a — half; — first — thing — it — said — was — bow — wow — wow — like — a — dog. — appears — to — be — a — girl. Maria — doing — as — well — as — could — be — expected. J. Toodles.* (Welcome, little chap — it's a good, jolly old world, ah me!) *My — child — don't — break your — old — mother's heart! Come back — come — back. — I am — old — and — forsaken — and — desolate.*

# II

# *Cap'n Simon Wheeler, The Amateur Detective. A Light Tragedy*

(1877)

Editor's Note: Twain's play about Simon Wheeler, basically a burlesque of Allan Pinkerton's detective stories, was written at Quarry Farm, Elmira, between 27 June and 11 July 1877. The various progress reports to William Dean Howells give the impression that, although the principal character, Wheeler, was somewhat older, the play itself was conceived, plotted, and written in those two weeks of enthusiastic and energetic composition. But the actual case is somewhat different: Twain had instead finally succeeded, after one or two previous attempts, in weaving his Simon Wheeler character, by now some three or four years old, into a fabric derived from the Brummel-Arabella plot.

The literary possibilities inherent in a character such as Simon Wheeler had apparently been for some time a topic of conversation between Twain and Howells. Such is the implication of Twain's reference to the chief character in his first letter to Howells about the play: "To-day I am deep in a comedy which I began this morning—principal character, that old detective—I skeletoned the first act & *wrote* the second, to-day; & am dog-tired, now. Fifty-four close pages of MS in 7 hours."[1] A similar implication appears in a later letter in which Twain describes in part his efforts to secure a producer for the play. During the interview with Dion Boucicault, Boucicault had pointed out the odd concidence that he, Boucicault, was currently rewriting a detective play with a minor character named Wheeler, a play he had originally written three or four years ago. In parentheses, Twain commented to Howells, "My detective is about that age, you know."[2]

Such comments indicate that Twain had been seeking a suitable vehicle for such a character as Simon Wheeler since 1873 or 1874. At least once, possibly twice before the summer of 1877, he thought he had succeeded and committed his idea to paper. Early in 1876 he devised what, from the surviving evidence, seems to have been a plot outline for a detective play and sent it to Charles Reade, apparently seeking encouragement to expand it into a play to be produced by Reade in London. The only remaining record of this transaction is a note from Reade dated 6 August 1876: "I beg to acknowledge your detecting plot. It is full of Brains but improbable on the stage and not popular. The public want to see the plain realities of life reflected on the boards. All on acting is a bad card. Put in a story."[3] The evidence remaining of this transaction is so vague that one cannot be at all sure that the plot submitted to Reade involved the character later named Wheeler, but, if it did, Reade's rebuff did not deter Twain for long, for in the autumn of 1876, during a conversation at the St. James Hotel in New York, he outlined to Chandos Fulton a plot which undoubtedly revolved around the idea of his amateur detective. Fulton encouraged him on the spot and in a note dated 12 March 1877, again urged him to fill out the plot and submit the play for production: "Was that a fanciful coinage of your imagination the plot which you sketched to me one autumn afternoon last year at the St. James' Hotel? As I told you then there was the germ of a good acting play, especially as the plot would be so new. I want a piece for two comedians. It strikes me there was the material there,—one the detective, the other the man of disguises."[4]

---

[1] SLC to Howells, Elmira, 27 June [1877] (*MTHL,* I, 184).

[2] SLC to Howells, Elmira, 29 August [1877] (*ibid.,* I, 200).

[3] Original in MTP. The key word of this note, "detecting," like the rest of the note is in Reade's almost illegible scribble. The first three letters, "det-," are clear, and the remainder is probably "-ecting," since the only other possible reading, "-ailing," makes no sense in the context.

[4] Original in MTP.

It was probably Fulton's note which sent Twain to Quarry Farm in the summer of 1877 brimming with enthusiasm and anxious to begin work. After arriving at the Farm on 7 June, he devoted his first few days to the final installments of "Some Rambling Notes for an Idle Excursion," the last of which he completed on 26 June. The next morning, as we have already seen, he began his play with the chief character named first Neddy, then Gideon ("Giddy") Swash, and in some seven hours of work outlined the first act and wrote the second. By 4 July so he reported to Howells in a letter of that date, he had completed the first and the fourth acts, piling up a total of 151 manuscript pages (including the second act previously written). He estimated that in two more days he would complete the third act and the play. Such was his enthusiasm, he asserted, that he had written over thirty pages a day since he began work on the play: "Never had so much fun over anything in my life—never such consuming interest & delight." [5] To this letter he added a postscript dated 6 July in which he exultantly announced the completion of the play, a four-act comedy "conceived, plotted out, written & completed in 6½ working days of 6½ hours each; just a fraction under 250 MS pages besides the pages that were torn up & the few pages of odds & ends of notes, such as one sets down in the midst of his work for future reference. . . ." [6]

As reported to Howells, the accomplishment seems prodigious, and it was—but not quite so prodigious as Twain made it sound. The implications of the "conceived, plotted out" must be tempered by the realization that, as we have already seen, both the plot and the principal character had been fermenting in Twain's imagination for some time. And the word "completed" also needs some qualification: apparently Twain really meant he had turned out the last page of a rough draft. On 11 July five days later, he again wrote to Howells: "It's finished. I was misled by hurried mis-paging. There were ten pages of notes, and over 300 pages of MS when the play was done. Did it in 42 hours, by the clock; 40 pages of the Atlantic. . . . Those are the figures, but I don't believe them myself, because the thing's impossible." [7] (For a slight correction of Twain's reports to Howells, see Appendix A.)

Shortly after composing and dispatching an application for copyright on 12 July, Twain left for New York to find a producer. He first went to Hartford to investigate reports of burglars around his house, and

[5] *MTHL,* I, 187.
[6] *Ibid.,* I, 187–188.
[7] *Ibid.,* I, 188–189.

while there read the play to Joseph H. Twichell. He was in New York by 18 July. Before his return to Elmira on 2 August he revised *Ah Sin,* the play written in collaboration with Bret Harte, attended the first two performances, and visited several producers with "Cap'n Simon Wheeler" under his arm. He sought out Dion Boucicault, John Brougham, and Augustin Daly as possible producers, and later tried to interest Sol Smith Russell in the title role, but all managed to find reasons for not getting involved.[8] Oddly enough, there is no record that he ever showed the completed play to Chandos Fulton, the man who originally wanted such a play.

The play survives in two forms: the holograph manuscript and an amanuensis copy apparently made in late 1877 or early 1878 (see headnote to the Simon Wheeler novel, below). The text reproduced here is that of the holograph manuscript, but in matters of dramatic format (italicizing of stage directions, etc.) I have followed the style of the amanuensis copy. Since the amanuensis copy is not entirely consistent, I have, in those few instances of omission, silently supplied the missing italics or other marks necessary to complete the format.

---

[8] SLC to Howells, Elmira, 29 August [1877] (*MTHL,* I, 200) and Russell to SLC, 25 and 28 August 1877 (originals in MTP). Russell's note of August 25 indicates that at this time Twain was calling his play *Clews.* Russell, of course, was the actor who had played Colonel Sellers in the stage version of *The Gilded Age.*

# *Cap'n Simon Wheeler, The Amateur Detective. A Light Tragedy*

## 1st Act.[9]

*Front Scene*—Where villagers might reasonably promenade.
*Rear Scene*—Open space in a wood. A thicket R.

## 2d Act.

Outskirts of a village—Capt. Wheeler's dilapidated cottage, with front door near C—perspective of country paths and cottages.

## 3d Act.

*Front Scene*—Signs: "Public Square"; "Keep off the Grass"; "Dogs not Allowed"; "Don't Sleep on the Benches."
*Rear Scene*—Interior of Justice's Office, opening on Public Square.

## Costumes

Front Scene, 1st Act, Hugh and Charles are in white linen from head to foot—with white linen or straw hats.

[9] When Clemens read the MS to Twichell in mid-July 1877, he jotted a record of the time consumed in reading each act on the title page: [after 1st Act] "reads 15 min."; "Top of 232 I was absolutely correct.—2 hrs." Just under the title he wrote, "The whole play reads 2. hours and 20 minutes."

Hugh remains in white linen until he changes clothes with the tramp.

But when Charles is out hunting he is dressed in full suit of blue navy flannel, with pants stuffed into boot-tops; black slouch hat; gun; rabbit slung over shoulder if he chooses, but no flummery of game-bag etc. The costume should be merely rough-and-ready, with nothing of the dandy sportsman about it.

## CAP'N SIMON WHEELER

### THE AMATEUR DETECTIVE.

---

### PERSONS REPRESENTED.

---

Cap$^{n}$ Simon Wheeler, Am. Detective.
Mr. Horace Griswold.
Hugh Burnside, a Poet.
Charles Dexter, his cousin.
Detective Baxter. } Professional
Detective Billings. } detectives
Detective Bullet. } from New York.
Jake Belford, a fugitive Desperado.
Tom Hooker, a Newspaper Reporter.
Lem Sackett, a Telegraph Operator.
Jake Long, a Police Officer.
A Newsboy.
A Magistrate.
Miss Clara Burnside.
Miss Millicent Griswold.
Mrs. James Burnside.
Mrs. Matilda Griswold.
Mrs. Jenny Wheeler, wife of the Cap'n.
Widow Higgins.

## Act. 1.

*A front scene. Barrel or something there. Chas. and Hugh discovered.*

*Chas*—But if I get an early start in the morning I'll bag that wolf, sure. This morning his tracks—

*Hugh*—'Sh! (*Low voice.*) Say, Charley—that old fool that imagines he's a detective, is spying around, yonder—(*pointing off*)

—I'm almost sure it was he. Let's go off pretending to quarrel—see what he'll do.

*Chas*—'Greed! (*Raising his voice.*) *I* say you *did* do it!

*Hugh*—It's false—I never dreampt of such a thing!

*Chas*—You *did!*—and it was as mean, and low, and underhanded as it could be!

*Hugh*—You're a coward to say it!

*Chas*—That word shall cost you dear.

*Hugh*—Pah! I don't fear you.

*Chas*—I *warn* you, I warn you to look out for yourself! (*Going.*)

(*As they go, Chas. glimpses Mr. and Mrs. Griswold.*)

—Hello, Hugh, there are the Griswolds—what'll *they* think? (*Exit—both laughing.*)

*Enter Mr. and Mrs. Griswold.*

*Mr. Griswold.*—Threatening words? A quarrel?

*Mrs. G.*—Charley's quick, and high tempered, but I shouldn't expect *these* two to be quarreling. Hugh's a poet—and *they*'re PEACEable folk.

*Pa*—But there's their uncle's *will.*

*Mrs. G.*—Yes, but *they* know Charley's to have all the property. There's nothing for *him* to quarrel about. O, dear, dear, dear!

*Mr. G.*—Now, wife, don't do that. I know what that means.

*Mrs. G.*—Poor Hugh loves our Millicent so—and she loves *him.* I do wish you—

*Mr. G.*—(*Interrupting*)—No, it's no use. He hasn't got ten thousand dollars to his name. He'll never be rich till his mother dies—and she'll outlive him. A *poet*'s bad enough; but a *poor* poet! (*Lifting his hands.*)

*Capt.*—(*Yawning, and stretching, protruding head, with sacking thrown over it, to conceal face, from barrel.*) Hallo, have I been asleep? Well, it's the *first* time I ever forgot myself since I've been an amature detective. Hello, who's this? Old pap and mam Griswold. (*Conceals himself again.*)

*Mrs. G*—Well, well, I see your mind's made up.

*G.*—It is. I've given Millicent her orders—and she'll obey. (*Sits down on barrel.*)

*Mrs. G.*—She will. And be sorry for it the longest day she lives, too.

*G.*—Come, Matilda, this smacks of insubordination. (*Punches Capt. in eye with his umbrella.*)

*Mrs. G.*—Call it any name you want to. I loved my father, and respected him; but do you think I'd have let him tell me who to marry and who to let alone? I think I *see* myself!

*G.*—*I* think Charley has a leaning toward Millicent—and I hope it's *so*.

*Mrs. G.*—Much your instinct is worth! He's not in love with *any*body;—else *I* should have seen it.

*G.*—So much the better. Then he *may* fall in love with Millicent.

*Mrs. G.*—Mf! Much good it would do him. You're *just* like a man! You set up a *man's* premises, and then argue from them what a *woman* would do.

*G.*—Well, what of it? Given the same premises, ain't the conclusion the same in both cases?

*Mrs. G.*—*No,* sir. Here's the difference. Granted that a woman's in *love:* That's the *end* of it. Granted that a *man's* in love: He'll *change* if he can make ten cents by it.

*G.*—Pah! you talk too much!

*Mrs. G.*—M'f! Don't *every*body that gets the best of an argument?

(*Exit.*)

*Capt.*—'Gad, she had him there! These quarters are getting too warm. I guess I'll climb out and hide in a cooler place. Hold on—somebody *else* coming. (*Retires again.*)

*Enter Hugh and Millicent.*

*Hugh*—O,[10] I cannot bear it. Do give me some little shred of hope to cling to!

*Milly*—Hugh, I cannot, though you *know* it breaks my heart to give you up. My father's commands are positive.

---

[10] Originally "O, Millicent. . . ." Twain deleted "Millicent" in the manuscript, but it was restored in the amanuensis copy made early in 1878 (see headnote to the Simon Wheeler novel below).

*Hugh*—(*Staggers toward barrel, sits down, covers face with hands*). O it is too hard! To be beloved by you, and yet forever barred from hoping!—Give me one little hope—one little, little hope!

*Milly*—O, so *gladly* I would!—but it cannot be.

*Hugh*—And will you, *can* you obey your father's will at cost of your life's happiness and mine? (*Springing up.*) You cannot do this thing—you cannot commit this wickedness, this crime, if you truly love me!

*Milly*—(*Bridling.*)—What are these words you use?

*Hugh*—(*Still excited.*) It *is* a crime! And your love is but a pretense if you can do it! (*Bitterly.*) Ah, confess—confess that my comparative *poverty*—

*Milly*—For shame!

*Hugh*—(*Trying to seize her hand.*)—O forgive me!

*Mill*—Do not *touch* me! (*Stamping her foot.*) For all my grief, for all my love—which you *never* had a right to doubt—my reward is an *in*sult! (*Going, crying.*) All is over between us!

*Hugh*—(*Handkerchief to his eyes—grandiloquently and broken-heartedly.*) You have *said* it. So *be* it. When I am no more—(*breaks down in handkerchief.*)

(She is moving away, crying—glances back, occasionally and furtively, hoping he is coming—catches his eye once, twice—he coldly turns his back on her—she bursts out sobbing and runs off.)

(*Exit.*)

Hugh sits down on the barrel and cries and groans into his handkerchief—Capt. uncovers his eyes to look up—Hugh unknowingly squeezes a flood of tears from his handkerchief into them—gets up and goes weeping away. Says—solemnly: (*Aside.*) I will wring her hard heart! If it's the last act of my blighted life, I'll commit suicide.

(*Exit, sobbing.*)

*Capt.*—(*Uncovering head*). *He's* put my *other* eye out. If those were *tears,* I judge he lives mostly on salt mackerel. I can't *stand* THESE quarters. Hullo, here's somebody *else* coming! *Every*body's taking a summer twilight walk this evening—*rot* them!

*Enter the Griswolds and Mrs. Higgins.* R, *Mrs. H. has a small basket. Enter Mrs. Wheeler,* E, *unperceived, and sits at wing peacefully knitting.*

*Mrs. Hig.*—Yes, it's *so,* just as sure as you're born. The news has just come. O, they ain't any mistake about it, you can depend on't. I just been on the trot amongst 'em, ever since I heard 'bout it, and I lay I'm *dog*-tired. (*Sits down on the barrel.*) Hank Slocumb was there and he heard the will *read*—he's just got back. He told his wife, and she told Spence Buckner, and Spence told Bull Wilkerson, and Bull told Bub Stavely, and Bub told Puss Leathers, and Puss told me, and I went straight to Hank Slocomb and sure enough it's just as I say. The will gives every red cent to *Hugh,* and leaves Charley out in the cold.

*Mr. G.*—(*Aside.*)—(*Annoyed.*) If I'd kept *still,* and let Milly *alone*—

*Mrs. G.*—(*Puts arms akimbo and smiles ridicule upon pa.*) (*low voice*)—Pah! you *talk* too much!

*Mrs. H.*—Well *I* knowed how 'twould be, *long* ago. I *said* so to myself, time and time again. Says I, them boy's uncle is the most indefinite old potato-bug this side o' Kansas. Says I, they ain't no de*pend*ing on *him,* says I. *Hugh*'ll get that money dead *sure,* says I, just because he'd always hinted he was going to give it to *Charley. He* never done a thing in his life he *said* he would.

*G.*—What do you reckon made him change his mind?

*Mrs. H.*—Mf! Pure cussedness! Reason enough for *him.* And Charley's *temper.* Charley wouldn't ever take sass from him nor anybody else. Time now for that ignorant old amature de*tective* to mix in and make a *mystery* out of it.

*Mrs. G.*—O, I haven't seen him around for a day or two.

*Mrs. H.*—That ain't no sign the work-house has got its due! I warrant you the old cretur's hid around the neighborhood som'ers spying out what's going on and mixing it all up in his poor old mushy *head.* Say—(*in low voice, nodding head toward Mrs. Wheeler*) what d'I tell you? Wherever you see that patient simple wife o' his'n knitt'n around, you can depend on't *he* ain't fur away. Follers him around like a dog; *he* thinks she's just built out o' sweetbreads and *pie,* and *she* thinks you could double the 'luminatin' power of a whole Congress just with the drippin's from his *intellect.*

*Mr. G.*—Why they say you had a pretty perceptible weakness for him before *she* got him, widow?

*Mrs. H.*—Mf! *Likely* story!—Go hence to git the home news, as the 'postle says. S'pose *he* told that around—nob'dy *else*'s got *time.* Gropin', maunderin' old bat! They say he don't do anything but read them sappy, lying detective yarns and imagine *he's* a detective! *Clews!* he's always after *clews!* Clews indeed! He couldn't follow an elephant's tail and find the elephant! I never see a detective that *could.* My land, I do believe some of these eggs is spoilt! Smell so, anyway. (*Holds an egg up, looks through it with one eye, or shakes it, slams it down on Capt.* [*Wheeler's*] *head.*) People do cheat so in aiggs.

*Mr. G.*—They say the hit bird flutters, widow. You seem to flutter a good deal when Capt. Wheeler is mentioned.

*Mrs. H.*—*Me,* indeed! I des*pise* him! (*Looking through another suspicious egg*). I only wisht I had his addle-head for a *mark.* (*Slams the egg.*) They ain't no dependence to be placed in aiggs now-a-days. You going? Wait a minute—*I*'m rested, now—I'll go 'long with you. And as for Simon Wheeler, if he's been going around letting on anything about me, and I catch him out, I lay I'll give him a hunk of my mind, the tor*men*ted old ash-cat!

(*Exit the* 3.)

*Capt. Wheeler*—(*Removing the defiled sacking from his head*) —Ach! Smells like a cat's *breath!* A detective's got to put up with all kinds of places, in the way of business, but I've had enough of this one. (*Looking.*) Drat if there ain't another gang a-coming! (*Covers head.*)

*Enter Charley and Clara. His arm around her waist. They sit down on the barrel. They do not observe Mrs. Wheeler.*

*Char*—Why it seems like a dream, Clara darling.

*Clara*—O, Charley, dear, I loved you—O, ever so long! And you never suspected it once?

*Char*—Never! For weeks and weeks I've thought you and Henry Savage—

*Clara*—(*Laughing.*) O, the idea! Henry Savage! And were you loving me all that time?

*Char*—From the very day I got here. In twenty-four hours I was head over heels in love—and then—

*Clara*—Then you imagined you saw something between Henry and me, and—

*Char*—Just so.—My heart nearly broke. *Would* have broken if I hadn't had Henry Savage to hate.

*Clara*—Why you never showed a sign, Charley dear.

*Char*—What was the use? *I* was unhappy enough; I didn't want to spoil *your* happiness.

*Clara*—You're a noble fellow, that you are. And how did you come to make love to me this evening, Charley?

*Char*—I just detected something in your darling old[11] eyes that—

*Clara* (*Putting her hand over his mouth*). There! you naughty creature! But never mind, my heart sings for joy, and I forgive you.

*Char*—(*Taking from pocket.*) See this ink and this paper? Know what I [have] been trying to do with 'em?

*Clara*—*What?*

*Char*—Been harassing my brains for a week, roosting around in the woods, trying to contrive a beautiful farewell letter to you that would be worthy of you, and then leave the country forever and go off and die somewhere.

*Clara*—O, Charley!

*Char*—It's a fact. That's the very identical ink.

*Clara*—Throw the hateful stuff away—I can't bear the sight of it.

*Char*—(*Motioning to throw bottle—Capt. uncovers face to look.*)—O, no—let's pour a libation in honor of our deathless love! (*Pours it in Capt's face.*)

*Clara*—There! Now we're betrothed in due and ceremonious form!

---

[11] "Old" is omitted in the amanuensis copy.

*Char*—True as you live, sweetheart! Clara dear, what'll *Hugh* say?

*Clara*—Won't he be glad! O, he's the best brother to me! He'll write some poetry about it, *won't* he?

*Char*—*Acres* of it! Let's go and hunt him up and tell him now. (*They rise and start*).

*Clara*—O good! [12] No—I know what we'll do. Tomorrow's his birth-day. You come, right after breakfast, and we'll make him a birth-day present of it together. We won't tell a *soul,* to-night!

*Char*—I'm agreed! O, what's peaches and cream to *this!* (*They skip or waltz off, arms around waists. They bow to Mrs. Wheeler, who half rises and curtsies respectfully.*)

(*Exit.*)

*Capt.*—(*Uncovering inky face.*) This is beastly. A detective ain't valued and looked up to as he ought to be. The world little knows what we have to go through to—(*groan*)—here's some *more!* (*Hides head.*)

*Enter Lem (Telegraph Operator) and Tom (from opposite direction.)*

*Tom* (*Reporter.*) Well, Lemmy, son of the lightnings, how's trade? Had any telegrams over the wires this week, hey?

*Lem*—'Bout as many as you've had sappy items for the paper, I reckon. Old boy I should [think] you'd come with apologies in your mouth instead of sarcasms.—You kicked me out of bed again last night.

*Tom*—Did I? I didn't know it. But ain't you ever going to get used to that?

*Lem*—(*Injured.*) Get *used* to it! Hang it, I *can't* get used to it.

*Tom*—Hang it, you don't *try.*

*Lem*—*Me* try! I *like* that. Why the nation don't *you* try to break yourself of that repulsive habit?

---

[12] In the top margin of MS p. 19, above this speech, Twain has written and then crossed out "Sh—That old fool detective's hid behind this barrel—let's quarrel!" The note may mean that Twain at one time considered using the same device with Clara and Charles as he used at the outset of the act with Charles and Hugh.

*Tom*—There's nothing repulsive *about* it but the m-mere action. It is always the outward and unconscious expression of some sweet fancy in my *dreams.* (*Pensively.*) I *always* kick when I dream.

*Lem*—*Mf!* Likely you dream you are an ass. You don't *miss* it much.

*Tom*—I don't mind it so I don't miss *you.* Come, now, my boy, I guess neither of us has any of the best of the other. Whenever I kick you out you always get up and pound me beyond all reason before I can get my faculties together. But a truce to trifles—my soul is full of trouble. (*Sadly.*)

*Lem*—*No!* Sit down here and tell me about it. We are sworn eternal friends and whatever bruises your heart bruises mine, whoever wrongs you wrongs me, whoever insults you has got to fight us *both!* (*They sit on barrel.*)

*Tom*—Spoken like yourself, old twin! Nothing shall ever sever our friendship. But—O, my! (*anguish—leaning forehead on Lem's shoulder.*)

*Lem*—What *is* it, old boy? Tell me—tell your own [13] Lem. (*This in earnest.*)

*Tom*—(*Sigh.*)—It is killing me. I have been *refused!* Support me! (*Falls heavily against Lem who shores him up the best he can.*)

*Lem*—O shame, shame—poor Tom! But let her name be *accursed!*

*Tom*—No—O, no—do not curse her, Lem. Rather let me suffer alone for what she has done.

*Lem*—It shall not *be,* my poor heart-wounded boy, my soul's friend. Let her be *accursed!* I say it *again!* May she sorrow, may she rot piecemeal, may she—What's her *name?*—who is this vile, this heartless, this this—

*Tom*—Clara Burnside.

*Lem*—(*Seizing him by throat*). What! Clara Bürnside! What! You purple-dyed villain, have you *dared* to aspire to that that divine—

[13] "Old" in amanuensis copy.

*Tom*—(*Interrupting.*) Unhand me, dog of an unbeliever! (*Struggling.*)—*You* love her, then?

*Lem*—She refused me last *night!* But I will *have* her, fiat justitia, though the heavens fall!

*Tom*—NO! reptile! 'Tis *I* that will have her, tho' I wade chin-deep in your heart's best blood!

*Lem*—You *lie,* caitiff! as deep as your midriff you lie!

(Struggling, they fall over the barrel, and they and the Capt. are a confusion of legs and arms and noise—Exit Mrs. W. in alarm. Then they separate and rise up—they two a trifle blood-stained, the Capt. inky, and his sacking eggy—he discards this, and seizes the youths who were about to escape, each by a wrist.)

*Capt.*—You rascals, you've broke the peace—and several of my bones! (*Tom is striking a match.*) No—you'll not get loose! I'll take you to an officer. (*Tom touches match to his hand*). Ouch! (*Lets go of Tom, who runs. Capt. drags Lem about, in chase.—Tom throws the long sack over his head, which reaches down to his feet and is covered with ink and eggs.*)

*Tom*—Run, Lem, run!

(*They exit.*)

*Capt. goes groping around, a walking tower.*

*Enter Mr. and Mrs. Griswold, Charley, Policeman Long, etc. and Mrs. Higgins and stand amazed—Mrs. H. frightened—Presently the Capt. turns deliberately down, stands on his head, and as the sack drops from him—(Or, he solemnly follows the frightened crowd off.)*

CURTAIN

sack kept open by hoops.

The sacking he covers his face with behind barrel may be an odd piece—or else ¾ of this sack may be *in* the barrel.

(*Change Scene.*)

## *First Act—Continued*
## [2D SCENE]

*Moonlight—time, after Midnight*

*Enter Hugh.* (*slow music.*) (*Under influence of strong sleeping-drug.*)

*Hugh*—(*hand on stomach.*) (*melodramatic.*) How it burns! (*Hand on forehead.*) O, what agony!—This, then, is death! Farewell, heartless one, farewell! May you not regret your dread work! ——(*Falls——dying.*) I——I——(*drowsily*) didn't think I ——was—taking so much! (*Seemingly dies.*)

*Enter Capt. Wheeler.*

*Capt.*—(*solus.*)—I knew by the way he hung around in the shadows by the drug store that he was up to some murderous villainy or other—got the cold eye of a pirate, that poet. See him slink *away* with the truck. He thought he was playing pretty sharp, but he had the old detective's eye on him—unerring as fate. But rot him, I've lost *track* of him. Can't start sign [14] of him anywhere. Well I'll just take a minute's rest on this log and think it over. (*Sits down on the body.*) I've lost him, but *my!* it's only for a minute or so—when I get on a man's track he might as well throw up the sponge—there ain't any escaping me—I'm as bound to trace him out and get him as if he was a spectator at a riot and I was a random bullet. There's something awful about being a detective—*night's* just the same as daylight to you—*whispers* just the same as *yells*—nobody can't hide a secret from you *no* way. Just give you a *clew* and that's all you want. Just an old glove's enough—or a footprint from a ragged boot—or an old cigar stub with the defendant's particular chew-mark on the end of it—and if a detective's got 3 or 4 little

[14] Amanuensis copy: sight.

clues like that, they just lead him as dead straight to his man as the poles would lead an *ord'*nary man to the telegraph office. Why when that great mysterious murder was done there in Brooklyn, what sort of clews did the detectives have? Nothing in the world but a sledge-hammer, and one of the criminal's boots, and his handkercher with his name on it, and his photograft, and some other little traps of his'n. That's all the clews they had. They've got 'm *yet.* Do you reckon that assassin 'll escape? Never—not if he lives long enough. This log's mighty warm. Sort of uncomfortable. (*Rising*) Now lemme see—how'll I go to work to track out this chap and find him. (*Moving to rear slowly.*) (*Stops and thinks.*) *I*'ve got it—in five minutes I'll lay my hand on him! (*Comes running, trips and falls over dead man, jumps up rubbing knees and limps off, saying,*) I'm as dead sure of him now as if I had him in my grip. In five minutes (*slow dumbshow of closing his fingers upon his capture,*) these old infallible nippers 'll take him into camp.

(*Exit.*)

*Enter Reporter, a little tight.* (*Sighing*) Ah, love, love! There's nothing like a broken heart to take the stiffening out of a man's legs! (*Observing body*). Hey? *Dead* man! Noble item—noble! Oh, no! *this* ain't any good *find,* I reckon! Why it lays over any item I've struck in 6 months. *Suicide,* I wonder? *'sassination,* I hope.—A suicide's a good thing in its way, but it don't begin with 'n assassination. You've got to be mighty reserved and respectful about a *sui*cide, else you'll have the surviving relatives in your hair. You've got to trim your item down pretty brief, and you've always got to say it's temporary aberr*a*tion. Temporary aberr*a*tion! (*derision*)—and half these suicides haven't got anything to *ab*errate! (*Sitting down on corpse and proceeding to load pipe*). But you let a man be assassinated once, and you can string him out to five columns. (*Scrapes match on corpse.*) [15] O, yes, a suicide's kind of lean stuff for literature, but (*giving corpse an approving slap*) *you*'re the right sort, old fellow! I wish they'd gashed you up a little. You'd show up a nation sight gaudier in print.—I wonder if it wouldn't be all fair

---

[15] Along the left margin of MS p. 35, Twain wrote, "The Capt mustn't scrape the match; better Tom, because he knows it's a corpse."

in the way of business to gash him up a little myself. No, tain't pleasant—I couldn't do it. Now half the time, (*scrapes another match on corpse*) what you take for a *sui*cide's only a *drunk*—and all of a sudden he comes alive on the inquest and rip goes your item. A bogus suicide's a disgusting object. But (*slapping corpse*) *you're* sound, old chap! You're a subject to feel proud of. I-George, I've got him all to myself, too.—Won't the other paper howl when I trot him out with thunder-and-lightning display lines in the morning! O, no, I reckon not! (*Slapping corpse*) M'fren', I wouldn't trade you for a crim. con. case and a riot on top of it! (*Lights match on him*) (*Pause.*) Hold on! It's a-way after midnight. Our paper's gone to press! Too late to get him into this week's issue! O, geeminy, this is too bad. (*Getting up and walking*) If he stays here, the other paper'll get him, too. O, *that* won't do. *I* found him. He belongs to *me*. Look here, can't I hide him somewhere till next week and then take him out of pawn? I know what I'll do. I'll lug him home. If my room-mate objects I'll lick him. I'll hide him under the bed till I want him. It's pretty warm weather, but I reckon he'll keep. (*Dragging him off.*) (*Dead man's hat drops off.*) It's the biggest dispensation I've struck in a year. Perfect *mine* of literature!

(*Exit.*)

*Enter Mrs. Burnside, Clara, Mrs. Higgins, Policeman Long and crowd of supes, with lanterns.*

*Mother Burnside*—O, my son, my son, shall I ever see him again?

*Clara*—Don't grieve so, mother, something has kept him out.

*Mrs. B.*—Till this time in the morning! He's *never* out so late. I know I shall never see him again.

(*Policeman Long looking around on ground, all this time.*)

*Mrs. H.*—Dear heart, don't take on so. You'll see him again, don't you be afraid. Laws-a-me, years ago when my Goliah disappeared, just the same way, says I, I *know* he's no more! and you might a heard me miles and miles I carried on so—but the dominie heartened me up and says he, Pray!—Prayer worketh all things!—and I done it, and if you'll believe me, right in the very midst of that prayer up he turns, alive and well as you be this minute, only *drunk*. You pray, sister Burnside.

*Mrs. B.*—If I prayed a year it wouldn't bring him home *drunk.* He is not that kind. O I never shall see him again! (*Weeps*)

*Clara*—O, mother, *don't!* I can't bear the thought. We *shall* see him again.

*Mrs. B.*—My child, I know what you *don't* know. I know that he went to see *her* for the last time.

*Clara*—What!

*Mrs. B.*—He *told* me so. He said if she refused him he—he—(*breaks down sobbing*)

*Clara*—(*frightened*)—Mother, mother, please go on. What did she do?

*Mrs. B.*—(*Sobbing*)—When he got home, he fell in my arms like a little child; and he asked me to fold him close; and said the world was nothing to him any more—and O, he looked so white and stricken!

*Mrs. H.*—(*wiping eyes with apron*)—Just the way my poor Goliah done, to a *scratch!*

*Clara*—(*sobbing*)—O, Mother, why *did* you let him go out of the house in such a state?

*Mrs. B.*—(*Sobbing*)—O, I comforted him all I could, and he kissed me good-night—O, over and over again, poor lost child, and I thought he was going to his room.

*Mrs. H.*—(*Sobbing*) My son Goliah done jes' so, jes' so poor lamb! (*Folding hands on Mrs. Burnside's shoulder and wailing aloud.*)

*Clara*—And hadn't you been to his room till you waked me?

*M*—O, child, how you talk! Could I forget his state? I haunted his door like a spirit! Twas always still—I said, he's sleeping his troubles away, poor boy and I'm so thankful.

*Mrs. H.*—(*Throwing her soul into another wail*)—*Me,* right over again!

*Clara*—And then—

*Mrs. B.*—(*interrupting*)—O at last there came a great dread on my soul:—*could* he sleep so, at such a time? I sprung through the door—not a sign of him!—hadn't been there at all! I fell like a person shot!

*Mrs. Higgins*—(*with a prodigious wail*)—Perfect facsimile! It all comes back to me like one o' them pagan boomerangs! (*Falls upon Mrs. Burnside's neck and is gently but firmly passed on from breast to breast.*)

*Policeman Long*—(*bringing hat, which he found on ground.*)—Madam, was this—

*Mrs. B.*—(*Shrieks and falls into her daughter's arms, but does not faint.—Gradually recovers, slowly and reverently takes the hat, kisses it—moves a step or two in a dazed way—turns, sees Clara, opens her arms, Clara runs and throws herself into them.*) You are all I have left, now! (*They go off weeping, the others following reverently.*)

(*Exeunt Omnes*)[16]

*Enter Tom and Lem.*

(*They bring the body and lay it down. They puff and blow and swab sweat. Both got blood on their faces. They hurriedly hide it in brush and cover it. Badly scared.*)

*Lem*—It's a nice piece of business—that's what it is. We'll *swing* for this.

*Tom*—Well it's your own fault!—skip out of bed and smash a fellow's nose (*feeling it*) for nothing. I never *saw* such a peppery devil.

*Lem*—For *nothing!* Slam a flabby corpse across a body when he's sound asleep! Call that *nothing!*

*Tom*—It was dark as pitch—I *stumbled,* you fool you! How could *I* help that?

*Lem*—What the nation d'you want to bring the grisly thing there for, *any*how?

*Tom*—Where *else* could I put him. In the *buttery?*

*Lem*—No—leave him where you found him, you flat-head.

*Tom*—Y-a-s (*with derision*) and let the other paper get him! *You'd* make a *gaudy* reporter, *you* would! You haven't got any more inspiration than a mud turtle! Confound you if we hadn't had the

---

[16] The discovery of the hat occurs on MS p. 47. Following this page in the manuscript Twain inserted an unnumbered page on which he jotted the following notations:

"The hat has no bloodstains on it—there was no easy way to get them there.

"The Capt thinks H fell out of tree head first because there's a dent or *bruise* in his hat."

fight and bloodied him, I wouldn't a lost this item. And the thing that grinds me (*half crying*) is that I've got to lose the item and get hung into the bargain!

*Lem*—(*shuddering*) O, Tommy, we're goners, I just *feel* it! He warn't dead, I *bet* he warn't. He was only stunned, I reckon. If we hadn't all tumbled together and jammed him against the furniture maybe he'd be alive now. But O my, we finished him! Nothing in the world can save us!

*Tom*—(*half crying*)—*Please,* Lem, don't talk so—it makes me shiver all over.

*Lem*—Such a state as that room's in!—furniture all crippled, blood everywhere—and look here, Tom! (*Starting*)—our noses have shed blood all the way here! It's a track that a detective—

*Tom*—(*interrupting*) A detective, your grandmother! A detective couldn't follow it if it was eleven foot wide. But other *people* will find us out!—the other *boarders,* O my goodness!

*Lem*—Bother the boarders, they sleep like the dead. But no matter, we ain't safe. *Some*body 'll hive us, sure. O, Tom, it's the awfulest night's work—we'll hang for it, just as sure as Moses!

*Tom*—Lem, you're taking all the *tuck* out of me. I can *feel* that rope!—why I can feel that rope just as *plain* as—

*Lem*—O, *don't,* Tom! (*Buries face in hands.*) Tom, we're blighted—two young innocent beings blighted, cut off in guileless youth, in the sweet dawn of life and promise (*sobs*)—let's swear eternal friendship and everlasting secrecy—

(*They embrace.*)

*Tom*—(*solemnly*)—We will be *brothers,* in heart and soul—

*Lem*—(*solemnly*)—In heart and soul—

*Tom*—With sealed lips from this sacred hour—

*Lem*—With sealed lips from this sacred hour—

*Tom*—So, breast to breast, heart welded to heart—

*Lem*—Breast to breast, heart welded to heart—

*Tom*—We walk hence, from this hour inseparable—to the *gallows!*

*Lem*—O! Ugh! (*shuddering*)—Yes—yes—to the gallows, Tom! O, the gallows, the gallows! (*Crying*)

*Tom*—Swear!

*Both*—W-e S-w-e-a-r![17]

*Tom*—*(they stand locked together)*—*(thoughtfully)*—What an item this would make!

*Lem*—Tom, let's go and straighten up the room and lie late and play sick and let on that we never stirred all night (*going*).

[*Tom*]—Right! We'll do it! (*Starting*) O, lordy, did you hear anything!

[ *Lem*]—O, come, Tom, *don't!* I wish I was DEAD!

(*Exit, precipitately.*)

*Day begins to dawn.*

*Enter Hugh from the thicket.*

*Hugh*—(*Solus*)—So I didn't quite manage to take enough, after all! I'm most honestly glad *of* it. If I don't turn up, that druggist will keep mighty still. If I *do* turn up, he'll tell on me and the village will ring with derision at my expense. (*Thinking*) I've got to mysteriously disap*pear*. Ah, that will be romantic! Ah, heartless Millicent, when you see what you have done, perhaps even *you* will be touched. (*Wretched hand-organ heard.*) Somebody coming? (*Steps aside.*)

*Enter limping beggar in a cloud of rags, blue goggles, cane, false whiskers, sign on his breast "Pity the Poor Old Soldier"—playing hand-organ—singing (or not, as is best.)*

*Tramp*—(*solus*)—(*Good-humoredly*) What show's an escaped desperado got *here!* And yet they call this a land of Bibles!——(*Examining himself*)——Mighty conspicuous disguise——(*Starts off, grinding his organ.*) Just my luck, to have a thousand dollars on my head—and not a *red* where I can get *at* it!

*Enter Hugh.*

*Hugh*—Where away, friend?

*Tramp*—(*lugubriously*) Many a hundred mile—*home,* to die, if I can only hold out to get there. Could you give a little something to the poor old soldier that fit and bled to keep up the old flag?

*Hugh*—(*gives him something.*) Now look here; business is business. What'll you take for your outfit?

---

[17] Along the margin of MS p. 54, Twain wrote, "All this scene in *real* solemnity."

*B*—How?

*Hugh*—I *mean* it. I want to have a lark. I'll swap outfits with you and give you a trifle to boot.

*B.*—Honest injun?—no joking?

*Hugh*—Honest injun. Come—would twenty-five dollars boot—

*B.*—It's a whiz! Mind you're to gimme all the clothes you've got on.

*Hugh*—To the last rag! Come in here and we'll exchange. All I require of *you* is that you give me time to get well away before you stir out of the wood again. (*Entering thicket.*)

*Beggar*—(*Chuckling and slapping his thigh—aside*)—If they'd only catch *him* and hang him in my *place* to-day!

(*Exit both into the thicket.*)

*Enter Capt. Wheeler, his wife following, knitting.*

*Capt.*—(*Scanning the ground.*) Jenny, they say they found his hat here.

*Jenny*—You'll get a *real* good clew out of *that, won't* you Simon?

*Capt.*—O, but *won't* I, honey. (*He goes mumbling up and down —pausing—nodding head, etc.—Jenny watching every movement with serene admiration.*) Jenny, I'm working up a theory that's perfectly beautiful.

*Jenny*—O, tell it to me, Simon!

*Capt*—Tain't only just begun, *yet,* you know—and I'll be altering it all the time. But as far as I've got, it stands about like this. He started out to commit *sui*cide. Well, a lot of things happened which I haven't ciphered out, yet, but anyway they inter*fer*ed. See these leaves?

*Jenny*—Yes. Are *they* a clew?

*Cap*—Well I should *think* so! Not to an *ord*'nary man, maybe, but to an old de*tective*——why they just *talk!* I found 'em down yonder. Shows 't he clumb a *tree!*

*Jenny*—*My!* I never would a thought of it!

*Cap*—Becuz you ain't a detective, Jenny.

*Jenny*—What did he climb the tree for, Simon?

*Cap*—Well there's a clew missing, as to *that.* But I judge he clumb it so as to have a quiet place to *think,* and fix up a new *plan.* See this piece of a limb?

*Jenny*—Another clew?

*Cap*—That's what *I* make out of it mighty easy.

*Jenny*—Does *it* talk to you, too?

*Capt*—(*impressively*) Jenny, it fairly yells!

*Jenny*—My *land!* What does it *say,* Simon?

*Cap*—He went to sleep and fell out of the tree. *That's* what it says.

*Jenny*—Simon, it's wonderful. I don't see how you can *do* it.

*Cap*—(*tapping his forehead*)—Tain't no merit in *me,* Jenny—*I* didn't put it here.—*Well,* honey, do you see this truck? (*Spreading his palm*)

*Jenny*—Yes—what is it?

*Capt.*—Lard.

*Jenny*—Lard?

*Capt.*—It's what it is—the true sediment of the translated hog.

*Jenny*—What do you make out of *it,* Simon?

*Capt.*—This. There was a man coming along under that tree—going home from market with his hat full of *lard.* This was just as Hugh was a-tumbling.

*Jenny*—Go on, Simon—it is *so* interesting.

*Capt.*—(*Impressively.*) He fell on that man!

*Jenny*—Gracious *me!*

*Capt*—Now did he come down head-first, or t'other way?

*Jenny*—Which way *did* he come, Simon?

*Cap*—What does the bruised place on his hat say? He bounced into that feller head *on.*

*Jenny*—It's as wonderful as a *tale!*

*Capt.*—It hurt him, it jolted his insides all up, it knocked him cold as an office-seeker's welcome;—so he must have fell sixty or eighty *foot.* Otherwise it wouldn't *stunned* him so.

*Jenny*—Yes, *that* looks plain.

*Cap*—Well, this stranger's lard was all squished out and *ruined.* He's mad as a march hare of *course.* What does he naturally do? He naturally lights into poor Hugh and *finishes* him. Then he buries the body and slopes. That's the theory *so* far, old sweetheart—subject to modification by fresh clews, you understand.

*Jenny*—O, Simon, I am not worthy of such a man! It's so astonishing—and it does seem to come so easy to you.

*Cap*—Jenny, if I make a strike on this, I wouldn't wonder if it was worth two or three hundred dollars to me.

*Jenny*—Why *Simon!* We'd almost be easy for life! I do hope and pray we may get the *half* of it!

*Cap*—Don't you worry, honey! Now the chap *I'm* after is this black-hearted left-handed *lard*-conveyer!

*Jenny*—Left-handed! Why what makes you think he's left-*handed*, deary?

*Capt*—Bless you child, if you'd read as many detective tales as *I* have, you'd know that pretty much *all* the murders are committed by left-handed people. In the stories, the detectives most always notice that the wound is made in a way that couldn't be made only by a left-handed man. 'Sh! (*pondering*)—Let me see—the parson, he's *right*-handed; the town clerk—*right*-handed, again. The butcher—(*Enter Mrs. Higgins hurriedly.*) Say!—old woman, have you run across a left-handed man around anywhere 't you've been gadding this morning?

*Mrs. H.*—I lay I'll make you think you've found *six* left-handed men if you old-woman *me* again! I've got a crow to pick with you, you slanderous old tramp, the first minute I get time. Have *you* seen the *doctor*—that's all I want out of *you,* now?

*Capt*—Caught a glimpse of a man 'way over yonder while ago with a *gun*—maybe *that's* him going for a patient medicine don't seem to fetch. Who's sick?

*Mrs. H.*—Couple of my *boarders* letting *on* to be—Tom and *Lem.*—*Why?* Are *you* a doctor, 'mongst your other idiotisms? (*Going*).

*Capt*—'Fst! (*with a gesture*)—*Mosey,* now, *mosey!*

*Mrs. H.*—(*Scornfully.*) *Detective! Always* blowin' and tootin' about *mysteries* and things that's right under your *nose* and you can't *see* 'em!——Perfect old *fog*-horn!

(*Exit with a toss of her head.*)

*Jenny*—The wicked old thing!

*Capt*—Why don't they tie up that old bell-wether!—(*musing—tapping forehead*) (*Looking off*)—Hello, yonder goes a man!—and he—yes—no,—yes! it's *so*, by George!—HE'S A SCRATCHING HIS HEAD WITH HIS LEFT HAND!

(*Exit in a hurry. Jenny following.*)

*Enter Charley with gun and game, stooping and tip-toeing.*

*Char.*—He must have run into that thicket! Something moving amongst the leaves (*creeping and raising gun slowly—fires!*) Got him! It's my *wolf*, sure! (*Darts into thicket. Staggers out again with hand to forehead.*) There he lies on his face—dead! My Clara's brother! O, this is the blackest misfortune! Poor Hugh—poor boy! (*Starting*) And I am a *murderer!* 'Sh! Was that a noise? What shall I do? I'm lost, lost—irretrievably! That unlucky sham *quarrel* last night—the *will*, that makes him the heir instead of me—his death, which makes *me* the heir again—O, nothing will persuade the world it was an accident! I—I must cover that awful thing up. 'Sh! I *did* hear a noise! (*Flies into the thicket.*)

*Enter Millicent.*

*Milly* (*solus*)—O, I cannot sleep, I cannot rest! I never shall forget his reproachful look! All night a horrible presentiment—

*Enter Newsboy.*

*N. B.*—(*interrupting*)—*Yer's* your Weekly Freedom's Banner extry!—all about the suicide, mysterious dissappearance and bloody assassination of young Burnside, the gifted poet!——O'ny TWO cents!

*Mil*—O, horror!

*N. B.*—Extry, Miss? (*she takes it, hands coin—he, feeling in pocket for change*)—(*yelling*) *All* about the *sui*—

*Mil*—O, *dear*, don't! Never mind the change!

*N. B.*—(*swinging away as usual*)—*Yer's* your Weekly Freedom's Banner extry, red-hot from the press! All about the suicide, mysterious disappearance and bloody assassination of young B[urnside,] the gifted poet——O'ny *two* cents!

(*Exit*)

*Mill*—(*Glances at paper, lets it fall, staggers but recovers*)—O, not dead, not dead! It only says he has disappeared. But that hideous word—*mysteriously!* Weak, foolish creature, to obey my father! But *now!*—O, *now* I am adamant! I will never love another! O, never, never, never!

*Enter Charley, sneaking away—sees her, drops gun and shudders. She perceives him—*

*Mill*—O, Charley I'm so glad to see you. I'm in such trouble—such misery!

*Char*—(*Coming, picks up gun, and trying to regain composure.*) Poor Milly! (*taking her hand*)—what is it, child? Tell me—can't I help you?

*Mill*—O, Charley, something's happened to Hugh! (*He starts, gasps, drops her hand, quakes*)—There, I knew it would shock you, for you loved him. You *did* love him, *didn't* you, Charley?

*Char*—O, I *did!* I d— I d— I *do* love him!

*Mill*—O thank you, *thank* you for wording it so! You don't think he's dead, *do* you? *Say* he isn't dead.

*Char*—O, (*a trifle choked*) he c— he c— he *can't* be—dead! (*Groan*).

*Mill*—You can't think what a comfort it is to hear you say those words!—And the *way* you say them—the *emotion*—makes them all the more healing and precious.

*Char*—(*Aside*) Every word she says is a stab in my heart!—(*Aloud*) But—but—what makes you think that—that—something has hap——

*Mill*—(*Handing the paper and burying her face in her hands*) There—read it, read it—and O, tell me *again* there's nothing to fear.

*Char*—(*The paper quakes and shakes in his hands—he mumbles over the item. The paper shakes still more violently.*) (*Aside.*) Then he was missing in the *night!*—they've been searching for him—they will find him!—I am *lost!* (*Drops paper.*)

*Mill*—O, Charley, Charley, my heart is so torn, so wrung. But you will be my friend. You will comfort me; you will talk to me about him; you will stay my fainting hopes; you will tell me he is not lost, not dead.

*Char*—(*Taking her arm in his and walking with her*)—Trust in me—lean on me—believe in me. He will s— soon be found. (*With a gasp.*)

*Mill*—O, my whole heart (*Hugh as beggar thrusts out his head*) thanks you for these words. (*Exit—Mill beaming up into C's face.*)

*Hugh*—O, perfidious girl! So soon, so soon! (*Reels out and supports himself at wing, looking after them. Grinds a slow note or two on organ*).

*Enter Capt.* (*Aside*) (*Swabbing face.*)

*Capt*—Hang him, he was *right*-handed, after all! *Dern* a right-handed man! All that long tramp for nothing! (*Percives Hugh.*) (*Fastens his eagle eye on him.*)

*Hugh*—(*Aside, discovering Capt.*) There's old Wheeler! Well, I'm in no danger from *him.*—I've got to keep my tongue still before everybody but *detectives.* Anybody else would recognize my *voice* in a minute.

*Capt.*—(*Fastening his eagle eye on him—aside*)—There's the murderer, for a *million!* He's got the mark of Cain all over him.—(*Hugh forgets all about the Capt and flourishes his stick left-handed vengefully in the direction of the retreating couple*)—Left-handed, too, by the holy poker! Now would a detective go and nab him and put him on his guard? O, no! (*Smiling.*) He'd ask him questions that are miles away from the *real* subject and don't seem to mean anything in the world—but they're deep—deep as the sea! (*Aloud*). Ah—I say, friend, have you seen anything of an old yellow tom cat going along here with a blue velvet collar on? (*Aside.*) I've got my eye on him.

*Beg*—(*Hesitating—aside*) Now what can he be driving at?

*Capt.*—(*aside*)—Aha! that shot went home—he don't know what to say.

*Beg*—Well no, I don't remember seeing the animal.

*Capt.*—Ah—you don't. Well, maybe you didn't come from down yonder way (*pointing.*) (*Aside*) See the guilty devil hesitate!

*Beg*—The fact is, I *did* come from that direction in a kind of general way,—that is, a while ago, but—ah—

*Capt.*—But what?

*Beg*—I was in the *woods* before that.

*Capt.*—(*Aside*)—Oho-o-o! Burying the *body?* (*Aloud.*) Been in the woods long? (*aside*) *'Gad,* he's got an evil eye!

*Beg*—No, not very. Only long enough to take a little rest.

*Capt.*—Ah, I see.—To take a little *rest.* (*Aside*) Calls it *resting.* (*Shudders.*) (*Aloud*) *Alone?* (*Significantly.*)

*Beg.*—Well-a—not entirely.

*Capt.*—(*aside*)—B'George he's walking right into the trap!—(*Aloud*).—(*carelessly*)—*Friend* with you, perhaps?

*Beg*—Well not exactly what you might call a bosom *friend,* but—

*Capt.*—(*Aside*) I should *say* not! (*Aloud*)—You left him there? (*Watching him furtively.*)

*Beg*—(*cheerfully*) O, yes, I hadn't any further use for him.

*Capt.*—(*starting, in spite of himself—aside*)—The unfeeling butcher!

*Beg*—(*Aside*) Now what can he be trying to get through his head?

*Capt.*—Well-a, I s'pose he-a—didn't have any further use for *you?* (*Aside*) Now—now let him look sharp!

*Beg*—Why of *course* he hadn't!

*Capt.*—(*Stunned—aside*)——Caesar's ghost!———This is the most abandoned villain that walks the earth! B'George, how neatly I'm drawing him on! (*Aloud*) You-a, you left him *comfortable,* I s'pose?

*Beg*—Well he didn't *say* he wasn't.

*Capt.*—(*Aside*)—Poor devil, I judge he *didn't.* O, but this is a grisly scoundrel! This is the very worst face I've ever seen in all my detective experience. Now for an entire broadside! If I don't make him jump clean out of his skin, call me no detective. (*Aloud*)—Say, friend, there's been a poet *murdered* here, last night! (*Hugh gives a start, but looks pleased*).

*Capt.*—(*aside*)—Why damn him, he looks *pleased!*

*Hugh* (*aside*)—O this is noble! Why I'll be a *hero!*

*Capt.*—(*aside*)—Come, this stumps *me.*

*Hugh*—(*aside*)—What a theme for a poem! I'll be hanged if I turn up again for a *year!*

*Capt.*—Say, Trampy, you going to lay around this village long?

*Hugh*—Maybe, if it *pays.*

*Capt.*—Well, you'll saw stove-wood stuff for grub, hey?

*Hugh*—O, yes. That's my line. Hot grub required—and a napkin.

*Capt.*—All right! Come along—want you to saw a stick for a nephew o' mine. (*Aside.*) This is a *deep* devil; 'twon't do to hurry things with *him*. But if I can keep him around under my eye a couple of weeks so't I can *pump* him—(*Aloud*). Well—come along, come along!

*Tramp*—(*Is absorbed in making a calculation on his fingers. Capt. waits.*) How many times you want that stick sawed in two?

*Capt.*—(*Aside*) *That* stick! Well that's good! But no matter. (*Aloud.*)—*Three* times.

*Tramp*—(*reluctant*) Must be a *long* stick. How much of it will you want done per day?

*Capt.*—W-h-e-e-w!——*Why?*—how much time would you like to have on such a job?

*Tramp*—Well, more or less—according to size and hardness of the stick.

*Capt.*—All right. You fix it to suit yourself. There ain't no occasion to *rush* the job.

*Tramp*—What kind of timber is it?

*Capt.*—There's *several* kinds. There's oak, there's hickory, there's—

*Tramp*—(*interrupts with a negative gesture of the hand.*)—(*with wounded dignity*)—Sir, I have done nothing to deserve this affront.

*Capt.*—*Affront?*

*Tramp*—Sir, there are *grades* in tramps. I am not a *hard*-wood tramp.

*Capt.*—Good *land!* What *is* your line?

*Tramp*—I do the delicate kindlings for the *parlor* stove.

*Capt.*—(*Bowing to the ground*)—I *beg* your forgiveness. Parlor kindlings is your line—

*Tramp*—(*interrupting*) When I am in *adversity*.

*Capt.*—O!——What's your line when you're in *prosperity*?

*Tramp*—I uncurl shavings for the *drawing*-room stove.

*Capt.*—(*Contemplating him with stupefaction*)—At how *much*?

*Tramp*—A shaving a meal.

*Capt.*—(*Puzzled—aside*). Wages has gone up. Well I've *got* to have him, what*ever* his terms are.—(*Aloud*). (*With great deference—fearing to offend again.*) Are——are you in adversity *now*?

*Tramp*—Alas, yes.

*Capt.*—(*Pleased*). Well, would you be willing to tackle a *pine* stick—

*Tramp*—(*interrupting*) *Kind* of pine, if you please?

*Capt.*—White—thoroughly seasoned—soft as butter—

*Tramp*—(*interrupting*) *Thickness,* if you please?

*Capt.*—Just the thickness of a *yard*-stick.

*Tramp*—(*Nodding satisfaction*)—To be sawed in two, three times.——(*Pondering.*) To do it *right*——I shall require three weeks.

*Capt.*—Done! It's a bargain! Come along.——Well?——What are you waiting for *now*?

*Tramp*—How far is it?

*Capt.*—Not over a hundred yards from here.

*Tramp*—(*Ponders a while.*)—Could you get a *hack?*

*Capt.*—(*Has to support himself to keep from fainting.*) (*Pleadingly.*)—O *don't* require that. I'm poor—*I* can't afford such things, you know.

*Tramp*—(*Mournfully, shaking head*)—I have conceived a great liking for you, sir; I would do much to accommodate you; but I must take care of my strength.

*Capt.*—(*in despair—and going*) (*aside*)—O, I've got to lose him —got to lose this noble chance, after all. (*Aloud.*) (*Face brightening.*) Here!—get on my back!—I'll *carry* you!

(*Tramp rides him off, pick-a-back, grinding the organ.*)

*Exit both.*

CURTAIN

## ACT. 2

*Enter Detective Baxter. Puts finger to nose awhile; next taps forehead and lifts eyebrows in token that he has "got it"—going off, makes cautionary sign with hand and says* 'SH!

(*Exit.*)

*Enter Detective Billings. Goes through about the same pantomime.*

(*Exit.*)

*Enter Detective Bullet. Goes through same pantomime.*

(*Exit.*)

(*After a moment*)

*Enter Capt. Wheeler, followed by his wife, knitting, ("disguised") as a pigtailed old sailor fashion of 18th cent. green patch over eye. Goes through the same pantomime, with earnest solemnity. Exits the same way, his wife following. After a moment comes deeply musing back again, his wife following.*

I'm a drawing the toils closer and closer around that tramp, Jenny; it's been a pretty satisfactory 3 weeks' work. Gimme a year and I've got him, sure. If I do it, it'll give me the biggest name in America. It'll spread to England—it'll be put in books!

*Mrs. W.*—That's good. You feel pretty sure about this fellow, I reckon?

*Capt.*—More and more sure every day, honey! It's pretty tough to be pitted agin the three most celebrated detectives New York can turn out. But I'll show 'em I'm their match, and maybe even lay over 'em a grain.

*Mrs. W.*—I always said your day was a coming, Simon, ever since you took up the detective business 5 years ago. I said, let the folks laugh if they like to, *you*'ll show them, yet.

*Capt.*—I bet I will.

*Mrs. W.*—Have you told the reporters what your new theory is, and who you suspect?

*Simon W.*—No.

*Mrs. W.*—Why Simon! You've always done it before. I thought detectives always told the reporters everything they find out, first thing.

*Simon W.*—Yes, they *do*. It's a good thing in some ways. It keeps your name in print and makes your theory of a case look wise and fine, but sometimes I've thought it might be bad, for this reason; the feller you're after takes up the paper and reads your theory and your plan, and then dern him he goes and changes his *own* tactics, and there you are, up a stump. I've suggested that to detectives but I couldn't seem to make 'em see it.

*Mrs. W.*—Well, I won't say anything, because you know best. But it seems a great risk, chancing a bran-new way that's never been tried, and this case so important.

*Simon*—It's so, Jenny, but I don't want those city detectives to find out who I'm suspecting. I want to play a lone hand.—And you mark my words—I'm a going to take every trick, as sure as you're born. I'm a going to throw out a feeler, here and there, on some *other* folks, just to make sure, though it ain't hardly worth the trouble. 'Sh! Trot, Jenny, trot!—Somebody's a coming!

*Exit Jenny.*

*Enter Charley, (moves across stage tolerably fast, but absorbed. Capt. slips up behind him, bends to his ear)*—

*Capt.*—*You*'re the man!

*Char.*—*(Staggers so, the Capt has to catch and support him.)* *(Aside)*. It's that odious old [18] sham detective *(Aloud)* W-What do you mean?

*Capt.*—*(Watching him)* I mean—You're the man to give an old sailor a light for his pipe, for you've got a kind eye, so you have.[19]

*Char.*—O, with pleasure. *(Hand trembles so he knocks half the matches out of his box—passes one.)*

*Simon W.*—Thanks, shipmet. Goin' a fishin'? *(Capt. falls to studying and forgets Chas.)*

---

[18] Omitted in amanuensis copy.

[19] On the reverse of MS p. 92, Twain made the following notation concerning the Captain's role as "an old sailor": "Always, *except when he is alone with Jenny,* the Capt. must *play* sailor while in this costume. He must throw his quid into his hat and put it under his arm, hitch up his trousers with both fore-arms, trip himself up, doing it, like Toodles, &c." Toodles, a sailor, is the title character in a popular burlesque extravaganza of the 1860's. The piece was the chief attraction in the repertory of R. G. Marsh's Juvenile Comedians, who toured California and Nevada in the winter of 1863–64. Twain saw the company and *Toodles* in Carson City in January 1864; see his letter to the Virginia City *Territorial Enterprise* dated 13 January 1864 (*Mark Twain of the Enterprise,* ed. Henry Nash Smith [Berkeley, 1957], pp. 131–132).

*Chas.*—No. Going up here to——to——*every*body flocking up yonder—don't know *what* it's *about.* (*Going.*) (*Aside.*) What a sickening shock he gave me!

*Exit.*

*Capt.*—(*Still pondering—shakes head*). (*Aside*) No—startles too *natural—he* ain't the murderer. (*Aloud*)—Say-a—why he's *gone*!

*Enter Lem* (*walking fast, his eyes gazing straight ahead.*)

*Capt.*—(*takes him by sleeve, leads him solemnly to footlights—shouts in his ear*)—*You* done it!

*Lem, skips a couple of feet into the air and flies.*

*Exit.*

*Capt.*—(*thinks a moment—then solus*)—No, that's the skip [20] of *innocence. He* ain't the murderer.

*Enter Tom.* (*Walking briskly.*) (*Notebook in hand.*)

*Capt.*—(*Observing him till he reaches middle of stage.*) Ship ahoy!

*Tom*—Do you mean *me?*

*Capt.*—(*Beckons with finger and head—Tom comes down front to him. Capt. shades his mouth with his hand, bends over, roars in his ear*—). *You* done it!

*Tom*—(*Flops instantly down on his knees, puts up his clasped hands and falls to working his lips rapidly as if in prayer to the Capt.*)

*Capt.*—(*Aside.*)—(*Knowingly*) Emotion too *sudden*—too *natural. He* ain't the murderer. It's that *tramp.* I'm nearly dead *sure* of it, now. (*Aloud.*)—Get up!

*Tom*—(*Rising with quaking legs.*) O, please, Capt. Wheeler,—

*Capt.*—Hello! you *recognize* me?

*Tom*—Only your voice. The *disguise* is marvelous.

*Capt.*—Do you think so? You've got brains and appreciation. (*Glancing at disguise.*) I ruther thought it was considerable of a success.

*Tom*—(*Getting over his fright*). Well I should *think* so. You look as if you'd just arrived in a ship—(*aside*)—with Columbus! O,

---

[20] Above "skip" Twain wrote, "(spring)?"

dear, I must be mighty sweet on this old scoundrel—he suspects me. (*Aloud.*) Captain, can't you favor me with a little something in the newspaper line to-day?

*Capt.*—Well, not to-day I reckon, but I'll have something for you before long. I'm a working up this big case, you know.

*Tom*—O yes, the mysterious disappearance of—

*Capt.*—Disappearance your grandmother!—MURDER!

*Tom*—(*Quaking*)—*O*, yes, I'm afraid it's so.

*Capt.*—O, *yes. Murder*—that's what it is. Will you do *me* a favor?

*Tom*—(*Eagerly*)—A thousand of 'em—a *million,* Captain!

*Capt.*—(*aside.*) See what it is to be *rising* in the world! This duck has always poked *fun* at me *before;* but now't I've got a big swell case to work up, see him come to his milk.[21] (*Aloud*). I want to know the theories of them New York detectives.

*Tom*—With the greatest pleasure in the world but keep it to yourself, of course. (*Aside*) I'm in for it *now*—I'm *bound* to lose that item. (*Referring to note-book.*) (*Aloud*) They've told me everything. Detective Baxter's theory is that his *mother* killed him. In a fit of temporary insanity. (*Signs of satisfaction from the Capt.*) Significant facts: 1. She doesn't *sleep* well, since; [22] 2. Cries, talks to herself a good deal; 3. Goes often to his room and turns over his things, weeping—sure sign of guilty conscience and remorse; 4. Enters into no gaieties—seems to have no stomach for them—mighty black sign; 4½—Loves to handle his hat and pet it—still blacker sign; 5—Wanders frequently to the spot where his hat was found—blackest sign of all.[23]

*Capt.*—By George it's mighty neat! Good close reasoning! Baxter come honest by his reputation. There ain't no getting around it, that man's a rattling detective. Well, what's Billings's theory?

*Tom*—(*referring to note-book.*) Billings's theory is that it warn't the mother that did it, but the *sister.* (*Signs of satisfaction from Capt.*) He argues in this way. Hugh was a poet, she was jealous of

---

[21] Above "milk" Twain wrote "(perfect old *pie*)?"
[22] Amanuensis copy: nights.
[23] In the amanuensis copy the last two items are numbered 5 and 6.

his gift. It got to preying on her mind, and finally she'd got carried away and done the deed before she thought. Significant facts: 1. She mopes around and shuns company and excitement; 2. She plays mournful music all the time; 3. She doesn't drink coffee any more—pretends it keeps her awake; 4. Can't bear the sight of his hat—when Billings thrust it suddenly under her notice, once, she fainted; 5th and blackest sign of all—she has thrown up her Sunday School class.

*Capt.*—Beautiful case; clean and clear as glass; reads right off, like a book. I tell you that man's got an awful intellect. There ain't a detective in the books that lays over Billings. What's Bullet's theory?

*Tom*—Detective Bullet's idea is, that it warn't his mother or his sister that murdered him, but his *sweetheart*—(*Signs of satisfaction from Capt.*) Millicent Griswold, you know. Bullet argues that she refused him, then got sorry for it and went and hunted him up in the night and offered to make up; he scorned her, and she killed him on the spot. Significant facts: 1. She likes to *talk* about him—wants to talk about him all the time; 2. She lugs his photograph around—Bullet picked her pocket and found out; 3. Every night at 10.45 she eats a pickle; 4. She is always sighing, like a person with a secret murder on his soul. 5. She won't go near the spot where the hat was found. 6th and blackest sign of all, she has taken a class in Sunday School.

*Capt.*—By George it's wonderful! Don't talk to *me!* That man knows his business. They're the three greatest detectives that ever lived. I'm proud to be a detective, though I ain't much known yet. It's an honor to be in such company.

*Tom*—They're pretty celebrated. That great lost child case raised their reputation a good deal.

*Capt.*—You bet it did. Kept their names always in the papers. Chances like that don't come often in a lifetime. Pity it's so, but it *is* so—children are lost too seldom.

*Tom*—Yes, I've often thought of it. How long have they been on the track of this child?

*Capt.*—Seventeen years.

*Tom*—They'll find it, won't they?

*Capt.*—*It!* It ain't *it* any more, it's a *man,* now. *Certainly* they'll find him—you can bet all you're worth on that. What does Baxter think was the way this murder was done by the mother?

*Tom*—(*Note-book.*) Thinks it was done with a broad-axe with a short hickory handle.

*Capt.*—Is he looking for the axe?

*Tom*—Yes. He has collected 13, and is spying around for more.

*Capt.*—O, that man's got a head on him! But could she use as many as 13 axes on one son?

*Tom*—No, he's only hunting for the *right* one.

*Capt.*—O, yes, certainly. What about Billings's idea?

*Tom*—(*Note-book.*) Billings believes the sister killed him with a *stove*-lid. Took it from some other house to mislead detectives. He has made a large collection; so most all the cook stoves in town *smoke,* now?

*Capt.*—Billings is a shrewd one. What's Bullet's idea?

*Tom*—(*Note-book.*)—Bullet had the hat, examining it for two days, and he came to the conclusion that the sweetheart killed him with a *hymn* book.

*Capt.*—With a what?

*Tom*—A *hymn* book. He wouldn't tell me *why* he thought so, but said he had a deep theory that would astonish people when he'd got it thoroughly worked out.

*Capt.*—Bullet's a trump. Bullet's as keen as a weasel. Got more brains than old Webster.

*Tom*—Well, I must go. Can't you let me have *your* theory, Captain?

*Capt.*—Not yet, my boy, not yet awhile.—(*Tom going.*—*Capt calls after him.*) But say—don't you drop a word to anybody that I said it, but you mark what I'm telling you now—they're all mistaken—*I* know who killed that man!

*Tom*—(*aside.*) O lordy! I just *knew* it! (*Staggers toward exit. Is met by the entering crowd.*) I *bet* I've lost that item! (*He remains.*)

*Enter Mrs. Higgins followed by the Griswolds, Millicent, Clara and her mother, Chas, Lem, the 3 detectives and the tramp. Mrs. H. out of breath. The crowd crowd around her.*

*Mrs. H.* (*Sitting down.*) I'll tell you in a minute. I've run every jump of the way.

*Griswold*—What *is* this important news?

*Mrs. H.*—O dear, Mrs. Burnside, they've found the body!

(*Millicent screams, and throws herself in her mother's arms.*)

(*Clara and her mother scream and fall into each other's arms.*)

*Tom and Lem*—We're goners! (*They fall into each other's arms.*)

*Charley*—(*reels away and supports himself against something.*) I'm doomed!

*Baxter*—(*aside.*)—See that mother's agony—my theory's right for a hundred and fifty, *gold!*

*Billings*—(*aside*)—See that daughter's remorse—my theory's right, for a *thousand!*

*Bullet*—(*aside*)—Hear that blood-dyed sweetheart scream—my theory's right, for a *million!*

*Capt.*—(*aside*)—Look at that game-legged black-hearted cheerful devil! He's the murderer, for a *billion!*

*Mrs. H.*—Yes, they found the body in that thicket right where the woods begin. Just his own poor white clothes—every rag of 'em but the hat—and all soiled and sodden. Poor boy, poor lad.

*Tramp*—(*aside*).—It's delicious to be grieved for like this. (*Touches eyes with a rag.*)

*Mrs. H.*—Why it even makes this poor game-legged *tramp* cry. (*To Mrs. Burnside*)—There, there, poor thing, it's all for the best. (*Petting her*)—He's amongst the angels if ever a human cretur *was.*

*Mrs. B.*—(*Weeping*) O, but it's so hard to lose him, and he so young and gifted.

*Mrs. Griswold*—(*Weeping*) O a dear good noble heart he was.

*Clara*—(*Weeping*) O my precious, precious brother!

*Tramp*—(*Weeping*) (*Aside.*) O, I never half appreciated what I was!

*Capt.*—(*aside*) Now *look* at that bloody-minded crocodile!

*Tom*—Lem, now that they've found *him,* they'll never let up till they find *us.*

*Lem*—I know it, Tom, but *don't* let's talk about it. Say—we'll stand by each other, *won't* we?

*Tom*—(*Solemnly*) To the day of doom. Put it there!—(*extending hand.*) (*They solemnly shake, and both cry.*)

*Mrs. H.*—Those tears are a-doing you *honor*, boys, though as a general thing you're a pesky hard lot, if I *must* say it.

*Capt.*—(*aside*)—I can't *help* it! This scene fetches even *me*, hardened old detective as I am. (*Bawls out crying like a great calf, and keeps it up, with streaming eyes which he mops with his sleeve.*)

*Mrs. H.*—Poor old cretur, how he *do* take on.—(*Aside*) My land, why it's that old *foo*-foo!

(*The whole crowd, pretty much, are absorbed in crying, now.*)

*Enter Policeman Long.*

*Long*—(*to Mrs. Higgins*) Madam, I found the body and—and —if you wouldn't mind speaking to *her* (*indicating Mrs. Burnside*) about—

*Mrs. H.*—About *what?*

*Long*—Well, you know there was—a—certain sum—

*Mrs. H.*—You miserable *cretur!* Do you mean to say 't you've come here to worry that poor thing about that reward b-before—O I *wish* I was a man!

*Capt.*—(*taking Long by the ear and leading him off*)—Now mosey!—and if you chirp *once* about that money inside of ten days, I'll drown you like a *cat!*

*Long* (*threatens in dumb show, and*———

*Exit.*

*Capt.* (*resumes his weeping*)

*Mrs. H.* (*looking at Capt.*)—(*aside*). I declare to goodness I believe there *is* something good about that old thing! (*Returns to Mrs. Burnside and they talk.*)

*Chas.*—(*to Clara, who is passing near him.*)—O, Clara, won't you speak to me?

*Clara*—(*shrinking from him with some show of scorn.*)—Does your late conduct invite it?

*Char.*—Clara, if you only knew—

*Clara*—(*interrupting*) It is sufficient for me to know that through all this great trouble you have scarcely visited me.—

*Char.*—O it was not because—

*Clara*—I know and care nothing as to the becauses, I know the *fact.*

*Char.*—O, I worship you, and your words kill me! (*Eyes still down.*)

*Clara*—Is it worship to avoid me in [the] time of my desolation? —to avert your face when I have begged for one poor little word of encouragement?

*Char*—O, darling I *knew* you would never more—(*aside*)—What am I saying!

*Clara*—You *knew!*

*Char*—(*confusedly*)—I——thought——I——believed—that is, I mean I *feared* for—for the worst.

*Clara*—*Why?* Everybody *else* encouraged me. Only you—*you* who should have considered it a sacred *duty* to give me heart and courage, gave me neither! *More!*—wrung your distressed and impotent hands, and more needed heartening than the weakest woman of us *all!*

*Char*—O, Clara, Clara!

*Clara*—When I *told* you, the very day of the calamity, that the desperado who was to have been hanged that day at the county seat had escaped and—

*Char*—(*interrupting*) I *know* it, I *did* say he could not have committed it—

*Clara*—The idiot *detectives* said the same, and now, *now* the wretch is hundreds of leagues away and safe from justice!

*Char*—Have some pity!

*Clara*—Poor Hugh loved you. If you had been there in his bloody bed, and he here, would *he* have been coldly indifferent like you?—No—for (*scornfully*) there was something of the *man* in *him!* (*She moves on some steps and stops, patting her foot with indignation.*)

*Char*—(*aside*)—How can I go on living thro' horrors like this! Poor child, I would confess, this instant, but that it would *double* her calamity—and she cannot bear more than she *is* bearing.[24]

[24] Twain partially circled the last portion of this speech, from "I would confess" to the end and struck one line across the text, apparently intending to delete it. He did not complete the deletion in his usual thorough and heavily inked fashion, and the passage is retained in the amanuensis copy.

*Billings*—(*aside*)—Her heart's consuming with remorse!

*Tramp*—(*aside*)—Now what's the matter with *her,* I wonder?

*Capt*—(*aside*) Gad he's got his blood-thirsty eye on the *sister!* But *I'm* here!

*Lem*—(*moves to Clara*) (*humbly*)—If you would rest your suffering heart upon this——this-a——suffering heart—no, this ——this boiling—no, I mean—

*Clara*—(*impatiently*)—O *do* go away from me!

(*Lem retreats in dismay and crestfallen.*)

*Tom*—(*moves to Clara*)—(*Clasping his hands before him*)—If the devotion of a heart that——that-a——if the devotion of a life——of which——of which——that is, if the devotion, *any* devotion, that——that could, if serviceable, could be of service to one who-a ——who—

*Clara*—(*impatiently*)—*Don't* annoy [25] me!

(*Tom retreats, in dismay and crestfallen.*)

*Mr. and Mrs. Griswold pass near Char*—

*Mr. G.*—(*low to Char. scornfully*) I wish you *joy* of your new wealth!

*Char*—Sir!

*Mr. G.*—'Twas the quickest way to get it—and the *manliest!*

*Mrs. G.*—*Don't* talk to him so, poor fellow. His heart is breaking for it—anybody can see that. No court shall ever wring a word of evidence out of *me,* Charley.

*Mr. G.*—As far as *that* goes, you are safe from *me,* too—but let your conscience have full play—what there is left of it. (*Going*)

*Chas*—(*aside*) *What* had I done that I should be fated to fire that unfortunate shot!

*Millicent*—(*approaches Chas. and gives her hand, smiling through her tears*)—

*Tramp*—(*snuffling*) Heartless, heartless girl!—She might at least have waited till my poor murdered remains were in the tomb!

*Mill*—(*low voice*) Ah Charley, it is good to look into your face, it is so full of grief for my poor Hugh!

---

[25] Above "annoy" Twain wrote "?(bother)."

*Chas*—I would give the world to bring him back! The *world!*—the phrase is poor and weak!—I would *gladly* give my own *life!* (*aside*) How true that is!

*Mill*—You generous heart!—I had such a foolish dream last night—I dreamed I saw the murderer standing over him; and when he turned around, it was *you!*

*Chas* (*starts violently*)

*Mill*—(*simply*) Why what is the matter? Do dreams frighten *you*, a *man*? They don't frighten *me*. Good-bye—let your compassion still abide with me and your friendly affection not forsake me.

*Char*—Trust me—*always*. Good-bye. (*Shake hands*).

*Tramp*—(*aside*) O look at her! Would that the inquest was over, and my sore heart and my mangled corse at peace in the silent tomb! (*Weeps*) [26]

*Capt.*—(*aside*)—O, if *tears* is your style, *wait*—I'll wring 'em out of you like a *sponge!* [27]

*Mrs. Higgins*—(*supporting Mrs. Burnside.*) Come, dear, you must go take some rest. You're most broke down.

(*Mrs. Higgins and Mrs. Burnside move aside talking and weeping.*)

*Bullet*—(*to Tramp*)—Say—in tramping around this village, if you should run across a *hymn* book anywhere—a Plymouth Collection—

*Tramp*—(*interrupts with the signs and noises made by deaf mutes.*)

*Bullet*—O, I forgot the stupid fool's *dumb*.

*Capt*—(*in low voice to Tramp*)—You play deef and dumb on the whole camp, and you do it *successful*, too—but there's *two* you can't come it over, my boy. One of 'ems *me*, and if you should run acrost a considerable of a detective around here by the name of Capt. Wheeler, I'd advise you not to try it on *him*, nuther!

*Tramp*—(*low voice*) I know him, hang him—he's as sharp as a razor. (*Aside*) The transparent old muggins!

---

[26] This speech is omitted in the amanuensis copy.

[27] Attributed to the tramp in the amanuensis copy.

*Capt.*—(*turning away—aside*—)—He little thinks that I'm one and the same relentless being, and always on his track!

(*The Griswolds, the Burnsides, and Chas, have been moving slowly out conversing—the Tramp stumps after them now and exit. Tom and Lem, who have been busy with their note-books for some time, start, now.*)

*Tom*—(*mournfully.*)—Lost that item. But what's items to a doomed person!

*Lem*—It's just all up with *us, now.* Burnt *brandy* can't save us. Say—let's slide out of the country, Tom.

*Tom*—And just make suspicion *boom*? You're a *fool,* Lem.

*Lem*—You're an*other* and a *fighting* one.

*Tom*—I *am,* am I? You take that back, or I'll—

*Exit quarreling*

*Billings*—(*to Bullet*)—Going to be a fight!

*Bullet and Baxter*—Looks like it!

*Exit 3 detectives and Capt.*

(*Stage vacant.*)

*Enter Policeman Long, running. Long*—Who's making that row?

*Enter Newsboy.*

*Newsboy*—*Yer's* your red-hot Weekly Hallelujah extra! *All* about finding the body of—

*Huge Policeman Long*—(*to Newsboy*)—Here! didn't I order you not to yell so loud? (*seizing him.*)

*Boy*—Please, I was *trying* not to holler loud.

*Pol*—(*Whacking him over head with club.*)—Well you warn't succeeding—I *arrest* you—come along! (*Whack, whack, whack!*)

*Boy*—O, please, don't—I'll go peaceable!

*Pol*—(*Dragging him roughly by collar.*) I rather think you *will!* (*Whack!*) Who said (*Enter Capt.*) you *would*n't? (*Whack, whack, whack!*)

*Capt*—Hi!—belay that, you tun of rancid blubber! Let the boy go!

*Long*—(*Still holding boy*)—I've *arrested* him!

*Capt*—Don't *answer* a question till somebody *asks* you one. Let the boy go!

*Long*—By what authority to, do *you* order me?

*Capt*—(*Very simply*) (*no pow-wow*) By the authority that's vested in every man that *is* a man, to protect a weakling that's in trouble.——Let him *go*.

*Long*—(*angrily*)—(*with threatening finger*)—I'll make you a mighty sick *man* first you know.

*Capt.*—(*Plaintively*)—*Must* I proceed to violence? (*Brushing away a tear and turning up his cuffs.*)

*Long*—(*Reaching his hand to his revolver*). If you come near me to interfere with my official business I'll put a bullet thro' you.

*Capt*—(*Approaching—keeping his eye on him*).—(*Pol. draws the pistol*)—I don't scare worth a dern—(*pistol raised*)—(*Capt. instantly snatches his wrist and turns pistol upward—it goes off in the air—Capt. wrenches the pistol away and throws it aside.*)—Go 'long, boy—yell all you want to—it's a free country!

*Boy*—(*Going*) *Yer's* your day before yesterday's papers, cool and nice from the press! All about how a bold policeman 'rested an infant and let him go again out of the *pu-u-u*-rest unselfish generosi-tee! *On'y* 2 cents!

*Exit*

*Capt*—(*Moving toward front, beckoning with finger for officer to follow.*) Say—what did you bat that boy over the head for?

*Long*—(*Moodily*)—*City* cops always do it.

*Capt*—When a prisoner ain't resisting?

*Long*—*Any* time.

*Capt*—Looky-here. 'Tain't right. 'Tain't right.

*Long*—(*Moodily*)—Well what you going to *do* about it?

*Capt*—(*impressively*) I'm a sweet disposition, and slow to wrath; but if you do it again I'll *bile* you. I'll bile you in biling *oil*, same as they did the prophet Deuteronomy. Now *mosey!*

*Long*—(*Moodily*) You better let me *alone*, Si Wheeler,—that's all. (*Going.*)

*Capt.*—(*pointing to pistol*) Say—you've forgot that. (*Policeman picks up pistol.*) You might want it to arrest a sick *girl* with.

*Long*—(*Going*)—All right—a time will come.

*Capt*—'Sh! Take a walk!

*Exit officer.*

*Enter Baxter.*

Baxter (*takes Capt. by lapel, leads him mysteriously down to foot-lights, glances over shoulder several times to see if anybody is near—puts finger to lips—bends to Capt's ear—*) 'Sh!——I can make it worth your while, old man, if you can tell me anything about the character and habits of that Mrs. Burnside when she was an infant—'Sh!—and what sort of a person her grandmother on her father's side was. 'Sh!—and whether her father's grandfather had warts or not!—'Sh!—These are important matters to know just at the present time. Come—tell me. 'Sh! speak low.

*Capt*—(*In a huge voice inquiringly*)—Ho-hasha, wan-wanka no-kami hi-hoppy no-swotty k'swosh? (*Imitate a sheep or guinea-fowl, or rooster.*)[28]

*Baxter*—(*standing off in dismay.*)—WHAT?

*Capt*—(*Repeats it, with zealous and eager interest.*)

*Baxter*—(*Puts hand on head as if stunned*) Good gracious——what——what country man are you?

*Capt*—(*Getting close up and talking with great interest*)—K'whoopy so-longy kwongsocky moosucksum ho-qua-a-h? *Hey?* Miaw-wow! (*cat.*)

*Baxter*—(*irritated*) Hang such a jibberish! Don't you know a *word* of English?

*Capt*—(*following him up and emphasizing with gestures*)—Barka barka so-waukee chow-sht! chow-*ow!* Yowrk! (*Dog that has got a kick.*)

*Baxter*—(*still retreating—puts fingers in ears.*) There, there, don't please, *don't!*

*Capt*—(*following him to the wing*)—Soop-hocky wonkawong tsum!—slop-swoshrum, r-r-r-r-asho! Korow-korow-ow whoosha! Sab-beldoomer-bumborooker muckarora (*imitating jackass*) waukee! waukee! waukee! waukee! (*jackass.*)

(*Exit Baxter.*)

*Capt*—(*solus*)—O no! I reckon I didn't learn Choctaw for nothing. Much information *he* got!

*Enter Billings.*

---

[28] Along the margin Twain wrote, "All through these speeches Capt. interlards cries of bird and beast."

*Billings*—(*takes Capt down to footlights mysteriously, finger on lip.*) 'Sh! (*looking furtively over shoulder*). Old man, I can make it worth your while to tell me what you know about that young Miss Burnside's antecedents. 'Sh! Not *loud.*

*Capt*—(*feigning idiotcy*) Eh?

*Billings*—'Sh! When she was a child did she stuff her dolls with *rags*, or *sawdust*? 'Sh! Be careful—think—for this is of the last importance in the present circumstances.

*Capt*—Eh?

*Billings*—(*aside*) Confound the old idiot! (*Aloud*) Come—jog your faculties! Wake up!—Did she——did she as a child use chewing gum?

*Capt*—Eh?

*Billings*—(*Aside*) Perfect flat-head! (*Aloud*) O stir up your brains—just this once! Answer me *one* question. Did her ancestors eat cold *pie* for breakfast? Come, *try* now. *Do.*

*Capt*—Eh?

Billings—(*Going*) What a disappointment! And I promised myself so much—(*moving toward wing—Capt humbly and stupidly following*)—(*turning*) Say—do you know *any*thing at all? Can't *any*thing stir you out of your stupor? If I were to tell you Gen. Grant had shot the queen of England or burned Paris down do you think you could manage to be startled by it?

*Capt*—(*stupidly*)—Gen. Grant?

*Billings*—Come, this is an improvement—Yes—Gen. Grant.

*Capt*—(*in reverie*) Grant——Grant——*Genl* Grant——I can't remember hearing the name before.

*Billings*—Well this beats my tune! Maybe you've never heard of Queen *Victoria?*

*Capt*—Victoria——Victoria——no, I don't seem to remember hearing the name before.

*Billings*—My soul! Nor the Emperor *Napoleon,*[29] I suppose?

*Capt*—Napoleon——(*gently shaking head*)—Napo—

*Billings*—(*impetuously and coming toward Capt.*)—Look here, you in*cred*ible ignor*amus*, did you ever hear of *Adam!*

---

[29] Amanuensis copy: Emperor of Napoleon.

*Capt*—Adam?——Adam?—a—a——What was his *other* name?

*Billings*—(*dumb show of giving it up.*)

*Exit*

*Capt*—(*solus*)—*He* didn't make more'n about *four* times, I reckon!

*Enter Bullet*

*Bullet*—'Sh! Old man, (*leading him down, finger on lip*) I can make it worth your while to give me a little information about—

*Capt*—(*hand to ear, pretending deafness*) A little louder, please.

*Bullet*—(*raising voice a little*)—I want to find out something about—

*Capt*—A *little* louder, please.

*Bullet*—(*still louder*) About that young lady, Miss—

*Capt*—Eh?

*Bullet*—(*shouting in his ear*) Something about the early life of Miss Millicent *Griz'ld!*

*Capt*—Ah? *Who's* mizzled?

*Bullet*—(*aside*)—Deaf as an adder! (*Shouting*) As a child did she eat oatmeal, or milk, or was she fed *meat?*

*Capt*—Dead *beat?* You're another!

*Bullet*—(*shouting*) No, you don't understand. I mean did this *girl*—did she eat hearty—as a *child?*

*Capt*—O, I see! I didn't under*stand.* It *is* pretty *mild.* Going to have rain, I think.

*Bullet*—(*aside*) O, this is up-hill work.—(*Shouting*). Did they stupefy her intellect in unventilated rooms?—did they smother her with air-tight (*this very loud*) *fires and coal gas?*

*Capt*—(*injured*)—*Me* a tiresome old ass?—What do you think of your*self?*

*Bullet*—(*shouting*) *Can't* you tell me—

*Capt*—Louder, please.

*Bullet*—(*shouting louder*) Just *any* little information—

*Capt*—Eh?

*Bullet*—*Any* little trifle—

*Capt*—(*hand still to ear*)—Eh?

*Bullet*—(*puts his mouth to Capt's ear, shades it with both hands —and yells*)—Go to the *devil!* (*Going.*)

*Capt*—O yes, my head *is* pretty level. (*Aside*). Too level for *you.*

*Exit Bullet disgusted.*

*Capt*—(*solus*) Now he can take *his* change.——Hullo, here it's *night,* and that tramp's given me the slip. I got to go and *shadder him.*

(*Exit.*)

*Enter Lem and Tom, rolling a powder-keg.*

*Lem*—Tom it's an *awful* thing to do. Suppose we get found out?

*Tom*—(*impressively*) Lem, we've *got* to scare old Wheeler out of this camp, or—(*dumb show of being hanged*)

*Lem*—O *don't,* Tom, it gives me the cold shivers.

*Tom*—Lem, I tell you that old fool's an *awful* detective. I never imagined it—*nobody* did. But as sure as you're born he's on our track.—Night and *day!*

*Lem*—I know it, O lordy I know it, Tom!

*Tom*—He took me all of a sudden and says he, *You* done it!

*Lem*—So he did *me!*

*Tom*—No, *did* he though?

*Lem*—I wish I may die if he didn't.

*Tom*—By George! We're *goners,* Lem!—(*Impressively*) Lem, when he said that, my heart skipped up into my mouth so't if I hadn't snatched my teeth together (*illustrating*)—I'd a *lost* it!

*Lem*—O, Tom, when he said it to me my heels—O I just *vanished,* disap*peared*—fst! (*Snaps fingers*) as if I'd been shot in the back with a keg of nails!

*Tom*—(*Thoughtfully*) Lem, dog'd if I don't believe it would be better, and *surer,* to blow *him* up.—No—no, that wouldn't do. That would be *murder.*

*Lem*—Tom we got murders enough on our hands *now* with that pelican we *did* do for. Poor Hugh!

*Tom*—Well, we can't fetch him back, Lem. (*Thoughtfully*) Where do you reckon he is?

*Lem*—O, they *say* he's in heaven. They say that about *all* dead people *I* ever struck.

*Tom*—Yes, that's so. I wish *I* was there.

*Lem*—(*Plaintively.*) Don't I wish *I* was. No more trouble, no more disappointed love, no more 'Sociated Press—

*Tom*—No more nightmare, no more crime, no more local items—

*Lem*—(*Doggedly*) What's the *use*? *We* ain't ever going to get there after what we've done. Tom, let's not *think* about it. It's too kind of *dismal.*

*Tom*—*I*'m agreed. Let's get at *this* business. Ain't you afraid Mrs. Wheeler is at home?

*Lem*—She? Why she's never home nights, now; has to help 'em at her son-in-law's—perfect *hospital* there.

*Tom*—S'pose old *Wheeler* was to come around?

*Lem*—Shucks, he's always *detecting* till midnight. But if you're willing to give it up, I bet you *I* am.

*Tom*—But I *ain't.* If we can scare him so he'll leave this camp, we'll stand some show. Otherwise—(*dumb show of hanging*)

*Lem*—*Don't* do that, Tom! Hain't you got any feeling?

*Tom*—(*Putting the powder-keg against front door of cottage*). All right—light the *slow*-matches.

*Lem*—(*strikes a match and tries to hold the ends of two long slow-matches in the flame, but he quakes all over and can't manage it.*)—Say, Tom, we don't want *two,* do we?

*Tom*—O yes, better have two—one might go out.

*Lem*—(*still quaking, can't light them.*)

*Tom*—(*taking the slow-matches*)—Here! You've got the buck *ague!*

*Lem*—Buck ague, you sap-head! I done it a-*purpose!*

*Tom*—(*thrusts the lighted slow-matches into the keg, one on each side*) (*angrily*)—*Who*'s a sap-head?

*Lem*—(*Firing up*) *You* are!

*Tom*—I'll *brain* you! (*Kicks Lem behind*)

*Lem*—(*they light into each other with their fists and go fighting off the stage exclaiming*)—O you will, will you!

*Tom*—Call me a sap-head, will you! (*Blow.*)

*Lem*—THERE! (*Blow.*)
*Tom*—Aha, take that! (*Blow.*)
*Lem*—*Like* it? (*Blow*)
*Tom*—Darn you! (*Blow*)
etc., etc.

*Exit.*

*Enter Capt.*

*Capt.*—Hello, what's *this?* Some kind of a *kag.* (*Sits down on it.*) Why lemme *see*——I reckon it's *soap*—or *bluing,* or saleratus or something my Jenny's ordered. Why *she* knows I moved out of here last *night.* I reckon tain't *her* fault, it's that *grocer's.* He can't ever get anything right. (*Proceeds to load his pipe.*) Consound that *tramp!* (*smells something—sniffs*)—something *burning* around here som'ers. I lay if I get my hands on him he won't gimme the slip *again.* But laws-a-bless you *he* (*sniff, sniff, sniff*) I wonder what *is* that? *He* ain't a-going to give *me* the slip! Might as well try to give the *sun* the slip! (*sniff*) Why on'y let him *try* it! (*Putting out hand*)—Dark or daylight—don't make no difference (*sniff, sniff*) to a simon pure detective—just go *any* time, straight as a bee-line, lay my hand on him; says I, "Young *man*"—(*sniff, sniff.*) (*Looking about*)—Lay my hand on him, and says I, "Young *man*"—(*his eye slowly follows a wreath of smoke*)—I think I got a clew!—(*along down to where it issues from one of the slow-matches. His face lights up with pleasure.—Lifts his hand with a wave*)—I done it like a born *detective!*—(*Glances at keg*)—Look here!—*this* ain't no saleratus!—excuse *me,* it's *powder!* (*Deliberately removes the slow-match and holds it before him*)—Aha! *now* stink at your *leisure!* Well, now, (*deeply studying*)——What's this *for? That's* what your true detective always asks, What's a thing *for?* A detective knows that there's always a *meaning* about things. Yes, sir—even as little a thing as a kag of powder and a *slow*-match reposing around a man's front *door*'s got a *meaning* about it—*som'*ers. Question is—lemme *see*——(*deep study—nodding head—lights his pipe with the slow match and throws it down—shakes head, nods it, etc.*)

(*Enter Lem and Tom at the wing*)

(*They fall into each other's arms in dismay.*)

*Tom*—(*Gasping*)—O Lem, *yell* at him! *I* can't get my *breath!*

*Lem*—(*Gasping*) Neither can *I*. O Tom we're in for *another* murder!

*Tom*—Let's run around behind and throw a *stone* at him.

*Lem*—'Greed!—What a head you've got!

*Exit both.*

*Capt*—Oho! *now* I see it! It's that *tramp!* (*Laughing to kill, at the idea.*) Sharp scoundrel—he twigs that I suspect him! He—he—(*can't talk for laughing*)—he thinks I'm living here *yet!* (*Laughing*) Was going to blow the old man up! (*Laugh*) He—he—(*laughing*)—he *could* a blowed an *ord*'nery man sky *high,* but a detective—(*picks slow-match up from floor, holds it aloft, suffocating with laughter as curtain slowly descends and the other slow-match sizzles furiously*)—

CURTAIN.

(*A tremendous explosion. Curtain rises showing wreck of house and the old man sitting on floor at some distance, face all black with powder, rubbing back of his head ruefully.*)

*Capt*—It's mighty lucky that stone made me skip out of that when I *did,* or we'd a been a detective *short!*

CURTAIN.

## THIRD ACT

*Enter Charles* (*expectantly*) [30]

*Chas.*—(*solus*) Not *here!* I am sure it was she I saw (*glancing off*)—If she would only speak one single kind word to me!——(*Looking off.*) *There* she is. *I* have committed no crime! Is a man so constructed that the mere *concealing* of such an act makes him feel like a criminal.

---

[30] The third act begins about halfway down MS p. 170; in the blank space above, Twain wrote two notes. One, subsequently deleted reads, "Tramp has crutches and a short leg." The other remains as an unresolved speculation about the stage setting: "Front scene? To slide back by and by and expose Justice's office?"

*Enter Clara.*

*(Musing—she is in mourning. She passes along, with head down —Chas stands with his head humbly ducked, observing. She does not see him till she is against him—draws her skirts aside in scorn as if escaping contact with a reptile, gives him a crushing look and passes on—halts with her back to him—he puts up his hands pleadingly hoping she is going to speak—she) (aside)*—I *hate* him! ——I *despise* him!——O, I *wish* I didn't *love* him! *(goes sobbing away)*

*Exit.*

*Chas*—*(solus)*—Not one word!—It is enough to break a *dog's* heart!——*(Walking up and down in a state of mind)*—It is misery to stay in this village——to leave would rouse suspicion ——what *can* I do?—what *ought* I to do?——

*Enter Baxter*

*(Carrying arm full of broadaxes—drops one—picks it up—drops another—picks it up, drops 3—picks them up)*—

*Exit.*

*Enter Millicent and her parents. The parents pass close to Chas.*

*Mr. G.*—*(low voice)*—You are going?

*Chas*—Yes, I—I—am on my way there.

*Mr. G.*—*(sarcastically.)* Necess*arily*. Relationship—and other circumstances—make you one of the chief mourners.

*Mrs. G.*—*(low voice)* Horace, you are *cruel!*

*(They turn aside conversing acrimoniously, leaving Mill and Chas together.)*

*(Hand-organ heard.—Enter Tramp.)*

*Tramp*—*(aside)* At it again! Heartless girl! Within one short hour of my *funeral! (much affected.)* Nothing can touch that icy heart. *(Grinds a bar on the organ.)* Alas! music cannot interpret what *I* feel!

*Mr. G.*—*(to his wife)*—Damn that organ!

*Mrs. G.*—'Sh! *Don't* use such language!

*Tramp*—*(aside)* I must tear myself away from this harrowing sight. I will strike a mournful strain—possibly *it* may touch her. *(Grinds a bar.)*

*Enter Bullet. (Carrying a pile of hymn books that reaches up to his chin—walks slow—funereally—and very carefully—hitching this way and that to keep books from falling.)*

*Tramp—(unconsciously drops into his wake and keeps step with him across stage, grinding very slow music.)*

*Exit Bullet.*

*Tramp—(aside)* I cannot go—the hateful sight holds me with its baleful spell, while it sears my eye-balls. *(Ranges up near Chas and Mill, unknown to them.)*

*Mill—(takes Chas's hand)*

*Tramp—(Dumb show of grief)—*

*Mill*—Poor Clara, I saw her on her way there a moment ago—her heart is broken.

*Tramp—(Weeps.)*

*Chas*—Poor child—poor Hugh!

*Tramp—(Scowls.)*

*Mill*—Everybody is bringing flowers—the whole region round about will be at his funeral.

*Tramp—(Thumb in arm-hole—smiles—dumb show of flattered vanity and exultation.)*

*Chas—You* bear up well, under the blow, Milly.

*Tramp—(aside)*—Don't she, though!

*Milly*—The others weep—I do not.

*Tramp—(aside)—(Weeping)*—I don't wish to live!—I'm *glad* I'm murdered! *(Rocking in agony.)*

*Milly*—There is that within me which sustains me—

*Enter Billings carrying great pile of stove lids very carefully.*

*Milly*—Tears are not for me—but *joy!*

*Tramp—(aside—sobbing and rocking himself)*—Monster!

*Mill*—Joy that I *loved* him, *alive—*

*Tramp—(starting)* Eh!

*Mill*—Joy that I love him *still,* now that he is *gone*—joy that I shall love his dear *memory* forever!

*Tramp—(aside—reeling, sinks to the earth.)*—This is bliss!

*Billings—(stumbles over Tramp and spills stove lids around. —While he gathers them up and)*

*Exits*

*Milly, Chas and the Gibsons*[31] *crowd around the tramp.)*

*Enter Mrs. Hig. Tom and Lem, the Newsboy and the big Policeman and crowd around also—(the males with long crape scarf on the arm.)*

*Mill—(bending over Tramp)*—Poor fellow, are you hurt?

*Tramp—(Makes signs and utters deaf and dumb noises.)*

*Mrs. Hig*—Laws, it's that poor deef and dumb Tramp—there ain't a bit of harm in him, Miss.

*Mill—Poor out*cast,—and to be so afflicted!—Isn't there anyone that knows the deaf and dumb signs?

*Chas*—Yes, I know them.

*Tramp—(aside), (with apprehension)* I wish *I* did! I wasn't expecting this.

*Mill*—Please ask him where his *home* is.

*Chas—(makes the graceful mute signs.)*

*Tramp—(Proceeds to make absurd signs and say "Goo-goo" etc.) (Aside.)* George I've got him *stumped!*

*Mill*—What does he say?

*Chas—(Puzzled)* Well somehow his signs are so peculiar that I—a—I—

*Mill*—Try again. Ask him if he has no friends—none to care for him.

*Tramp—(aside.)* Bless her heart!

*Chas—(signs)*

*Tramp—(extravagant signs and noises).*

*Mill*—What does he say?

*Chas—(Scratching head in shame and perplexity)* Well, *I* never saw such inhuman signs! Either I know the sign-language and *he* doesn't, or he knows it and *I* don't.

*Mill*—It seems strange. How can you account for it?

*Chas*—It's clear beyond *me.*

*Mrs. Hig*—Why bless your heart, I reckon he's a poor misable *foreigner.* Likely they're *Dutch* signs. Dutch *words* do work a Christian's *jaw* turrible, so I reckon it works a body's *arms* considable to do 'em *that* way.

---

[31] I.e., Griswolds. Twain made a similar mistake earlier in the manuscript but corrected himself.

*Mill*—Perhaps there *is* something in that.

*Mrs. Hig*—Like enough he tried to do 'em with his legs, and *crippled* hisself.

*Chas*—*I* thought the *sign*-language was uni*ver*sal. There *can* be no universal language *but* it. And it is so beautiful, so simple, so clear, and it so compacts and compresses ideas. It is unspoken *short*-hand. It has been my dream that some day in the future a man might traverse the whole broad earth conversing with ease with all he met, Christian and savage, learnéd and ignorant, in this dumb marvelous tongue! But now my noble dream is dead! (*Sadly.*)

*Tramp*—(*aside*)—Aha! Score one for the undersigned!

*Mill*—Well there *is* one sign that is universal—the symbol of compassion. (*Puts a coin in the tramp's hand.*)

*Tramp*—(*Kisses the coin—kisses the hem of her dress—aside*)—Bliss! Perfect bliss! (*Signs and "Goo-goo" of gratitude.*)

*Mill*—There, Charles, my *ignorance* has shamed your *learning*.

(*Tramp gets up.*)

(*Bell tolls*)

*Mr. G.*—Come, daughter—there is the bell.

*Mrs. G.*—Yes, come. (*The crowd going.*)

*Lem*—Tom, the old man's around, all right, this morning. I'm so *miser*able!

*Tom*—O Lem, he don't scare worth a *cent*. I think I'm just gradually *dying*. I feel as if he's creeping in my tracks all the *time*.

(*Exit crowd—Tramp follows, grinding organ briskly in contrast with tolling bell.*)

*Enter Capt. elaborately gotten up as a negro—Jenny following, knitting.*

*Capt.*—Hang him, I can't seem to light on him, somehow. I was most sure I heard that hurdy-gurdy—didn't *you*, Jenny?

*Jenny*—I heard *something*, but I'm so near-sighted I never can hear a noise 'thout I happen to be *listening* for it.

*Capt.*—Well I think I heard it. We'll rest a bit, anyway, and see if he don't come along. Like enough he'll lay for the funeral procession and *levy* on 'em. I'll just run over my theory a little, in my head.—(*Walks—stands—shakes head—puts finger beside nose*

*—laughs—starts—frowns—scratches—traces figures on floor, inspects them wisely—etc., etc., etc., like a man thinking out a problem. His wife sits by, gloats on him admiringly, unconsciously nods her head, pleased, when he does, looks sad when he shows perplexity, etc.—Finally she says)—*

*Jenny*—(*simply and admiringly*) Husband, you do go through the motions as elegant as any detective I ever saw.

*Capt.*—Yes Jenny, and it's a big part of the business, too, to do it right.—I mean when there's people looking at you. Ah, when a detective's under the public eye, it's *beautiful* to see him go through the motions—*beautiful!* Why Jenny dear, you watch a detective, and you can follow his line of thought right straight through, just the same as a deef and dumb scholar can foller his teacher's meaning when he stands on the school platform making *signs*. Now here—I'll do the head-shakes and nods, and so on, and I'll give you the *language* of each one as I *make* it—now you just imagine that the biggest and bulliest detective in New York or Chicago is before you:——(*long impressive pause*). *Now*—(*tapping forehead*) the great detective brain begins to work;——the clew——is obscure——but never mind that.——Did the burglar enter the *house?* ——(*long impressive pause, finger on face somewhere*)——or did the house enter the *burglar?*—A deep, difficult question there—requires thought——Ah those villagers are observing me!——the clew grows clearer——Ah, I see!!——No (*shake head*)——No—(*shake*)——Ah (*smiling,*) so you thought you'd con*fuse* me, did you——shrewd, shrewd burglar?—Ex*cuse* me.——HULLO!—*Is* it? ——It *is!!!*——Of *course!!!*——But wait——wait——(*nose in the air, eyes nearly closed, thinking for a minute, forefinger of right hand resting on little finger of left*)——*would* he, *would* he break through the jewelry store to get at the blacksmith shop——to get at the blacksmith shop and steal an anvil?——'m——'m——'m ——(*slowly working head up and down.*) Now the jewelry store *was* broken open——the *black*smith shop was broken open——but there the *clew* fails——*I* maintain that he stole an anvil——the blacksmith contends that he *had* but one anvil and he's got it YET. ——But shall we value this man's mere low *fact* above intellectual demons*tra*tion?——Ah-h-h!——(*slaps thigh vigorously, then covers forehead clear across with the same hand*)——he *did* steal the *anvil,* he found it wasn't the size he wanted, and he took it back!—Clear as DAY! (*Walking the floor rapidly, excitedly, slapping himself on top of head with his hand*)——I'GEORGE! When I've finished working up this case it'll be worthy a chapter in one of Allan Pinkerton's great detective books!——The villagers still observe me with admiration—(*suddenly casts eye on ground, slowly follows a sinuous imaginary track here and there—then springs away like a hound on the scent and*)

*Exit*

*Capt—Re-enters at once.*

*Capt—There,* old girl, I'll bet a doughnut Allan *Pinkerton* couldn't do it better, him*self.*

Jenny—(*Kisses the hem of his garment, unknown to him*)—Simon, Simon, you were *born* for this very business, and I do believe you'll see the day that your name'll lead the detective list of this whole [32] *country.*

*Capt.*—I hope it's so, Jenny, I hope it's so for *your* sake as much as mine; for you've helped to make me what I am. You've stood by me like a *man* when everybody else turned up their noses and said I was a maundering old fool; you've put up with my five long years of *failures,* just as sweet and patient, and never dropped a word that hurt; a word that *hurt!*—bless your heart you've always rose up after every failure and said "Pick your flint and try it *again!*" (*Kissing her*). A man that couldn't succeed with such a wife to hold up his hands *ain't* a man! I wouldn't swap wives with the King of *Sheba!* ——and that's the word with the *bark* on it!

*Jenny*—Simon, (*a tear*) a body couldn't *help* but love you——and how anybody can try to dis*cour*age you is more than I can make out. You go right along with your appointed *work*—you've had a *call* to it if ever a man had, in this world; and you've got the *capital* for the business right there—(*reverently touching his forehead*)—*loads* of it!

*Capt*—(*Patting her head*) Thank you *hearty,* Jenny.

*Jenny*—Si, haven't you got the new theory fixed up, now, so you can tell me about it?

*Capt*—Yes, I think I've got it all mapped out, now, satisfactory.

---

[32] Omitted in the amanuensis copy.

The way I put it up is *this*. Hugh started out that night, to commit suicide—I see him buy the stuff myself. Well, he got to thinking things over, and his heart failed him and he concluded he *wouldn't*. Well, there's the pison left on his *hands*. "Throw it away?" says he. "No. No economy in *that*. What [to] do with it, then? What's the most *natural* thing for him to do with it, Jenny?

*Jenny*—Trade it back to the drug store for *hair* oil or something.

*Capt.*—(*smiling knowingly*)—Wide of the mark. Though it's what the unprofessional w[d] say. Guess agin, Jenny.

*Jenny*—(*Brightening*)—Feed it to the *cat?*

*Capt*—Try it again, lass. You're down on the un-detective levels yet.

*Jenny*—(*Simply*)—It *strains* me so to work my mind—*you* tell me, Simon.

*Capt.*—Well, I will. He'd given up killing him*self*. Very well. The detective instinct knows that the most natural thing for him to do with that truck *then,* was for him to conclude to go and kill somebody *else* with it.

*Jenny*—My *land!*

*Capt.*—That's about the *size* of it. Next comes the question, *who?* The detective mind says, the person he'd be most *un*likely to go for—in a *hos*tyle way. That's—who? Why his *mother,* 'course!

*Jenny*—Save us and sanctify us!

*Capt.*—His mother was the very party he had his eye on, Jenny.

*Jenny*—Detecting *is* the most wonderful thing in this world!

*Capt*—You'd say that and *more* if you'd had *my* experience, Jenny. Very well. He was a-going for his mother, when unfortunately he meets this tramp. Well, the tramp demands *money*—or Sunday School books or something—you can't ever tell what a *tramp*'ll want. *Some* have been known to ask for *work*—but (*absently*) they're *dead,* now. Hugh *declined*—maybe rather *rough*. Then what does this tramp do?—mind you, he's a deep, cunning tramp, this fellow, Jenny—what would he do? Take out his knife and run the resk of Hugh skipping into the bush and getting away? *Scasely*. Not that kind of a *spoon*. *No* sir—says he to Hugh, says he, "Let me favor you with a *mel*ody"—and don't you see, he's *got* him! 'Course *Hugh's* unsus*pect*in', you know—the tramp he fastens his eye on him—commences to grind—(*motion of grinding an organ*)—and grind—and grind out that same old stupefying, suffocating, soul-blistering tune—when—

(*Hand-organ heard*)

Hark!—fly, Jenny, fly! Here he comes!

*Exit Jenny.*

*Enter Tramp.*

(*To all but Jenny the Capt. talks nigger talk, and must do it well or ill as shall be funniest or most effective.*)

*Tramp*—(*aside*)—(*Snuffling*)—There warn't a dry eye in the *house.* I wouldn't missed my funeral for a *gold* mine. I never, never heard such a moving sermon in my life.——Ah, it's a big day for me—a mighty big day. (*Thoughtfully*) I'll never forget my funeral, till I have *another.* How they cried! How *she* cried! Darling! *Such* a sermon! Why I never *begun* to imagine I had so many virtues!—I didn't know there was *half* so much *to* me! I knew I was pretty so-so, but I hadn't any idea of the *mag*nitude of it. I didn't know I was so universally respected and looked up to. And my *talents*—I didn't begin to appreciate myself in this life. That old poem of mine *fetched* them!—About the crippled cat and the bar of soap. Well it *is* pathetic! Hang'd if I mean to come alive till I read my *tomb*-stone! [33] I bet it'll crack me up till I wouldn't swap graves with Shakespeare! And then they'll all be *committed!* They can't go back on the record! (*Aloud*)—Hello!

*Capt*—Hello you *own* seff, Trampy!

*Tramp*—(*aside*) It's that old *fool* again! What a disguise!—

*Capt*—Been to de funeral?

*Tramp*—Yes.

*Capt*—Is it out?

*Tramp*—No.

*Capt*—Why didn't you stay?

*Tramp*—They were going to take up a collection.

---

[33] At this point, Twain wrote "(Supe crosses with tomb-stone on shoulder—sets it down to rest—steps off to get something—the tramp goes and reads inscription, sheds tears all over the stone, says, 'I never knew it before, but I can see *now,* it's so *true,* so *true!*'" then changed his mind and added, "No, leave this out."

*Capt*—(*Laughs consumedly*)—Dey couldn't collect from *you,* could dey?

*Tramp*—(*sadly*) No—nothing but *tears.*

*Capt*—(*aside*)—Hear the sanguinary butcher! (*Aloud.*) Only tears, eh? Den you might as well staid—you was *strapped,* I jedge.

*Tramp*—I am a *feeling* being. That sermon would a *killed* me if I had staid—(*Aside.*) Forever dogging me and *quest*ioning me. (*Suddenly bursting into a laugh all to himself.*) O I see it *all,* now! He suspects *me!*—thinks I murdered my*self!* O, this is good! I'll *help* his investigations! (*Yawns and stretches.*)

*Capt*—Is you tired?

*Tramp*—I'm *always* tired. Hard work, hard fare—the cold neglect of the world—

*Capt*—Hard *work!* What you been doing? Sawing a *lath* in *two?*

*Tramp*—No. *Con*templating it.

*Capt*—(*Exhausting laughter*)—Did *dat* tire you?

*Tramp*—*No*—the *work.*

*Capt*—But you didn't *do* de work.

*Tramp*—No.

*Capt*—Den how did it tire you?

*Tramp*—The antici*pation* of it.

*Capt*—(*Huge laugh*). Well if de mere an*ticipa*tion wore you out so, what would a become of you if you'd actu'ly *tack*led dat lath?

*Tramp*—There'd a been *two* funerals to-day.

*Capt*—(*throws up hands*)—I gives in! A body dat wouldn't pity you is a *dog.* Lay down dah and take a nap. (*Aside.*) Don't I wish he *would!*

*Tramp*—Somebody might run off with my instrument.

*Capt*—Anybody dat would steal dat thing would steal a *mad*-dog. Go to sleep—*I*'ll watch it.

*Tramp*—(*lying down, yawning*)—Thanks, I'll trust you. You have an honest look. (*Nearly asleep—slow music—says, thickly.*) Call me when the funeral procession comes. (*Sleeps.*)

*Capt*—I'll do it, honey.——He's beginning to snore. (*Approaches, gets down by Tramp's ear*)—(*aside*)—sound as a drum.

Sleeps like a *plumber*—at *work.*——What's the surest text to give him to make him *dream* right?——I've got the word that'll set the remains of his conscience blabbing!——(*Hoarse whisper in Tramp's ear:*) MURDERER!

*Tramp* (*squirms and writhes in agony.*)

*Capt*—(*aside*)—It *fetched* him! See him squirm!—curls him up like a worm on a hot shovel!

*Tramp*—(*murmurs in sleep.*)

*Capt*—(*aside*)—Now it's coming (*Ear close down to Tramp's face.*)—(*his exclamations increase in loudness and horror as the Tramp's inarticulate mumblings go on*)——There, there, he's on the right track——no, wanders from it——now he's pinted right again——warm!——cold!——warm!——hot!——*hotter!*——*red*-hot!!——George I b'leeve he's coming right *to* it!——(*listening intensely for ten seconds or more—that is to say, whatever is the limit of suspense that is effective with an audience—then springs up*)——Good, *he's* the murderer! *Says* so! ac*know*ledges it—perfectly free and frank, like a gentleman! I'm a made man, I'm a made *man!* He's my bene*fac*tor. I want to *hug* him—I've *got* to hug him! (*starts thither*)——No—*that* won't do—'twould wake him up. But I must do *some*thing to show my appre——I'll ar*rest* him. (*Starts to do that.*) Hold on——s'pose he took it back when he come awake!——But couldn't I hang him on the confession he made when he was *asleep?* I don't see *why* I couldn't. You catch a tramp telling the truth *except* when he's asleep!—(*Ponders.*)——To make everything dead sure, I reckon I better go for him *awake,* now, and inveigle him somehow into a confession he can't go back on.——(*Pensively*)—There he lays, sleeping as ca'm and sweet (*gentle snore*) as a little child, and me a-hangin' over him with a halter!——I've eavesdropped, like a low, mean cuss, and——it's a dreadful business! Poor devil, *he* ain't ever done *me* any harm—and here I've hounded him and hounded him day and night and—(*nearly ready to blubber*) why one day he most sawed a *match* in two for me without charge—a *real* accommodating hellcat—and I wish I'd never started in on this miserable, treacherous——Hold on! 'Vast there, man! (*thumping chest*)—DUTY!!—Duty to the State, duty to your noble profession, duty to your citizenship!—*Now* I've the detective's stern, implacable heart again; and I move to my great work pitiless, in*ex*orable!——When he wakes, and sees me, won't he suspect that I——I know what I'll do. (*Meantime he is undoing a small parcel while he talks; takes from it a woman's dress which has the skirt rolled up and pinned at the waist, so that to the audience he seems to be putting on a round-about or blouse; turns his back to audience, bends low, slips on a woman's wig that has a queer Irish woman's bonnet or cap perched on top of it, rubs a handful of powered chalk over his black face, snakes out the pins and lets the dress-skirt fall down and hide his legs as he turns toward the audience. Sits down beside the sleeping tramp, tilts back, puts his heels on something about as high as his head, hitches his gown to expose his legs to the knees, and says with satisfaction in a rich Irish brogue*)—Bedad he won't know me now. He'll think I'm his g'yairdyan angel. Now lemme *see*——when he wakes I'll lead him on, in a cunning way, and just at the right time I'll come a little dodge that'll be in the nature of a koop-de-*tat* as the Irish say, and I'll be ruther theatrical, too.—

## ACT 4 [34]

(*Still in the Public Square or Park.*)

(*Irishwoman and Tramp discovered as before.*)

*Tramp*—(*stirring and stretching*—*aside*)—By George I *have* been asleep, sure enough!—Hel-lo, what sort of a ghost is this! (*aloud*) Say—madam, what went with that nigger that was here?

*Capt*—A *nagur,* is it? Bedad I haven't seen him, yer anner.

*Tramp*—(*aside*)—Hang'd if it ain't that old fool in a *new* masquerade! (*Aloud*) He said he'd watch my hurdy-gurdy! (*Starting up*)—If he has cabbaged that instrument I'll—

*Capt*—Is it the little py*anner* ye mane? It's over beyant ye here, fernenst, honey—and an illegant wan it is, at all at all.

[34] Thus in the amanuensis copy. In the manuscript, Twain wrote the scene designation first, then "(Fourth Act)?"

*Tramp*—An honest fellow! I was afraid the temptation would be too strong—though he had a good face. (*Straps his organ on.*) Well I'll go meet the procession.—

*Capt*—Mayhap ye knowed the poor young man before he was ——(*Gazing fixedly in his face*)

*Tramp*—(*Dropping his eyes slowly—after a pause*)—(*low voice*) Before he was *what?*

*Capt*—(*Impressively*) (*right at his ear*)—MUR—DHERED!

*Tramp* (*starts violently*)

*Capt*—(*aside*) *That* took! (*Aloud.*) That's the word for't.

*Tramp*—(*uneasily—trying to move on—Capt apparently without intending it keeps in his way*)——Is——is——any particular person——suspected?

*Capt*—There's *wan* is?

*Tramp*—(*Distressed.*) No! How——how did they come to——to——suspect him?

*Capt*—(*in his ear*).—Be jabers, young man, he—talked in his *shlape!* [35]

*Tramp*—(*staggers, puts hand to forehead, partly recovers, makes determined effort to leave*)—Out of my way, woman! Stand back! [36] —I have business in the next *town!*

*Capt*—(*taking firm grip on his wrist*)—The business'll kape!

*Tramp*—(*in great distress*) O what do you mean? You don't mean to——to——

*Capt*—(*tugging him forward—he gently resisting—stops—impressively*)—I mane—this:—it was *yerself* that talked!

*Tramp*—(*frightened*) Who heard me! There was nobody here. Could it be——it *must* have been that negro! Aha! Who cares!—ten to one he's an escaped convict! Had the guileless *face* of a convict!—He can't testify in a court!

*Capt*—(*smiling*)—So then bedad, ye think ye're *safe?*

*Tramp*—Not a doubt of it! Let me go, let me go!

*Capt*—(*impressively—speaking without the brogue*)—You are lost! The nigger, the Irishwoman and Capt Simon Wheeler the detective are one and the same being! (*Strikes an attitude.*)

---

[35] In the amanuensis copy after this word, in a very shaky hand not Twain's is the note "Not Irishy."

[36] Omitted in the amanuensis copy.

*Tramp*—(*staggers*) I *am* lost! But wait! I am *not* lost! You've no *proofs!* The empty talking done in *sleep* is valueless!

*Capt*—*Is* it though? Listen to me. (*aside*) Now I'm on dangerous ground; he didn't give me a single detail of how he done it or when or what with—only just said he *done* it. I'll pour my new *theory* into his ear, particular by par*tic*ular—if that theory's wrong, I'm busted—ruined! (*Aloud.*) Listen to me. There's other ways, and better ones than a man's talk in his sleep to furnish a detective the facts of a crime.

*Tramp*—(*pleadingly*) *Whisper* it—might be somebody hid here.

*Capt*—Just as you say. Well, (*mumbles in Tramp's ear.*)—(*with excited gestures as he warms to his work.*)

*Tramp*—(*during the mumbling, exclaims*)—O, *how* could that have been discovered!——Heavens, this is amazing!——*Can* I believe my ears!——(*aside*) This is certainly the absurdest rigmarole that ever lunatic[37] devised! (*Aloud*). Amazing, amazing! —I am lost beyond redemption!——Why how in the *world* was *that* found out! (*Aside.*) The superhuman idiotcy of this rubbish would make a *corpse* laugh!——I did *that,* too—and just exactly in that way!——Stupendous!—just precisely the way it happened! There—there—(*despairingly*) no more, no more. It is useless to deny. I CONFESS!

*Capt.*—(*delighted*)—Do you though? Honest?

*Tramp*—(*dejectedly*). I do. Do with me as you will.

*Capt.*—(*Hugging the tramp to his heart and whitening his face with chalk*)—Say it again, say it again!—it's *mu*sic!

*Tramp*—Alas, I murdered him.

*Capt.*—(*Hugging him—with effusion*)—O my friend, if my honest heartfelt gratitude can repay you for the trouble you were at—

*Tramp*—(*interrupting—sadly*)—Don't *men*tion it.

*Capt.*—No I don't mean that. I mean—(*taking both his hands and gazing on him with deep affection*)—My bene*fac*tor!——I'm a *made* man!—and I owe it all to *you!*

*Tramp*—Now tell me—this mystery stupefies me. How did you find all that out?

---

[37] Amanuensis copy: lunacy.

*Capt.*—(*pleased*)—How did I find it out? Was it pretty correct?

*Tramp*—*Pretty* correct! It was *absolutely* correct!

*Capt.*—'Twas put up about *right,* was it?

*Tramp*—Who ever told you that, had only *one* way to find it out. He followed right at my elbow and saw every single thing that happened, in broad daylight, and I never saw *him once!* Who was it followed me? Was it you?

*Capt.*—No.

*Tramp*—Who then?

*Cap*—Nobody.

*Tr*—*No*body!

*Cap*—Nobody.

*Tr*—Then who told you I did those things?

*Cap*—Nobody.

*Tr*—This is astounding! Then how did you know I did them?

*Cap*—Well, some little things informed me.

*Tr*—*What* little things?

*Cap*—Clews.

*Tra*—You don't mean to tell me—

*Cap*—Yes I do. I never had a *thing* to help me but a few little odds and ends that we fellows call *clews*—nothing else.

*Tr*—And you—

*Cap*—I just took these little clews and traced along from one to tother—put this and that together, and hunted you straight to your *hole.*

*Tr*—This is wonderful! Perfectly stupefying!

*Cap*—(*Serenely*)—And yet they warn't clews that would amounted to anything in the hands of an unprofessional.

*Tr*—(*sorrowfully*)—I never believed much in detectives be*fore,* but I know now to my cost that they are gifted like the *gods.* (*Sadly.*)—Well, I have run my course.——The sun of my life is setting——

(*Cap shows symptoms of distress*)—

*Tr*—Death has found me at last——*Death!*—(*with a shudder*).—I wonder if it is hard to die!—I wonder if the grisly rope—

—the pitiless knot——the awful sense of suffocating——(*goes on mumbling to himself*)

*Capt*—(*aside*)—O, now't I've *got* my triumph, I wish I *had*n't got it! Poor devil, poor miserable devil, he would have got away, but *I* hounded him down and hadn't any pity! I'm a taking away his life that's as sweet to him as mine is to me, and he never done me any harm! I wormed myself into his confidence[38] with a *lie*—I trailed him on and on, him never suspecting, and betrayed him like a *dog!* O dear, O dear, like a mangy, low-born treacherous dog! I—I can't ——I *won't*——(*rushing excitedly to tramp*)—(*Aloud*)—Here, here, (*putting money in his hand*) You poor god-forsaken, bloody-minded villain, *leave! fly!* Nobody knows it but *me,* and they may *roast* me and *I* won't tell! (*Shoving him along*)—Go—go—*van*ish!

*Tramp*—Wait!—I'll not stir!

*Cap*—(*Astonished*) You *won't!* Not to save your *life?*

*Tr*—Not to save my life.

*Cap*—Say—what do you mean? What *do* you mean?—What's the *matter* with you?

*Tr*—I mean *this.* I'd rather die than be hunted any longer.—Nothing can save me. I'm a doomed man. Do you know who I am?

*Capt*—You? *Who?*

*Tr*—I'm Jack Belford, the fugitive desperado!

*Cap*—That *pirate!*

*Tr*—That *pirate.* I was to be hanged. I broke jail and murdered this young man.

*Cap*—Why the advertisements described you very different—said you had on *jail* costume.

*Tr*—Did the idiots suppose I'd *keep* it on? The ordinary detective *would.* I'm *safe* from *them*—but the *people* will catch me, yet.—Now look here; I'm going to give myself up *any*way.—Hadn't *you* better capture me and have the credit of it and the reward? You've been *kind* to *me.*

*Cap*—Gimme your hand—you're the whitest scoundrel I ever struck! (*Shake.*) I'm glad you're willing to go—it's a great favor, I

[38] Amanuensis copy: conscience.

*tell* you. The minute I take you into camp, I'm a made MAN. (*Aside*) Darn him—to think of him being that awful desperado and I never once suspected it.—

*Tr*—Well, I'm ready to go with you.

*Cap*—(*Ponders.*) Look here, Belford, just do me *another* favor. You just keep mum, and knock around where you'll be handy when I *want* you. In our business considerable depends on a big *show*-off. We lay for the dramatic ef*fects,* you understand. Now I'll put my hand on you and arrest you just at the right moment to make the biggest sensation, the bulliest *situation*—see?

*Tr*—I get the idea.

*Cap*—And you're agreed?

*Tr*—I'm agreed.

*Cap*—Give us your hand, Jack! (*Shake.*) Now when I think it's the right time, I'll *whistle*—so. (*Some sort of peculiar whistle*)

*Tr*—I'll keep my ears open for it.

*Cap*—Good *boy!*—good *boy!* (*Bell tolls.*) Hello, there's your poor victim starting for his long home. Stand away, now, and don't seem to know me.

*Enter procession, coffin covered with a pall and loaded with flowers.*

*Mr. Griswold, chief pall bearer.*—Let us rest a moment and gather strength.

(*People group themselves about, weeping and talking.*)

*Cap*—(*at a distance, front—his back to the group.*)—(*aside*)—Poor lad, poor boy, cut down so young! He was always good to me, poor chap. I wish they wouldn't *cry*—it fetches *me,* and I hate to cry before folks.

*Mrs. Hig*—(*leans forehead on Mrs. Burnside's shoulder a moment*). If there ever was a dear sweet soul in this mortal world it was *him!* (*Boo-hoo!*) But he's better off where he is! (*Boo-hoo.*)

*Mrs. Burnside*—O yes, far better off—no more sorrow, no more disappointment, no more heart-ache, my poor poor boy! (*Cries.*)

*Tramp*—(*Weeping*). (*aside*) This is luxury!

*Clara*—I feel that his dear spirit is near! (*Weeps*)

*Tramp*—(*aside*) (*Weeps*) It makes a body better and purer and nobler to be lamented so!

*Mrs. Gris*—O, I can almost *see* him, as he used to come bounding up the back yard, his face all lit up with the theme for one of his immortal poems! (*Loud weeping.*)

*Capt (begins to snuffle—struggles to keep it down.)*

*Tramp*—(*Weeping aloud with the rest*)—(*aside.*) O, that it might never end!

*Mill—(Comes reverently—in deep mourning—handkerchief to her eyes—deposits a bouquet on the coffin—embraces Mrs. Burnside and Clara).*

*Tramp*—(*aside—weeping.*) It discounts *Paradise!*

*Mrs. Burnside*—(*to Mill*)—And did you love him so much, dear?

*Mill*—O, I never *knew* how I loved him till I lost him!

*Tramp*—(*aside—weeping*)—O hear that! I wish I could have such a funeral every day of my life!

*Clara*—(*to Mill*)—O my sister—*let* me call you so! (*Embracing.*)

*Pall bearers take up coffin. (Bell tolls.)*

*Mrs. H.*—O that awful sound! (*Bursts out crying—everybody follows suit.*)

*Capt*—(*aside*)—I *can't* help it! (*Begins to bawl like a calf.*)

*(Procession moves out, everybody weeping—bell tolling, Tramp drops into rear, grinding his organ and crying—Capt follows him bawling.)* *Exit all*

*Enter Baxter, with a broad-axe.*

*Baxter*—(*solus*) Hah! The procession is entering the *grave*-yard. I'll watch her face beside the grave. At the right moment I'll slowly raise this accusing weapon (*suiting action to the word*) before her gaze—if she so much as *winces* I'll *arrest* her on the spot! *Exit.*

*Enter Billings with a stove-lid.*

*Billings*—(*solus*)—They're there, now. Now I play my *last* card —my ace of trumps! Her conduct at the grave shall decide her fate. I'll fix my eye on her guilty face—and I'll slowly raise (*illustrating*) —this awful implement aloft. If she flutters—she's *lost!* *Exit.*

*Enter Bullet with a "Plymouth Collection."*

*Bullet*—The great tragedy draws to its fearful close! Every link is complete. Now, steady, steady heart!—be true, brain!—be vigilant, eye that never failed me yet! Not a shade of expression shall flit across her face but I shall *mark* it. At the pregnant moment I will slowly lift into the blue empyrean this dismal instrument of torture and destruction (*illustrating.*) If she but *shrinks,* upon her defenceless head falls the avenging hand of the *law!* *Exit.*[39]

*Enter Justice of Peace and Policeman Long.*

*(Long comes from the direction of the grave-yard.)*

*Justice*—Well, you have *news* in your face!

*Long*—Big news it is, too, your honor!

*Justice*—What is it? What is it?

*Long*—Just met one of the detectives. Says he'll have young Burnside's as*sas*sin under arrest in 5 minutes!

*Justice*—Prodigious! Who *is* it?

*Long*—He didn't say. He was *running.* So I rushed here to pre*pare* your honor.

*(Turmoil outside.)*

*Justice*—There!—What is that?

*Long*—(*Looking off.*)—Here they come! The whole *crowd.*

*(Justice seats himself.)*

*The crowd swarm in before justice of peace.*

*Mrs. Higgins*—(*to Mrs. Wheeler*)—O my *land,* they say one of them New York detectives has been making an arrest—wonder who 'tis.

*Mrs. H.*[40]—Here comes one of 'em *now.*

*Enter Baxter with Mrs. B. in charge.*

*Baxter*—(*to justice*) I charge Mrs. James Burnside with the wilful and deliberate *murder* of her *son!* (*Sensation—groans in the crowd.*)

*Mrs. Hig*—For shame, you ignorant reptile! (*Applause.*)

*Justice*—*Order,* if you please!

*Tom*—Lem, I never looked for *this*—I can't *stand* it.

*Lem*—'Sh! Keep quiet, don't budge—remember the *oath!*

*Baxter*—I charge that this woman did, on the 9th day of June, with a blow on the temple—

---

[39] After this Twain wrote, "Slide scene?" According to the broadside prepared for entering copyright, Twain indicates a shift of scene at this point to "Magistrate's office."

[40] Omitted in amanuensis copy.

*Tom*—Lem, I can't *stand* this!

*Lem*—(*Holding him by his arm and shaking with fear*)—*Don't!* —we're *dead* if you yelp!

*Baxter*—with the murderous weapon which I now offer in evidence (*displaying short-handled broad-axe*)—

*Tom*—Let go my arm, will you!

(*Lem tries to keep hold*)

*Baxter*—murder her son Hugh Burnside!

*Tom*—(*tearing loose from Lem and springing forward*)—It's a lie! If murder's been done, put it on *me,* where it belongs! (*Sensation.*)

*Capt*—(*greatly put out—aside*)—O, this is a d—d swindle! (*Gives peculiar whistle.*) (*Judge says "Order!" every time he whistles.*)

*Mrs. B*—O, you good manly soul, how *could* you do it, how *could* you!

*Mrs. Hig*—*Good* for the *boy!*—he ain't a *sneak,* if he *is* a murderer!

*Baxter*—(*to justice*) Your honor, I am a detective of *national* reputation. I cannot permit this gushing lunatic to undermine that reputation with a frivolous confession which will not hold water an *instant* before the overwhelming chain of circumstantial evidence which I shall bring to bear against this bloody and unnatural—

*Enter Billings with Millicent in charge.*

*Billings*—(*interrupting*) Way for the red-handed murderess! (*Sensation—murmers.*)

*Mrs. Hig*—What a wooden *fool!*

*Lem*—(*aside*) SHE! O I can't stand *this!* The noblest creature that ever—when I was dying with cholera and the doctors wouldn't allow me so much as a pellet of bread to keep me from starving, she succored me with a peck-basket of fried pork.

*Billings*—I charge this girl, Millicent Griswold, with the brutal assassination of Hugh *Burnside!*—

*Mrs. B'side*—O she *couldn't,* she couldn't!

*Lem*—O, if I had *Tom's* grit! (*Struggling with himself.*)

*Billings*—I charge that upon this vile, this abandoned, this inhuman girl's soul lies—

*Lem*—(*Springing forward*)—*You* lie, your*self!* And *Tom* lied!

*I*'m the only guilty one! O please string me up quick and get me out of it—I can't stand the suspense!

*Mrs. H.*—Good! *My* boy again!

*Tom*—Judge, he never told the truth in—

*Capt*—(*aside, plaintively*—) O here, these mean underhanded liars will just *ruin* me! (*Whistles—and looks off anxiously.*)

*Judge*—(*to Capt.*)—Order!

*Billings*—Your honor this silly, this absurd confession must not, *will* not be allowed to bring shame upon a reputation like mine. I will *prove,* overwhelmingly, that this girl did brutally assassinate her defenceless lover, at dead of night with the dismal weapon which I hold in my hand! (*Displaying hymn book*). And I demand—

*Enter Bullet with Clara in charge.*

*Bullet*—Way for the crimson *assassin!* (*Sensation—murmers.*)

*Mrs. Burnside*—(*Shrieks and flies to her daughter*). O, my child, my child!

*Mrs. Hig*—O, the blithering numscull!

*Bullet*—I charge that this heartless, unnatural

*Enter Chas—and by another entrance, Mr. and Mrs. Griswold.*

and bloody-minded girl, Clara Burnside, did with foul malice murder her own brother on the night of—

*Charles*—(*stepping forward and lifting his hand to impose silence*)—*I* am the murderer! (*Sensation—murmers.*)

*Capt*—(*aside*) (*plaintively*)—Lord, have I got to divide the honors among seven? (*Whistles.*) Dern that tramp—ain't he *ever* coming?

*Mrs. Hig*—Well for the *land's* sake!

*Mr. Griswold*—Good! That's manly!

*Mrs. G.*—I *knew* he'd come out!

*Clara*—(*Springing toward him with clasped hands*)—O Charles, you are destroying your*self* to save—

*Chas*—I wish it were so, but it is not. *Now* you understand why I could not bear your eye, why I could not—

*Clara*—(*interrupting*)—O say it was by *accident!*—I will bless you all my *days!*

*Chas*—It *was* by accident, wholly!

*Clara*—(*Throwing herself on her knees*)—O, out of my heart of *hearts* I thank you for the words!

*Capt*—(*Aside*) O my, why don't that tramp come! (*Whistles.*)

*People say*—"Look at old Wheeler!" "What's old Wheeler whistling about?" [Written along margin.]

*Judge*—Order!

*Bullet*—That is all stuff and *folly* your honor! That atrocious girl, with the solemn weapon which I hold in my hand (*elevating stove-lid*)—

*Hand-organ heard—enter Tramp.*

*Capt*—(*collaring him joyously and marching him forward*)—'Vast heaving and *belay! Here's* the only true and genuine assassin of the poet Burnside!—*here* he is!—the original *Jacobs!* And *his* confession knocks all the other confessions galley-*west!* Annuls 'em! annuls 'em!—by priority, seniority, first mortgage—becuz HE confessed more'n an hour ago! Don't you be afraid, Trampy—you stand your ground—I'm a backing you agin the field! *I*, detective Wheeler! (*Stripping off dress etc.*) Your claims lays over 'em *all!* And who do you reckon he is? (*Looking around*). Stand by for a surge!—stay in your clothes if you can!—It's the bloody desperado Jack Belford! (*Tremendous sensation—people crowd away from him.*) It's the black-souled pirate him*self!*—disguised like an honest man! *He* done it! Judge he done it with his own hand—none of these frauds were *around!* (*indicating the others with a sweep of his hand*)—He played that pison old tune to him till he'd got him weak and helpless and then he up and batted him over the head with his deadly hand-organ! Go forrard like a man and *tell* 'em you done it! (*Tramp moves slowly forward with downcast face till opposite Judge.*) I'm a *made* man! I'm a *made* man Jenny!! (*Washing his hands delightedly.*)

*Tramp*—Alas! I *am* the only guilty one!—(*Strips off disguise.*) (*He ought to bend and cry into his hands and so slip off his whiskers, goggles etc.,*—then *say "Alas etc."* as he raises his head, *because his voice would betray him to his friends if he spoke* before *undisguising himself.*)

*Capt*—O, that thousand dollars is gone!

*Millicent*—Hugh! O my darling! (*Hurls herself into his arms.*)

*Mrs. Burnside.*—O, my son! my son! (*Hurls herself upon him.*)

*Clara*—O forgive me, Charles! (*Hurls herself upon Charles.*)

*Tom*—We're *saved,* Lemmy! (*Hurls himself upon Lem.*)

*Lem*—(*Embracing and kissing.*)

*Capt*—(*Walking up and down wringing his hands*) Ruined, ruined! ruined! But that's a matter of *de*tail.

*Mrs. Wheeler*—(*Clinging to him, comforting him*)—*Don't* be disheartened! You've done all a man could! I shall live to see you have a name yet!

*Capt*—O, no Jenny, it's another failure! (*Still walking*)—and the boss failure of the old detective's life!

*Mrs. Burnside*—(*Rushing forward*) Who talks of *failure!* It's the noblest *success* man ever achieved! You've given me back my dead son a*live*—take the reward! (*Passing check or notes*)

*Capt*—A thousand dollars! I *am* a made man, Jenny (*kissing her*)—I'm a made man *sure!*

*Hugh*—(*comes and throws hand organ strap over his neck and piles goggles, wigs etc. on top of it*)—There, old chum, take 'em and be happy! They're invaluable to a detective!

(*Hugh and Chas put heads together a moment.*)

*Hugh*—I'm perfectly *sure* of it—I traded clothes with him that very morning.

*Charles*—(*Coming forward*)—You shan't go without a testimonial from *me,* I can tell you! There's a thousand dollars offered for the capture, dead or alive, of the desperado Belford, whom my accidental bullet saved from the gallows. *Take* it!—and my blessing! (*Shakes him by both hands.*)

*Capt*—I'm a made man, Jenny, there ain't no question about it!

*Clara*—(*rushing up*)—O, you dear old dear, if I *only* had something to give you!—O, *I* know! (*Suddenly tip-toes, takes his face between her hands and kisses him*). (*Applause.*)

*Capt*—Lord that's worth all the trouble I've been at!

*Millicent*—(*Rushing up*)—Bless your old heart! (*Suddenly tip-toes, takes his face between her hands and kisses him twice, vigorously.*)

*Capt*—O I'm *richly* rewarded!

*Mrs. Higgins*—(*Rushing up passing a wipe of her apron across her mouth*)—Throw prejudice aside for this once! (*Suddenly snatches the captain's face in her hands and gives him 3 sounding smacks before he can struggle loose.*) (*Applause.*)

*The captain's cheek whitens all these women's faces.* [Written in margin.]

*Capt*—(*Resignedly.*) I'm *more* than rewarded! Well, take it all around, Jenny, it *ain't* a failure! To track out a *murderer* ain't much but to track out a lost [41] *corpse* and fetch him home alive and good as new, takes *genius!* Come—fall in, fall in! We'll take the boy home and have a tearing jubilee! Fall in! (*They fall into procession*) Mark time! (*They mark time.*) FOR-ward march! (*He brings up the rear, his wife on his left arm, he strikes up the same old tune on the hand-organ.*)

CURTAIN.

*Have a dance, if preferred.*

---

[41] In parentheses Twain suggests the alternate "mislaid."

## *Working Notes for*
# Cap'n Simon Wheeler, The Amateur Detective

## Notes for Plan I

[Nine pages of notes on Crystal Lake Mills paper, the first page unnumbered, the remainder numbered 2–9.]

Telegraph op.—(*t'other feller*)

15m Love scene in parlor with reporter. Fire! (*Lewis*)[42] *Chas Warner?*[43] [in left margin].

15m Love scene there with somebody poet.—No! I love him, but my father—(He goes away to suicide.

15 Arrival of Mrs. Halliday and trunks just in time to prevent this chaffy, lightsome young fel from carrying his point. (Not that she desired it, however. She begins to lie and slander and talk for him.)

This man must be glad of an opportunity to go into hiding; he will be ashamed of his suicide, but more particularly he wants to enjoy the delight of seeing Mary mourn for him, and also see the remorse of those 2 young fellows, Reporter and tel operator are always lugubriously striking hands and saying "Put it there!—there's a bond of blood between us—the trade-mark—I mean the mark of Cain is on us—let us swear to stand by each other and keep the dread secret until death."

---

*Alfred*

Ah, I perceive—this young poet is so romantic that this being dead in the midst of the world and life, charms him.

---

[42] Presumably John T. Lewis, the Negro farmer employed by the Theodore Cranes, owners of Quarry Farm, Twain's summer retreat near Elmira, New York.

[43] Charles Dudley Warner, Twain's friend and neighbor in Hartford, collaborator with Twain on *The Gilded Age*.

Mrs. H is very unwelcome until she drops into the old gentleman's ear the news that a fortune has been left the poet. *Here's* your reason for detectives! If it can be proved that Af is dead, his rascally cousin John Hooker gets the money.

Hooker makes friends with Mrs. H who tries to get up engagement for him with Mary.

---

A call in that parlor among 3 or 4 Devils that shall do all the "history" with plenty venom and envy.

Then Enter the old gent

Wife

Daughter. Then Exit all but latter.

---

GHOST of dead man appears to the 2 criminals every now and then.

---

Each time just in time to break up some almost completed plan.

---

At the end of trial, last act both these fellows confess the murder in the most grandiloquently heroic way, and weep upon each other and each says " 'twas I that struck the fatal stroke!" (Their mothers, sisters, sweethearts and the mourning girl are there all crying—the villain cousin trying to help the latter)—when the old Capt. strips deceased. *Tableau.*

---

Dead man must use falsetto voice before death and natural voice afterward.

---

In one place let the old man explain the poet's relationship in the confusing fashion of S in a fix.

Father of girl—S. Gillette [44]

---

Wakeman is Nobleman of Steppe [45]

---

Barrel of Gunpowder placed at Wakeman's door by those 2

---

[44] Probably the Sol Gillette mentioned in Typescript Notebook 14, p. 47, but there is no further identification of him. Possibly he was a relative of Francis Gillette, Twain's Hartford neighbor and one of the original purchasers of Nook Farm.

[45] The allusion is to one of Ivan Turgenev's "Sportsman's Recollections" entitled "The Nobleman of the Steppe," which appeared in *Scribner's Monthly,* XIV (July 1877), 313–338.

scapegraces who are terrified at his investigations—their hearts fail them and they rush back to pull out slow-match and observe W. sitting on it. "Oh, John, speak to him!" "No!—he'll suspect me!—I'll step aside and *you* do it! Let's be men!—let's *both* do it! The[y] start, first one pulling back and then the other—You warn him—I can only gasp—got no voice—meantime the Cap bragging about his keen detective scent and the match burning under his nose—takes it out—glances at it, then at keg—"Powder keg, by jingoes!"—gravely lights pipe at slow-match—then finger on nose (deep thought)—"That keg of gunpowder placed there is significant—that never come there by itself—that *means* something—the common run of detectives wouldn't see anything significant about that barrel—very few of them see the *barrel*—but nothing escapes *me*. There was a deliberate purpose in putting that barrel against my house—it was to kill somebody.—Now let me see; nobody ever comes to my house that there'd be any object in killing.———O!—I see!—curious I didn't think of it at once!—They've made a mistake and put it at the wrong house. Now that barrel's a clue—a little vague, but still a clue—and with no better finger-post *I'll* unravel this mystery.

Sh! I've got an idea! I'll light and replace the fuse. The villain will come sneaking back presently to see how his work's going on, and I'll nab him! It's that villain for a million! (Hides behind bbl.)

*Poet enters* tickled to death at meeting his 2 murderers flying,—"The moment I appeared to them, they fairly flew!"

The Capt. glides up, lays a grim hand on his shoulder, says: "It's just as I expected! My instinct's never wrong! Now you've got accomplices—I'm going to hide in the bush (placing him on barrel) when they see you they come for'ard—else they're not *men!* (Ties his legs around barrel). Now (impressively—and going)—you set perfectly quiet—if you make a sound or raise a whisper, I'll *eat* you, body and soul. (*Exit tip-toe.*)

*Poet*—O, this is too good! Just as usual, he suspects me of some crime or other. (Mf!—what is that smells so?) But this suits me—my legs are tired to death. (Cleaning out his pipe with his knife)—I'd as soon roost a couple (sniffs around) a couple (sniff) of hours on this (sniff) this onion barrel—(discovers slow-match)—(Yell after yell of Murder)—

Enter Capt, dragging Mrs. H.—

There! *There's* your bloody pal!

(CURTAIN)

## Notes for Plan II
(Final Version)

### Group A

[Two sheets of Crystal Lake Mills paper numbered 1 and 2. In upper right corner of p. 1, Twain wrote "2$^{d}$ *act.*"]

1

Send a broken heart by ASS Press

Clara and Chas.

Swash in disguise and Millicent. S—don't betray me.

Swash and her Parents and Mrs. Higgins.

Swash and the Tramp.

" and detectives—he deaf.

The Reporter tells Lem about the theories of the 3 or 4 N.Y. Detectives—scared because can't get Swash's theory.—They are sure he suspects *them.*

Tom and Clara

Lem and Clara.

They both scared to death when she speaks of murder.

Swash and Clara.

*You* did it! (boys jump.)

Clara—I know he did it. If you love better to shield a vile murderer than help me to bring him to justice—

Pa and Ma—They look darkly on him, but say privately Poor fellow, we will say nothing.

*You* did it, etc. Swash always misinterprets the boys' guilty looks and actions.

---

Confession of Hugh.

---

The Body found.

Group B

[Two sheets of Crystal Lake Mills paper, the first, unnumbered, headed "Last Act," the second numbered 2 and headed "*Last*" in upper left corner. The discontinuity of text between the two sheets, however, suggests that these were written separately, the first a revision of a text continuous with the second.]

[1]

Last Act

Swash chuckling over this scene.

3 detectives bring in the mother, sister and sweetheart charged with the murder, one after another.

When sweetheart is charged, Tom confesses and is taken into custody. [deleted later]

Tom, Lem and Chas. brought in in detail.

When Clara is weeping and protesting, Tom folds arms grandly, steps forward, I am the murderer! (Sensation and app)—Lem ranges up a trifle in advance—*I* am the murderer! You lie! Another etc.

Chas—I cannot let these youths die for a crime which is not theirs!

2

theirs—I am the murderer!

Clara—*You!* Say it was an ax—O say it and I will love and adore you to the grave!

Swash—Excuse me—he didn't do it. None of 'em did. *I*'ve got the true and *only* murder of the poet Burn—the original Jacobs! And if I do say it myself it's the biggest and the bulliest and the ingeniousest detective job the universe has ever seen. Come up here and add your confesh$^{n}$

Beg—Alas! I confess it. I am the murderer—the only one! (Buries face low in hands and sobs aloud) (everybody affected, espesh Swash)—When he comes up his disguise is gone and he is Hugh.

Group C

[Two sheets of Crystal Lake Mills paper, the first unnumbered, the second numbered 2 and headed "(3d act)."]

[1]

Capt. says "Night—must go for Tramp—must keep eye on him. [")]

Enter Tom and Lem with powder, 2 slow-matches.

Blows up when curtain is down—curtain raises again, displaying wrecked deserted house. Capt—face all black—By George it's well I left that place when I did.

Tramp has crutches—and one leg shorter than the other. [The preceding notes were written in the top margin.]

*3d act*

Capt. tells his theory to his wife.

Capt as Irishwoman questioning Tramp.

Tom and Lem—talk about Capt's suspish—plot to blow up his house that night—they end with a fight.

1st D—passes with armful of broadaxes; 2d with stove lids; 3d with hymn-books.

Chas and Clara meet—Clara won't recognize him. She drops an aside that she loves him, though.

Chas and Melissa (Tramp overhears her avow her love for him. O, this is bliss—I hope the mystery'll hang on a year.)

*Tramp* (solus) That old fool thinks I'm my own murderer. He's coming—I'll talk in my sleep

2

and help him keep up the delusion. Talks in sleep. Capt. leads him on with questions. Capt. resolves to dress as negro and make him confess awake what he did asleep. "Poor devil, my heart begins to get soft for him now—psh! I must be firmer! Like a detective. Business is business." (Goes off sighing).

*The funeral—*

Tramp joins it crying—Capt. ditto.

The boys blow up house.

Curtain.

*4th act*

Capt. as negro, makes Tramp confess. Says the other arrests are to be made presently. Plans grand surprise when he brings in a *confessed* murderer—theirs only suspected ones. [The remainder written interlinearly.] Capt. is immediately sorry he hounded him to death's door—says you're sorry ain't you? Here's money—fly. "No—I'm the desperado that escaped tother day—my crimes make me tired of life—I'd rather die." Capt.—This is a big thing—$100 reward for this desperado.

Capt—But he was advertised as being sound and dressed in prison rig. "Fools, my leg's false—I borrowed this disguise."

Newsboy—all about the funeral!

Group D

[Two sheets of Crystal Lake Mills paper numbered 1 and 2]

Tramp talks in sleep for benefit of Capt.

---

Confesses.

---

Clara mentions escaped desperado to Charley.

---

Bastile *Capt* distin

Never heard of a *poor* prisoner falling out of Ludlow St. Sheriff was blind and didn't see the money, warden was deaf and didn't hear the door open; so the poor fellow went along unsuspecting and fell out.

Why say ring thieves *and* lawyers?

You see he took the Nation 5 years, and made it his Bible; tried to live in all ways humbly and sincerely according to the Nation; What's the consequence? First 3 months he was a Prot; next 3 a Cath; next 3 a Univer; next he was totally out of religion and short of a God; to follow the nation he went from a brown stone front to all the different sort of houses there are—busted at last he fetched up in the poor house.

Perplexing as a compliment from the Nation newspaper—you can't reconcile it to your reason any other way than as a typographical error.—You can't persuade yourself that it ain't a typ°—you can't account for it any way but as a—[interlinearly with above] Mr. Griswold—a bitter, sarcastic man. Says Mrs. G's a *cat* when started.

---

Huge policeman clubs the newsboy for selling papers on Sabbath—comes into justice office clubbing him—every word says *Will* you be quiet and bangs him—says it is N.Y. style.

Group E

[Miscellaneous notes jotted on four sheets of Crystal Lake Mills paper and two postcards.]

Capt. Gideon Swash.
Mrs. Jenny Swash.

---

Mr. Horace Griswold.
Mrs. Matilda Griswold
Miss Millicent Griswold.

---

Hugh Burnside
Mrs. Burnside.
Miss Clara Burnside.

---

Widow Higgins.
The Newsboy.

---

Tom
Lem.

---

Detective Baxter
" Billings
" Bullet.

---

1st Drug Clerk
2d Drug Clerk
Policeman Jake Long.
Justice of Peace.
Desperado.
Charles

[In the list above, all but Mrs. Swash and Widow Higgins have been crossed through.]

No. 1. Baxter, 2 Billings, 3 Bullet.

Lem Dunlap, tel op.

Clara, Mrs. and Hugh Burnside.

Negro,—old sailor etc. very deaf Irish woman

Tram—the tramps are marching.
Cheer up comrades we will go go go /swarm/.
Where the people are not mean and
philanthropists are green
*And* the loathesome tramp is welcomed like the morn.

---

I always had an unaccountable prejudice against suicide.

---

These boys must always wind up with a fight about a triviality.

---

3 silent detectives.

---

Served on a canal in a storm  Low bridge

Consider the having a sweet believing wife to talk his asides to. Hugh engages to give him $1000 to keep his mother still.

Tom and Lem—He was only stunned—his eyes opened—when we tumbled in a pile from the bed, his head must have struck something and killed him.

*Note.* When news of the finding of the body comes, it is accompanied by word that a note in an unknown hand says the finder will call upon Mrs. B when her grief is somewhat assuaged, for the $1000—this note is to Editor of the paper.

("Tom, tother paper's got it!") [The note above was later canceled.]

$1000 reward for finding him.

Tramp—Who found it—

Capt—Old Truman Jones.

Tramp—Meanest miser in town. Has he got the money?

Capt—He wanted to go for it right off—people said they'd lynch him if he didn't wait a month for decency sake.

Irish woman after confession—I've betrayed you. Fly,—here's money—I haven't the heart to hang a man I've wormed confidence treacherously out of—

Tr—No—I'm tired of life—I'm the desperado Belford Bros [46]—I killed the poor boy and robbed him—I'd *rather* die—You've been kind to me—you've fed me—give me up and take the reward and the honor  $1000

Cap—My theory's right!

Capt

This is the desperado—he killed Hugh. (Tearing off clothes)—and I'm Swash the detective.

Judge—Why everybody knew you.

Detectives question Capt., who is deaf.

---

[46] Belford Brothers was the Canadian publishing firm which, by taking advantage of a loophole in British copyright law, had successfully pirated *The Adventures of Tom Sawyer* despite the fact that it was covered by a British copyright.

Glad the tramp plays dummy to all but me, says the Capt.

He bawls at end of funeral and so closes act—others signing to him "not so loud."

Hugh has been kind to the Capt—hence his grief.

Some detectives think they've played thunder when they track out a man that's killed another man; but that don't mount to much 'longside of a detective that can track out a murdered man and fetch him alive again.

Capt—$100 Jenny would keep us a year—$200 2 years—then we're safe—

# III

# *Copyright Application*

[Title Page.]

CAP'N SIMON WHEELER,

THE AMATEUR DETECTIVE.

---

A Light Tragedy,

By

MARK TWAIN (SAMUEL L. CLEMENS).

---

PERSONS REPRESENTED.

Cap'n Simon Wheeler; Mr. Horace Griswold; Hugh Burnside (a poet); Chas. Dexter (his cousin); Detective Baxter, Detective Billings, Detective Bullet (these three being professionals from New York); Jake Belford (a fugitive desperado); Tom Hooker (a newspaper reporter); Lem Sackett (a telegraph operator); Jake Long (a police officer); A Newsboy; A Magistrate; Miss Clara Burnside; Miss Millicent Griswold; Mrs. James Burnside; Mrs. Matilda Griswold; Mrs. Jenny Wheeler (wife of the Cap'n); Mrs. Higgins (a garrulous, good-natured widow).

The scene is laid in an obscure mountain village, supposed to be three or four hundred miles from New York.

PLOT AND INCIDENTS.

Summer twilight promenade of citizens; Cap'n Wheeler concealed, taking observations. Charles and Hugh pretend to quarrel, in order to fool him—exit. Enter Mr. and Mrs. Griswold: "The Uncle's will will leave everything to Charley; our Millicent shall refuse Hugh."—Exit.

Enter Hugh and Millicent.—She refuses him; the sap-head resolves to commit suicide.—Exit. Enter the elder Griswolds and Mrs. Higgins. —The latter has discovered that the will gives the property to Hugh, *not* Charley.—Exit. Enter Charley and Clara, and pour a libation (of ink) to their betrothal. Will give the news to her brother Hugh, as a birth-day present, in the morning.—Exit. Enter Tom and Lem (bosom friends).—Both been refused, the night before, by Clara; they fight, and tumble on the Cap'n, who tries to capture them, but they assist each other and escape. Tableau.

SCENE 2. *Open place in a wood, moonlight, midnight.*

Enter Hugh, poisoned; apparently falls dead. Enter Cap'n, on his track; sits down on him to study out the best way of hunting for him; rises and continues forming plan; thinks he is on the right track now, starts off, stumbles over the body, but hurries on, not observing what it is.—Exit. Enter Tom, tight, discovers body—a good item; sits down on it to smoke and glorify his good fortune; drags the body home, to keep rival journal from getting the item. Enter Mrs. Higgins, Mrs. Burnside, and others, seeking the missing youth; find his hat.—Exit in grief. Enter Tom and Lem, with the body, and conceal it in a thicket; have fought in their room and bloodied it; fear they will be hanged for murder; they swear to be mute, and stand by each other henceforth, to the gallows.—Exit. *Day dawns.*—Enter Hugh, from thicket; glad he did not take enough poison; fears ridicule; resolves to mysteriously disappear. Hand-organ heard. Enter fugitive desperado, Jake Belford, disguised as a tramp; Hugh buys an exchange of clothes, etc., for cash.—Exit, to make the exchange. Enter Cap'n Wheeler, his wife following, knitting (as usual). The Cap'n's marvelous theory of the disappearance, which compels simple Jenny's worshipful admiration; the murder must have been done by a left-handed man, because "most of the murders in detective stories are done by left-handed people;" Cap'n sees a man in the distance, scratching his head with his left hand.—Exit, excitedly, followed by his wife. Enter Charley, with gun and game, on track of a wolf; fires into the thicket and "gets" the newly disguised desperado, who falls dead *on his face.*—Exit Charley, and covers the body; thinks it Hugh. Enter Millicent, sorry she obeyed her father and discarded Hugh. Enter Newsboy, and sells her an extra, "All about the mysterious disappearance, etc., etc."—Exit the boy. Enter Charley, in a panicky state of mind; the distressed Milly shows him the extra, which pretty nearly "fetches" him.—They exit, arm in arm, he keeping his secret, but trying to encourage and comfort her. Enter Hugh, as a tramp, and sees them disappearing in this very friendly conjunction. Enter Cap'n, whose man was right-handed, after all; is overjoyed to see the tramp shake his stick, *left-handed,* at some invisible object (the retreating couple); questions the tramp in an absurd way, after the supposed manner of professional detectives; thinks the answers show guilt; wants to haunt this tramp till he is sure; tramp contracts to saw a white pine stick in two, three times, for hot meals and a napkin—requires three weeks to "do it right" in; must be conveyed in a hack; the Cap'n takes him home on his back.

SCENE—*Outskirts of the village—some cottages*

*Several Weeks Later.*—The three detectives and Cap'n cross the stage one after the other, making idiotic gestures signifying that each is hot upon the murderer's track. Cap'n is disguised as a sailor of about Columbus's time. Cap'n returns. Feels pretty sure of the tramp's guilt, but thinks best to throw out a random feeler here and there on other people, so as to make certain. One at a time Charley, Lem and Tom pass by, having heard wild, undefined rumors of something going on "up yonder." Cap'n tackles each in turn and frightens him to death by slipping up behind him and suddenly shouting in his ear, "*You* done it!" He ponders over the results and decides that these are not murderers, because their fright was too "ghastly and sudden and *natural.*" Tom the reporter informs him that detective Baxter's theory is that Hugh's mother killed Hugh, with a broad-axe; Billings's is that Hugh's sister killed him, with a stove-lid; Bullet's is that Millicent brained him, with a hymn book. Cap'n declines to give Tom his own marvelous theory (a new one) yet a-while, but reveals it to Jenny—has no secrets from her. Enter *all* the characters, with news that the body is found! Dismal joy of Hugh the pretended tramp, over the grief, and praise of himself, and general public suffering which the discovery of his decayed remains elicits. Fright of Charles, Tom and Lem; each considers himself secretly hunted, and infallibly doomed. The three New York detectives see signs of guilt in the grief of the three women; the Cap'n sees the same evidences in the moist but cheerful demeanor of Hugh the tramp. Clara despises her affianced, Charles, because he avoids her, in her trouble, and never encouraged her with a hope, while all others did. The elder Griswolds suspect Charley, because of the sham quarrel, (a little of which they overheard,) and because the death of Hugh makes the property *revert to Charley;* they do not conceal their suspicions from him, but do from all others. Hugh the tramp plays deaf and dumb on everybody but "detective" Cap'n Wheeler; he is not afraid of *his* recognizing his voice, although Wheeler has known him all his life. Charles, who knows the sign-language of mutes, tries to ask some questions, at Milly's request, but is "stumped" by Hugh's intricate and marvelous signs in reply, Hugh's system of signs being an entirely fresh and original one. Officer Long comes shamelessly to collect the reward for finding Hugh's body, and is ejected and advised to wait a decent time, by the Cap'n. Tom and Lem end their terrors with their customary fight—exit all, but Cap'n. Re-enter Long to see about the row. Enter newsboy with extra about finding body; Long arrests him for yelling too loudly; clubs him for not resisting (because "city cops do it"); boy forcibly released by the Cap'n, "by the authority vested in every man that *is* a man, to protect a weakling when he's in trouble." Enter detective Baxter; tries to get information out of the apochryphal sailor, who defeats him by replying in the Choctaw language. Exit Baxter. Enter detective Billings on the same errand; the Cap'n pretends idiotcy. Exit Billings, defeated. Enter detective Bullet on the same errand; the Cap'n pretends to be stone deaf—exit Bullet, defeated. Exit Cap'n, to spy further on the tramp. *Night.* Enter Tom and Lem with a plan to scare the dreaded Cap'n out of the camp, (by blowing up his cottage,) and thus stop him from (as they imagine) haunting their guilty track. They put a keg of powder against his cottage (not knowing that he moved out of it the night before). They first ascertain that no one is in the house; they light two slow-matches and stick them into opposite sides of the keg; "one might go out"; they quarrel, and exit fighting. Enter the Cap'n and sits down on the keg to ruminate; smells something burning; presently discovers one slow-match; removes it, delighted to think he has outwitted the *tramp's* deadly designs upon him; holds it up—"Now stink at your leisure." Lights his pipe with it and throws it down. Lem and Tom appear, and cannot muster voice enough, in their terror, to warn the Cap'n to get off the keg before the other slow-match sends him to heaven. They conclude to retire to the rear and dislodge him with a stone. Slow-match sizzling viciously, the Cap'n calmly mapping out new plans against the tramp—curtain slowly descends. Prodigious explosion. Curtain rises, displaying the wrecked cottage; Cap'n, powder-blackened, sitting on the ground at a distance, rubbing the back of his head: "Lucky that stone made me skip out of that when it did, or we'd 'a' been a detective short."

SCENE—*A part of the Public Square.*

*Next Day.*—People straggling to the funeral. Baxter crosses stage with armful of broad-axes (collected in his search for the right one); presently, Billings with pile of stove-lids; after him Bullet with stack of hymn-books. Charley and Millicent talking; Tramp jealous and distressed; presently he overhears her say she "adores his memory." Tramp faints for joy; Billings stumbles over him and spills his stove-lids. Conversation; then exit all, to the funeral, the joyous tramp following, grinding hand-organ briskly in contrast with the solemn tolling of the bell. Enter Cap'n, disguised as a negro, his wife at his heels. Cap'n shows her how a professional detective goes through a "theory" in dumb show when said detective knows people are looking at him, (though he pretends he doesn't). Unfolds to the admiring Jenny his wonderful new theory. Exit Jenny; enter tramp, overcome by the affecting nature of his own funeral sermon, and the laudations his doggerel received in it. Sees through the Cap'n's disguise (as usual); perceives that the Cap'n suspects him of being the murderer (of himself); resolves to *help* him in his investigations. Takes a nap, and confesses the murder in his sleep. Cap'n disguises himself on the spot as an Irishwoman, overlaying his black complexion with flour or chalk, and purposes inveigling tramp into repeating the confession awake. The tramp wakes; is charged with confessing in his sleep; tramp cares nothing for that. Cap'n boldly pours his absurd "theory" into tramp's ear; tramp pretends it is correct in every detail; in despair he confesses again. Cap'n is distressed, now, to think he has trapped the hunted victim to his death by lies and treachery; suddenly offers him money, tells him to fly, shoves him along. Tramp refuses to go; says it is useless, his doom is sure. "Do you know who I am? I am Jack Belford, the fugitive desperado!" (Amazement of the Cap'n). It is agreed that the tramp shall stay around within sound of a whistle till the time comes when the arrest will be most theatrical and make the biggest "situation"; the Cap'n will then give the signal, make the arrest, and pocket both of the thousand-dollar rewards—one for finding the body of the "late" Hugh Burnside, and the other for the capture of Jack Belford "dead or alive." *Bell tolls.*—Enter funeral procession with coffin covered with flowers. Much grief, much glorification of the "late" poet. Tramp, in tears of melancholy enjoyment: "I wish I could attend my funeral every day of my life." Exit procession, bell tolling, tramp grinding his hand-organ, the Cap'n closing procession at his heels, bawling inconsolably. "He was always good to me, poor young chap." Enter Detective Baxter, with a broad-axe; going to suddenly thrust it before Mrs. Burnside, at the grave, and if the guilty creature "but winces," arrest her on the spot; exit. Enter Billings with stove-lid—going to convict Clara at the grave; exit. Enter Bullet, with "Plymouth Collection;" going to confront Millicent with this "dismal instrument of torture and destruction" at the grave-side. Exit.

*Magistrate's Office.*—Enter Officer Long; has just met one of the New York detectives, who said he would have the assassin of Hugh Burnside under arrest in five minutes. Turmoil outside. Enter excited crowd. Enter Baxter with Mrs. Burnside and the fatal broad-axe; he charges her. Tom: "It's a lie! if murder's been done, put it on *me,* where it belongs!" Cap'n (*aside*), "O this is a d—d swindle!" (Gives a peculiar whistle—but the tramp does not come.) Enter Billings, with Millicent and the deadly hymn book: "Way for the red-handed murderess!" He charges her. Lem: "No! *I*'m the only guilty one! (*pleadingly*), and do please string me up quick and get me out of it—I can't stand the suspense!" Cap'n (*aside—plaintively*), "O these mean underhanded liars'll just ruin me!" (Whistles—but tramp doesn't come). Enter Bullet, with Clara and the fearful stove-lid: "Way for the crimson assassin!" He charges her. Enter Charles, and raises his hand to command silence: "*I* am the murderer!" Cap'n (*aside—plaintively*), "Consound the luck; have I got to divide the honors among seven?" (Whistles; no result: "Dern that tramp!") Clara (to Charles), "O say it was by accident, and I will bless you all my days!" Charles: "It *was* by accident, wholly." Hand-organ heard; enter the tramp; Cap'n collars him joyously: "Stand back, frauds, the lot of ye! *Here's* the only true and genuine assassin of the poet Burnside! here he is—the original Jacobs! And his confession annuls all the others—by priority, seniority, first mortgage!—for *he* confessed more'n an hour ago! Don't you be afeared, trampy; you stand your ground—I'm a backin' you agin the field!—I, detective Simon Wheeler! (*Stripping off Irishwoman's disguise*); and who do you reckon *he* is? Stand by for a surge—it's the bloody desperado Jack Belford in disguise! He killed him, Judge; he played that pison old tune to him till he'd got him weak and helpless, and then he up and batted him over the head with his deadly hand-organ!" Hugh the tramp: "Alas I *am* the only guilty one!" (*Strips off disguise*). General explosion of joy and indiscriminate embracing. Cap'n (*aside, plaintively*): "It's all a fraud—and away goes all them rewards." Jenny tries to comfort him.

Cap'n: "Tain't no use, Jenny; it's another failure—and a boss failure of the old man's life, too." Mrs. Burnside: "Who talks of failure? It's the grandest *success* man ever achieved! You've given me back my dead son *alive*—take the reward!" Hugh contributes hand-organ and tramp's disguise: "They're invaluable to a detective, old Chum!" Charles: "I accidently killed the desperado Belford; thousand dollars offered for him, dead or alive—take it, old man!" Clara: O you dear old dear, if *I* only had something to give you!" (Suddenly tip-toes and kisses him.) Cap'n: "That's worth all the trouble I've been at!" Millicent: "Bless your old heart!" (Suddenly kisses him a couple of times.) Cap'n: "I'm *richly* rewarded!" The ancient widow Higgins, passing a wipe of her apron across her mouth: "Throw prejudice aside for this once!" (Suddenly gives him three sounding smacks, before he can struggle loose.) Cap'n: "I'm *more* than rewarded! Well, take it all around, Jenny, it *ain't* a failure; to track out a murderer ain't much, but to track out a mislaid *corpse*, and fetch him home alive and good as new, takes genius! Fall in! fall in! we'll take the boy home and have a tearing jubilee! Mark time—forward march!" They file away, the Cap'n closing the rear, grinding stirring music from the hand-organ.

CURTAIN.

# IV

# *Simon Wheeler, Detective*

(1877–1898?)

Editor's Note: The surviving documents do not indicate whether Twain's faith in his play was shaken by the adverse reactions of the producers and actors to whom he showed it. But, if so, his enthusiasm soon rekindled when William Dean Howells visited him in Hartford in the latter part of October, considered the play, and urged him to turn it into a story or a novel. After he returned to Cambridge, Howells wrote that he had given further thought to the amateur detective and that it seemed to him Wheeler should be "as like Capt. Wakeman as you can make him. Why not fairly and squarely retire an old sea-dog, and let him [take] to detecting in the ennui of the country? This is what you first tho't of doing, and I don't believe you can think of anything better. I want the story for the Atlantic." [1]

Twain began turning the play into a novel, while, however, still dreaming of a brilliant success on the stage. To Thomas Nast he wrote on 12 November 1877, that he was engaged in writing a book which he planned to "have ready for the printers and the dramatist (for I want it dramatised) by the end of January." [2] He may have been referring to *The Prince and the Pauper,* but it is more likely he had in mind the

[1] Howells to SLC, 31 October 1877 (*MTHL,* I, 207). Captain Edgar Wakeman was the captain of the *America,* the ship on which Twain sailed from San Francisco to the Isthmus in 1866. He was the model for Captain Blakely in *Roughing It,* Captain Hurricane Jones in "Some Rambling Notes of an Idle Excursion," and Captain Stormfield in *Extracts from Captain Stormfield's Visit to Heaven.*

[2] Original in the Berg Collection, New York Public Library.

novel mentioned in his 5 February 1878, letter to Mrs. Fairbanks: after describing *The Prince and the Pauper,* he added, "Of course I am doing some bread-&-butter work. . . . To-wit, a novel of the present day—about half finished. A talented young fellow here is dramatising it from my MS (I have just finished hurling a few sentences into his 1st Act here and there, this afternoon.) I expect to put the play & the chief character, into the hands of Sol Smith Russell." [3]

Originally Twain may have hired this "talented young fellow" with the intention of having him produce a dramatized version of the novel, but the traces of his work still visible in the Mark Twain Papers indicate that he soon became a general secretary whose principal task was to make a copy of the play written at Quarry Farm. In addition to the amanuensis copy, the Papers contain several routine letters and notes in the same hand signed "Sam' L. Clemens, per F. C. H." He apparently also took charge of remittances to Orion, for Orion, annoyed at receiving communications signed by a secretary, wrote Clemens on 5 February, "Please accept my thanks for the $42 drafts—three—and give my acknowledgments to your secretary for her autograph." [4] The details concerning the copy of the play and the secretary's rights therein were apparently not entirely settled when the Clemenses departed for Europe late in March, and Twain left them in Howells' hands. On 2 June, Howells sent a letter after Twain announcing the satisfactory settlement of the question of rights: "I have had a very pleasant letter from your cub-dramatist in Hartford, renouncing—or rather disclaiming—all right and title to Clews" [an alternate title for *Cap'n Simon Wheeler*].[5]

The Simon Wheeler novel was probably abandoned shortly after the 5 February letter to Mrs. Fairbanks in which he described the novel as "half-finished." Throughout his life he regarded 800 half-sheet manuscript pages as the equivalent of a one-volume book. Thus "half-finished" would describe a manuscript some 400 pages in length. The manuscript preserved in the Berg Collection of the New York Public Library consists of 541 pages and thirteen pages of notes. Despite the fact that the text has been much revised, the evidence of ink and paper indicates that with the exception of a few minor revisions the

---

[3] *MTF,* p. 218.

[4] Original in MTP. Orion presumably mistook the sex of the secretary because of the handwriting, which might easily be mistaken for a woman's.

[5] *MTHL,* I, 232–233.

manuscript was composed over a relatively short span of time. Such evidence suggests strongly that Twain ceased work on the novel prior to his departure for Europe in March 1878.

Although he never returned to the manuscript long enough to advance the story, he did frequently revert to his amateur detective in his thoughts over the next twenty years and from time to time tinkered with the text already written. Apparently he started for Europe with the intention of completing the novel while gathering materials for *A Tramp Abroad.* And apparently he used it to divert his attention from the frustrations he experienced in the composition of his travel book, but, perhaps because of the frustrations, he was unable to recapture his enthusiasm for the novel and finally he decided that the task was beyond his capabilities. On 21 January 1879, he wrote Howells:

> I have given up writing a detective novel—can't write a novel, for I lack the faculty; but when the detectives were nosing around after Stewart's loud remains, I threw a chapter into my present book in which I have very extravagantly burlesqued the detective business—if it *is* possible to burlesque that business extravagantly. You know I was going to send you that Detective play, so that you could re-write it. Well I didn't do it because I couldn't find a single idea in it that could be useful to you. It was dreadfully witless & flat. I knew it would sadden you & unfit you for work.[6]

Such a sweeping condemnation undoubtedly derived in part from the jaundiced condition into which the struggles with *A Tramp Abroad* had thrown him, for, returned from Europe, his travel book at last nearing completion, he regained his faith if not in his story at least in his character. When a now unidentifiable friend wrote to suggest a collaboration in a broad comedy, he wrote to Howells on 15 September

---

[6] *Ibid.*, I, 246. The chapter written for *A Tramp Abroad* was later deleted. It became instead the title piece for *The Stolen White Elephant,* published in 1882. In this burlesque Inspector Blunt, like Detective Bullet of "Simon Wheeler," is a caricature of Allan Pinkerton's New York superintendent, George H. Bangs, who headed the Pinkerton investigation of the bizarre episode on which *The Stolen White Elephant* is based. On 7 November 1878, the body of Alexander T. Stewart, a wealthy New York merchant, was stolen from a vault in Weehawken Cemetery. The police and numerous private detectives, including the Pinkertons, launched a massive investigation and search—to no avail. Finally in July 1880, the body was returned upon the payment by the family of a presumably large ransom. The sum was never disclosed, but earlier the family had offered a ransom of $50,000. Despite all the police activity, the body-snatchers apparently were never apprehended.

1879, asking Howells to join with him in writing a play with "Old Wakeman (Amateur Detective)" in it.[7]

In subsequent years, Twain reviewed the manuscript at least once and at least twice returned to it apparently with serious intentions of continuing the story. The first effort to continue was made sometime between 1885 and 1895, probably in the early 90's. At this time he reread the manuscript, made some minor revisions (usually of only a word or two), and projected the conclusion outlined in Group C of the working notes. The paper on which this conclusion was plotted matches various samples in letters and manuscripts preserved in the Mark Twain Papers which indicate that the paper was used extensively in the late 80's and early 90's. A notebook reference shortly after 29 May 1891, shows that the story had been recalled to his mind: "Gave Mr. Hall 'The Californian's Story' to be [typed] & kept. Also gave him the Wheeler detective story."[8] The reference suggests that the conclusion may have been drafted at about this time. But it is equally possible that the work was done in 1894, when Twain reviewed the manuscript and decided that a portion of chapter 10, Wheeler's dream-visit to Heaven, might be used on a program during his forthcoming around-the-world lecture tour. In his notebook he listed a number of program suggestions, and among those jotted under the heading of 4 November 1894, he included "Si Wheeler's arrival in heaven."[9]

Sometime after 1896 he again returned to the manuscript and made another, if feeble, attempt to continue. This attempt is reflected in a number of minor penciled revisions throughout the text and in a note in the top margin of page 433 of the manuscript: "Gillette's SS speech," probably a reference to a speech in William Gillette's play *Secret Service* (produced in 1895), Captain Thorne's major speech of the play in the last act. Captain Thorne, whose dilemma in the play is somewhat analogous to Dexter's in the novel, expresses here emotions similar to those of Dexter in the portion of the manuscript where the note appears. One may assume that the note reflects Twain's intention to recast this section of the novel in order to bring such emotions more sharply into focus, using Captain Thorne's speech as a model. Since Twain probably did not see *Secret Service* before its London run in

[7] *MTHL,* I, 269.

[8] Typescript Notebook 25, p. 44, MTP. Frederick J. Hall, partner in Charles L. Webster and Company, Twain's publishing firm, became its manager in 1889 when Webster withdrew.

[9] Typescript Notebook 27, p. 35, MTP.

1896 with Gillette, his friend and former protégé, in the role of Captain Thorne, the likelihood is that the work on the novel was done after 1896.

In fact, most probably the work was not done until after 16 August 1898. On that date Twain wrote to Howells a letter which contains his last surviving reference to the novel:

> In 1876 *or* '75, I wrote 40,000 words of a story called "Simon Wheeler" wherein the nub was the preventing of an execution through testimony furnished by mental telegraph from the other side of the globe. I had a lot of people scattered about the globe who carried in their pockets something like the old mesmerizer-button, made of different metals, & when they wanted to call up each other & have a talk, they "pressed the button" or did *some*thing, I don't remember what, & communication was at once, opened. I didn't finish the story, though I re-began it in several new ways, & spent altogether 70,000 words on it, then gave it up & threw it aside.[10]

Twain's recollection here differs markedly from the facts. The mesmerizer-button business may be a faulty recollection of Lem's pocket-telegraph in the Brummel-Arabella fragment, and it is always possible that some such variation upon the pocket-telegraph was worked into the outline sent to Reade or the version described to Chandos Fulton, but it is doubtful that he wrote as many as 40,000 words on that early version. That total more nearly describes the novel *Simon Wheeler, Detective.* Obviously the recollection is one made from some distance and in which several story lines and stages of development have been commingled. The inference is that he had not yet reviewed the novel after seeing Gillette's play. One may surmise that this recollection sent him back to the manuscript to see if the tank had filled up. He revised slightly, jotted the note, and decided, this time finally, that the story would not work itself out.

---

[10] *MTHL,* II, 674–675.

# *Simon Wheeler, Detective*

## Chap. 1.

THE SCENE of this history is a sleepy little Missouri village hidden away from the world in the heart of a cluster of densely wooded hills, where railways and steamboats were not known; where tourists and travelers never came; where the telegraph intruded not; where the only journals were a couple of [11] chloroformed weeklies whose sole news was "local," whose advertisers paid in trade, whose subscribers paid in cord-wood and turnips, and whose editors discussed nothing but each other, and not in Sunday-school terms either. In this drowsing hamlet nothing had changed during a generation; the weather and the crops were the staple of conversation, as they had been always; Ossian and Thaddeus of Warsaw [12] were still read, fire and brimstone still preached.

This village of Guilford ended suddenly at its northern extremity, and one found himself at once upon the threshold of wild nature; a charming expanse of woods and hills lay before him,[13] with green meadow-glimpses here and there, two or three scattering cottages in the distance, and a crooked and rugged gorge that reflected its vines and crags in a tranquil little river.

Leading northward from the village was a broad and well worn

[11] At the top of MS p. 2, Twain wrote in parentheses "not Saturday but Monday." In accordance with this note, he deleted a paragraph which specified the time as Saturday. The day was changed to allow time for the Guilford newspapers, weeklies issued on Friday, to reach Drytown for Hale Dexter's perusal upon his arrival there (see chap. 2).

[12] A highly successful historical novel by Jane Porter (1776–1850) published in London, 1803.

[13] Above this clause, at the top of MS p. 3, Twain wrote, "(moonlight, now)."

footway, which faithfully followed the windings of this stream, threading its way among occasional great boulders, stealing through the twilight mystery of brief forest patches, marching across open grassy levels, and rustic bridges that spanned limpid, brawling, knee-deep tributaries—and so, on and on, until, having traversed a mile and a half of varied prettinesses and charming surprises, it entered the gorge. Thence forward its surroundings were as rugged and picturesque as they had before been simple and pleasing. This river-path was a favorite resort of the villagers on moonlit evenings in summer or the earlier gloaming. It had several names. The practical called it "Drytown Trail"; the romantic called it "Lover's Ramble"; a few super-artificials referred to it as "La Belle Promenade."

The two wealthiest families in Guilford were the Griswolds and the Burnsides.—"Judge" Burnside [14] had never been on the bench; but that was no matter; he was the first citizen of the place, he was a man of great personal dignity, therefore no power in this world could have saved him from a title. He had been dubbed Major, then Colonel, then Squire; but gradually the community settled upon "Judge," and Judge he remained, after that.

He was sixty years old; very tall, very spare, with a long, thin, smooth-shaven, intellectual face, and long black hair that lay close to his head, was kept to the rear by his ears as one keeps curtains back by brackets, and fell straight to his coat collar without a single tolerant kink or relenting curve. He had an eagle's beak and an eagle's eye. He was a Kentuckian by birth and rearing; he came of the oldest and best Kentucky Griswolds, and they from the oldest and proudest Griswolds of Virginia. Judge Griswold's manners and carriage were of the courtly old-fashioned sort; he had never worked; he was a gentleman. He so entered himself in the census list. To him that abused word still possessed what he called its only warrantable meaning. In his eyes, a man who came of gentle blood and fell to the ranks of scavengers and blacklegs, was still a gentleman and could not help it, since the word did not describe character but only birth; and a man who did not come of gentle

[14] Note that in the next paragraph and henceforth the name shifts to "Judge Griswold."

blood might climb to the highest pinnacle of human grandeur but must still lack one thing—nothing could make him a gentleman; he might be called so by courtesy, but there an end. In his younger days nobody had lightly used the word in the south; our modern fashion of speaking of everybody, indiscriminately, as ladies and gentlemen maddened him; and once when he read in a paper how that a hostler had clubbed "another gentleman" for talking disrespectfully of a tavern chambermaid and "another lady," he swore the first oath that had ever passed his lips, and followed it up with a lurid procession of profanity that was five-and-forty minutes passing a given point.

The Judge was punctiliously honorable, austerely upright. No man wanted his bond who had got his word. He was grave even to sternness; he seldom smiled. He loved strongly, but without demonstration; he hated implacably. He decorously attended church twice a month; but if he had a religion it was his own secret; religion was a subject he never mentioned.

His wife was about fifty; she was gentle, loving, patient, pious, and believed everything her husband believed about everybody and everything except the hereafter; no doubt she would have adopted his belief about that, too, if he had revealed one.

They had buried all their children but one: Milly, a simple little beauty of sixteen, with light hair hanging down her back in two long plaited tails tied at the ends with blue or pink ribbon according to the gown they were to "match." Her actions and her rounded form were full of girlish grace; she sang the ballads of the day, she read romantic little tales and cried over them, she still cherished cats; she was not even wholly estranged from her last doll, though nobody knew that but herself. She was a very sweet and dainty and artless little maid, the idol of her father, who sometimes manifested this by a look or a word, but never kissed and never petted her. One perceives that this girl was still a girl, nothing more, and yet she lived in a region where hers was a womanly age—at least a marrying age.

Mrs. Burnside was a gracious and winning old lady, of fine family, whose life was wrapped up in her two remaining children, Hugh, aged twenty, and Clara, twenty-one. Clara had the delicacy and refinement of a woman, and the pluck, decision and spirit of a man. She was a beautiful creature, slender but shapely, a trifle above medium height, with brown eyes that were deep and tender when her soul was in repose, but burned with passion when it was stirred. Her usual humor was happy and sparkling; and in this mood she had a bird-like fashion of setting her head aside and glancing up a trifle coquettishly, which was pretty to see; but there were other times and rarer when she was too severely in earnest for idle graces and nonsense.

Hugh was an innocent. He was giddy and thoughtless, when he was not sappy and sentimental. At twenty he was, during three-fourths of every day, still sixteen. He would hunt and fish all day, taking no heed of anything but his pleasure; and then, as likely as not, go off in a corner and pout over some imaginary slight inflicted by somebody who was entirely unconscious of having offered him one. The world was hollow to him, then, and he was more than likely to shut himself up in his room and write some stuff about "bruised hearts" or "the despised and friendless," and print it in one of the village journals under the impression that it was poetry. He was the butt of the town and the apple of his mother's eye.

One day, in the spring, Mrs. Griswold said to her husband—

"The Burnsides are to have a visitor."

"Well?"

Judge Griswold did not look up from the book he was reading.

"From Kentucky."

The Judge said nothing, and gave no sign. Plainly the matter did not interest him. Mrs. Griswold added—

"It is Mrs. Burnside's nephew—young Hale Dexter."

The Judge laid his book down and faced about. There was a strange light in his eye. Said he—

"It needed no prophet to say that this would happen some day."

Mrs. Griswold paled. She washed her hands helplessly together, and said in a voice so weak that it was hardly audible—

"I had hoped and believed that that was all ended long ago."

"Ended!" said the Judge—and the light of battle was in his eye—"a Kentucky feud never ends!"

Mrs. Griswold began an exclamation, but it perished in a gasp.

"It never ends! This stripling is coming here to kill his cousin Hugh. Now look you, my wife, we have a duty to perform. We must save him—"

"Hugh?—O yes, O surely!" eagerly interrupted Mrs. Griswold, white and trembling.

*"Hugh?* No! Dexter! We must be ready with horses and men and spirit him out of the country when the deed is done!"

Mrs. Griswold was past speaking. She dropped her countenance; she was not able to endure her husband's flaming eyes. He went on fervently, as one who recalls the blessed memories of a vanished time—

"The feud between the Burnsides and the Dexters has lasted longer than I can remember [15]—it cannot end till one house is extinct. When the sister of Hale Dexter's father married a Burnside, some weaklings imagined it was York and Lancaster wedded again, and the wars of the roses finished. Wiser heads took into account the fact that Edward Dexter was an invalid, a prisoner in his bed. He remained a prisoner ten years. What did he do then? The moment he was on his legs he took his gun and came to Missouri—to this village, Madam!"

Mrs. Griswold looked up and gasped—

"Came here? I never knew it?"

"You were visiting at Hoxton. I received him in this house. He was travel-worn, tired, hungry; but he would touch nothing. He said, 'I will neither eat, drink nor sleep till I have warned my sister's husband and called him out and killed him.' I beguiled him with questions and random talk—miserable expedients to delay the news I had not the heart to tell him at once. But when this would not answer longer, I blurted it out, and awkwardly enough—'Burnside,' I said, 'is lying on his death-bed!' Poor fellow, he was unprepared for it. He sat where you are sitting now. He gave me such a look—so wounded, so stricken—his head fell listlessly against the wall, and he said, 'And I have waited ten years!' "

---

[15] At the top of MS p. 20, Twain wrote "(Mrs. G. doesn't know the D's, but loves D because her husband does—and pities him.)"

"God forgive him!" murmured Mrs. Griswold.

"Every day, and all day long, he watched the Burnside house from the attic window. He was too restless to talk; my presence only disturbed his thoughts. He cleaned his gun and reloaded it a dozen times a day. When he was not watching, he walked the floor and mumbled to himself. The servants thought he was crazy. I always carried him news of Burnside myself; but one day I had to send a servant—Mulatto Bob—with tidings that Burnside was better. Dexter embraced him furiously and gave him five dollars. Next day Bob begged to be messenger again, and I allowed him to go with the news that Burnside was worse. Dexter threw him down stairs and broke his leg."

Mrs. Burnside [16] had been in a recalling attitude for a minute. Now she said—

"They told me all about that, but *you* and *they* called that man Johnson."

"It was what he called himself, for better security. It was a dismal day for me, the day I had to go up and tell him Burnside was dead.[17] At first he raged about the room, cursing his ill luck. Then he quieted down and sat a long time thinking. By and by he asked about the Burnside family. I named the children and their ages. He brightened when I mentioned Hugh; saddened again when he remembered that Hugh could be only a little boy. He shook his head sorrowfully and said, 'Gentlemen do not war with children.' Presently he said, 'I have nothing more to live for.' We sat silent, then, an age. Finally Dexter said, not as one who consciously speaks, but only thinks aloud, 'I, too, am leaving a boy behind me; he shall finish the work.' Then after a time he muttered in the same way, and with a smothered sigh, 'It is like all of life—a hope that buds in a promise, and blossoms in a disappointment; I shall be glad to go.' When he started home I did not ask him if he wished to leave any message for his sister, and I knew his delicacy would not allow him to afflict me with one without the asking.—He was going to leave his gun, but hesitated, muttered something about his son and went

[16] I.e., Mrs. Griswold.

[17] Along the margin, Twain wrote, "Explain," apparently intending to expand upon Dexter's use of an alias "for better security."

into the house and got it again. Poor fellow, he dragged himself home and lay down and died."

There was a pensive silence for some seconds, and then Mrs. Griswold absently murmured—

"Poor fellow!"

"Ah, then you pity him, too?" said the Judge with interest.

Mrs. Griswold was confused. She said—

"Why no! I hardly know what I *did* feel. For the moment I seemed to pity him, but why, Heaven only knows. I think I felt for the disappointment, forgetting for the instant what the nature of it was."

The Judge heard the beginning, but not the end. He had drifted back into his old memories again. Presently he said—

"He was a fine man, Dexter—good old Kentucky stock, with a good old Virginian root. Brave as Richard, chivalrous as Saladin. We were always friends. You know that when I was young the Griswolds and the Morgans had been at feud for three generations—"

"Yes, I know. What was it about?"

"I do not remember—that is, I never knew. I think it never occurred to me to ask. But no matter; it is not likely that any of my generation could have told me. Besides, the feud itself was the only thing of consequence; how it originated was a circumstance of no interest. I was only taught that when I should meet a Morgan there was a thing to be done; it was very simple—kill him."

"Or be killed yourself?" said Mrs. Griswold, with a falling inflection and a shudder.

"*That* is understood. As boys, I and my brothers built Morgans of snow, in winter, and of rubbish in summer, and killed them. Later on, came the killing in earnest. No matter about that—it is not what I wish to speak of. The point I am coming to is this: two Morgans and three of their friends met me unexpectedly on the road, once, when I was twenty-five. I drew—they did the same. Dexter came riding up, saw how the odds stood, and being my friend he reinforced me, of course, though he had nothing against the Morgans. Between us we killed three outright; the other two lingered a month.—I was not a well man for more than a year;

Dexter was never a well man afterwards; at least he never was nearly so well as he had been before.—You perceive, I am under an obligation to him and his family. I am glad to keep it green in my memory. I shall be as a father to his son; I know you will be as a mother to him."

"You cannot doubt it—his father saved your life. His mother was my schoolmate and later friend. All that gratitude can prompt, and all that love can do, shall be done for him. This shall be his home; he shall be no guest, but one of us."

"You speak what I feel. I am glad, and thank you. Where is he?"

"Visiting that distant relative, old Humphrey, at Marley, for a few days."

"Is the old man any better?" [18]

"Worse, they say, but not really threatened with death."

"Still, he will not live long. His fortune will make Hale Dexter very rich."

"Yes, and all the villagers here very angry. They call him all sorts of hard names for leaving the money to a stranger whom they neither know nor care for, and who will carry it off to Kentucky. They say he might at least have divided the money, instead of giving it all to one cousin, to go to the other when the first recipient dies."

"Yes—both are so young that Hugh may likely find it weary waiting for Hale to die. Humphrey is a strange person and always was. When is Hale coming here?"

"His letter says day after tomorrow."

"We will make preparation." Then after a pause, "What name is he coming under?"

This gave Mrs. Griswold an electric shock, it brought the probable grim purpose of the visit back to her mind. But in another moment she said—

"His own."

Evidently the Judge was perplexed. He walked the floor a while, puzzling over the matter, then said—

---

[18] Beside this and the following three paragraphs, Twain drew a vertical line in the margin and wrote, "kill."

"There is some mistake. Look at the letter again."

Mrs. Griswold did so.

"No," she said, "he does not mention any fictitious name. He encloses a brief note from his mother, recommending him to me—now that I observe it closer there are tear-stains on it—but she calls him by his own name, too.—There is no suggestion of mystery anywhere, except that Hale mentions, as in the most casual way, that he will time his journey so as to reach here at night."

"Ah," said the Judge. "His purpose is plain, though his method is puzzling."

"O, I pray God you are mistaken. It is awful to think of. That poor Hugh is as harmless as he can be, and at bottom is a good child. It would be *double* murder—it would kill his mother. I will not, can not, have it that you are right."

"But I am right.—I know the Dexter blood. It has a long memory and a deathless purpose.—This youth comes on the business his father left him. We must protect him till it is done, then get him away. My life shall be freely forfeited in his defence, if need be. Wife, keep his coming a secret until he is here. He will tell us how to proceed then."

At this point Milly entered, and all the grimness melted out of her father's eyes. The conversation ceased. Milly moved about the room from place to place, humming an air in happy contentment, and got a needle here, a strip of perforated cardboard there and some colored cruels out of a basket, her father's eyes following her lovingly the while, then she sat down and began to embroider one of the fearful and wonderful book-marks of the period. During half an hour the Judge walked the floor, planning the rescue to follow the coming tragedy. Mrs. Griswold sat thinking, and saying to herself, "He was near being slaughtered, Dexter saved him, we are married thirty years and then he casually mentions it for the first time; and as usual I find I am only surprised that he ever mentioned it at all; he never explained 'Johnson' to me before; I can admire his reticence, and I do—to comprehend it is beyond a woman." Now and then she sighed and said to herself, "Poor Mary Burnside; poor Hugh—O my God!"

And all the while the young girl's soft music went on, and the book-mark grew. By and by she held it off, examined it with a critical eye, saw that her work was good, and blushed. Upon a neutral groundwork, within a half-completed, variegated border, it bore the word HUGH.

## Chap. 2.

HALE DEXTER had been something more than a day and a half in the saddle. It was becoming wearisome work, and tedious. He ceased to take interest in the scenery or anything else, and fell to drifting off into dreams and thinkings. About the middle of the afternoon he roused himself and looked about. He found himself in the midst of a maze of cattle paths—no road visible anywhere. He stopped his horse and considered. He could not remember when he had last observed the road; he did not know whether he had been out of it a long or a short time. He turned and looked back—nothing there but a web of paths that crossed and re-crossed each other in every direction. Here was a predicament. There was but one thing to do: try to return in his horse's hoof-tracks. He tried it, and failed early.—The horse had crossed grassy patches and broken the trail. It were as profitable to stand still as to move; but one can't stand still in such cases, therefore the young man moved—for a while in one direction, then in another, not making the matter worse, perhaps, but not bettering it any. At the end of an hour he was very tired of this, and very thoroughly vexed; and hungry and thirsty withal. One always gets hungry and thirsty as soon as he finds that food and water are far away.

Now he glanced rearward and saw two persons in the distance,—a welcome sight. He turned about and was soon with them. One of them was a stalwart young fellow with light hair and a good-humored face, the other a young lady. Young Dexter saluted; the young fellow bowed and said, "Good-day, sir," the young lady inclined her head slightly, but said nothing. Dexter's thought was,

"It was worth getting lost, to see this girl's face"; the girl's thought was, "The stranger is handsome." Dexter spoke—

"I am sorry to trouble you, but I am a stranger and I am afraid I am lost."

The young girl thought, "He has a fine voice."

The young fellow delivered himself of the sort of bubbling laugh that goes with youth and a soul at peace, and said—

"I shouldn't be surprised if you could put it stronger and say you know you are. Which way did you come?"

"I—well, the truth is I don't know."

"I said it! A stranger can't be expected to find his way through this place—it pushes a native to do it. We saw you before you saw us; we noticed which way you were going—which was towards nowhere in particular. We said, there's somebody that's lost. So we whipped up to overtake you."

"It was very kind of you, indeed. I got out of the Drytown road without noticing it, and have been wandering about here a good while."

The young man and the young girl turned their horses about and struck into a trot, the former saying, with another comfortable laugh—

"It's not so bad as I thought; you weren't hunting for a short cut, but only nodding. There are plenty of short cuts here, but none to Drytown. The regular road's the directest."

"But you are turning back on your own journey. Do not do that; I can't allow you to take so much trouble."

"Why my dear sir, it's good three miles and a half back to the Drytown road." The speed was not slackened.

"Then I *can* not inconvenience you so much—and the young lady." Dexter reined in his horse. "If you will kindly point—"

"Point the way? I will, of course; but I think it would be better if we went with you. And mind I tell you it's no easy thing to describe it so that a stranger—." He stopped, and searched the distance for a landmark. Shook his head. "It's a blind region—a mighty blind region. First you go—" He turned, with a perplexed look and found a smile on the young girl's face that suggested how considerably she was enjoying his difficulty. "Hang it, don't smile—that doesn't help any—give me an idea!"

The girl said—

"How can a body help but smile? Don't you know perfectly well that the route cannot be described so that one who has never traveled it can follow it? We are losing time."

She started her horse briskly forward; the gentlemen did likewise. Dexter said to himself, "More than half an hour to look at her in—it is worth being lost a week! I was in mortal fear they'd take me at my word and direct me instead of leading me." Then he made one more protest, aloud, about the trouble he was causing, but there was no heart in it. The girl's comrade said—

"O don't you bother about that. It's no inconvenience to me; and she—well, five or ten miles more or less is nothing to her; she don't mind it. Riding's no more to her than deciding; riding's nothing to me, but deciding's different—that is, when there's much of a puzzle about it."

The way was anything but straight. It wound hither and thither to avoid ridges, gullies and rocky outcrops, but the three were usually able to ride abreast. The broad young fellow had the middle place. While he discoursed cheerily about strangers who had come to grief in the mazes of this cattle-range, Dexter kept up an appearance of active interest by throwing in a "Yes?" or a "No?" or an "Indeed?" here and there in the wrong place, which encouraged the jovial story-teller to go on with his marvels, and left the stranger free to admire the young girl with charmed and furtive eye, and comment on her to himself. "How graceful she is—and beautiful! And her eye—ah, what an eye it is! So rich and deep and brown; so sweet—and sometimes so mischievous! Such character in the face! Then the voice—I wish she would speak again. Only half an hour of her! Only that—but even that is worth being lost a month. I never can have any luck—another man would have been twice as badly lost. That would give him an hour of her. There—I caught her eye. I believe she blushed—I wish I had the pluck to look and see. I wonder what she is to this young fellow. Sweetheart? She smiled on him so archly; she looked at him so affectionately; and he

—he spoke of her so proudly. Ah, that's it, that's it—I wish I hadn't thought of it."

Then his face lost animation; took on a dejected cast. He forgot to throw in his "Yes's" and "No's"; but the historian's tongue wagged cheerfully on, dead to everything but the charm of its own music.

Meanwhile the young girl stole an occasional glance and communed with herself. "Yes, he is very handsome. Finely formed and manly. There is spirit in his face—and strength. Black hair, black eyes. Black hair and black eyes suit some faces; they suit his. He rides well. An odd place to go to—Drytown. I caught his eye, then —I believe I am blushing.—Vexation!—why should I be so confused? There's nothing to be confused about. If he should discover it! He can't, if he is minding his own affairs. It is impertinent in him to look at me. Why should he look at me? I wish we had left him where he was. Can he have noticed? . . . But it's nothing—nothing; I do not care a straw. Still, I wish I knew if he . . . I *will* look again. Ah, now he is pouting; looks as injured and dejected as if somebody *else* had done something, when it's himself. Very well, let him pout; I'm sure *I* don't care. Hold up your head, won't you! and quit fretting at the bit! Take that! . . . Now then . . . stay quiet, or you'll catch it again. . . . I wonder if he is pouting yet."

Dexter—to himself:

"There—she's vexed; she looks it. Acts it, too—I ought to have that cut, not the horse. 'Twas I that offended. But I didn't mean any harm, I was only worshiping. She is very much displeased. Well, well, it's [a] villain world; nothing ever goes right in it—for me, anyway. *Is* she his sweetheart?"

The historian cuts short his tale with a—

"Hold up, sister, here we are!"

Dexter, to himself—

"*Sister!* There's music in his voice! One last look!"—

The sister, to herself—

"I will just take one glance at this creature and see if he—why he's radiant!"

Dexter, to himself—

"Bless me, how she lights up!"

The brother—

"We'll leave you here, sir—here's the road. Keep straight ahead—you're all right, now."

"Why, we have come very quickly! I am very grateful to you, sir; and to the young lady your sister; and if I have not taxed your kindness too far—"

"O, that's no consequence—none in the world. If anybody's to be thanked, it's she, not me. I shouldn't have had any more wit than to direct you and confuse you, and leave you and lose you again. It's more my place to thank you. I haven't had such a good talk in a year. Generally people don't seem to care to listen to me; but with you it's different, and I like it."

"Well, I can say in all frankness that if you have enjoyed talking, I have not less enjoyed being near you while you did it."

"Good! There—your throat-latch is unbuckled—keep your seat, I'll fix it. Now your hand—good-bye. Stick to the road and you're all right."

He shook hands heartily, turned his horse about, Dexter took off his hat and bowed to the girl, with some awkward half-audible thanks, which she received with a little inclination of the head and a not unpleased look, and the parties separated, the horses walking. After three or four steps, young Dexter ventured to steal a backward glance—and caught the girl in the same act.—She gave her horse a sharp cut with her whip, Dexter accommodated his animal with a spur-stab which expressed a trifle of vexation, and the distance widened rapidly between the new acquaintances. But presently Dexter got down to tighten his saddle-girth. He took hold of the strap, but paused to gaze; two figures were rising and falling to the undulating movement of a canter, and steadily receding. He watched them till they disappeared. Then he mounted again, with a sigh and moved on his way. But he hadn't tightened his girth.

He was full of thinkings. By and by he started—

"What a blunder!" he said, "never to have thought of asking the young man his name! A woman wouldn't have forgotten such a thing." Presently he said, "I like him. What a good-hearted, giddy chap he is! And she—what a numscull I have been!"

He drove the spurs home—though it was not really the horse's blunder.

The girl and her brother cantered on. The latter took up his history again with animation. The girl, listening without hearing, biting her lips, as one wrought upon by a secret vexation, by and by broke into the middle of a sentence, brightening hopefully as she spoke—

"Now suppose Mr. . . . er . . . er—"

"Who? That young fellow?"

"Yes! I was thinking, suppose Mr. . . . er . . . er—"

"Well, suppose he *what?*"

*"Nothing!"*

The historian proceeded.—After a little the girl severed the tale with another hopeful interruption—

"I suppose Mr. . . . er . . . er—whatever his name is!—is just passing through the country—not going to stop."

"Yes—maybe so. *I* don't know. As I was saying, Jones finally got mixed up, and judged he was lost—knew he was, in fact. Well, the first thing he did was to—"

"Didn't he *say* anything about it?"

"Who?—Jones?"

"O, plague Jones!"

"O, you mean the other fellow. No—yes. Let me see. Once when you were ahead a little, he said—he said—well, I'll remember it presently. He looked around and said—"

"Said *what?*"

"He didn't say *any*thing. He was *going* to say, 'I'm up a stump,' but—"

"There, there—you were going to remember. Then why don't you leave off a minute and *try* to remember?"

"Well, I will. I only wanted to get through that, first. He said—"

"Well?"

"*I* can't remember what he said." A long pause. "No—I give it up. I thought I could remember, but I can't. But I like him—he's a good fellow."

Here he dropped into history again. His sister fretted a while, then put on an aspect of resignation. The history proceeded till it reached this point: "Jones took to a tree, the bull after him—" when the girl cut in with—

"I should say he was of good stock."

"Only so-so. Comes from the same old Warren county tribe. They all do."

"Did he say so?"

"Who?—Jones?"

"Burn Jones!"

"Burn him? He's a mighty good man, if he *is* short-stock. Why once when Hank Miller got the cramp in the river—"

The girl dropped into a reverie, and the history rolled over her, wave after wave, but disturbed her not.—Finally she walled the tide with—

"If *I* had been you, I would have taken the trouble to ask him—"

"Well—ask him what?"

"O, nothing."

"Well, I did. As I was saying, they pumped and pumped—well, they pumped about a barrel of water out of him, and by and by, sure enough, he came to. It was all owing to Jones. Everybody says that. By the way! I believe I'll write to him and tell him about that."

"Write to *whom?*"

"Why, that young fellow. I forgot to tell it when I was talking. It's a prime story. I believe I'll do it—wouldn't you?"

The sister showed quick interest.

"Yes, I would," said she. "No—I wouldn't. He might not care for it, and then you are not well enough acquainted."

"Well, that's true. Yes, that's true. I won't write him. Jones told me once, that when he first came to this region—"

"But suppose you did know him well enough, and were going to write him—"

"Well?"

"How would you begin?"

"How would I begin?"

"Yes. Just begin, now, as if you were going to write him. You would be awkward enough about it, I fancy. Come—begin."

"It's perfectly easy. I should say, 'My Dear Sir: On the occasion that I had the honor to tell you some particulars about the region where you got lost, and where my sister and I had the good fortune and also the pleasure to—' "

"Why that is very good—very good indeed. I confess you could do it well. Next, how would you address the letter?"

"Address it?" The young fellow's face began to lose its animation and look blank. The young girl was watching it. When its change was complete, she lashed her horse suddenly and broke away, ejaculating, half audibly—

"I just knew it! He never asked him!"

Hale Dexter arrived at the wretched little tavern at Drytown a trifle after dark and found the landlord, a couple of negro servants and a dozen villagers grouped about the front door, in listening attitude and looking very uncomfortable. There was a fine row going on within. Said the landlord—

"Gimme your hoss, stranger, and stay wher' you are.—Three stage-drivers are layin' into old Si Wheeler, in there, and it's warm times."

"Three on one, and you people allowing it? Is this Missouri style? Come in, and require fair play."

But nobody followed him in. The bar room was in an uproar; chairs and benches lay wrecked about it. A well built man of near fifty, with short, curly, yellow-reddish hair and a bloody but smiling face, stood in a corner, barricaded with a broad table which he had drawn in front of him, flourishing a heavy oaken cane, or rather club, and saying, "O come on, don't mind old Si, *he* don't 'mount to much!"

The three burly and gory stage-drivers had turned to see who had opened and closed the door. One of them squared himself before Hale and said—

"Stop wher' you are! Mix in, or leave! Who're you for, in this fight? State it quick, or vammus!"

"For the old man in the corner!" He had his hands full in a moment.

"Huray!" shouted the man in the corner, clearing his table at a bound and bringing down an enemy with his club, "it's an even thing, now—two *men* against three imitations!"

He threw away his club and went at his work as one who loves it. As fast as his two men could get up they went down again under his vigorous fist. They remained down presently, and both called for quarter. The victor turned.

"Well?" said he.

"My man is satisfied," said Dexter.

"He looks it. Give us your hand—you're true grit, stranger."

The landlord and the populace entered; a negro servant was ordered to show Dexter to his room, Si Wheeler followed, took a seat, and chatted freely and comfortably while Dexter removed his battle stains.

"What had you been doing to those roughs?" said the Kentuckian.

"Me? *I* didn't do anything to them. I'm only here for a few days on a matter in my little line of business, and I hadn't ever seen them before. One of them picked a quarrel with a poor devil of a nigger hostler and that harmless old granny of a landlord, and when I said I judged I'd take a hand myself to sort of even the thing up a little, the other two told me to mind my own business or they'd mix in, too. Says I, 'Mix! You've come to the right shop.' So in I went,—and out went the nigger and the landlord. I could 'a' cleaned them all, retail; but wholesale they ruther held over me. 'Twas lucky for me you chipped in. Say—you're good grit; and you've got a prime muscle. They *do* raise that sort down Ozark-way."

"I suppose so. But I'm not from there."

Wheeler—to himself—

"That didn't take. I'll try him on another lay." Then aloud: "I should 'a' thought you was from there. But a body's so apt to be mistaken. Laws, as like as not I missed it a hundred mile."

"About that—yes, more than that."

Wheeler—to himself—

"*That* didn't fetch him. Well, I'll try something else and come back to that."—Aloud: "You'd be suprised to see what curious names some people have around here. I know some named Waxy, and Abble, and Mucker, and Ding—O, all sorts of odd names. Then again there's a lot that ain't odd at all—like enough it's so down your way. My name ain't odd. My name's Wheeler—Cap'n Si Wheeler."

Dexter—to himself—

"It's a queer old chap. If he wants to know my name and where I'm from, why doesn't he simply say so? Has an idea it wouldn't be polite, maybe." Then aloud: "Ah—Wheeler, is it? I'm glad to know it—and to know you. I ought to have mentioned mine, sooner, but I was absent-minded. My name is Dexter—Hale Dexter—from Kentucky. I am on my way to—"

A look of anguish spread itself over old Wheeler's face. "O, don't!" said he.

"What is the trouble, friend?"

"I wish you hadn't told me—it's such a pity—don't tell me any more."

"I am very sorry, Captain, but I had the idea that you wanted to know, and—"

"O, I *did* want to know, but not that way—not that way."

"Not that way? How, then?"

"O, there's better ways—more satisfactory. You see, I'm a bit of a detective; not a regular, you understand, not official, but just on my own hook—an *ama*ture, so to speak. Well, a detective don't like to be told things—he likes to find them out.—You look at the detective books—you'll see."

"Ah—I see my mistake, now," said Dexter, a good deal amused.

"Yes. Well, a detective don't ever ask a question right out about what he wants to know. He asks questions away off yonder, round about, you know, that don't seem to bear on the matter at all, but bless you they're deep—deep as the sea. First thing a man knows, that detective has got all the information he wants, and that man don't ever suspect how he done it. See?"

"Yes. It must be a wonderful art?"

"Detecting? You bet it is. Why if you'd 'a' let me alone, I'd 'a' pumped you dry, and yet never asked you a thing that ever seemed to refer to anything in this world or the next."

"Well I won't interfere again, Captain—I only did it this time through ignorance and simplicity."

A negro appeared at the door and said, "Supper's ready."

"Well, I'll go, now, Mr. Dexter. I'm going to be about here a day or two, working up a case, as we say, and if you're around day after to-morrow—"

"To-morrow afternoon I go on to—"

"There—you're at it again! You leave it to me—I'll find it all out. All I want's a clew—the least little clew in the world—an old comb with a tooth gone's a plenty—and I'll find out anything I want to about the owner of it. Don't tell me anything—just leave me alone. Good-bye. Shake."

They shook hands and Wheeler went. But he put his head in again, and said—

"Here's the Guilford papers. You might like to run your eye over them. They're splendid papers. There ain't any better around this region. So-long." (Meaning Good-bye.) As he moved away, he observed to himself, "It's Hugh Burnside's cousin, that they say is going to have old [Humphrey]'s [19] pile of money when he dies. Old [Humphrey] is sick again, and like enough he sent for him. There's where he's bound for now; I could 'a' ciphered out the rest of it as easy as I've done this, if he'd 'a' let me alone."

"This *is* an odd fish," said Dexter to himself. He threw the newspapers on the bed and went down to supper.

By and by he returned to his room and sat down to smoke and think. Of what? Of that young girl. Her form floated before his imagination as in a tinted mist, the sound of her voice came and went, in his ear, fitfully and soft, like the distant murmur of music.

After a while his eye fell upon one of the newspapers, and he took it up. It was a wretchedly printed little sheet, being very vague and pale in spots, and in other spots so caked with ink as to be hardly decipherable. The first column was occupied by "Original

[19] This meditation was inserted during one of the later revisions at a time when Twain had forgotten the name of the old man. In writing the insert, Twain here and in the next sentence left blanks to be filled in, but he never did so.

Poetry" of the sappiest description. The next four were occupied by a selected story which was as sappy as the poetry. The remaining column of this first page was made up of short paragraphs of vapid, heart-breaking, infuriating rot entitled "Wit and Humor." The other outside page was built wholly of advertisements; three columns consisted mainly of glorified quack-poisons, stereotyped in various measures, headed with blurred portraits of the assassins who invented the nostrums, and tailed with lying testimonials from people who had never existed; the two remaining columns were thrown into one, which sang the praises of "Bagley's Celebrated One-Price Emporium" in riotous display-lines of forty-line pica shot full of shouting exclamation points. This whole page of advertisements was *repeated* on the inside without a blush or an apology. The editorial page was of double-leaded small-pica, and the turned letters were so thick that it was nearly as easy to read it upside down as right side up. The other marvels of bad proof-reading covered all the vast possibilities, in that line, comprehensively, exhaustively, miraculously.

Dexter tried a specimen-editorial, to taste of its quality: [20]

"THE DES*p*ERADO JACK BELFORD.—This inhnman miscreaut who is ʇo be hnug next mouth and his cri*m*e-blackend sole seut to that place unmentiouaBle to eɐrs polite whəre it belon8s, and who hɐs twicə before triep to breɐk jail and wouɹd have &ucceəped buʇ for the vigilɐnce of the eveɹ-efficient Sheriff of ƃoggsville, the accomplisɥed and geuʇlemenly Maj. Hosʞins, who *k*nows hoʍ to retain the gnests oɟ his hospıtable little estalbishɯent wheu he oNce gets them inʇo it, and *w*ho came near murdering hea*d-k*eeper Hubbard the last tiMe he tried to bɹeak out, mɐde one *m*ore attempt last Thursday night, only the day before we wemt to press and so could not get it in type for last week's issne, tho' we issuep an extra Friday noon with ouɹ accostomed enterprise and de*v*otion to the inʇerests of our paʇrons, but flailed again, thanks to the ever-efficient, who was on hanp and uɒ to sNuff as usuaן in the discharge of his vigilant and onerus duties. We take tɥis occasion to ask, What does the cowardly, lyıng, black-heaRted, lily-livered

[20] On MS p. 79, Twain wrote, "(*Private*—Here let the compositor turn as many letters, mis-spell as many words, and scatter in as many wrong-font letters as shall be about right without exaggerating too much.)"

filɟh-dessemɪnator of the Guilford *Torch of Civili3ation* saʎ to the purity and efficiency of Whig office-holders *now*? Will be dəɥle the long-outraged public ear witɥ another deluɔe of his peculiar langoage from his intellectual cess-pool, his hell-engendeɹed brain, which no truly rebined Christian man or woman daɹe read, and even blacKguarps blush at?"

This being sufficient literary sustenance for his passing needs, and not feeling interest enough in the jail-breaking desperado to read further about him, Dexter returned to his musings about the afternoon's adventure and the girl.

## Chap. 3.

When young Dexter entered Judge Griswold's house in Guilford, the next evening, his head was still full of soft visions that refused to take their leave—and indeed they were not asked to. Mrs. Griswold received him with a warm welcome, though she paled a little and a momentary faintness passed over her as the thought of his possible mission recurred to her. But the thought and its signs went as quickly as they had come; admiration, beaming its expression from her eyes, took their place, and she said—

"What a fine manly creature you have grown to be, from the frail little lad you were seventeen years ago!"

"Yes, mother said she would have to certify me to you over her signature, to keep you from taking me for an impostor. She said you would be expecting a shadow."

"And no wonder, remembering how you began. People used to say they called you Hale because you weren't hale; since in this world the name never describes the man—the Cowards being always brave men, the Strongs always weak, and the Smalls overgrown."

The Judge said, courtly and stately, in a grave tone and without a smile—

"The son of my old friend is welcome. Consider yourself in your own house, sir, and at home."

This would have seemed a sort of funeral oration, but that the strong hand-grasp that accompanied it, translated it and gave it a very different and very agreeable meaning.

Young Dexter said—

"I thank you kindly, sir," and bowed.

A smiling, shrewd-faced young black, of eighteen or nineteen, was called in, and the Judge said to him—

"Toby, this is your young master Hale. You are his servant while he is here.—You will come and go at his beck and call; you will obey no orders but his. Take his keys and arrange his things."

"Yes, Mars. Helm."

"Your baggage arrived yesterday, Mr. Dexter. This is my daughter Milly—shake hands with Mr. Dexter, Milly."

Milly did so, with some diffidence and a blush.

Dexter thought, "What an earnest, gentle, pretty face it is!"

The girl's thought was, "If he is good to Toby, and can sing 'Roll on, Silver Moon,' I shall like him."

After some general talk, supper was announced. The Judge gave his arm to his wife, and the two young people dropped into their rear. Arrived at table, Mrs. Griswold bent her head, there was a moment or two of reverent silence, and then the meal began. As it progressed Dexter found himself growing more at home; Mrs. Griswold drew him on to talk, and his tongue presently got into smooth working order; Milly's shyness began to thaw and liberate a monosyllable here and there, then a brief sentence, then a clause, and finally her conversational ice-pack dissolved wholly and poured its shoal but fair and pleasant tributary to the general stream. The Judge did not give forth wastefully, or even in a fluid state, so to speak, but set a stately berg afloat, at intervals, that made up in frozen grandeur what it lacked in glow and warmth. By and by Dexter touched upon the great Californian gold excitement and the marvelous things one was hearing daily from that far-off, mysterious land; [21] and from that he fell to describing his experiences of a fortnight before in a fantastic camp of hopeful and hilarious emigrants, westward bound; and warming to his theme he forgot

[21] This reference to the California gold rush, of course, dates the events of the novel either in 1849 or early in the 1850's.

everything else and did his work so well that when he came to himself and caught something in the nature of surprised admiration in two pairs of eyes and almost a compliment in the third pair, he was very much pleased with himself and knew these were fine people and that he should enjoy being with them.

When the party returned to the parlor the acquaintanceship was already ripe, already complete, all angles gone, all stiffness removed.

By half-past nine o'clock the newcomer had won Milly's deep regard; for without betraying the suffering it cost him, he had sung Roll on, Silver Moon, A Life on the Ocean Wave, and several other villainous ditties of a like sort.

At ten the Judge's hot whisky punch was brought, and Mrs. Griswold said to Dexter—

"Milly and I will say good-night, now. We are all satisfied with you—write your mother that; she will know it means a great deal when it comes from me. You are a member of this family, now, as long as you will stay with us; this is your home, and you are welcome. And always after this, I shall call you Hale, as I did when you were a little child. Good-night."

The young man was pleased and touched; the cordial clasp which the lady's hand delivered with her closing words touched him still more; so he found it easier to express his thanks in his return-pressure than to speak them. The Judge moved forward, held open the door, and tendered his wife a courtly bow as she passed out, and a grave "Good-night, my daughter," to Milly as she followed her. Then he sat down to his whisky punch again, and began to mix a tumbler for Dexter. Dexter sat down beaming with pleasure. He was happy and content to the core. There was a brief silence. Then the Judge's spoon stopped stirring; he looked up, and said with solemnity—

"Of course you have come to carry out your father's wishes. We all know that. Command me freely in any and all ways, for your father was my friend."

The words smote upon the young man's gladness like a tolling bell, and it vanished away. He could say nothing for a moment. He was dazed, confused—like a sleeper roused suddenly out of a gracious dream and confronted with some vague and formless horror. Then he gathered his disordered faculties together and said in a voice that had little of life in it—

"Yes—I come for that."

"Ah, good—you are your father's son. *I*, also, am satisfied with you."

It was the same testimony, in the same words, that had given so much pleasure five minutes before; how had those words lost their virtue?

The Judge took up the grisly theme of the ancient Dexter-Burnside feud, and as he pictured one after another its valorous encounters and their varying fortunes in all their chivalrous and bloody splendor, his fervor grew, the light of battle was in his eye,[22] and it was as if the spirit of some old Gaelic bard had entered into him and he chanted the glories of a great past and of a mighty race that had departed and left not their like behind them.

The old man finished. The younger man's face had been undergoing a change—not swift but gradual. Shade by shade, depression had passed from it, and ray by ray a proud enthusiasm had occupied its place with light and life. Now his eye hardened with an iron purpose. He said—

"I will do my father's will."

"He charged you with it, then? I knew he would. He said he would."

"Yes—on his death-bed."

"What is your plan?"

"I have formed none—further than this. I wish to have him pointed out to me. Then I will name myself, and if he is not armed, wait till he arms himself."

"That is right. Your father's gun came with your baggage; I recognized it. Is it in order?"

"It seems to be, but I do not know. I will examine it."

There was a considerable pause; both men sat thinking. Then the Judge said—

---

[22] Twain checked this phrase in the margin and noted "kill former," referring to the use of the same description in chapter 1 when the Judge begins to explain the feud to his wife.

"In case of accident—have you made your will?"

"I have not a very great deal to leave, but—"

"You forget old Humphrey's fortune."

"If I fall, it goes to *him*."

"Ah—true."

"And if we both fall—what then?"

"That is easy—if one lives a distinguishable pulse-beat longer than the other.—If that should be you, your will would dispose of the property."

"Then I will draft a will."

"It is wisest."

There was a knock at the door, and a spare and severely neat lady [23] of about forty-five entered, bonneted and shawled. There was a mingled kindliness and austerity in her face, but the austerity had a trifle the advantage, perhaps. The gentlemen rose, the Judge bowed, then waved his hand toward Dexter and said—

"Martha, this is the friend we were expecting—Mr. Dexter. My sister Miss Griswold, Mr. Dexter."

The lady bowed, then said—

"Brother, I stopped at the post office this morning, and got a letter for you, but I was on my way to the church to help arrange things for the fair, so I put it in my reticule, and have been so busy ever since that I never thought of it again until I left the church a quarter of an hour ago."

While she fumbled among the chaos of odds and ends in her reticule, the Judge said—

"Where is it from, Martha?"

"I didn't notice."

"Why it might be from Hoxton!"

"True as the world!—and I never once thought of it, I was so full of the festival plans. Ah, here it is. Open it and see what it says."

The Judge opened it, ran his eye down the page and looked very grave.

"The news is bad!" exclaimed the lady. "How can I be always so absorbed and heedless! What does it say?"

---

[23] At the top of MS p. 96, Twain wrote, "Maiden sister of 40."

"She is very low."

"O, it is too bad! But I was expecting it."

"I was, too—but not so soon. Take it—but say nothing to Ruth about it to-night."

When the sister was gone, the Judge said—

"Her forgetfulness has saved my wife some hours of grief at any rate—so there was virtue in it. I sent to the post office just before noon; the idiot clerk said no letter had come. No news is good news, and my wife has been light of heart ever since. Now I am confronted with a difficulty. What shall I do? How can I surmount it? My wife's only sister lies very low, at Hoxton, three whole days' journey westward by stage, through a rough region.[24] My wife will go—that is of course, and as it should be."

"And you will go with her. That also is a matter of course, and as it should be. You were thinking of me?"

"Yes. An affair like yours is one which is so important, and so requires—"

"Do not think of me for a moment. I shall not allow it—I will not hear of it!"

"But—"

"Not for a single moment! You will go with her—you must go with her. My affair is very simple."

The Judge gave himself up to thought during some moments, then he said—

"I see a way of arranging the matter. I have a friend who would go through fire for me—Major Barnes, a distant relative of mine, and a thorough gentleman. No danger can shake his nerve, and no emergency find him wanting in expedients. He is younger and more vigorous than I, and therefore may be able to serve you even better than I could. Take him this note in the morning, and put yourself in his hands with entire confidence."

The Judge wrote the note and gave it to Dexter, with the remark—

"It is not a quarter of a mile; anybody can point you the way."

---

[24] In the margin, Twain wrote, "Refer to sick sister in earlier chap."

## Chap. [4]

DEXTER SAT late in his room that night; he drafted his will, he wrote his mother an affectionate letter which had no reference in it to the crime he was meditating; he cleaned and loaded his gun. With his murderous thoughts came the frequent suggestion, "My mother does not know; it will break her heart when she hears of it—there is the hardship of it all." Presently a question that had been floating, vague and inarticulate, through his mind, condensed itself into words: "Why do I want to kill this man?" It may have seemed only a small matter at first, this little question, but the more he examined it, and reasoned around it, and assaulted it with answers in front and flank and rear, the more compact and impregnable it stood. At the end of a long and harassing siege, he had to coldly confess that he was going to commit a crime of a dreadful nature partly in obedience to an authority which might possibly be questioned, partly because he must henceforth be despised by the Dexter clans if he refrained, and partly because there were witnesses that he had put his hand to the plow, wherefore he was ashamed to turn back now. So the thing was stripped of all its poor rags of justification, and stood naked before him: he did *not* want to kill this man; he had suffered no injury from this man—but, he would kill him.

The first gray of dawn had appeared before he finally dozed off into a dream-ridden, unrefreshing sleep. The last thing he was conscious of—and that but dimly—was the stage-horn and the sound of wheels. So he knew that the Griswolds were gone. He got up about the middle of the forenoon, ordered Toby to carry Judge Griswold's note to Major Barnes, then armed himself, and started down stairs; he heard a girlish voice below, singing some foolish ditty or other, and knew that Milly was coming along the hall. He stopped, like a guilty thing, and shrunk back out of possible sight.

His cheeks burned when he recognized that his act had been involuntary, and that without reasoning he had been ashamed to meet innocence face to face. Milly sang herself away again and left the road clear; Dexter was quickly in the street. As he moved along, hardening himself to his purpose, he was presently hailed from behind by a voice which he recognized, and Captain Simon Wheeler rode up.

"Morning, Mr. Dexter—Glad to see you again. I was on the wrong scent, up yonder, so I didn't stay. Got a clew or two, though. How'd you find the Burnsides?"

"I—haven't seen them yet."

"No? Got in at night and roosted at the tavern, I reckon. Well, it's the best way. Don't ever take anybody by surprise, my old woman says; there's two kinds of surprises, and a body might strike the wrong kind."

The captain rattled on. Dexter hardly heard him. He was busy thinking and planning. But this remark brought him suddenly to himself, with a cold shock—

"There's Hugh Burnside, now."

"Where!"

"In that door yonder. Good-bye—I turn off here."

Dexter moved diagonally across the street toward the man, and the thought shot through his brain, "It is no dream, then! and to think that this thing must be done, not tomorrow, next month, next year, but *now!*—it seems hideously sudden."

The man was stooping, patting a dog on the head. Dexter stood behind him a moment, waiting, then said in a voice that seemed not his own, so dreary and hollow it sounded—

"I will not take you at a disadvantage, sir, but—"

The man turned, and at sight of his face Dexter's speech died with a gasp. It was the jovial young historian of the cattle-maze. He seized Dexter's hand with a cordial grasp and exclaimed—

"Hello! Why it's *you!* This is splendid! Come right in!—don't stand on ceremony; once met is an introduction in this region. Hi! mother! Clara! This way!—here's the gentleman that was lost in the cattle-range! Here, take the rocking-chair—no, but you must—it's the seat of honor. Give me your hat. No, you needn't set your gun outside; I'll take care of her. Why look here! a minute ago you were as white as a sheet—now you're turning as red as the mischief. You ain't well—but never you mind, I've got some whisky that'll fix you."

The tremendous surprise of the situation had thrown Dexter's mind into a state of chaos. Only one thought took form and shape in this confusion. It was, "Thank God, the time has come and gone, and I shall never be a murderer, now."

The women entered. The daughter bowed, smiled, and said—

"You are welcome, sir; Mother, this is Mr.—"

"Hale Dexter, who is proud to be your relative."

Another surprise. The hand-shaking that immediately followed was hearty and general.

"By George!" said Hugh, "this is a wonderful state of things. So you are cousin Hale! Why look here! why the mischief didn't you say so, the other day?"

"Say what?" asked Clara.

"Why, that he was our cousin."

"How could he know it, then?"

"O, I didn't think of that. Come to think, I didn't even know enough to ask him his name. You said I was a—"

"When did you arrive, cousin Hale?" Clara broke in, while the color rose in her face.

"Last night."

"Then you stopped at the tavern," said the mother. "I hope you didn't rest well, for not coming straight to us. Come—tell me you had bad dreams and a troubled spirit."

Dexter felt the blood flowing into his own cheek, now, as he thought of his uneasy night and the reasons of it. He said—

"No, aunt, I did not stop at the tavern. I had bu-business—with Judge Griswold—"

"So you went there and cleared it off, and have come to us now, untrammeled and ready for a good visit and with nothing to interfere? Well, it was not a bad idea. You finished the business, did you?"

"Ye-s—it is finished. O yes, it is entirely finished."

"Good. What was it?"

Poor Dexter was speechless. The question set his face on fire, but it seemed to freeze the rest of him. The innocent old lady and her son saw nothing; the young girl saw the young man's confusion, but pretended she did not, and quickly turned the talk to other matters. Presently Mrs. Burnside said—

"We must send for your baggage; for you must move here now."

Dexter said he would be more than glad to come after a few days. He explained the close friendship existing between his mother and Mrs. Griswold,[25] which made it his duty to remain where he was until the Griswolds should return from Hoxton, as protector of their household.

Conversation drifted into pleasant channels and flowed smoothly along. Dexter was charmed with his relatives, and they with him. Now and then the talk got upon uncomfortably shoal water or encountered a snag. For instance, after inquiring after her old Kentucky friends in detail, Mrs. Burnside said—

"Of course I never think of the friends there without thinking of the old dreadful feud days, and feeling grateful that they are gone forever. Sometimes I find myself looking upon them as nothing but an ugly dream, they have drifted so far from our later life. Just think of it for a moment and try to realize it. You come now with that innocent gun, and nothing is thought of it; but if it were in the old days I should drop lifeless, because I would know you had come to kill my Hugh!"

"You put it in a fearfully vivid way," gasped Dexter.

"But *you* can't realize it,—now *can* you?"

"We-ll, ye-s—but perhaps not wholly."

"I should say not wholly, indeed! *I* can't, now; but once I could. Once I could imagine you coming to Hugh and saying, 'I am a Dexter—go arm yourself.' And I could imagine the rest of it too:

---

[25] On the left side of the top margin, MS p. 116, Twain wrote, "Better to be a stalled ox and feed on the vapors of a dungeon [continued in the bottom margin] vault than gain the whole world and lose thine own soul, as the saying is." On the right side of the top margin appear the notations "*Dam*-mascus blades" and "*Hell*-en's B." (cf. the "1,002[d] Arabian Night," pp. 105 and 109). *Helen's Babies,* a novel by John Habberton, enjoyed a tremendous popularity after its publication in 1876.

one or both of you stretched dead and bleeding on my threshold, and I standing there dumbly trying to realize the truth that my daughter's life and mine were blighted, wasted, ruined past help, by that wicked and useless act, when we had done no harm to any one —for in these hateful feuds a man's heart is cloven, but his wife's or mother's is broken—so the guilty is released with an instant's pang; and the long misery, the real suffering, falls upon the innocent."

Dexter thought, "If the subject could only be changed—to *any* thing, no matter what,—I should be so humbly grateful."

When the noon meal was about ready Mrs. Burnside said—

"Maybe you would prefer to have it put off a little, Hale, if you had a late breakfast. Did you?"

He said, with inward embarrassment, that he had not breakfasted at all; then added that he had not thought of it or cared about it. The old lady patted him on the shoulder and said—

"It was so good of you to be so impatient to come and see us"; and she accompanied this with a smile of such sweet approval and endearment that it fairly blistered the young man's remorseful heart.

An hour later, Hugh took up Dexter's gun and fell to examining it. This disjointed the visitor's pleasant chat with Clara at once and made him nervously uncomfortable. Presently Hugh said—

"What sort of game did you start out after? Not small, I judge?"

"N-o. Large."

"Deer?"

"No—I hadn't thought of deer particularly."

"I reckon not—in the middle of the day. What then?"

"Well, I—I hadn't really made up my mind about the sort of game I wanted to hunt," said Dexter, nearly aground for a reply.

"Maybe hereditary instinct was stirring blindly within you and Hugh was the game you had in mind after all, without knowing it," said Clara gaily. But when she saw Dexter redden with confusion under her random remark, she hastened to add, "O I am so sorry! It was only in jest, of course, but it was a cruel and foolish speech. Please don't be hurt; I am so ashamed of myself! You will not lay it up against me, will you?"

It was an easy promise to make; but it seemed to Dexter that he could almost bear another such shot for the pleasure of being so pleaded with again. By and by Hugh said—

"Sitting around here is dull. Let's go up into the woods and I'll show you where I'm on the watch for a wolf."

Dexter had been wishing that something might call Hugh away in his individual capacity. This proposition banished that hope. For a moment he imagined he detected a look of disappointment in Clara's face, and this raised his spirits; but the next moment she said with a cheeriness that blighted his self-complacency—

"I'm glad you thought of that, Hugh, for I want some wild flowers. Please see that he gathers them, cousin Hale, won't you?"

When the young men were gone, she said to herself, with a sense of injury, "I think it might have occurred to them that if it is dull here with three or four people, it might be still duller when two of them go away."

Dexter wished to go by Judge Griswold's and make his excuses for his absence from breakfast. Hugh assented with alacrity. They found Milly in the parlor, at work at some trifle with her needle. She and Hugh did not seem to be aware of each other's presence after the first glance. Dexter said a word or two and then stepped out of the room to seek the aunt. Hugh now went to Milly and began to inquire into the nature of her work, evidently less to lay up information than to be near her. She explained that it was called hemistitching.

"Why no! is it?"—with surprised admiration.

"Certainly it is. There—don't you see?"

He drew his chair very close and bent over the work with intense interest.

"So *that* is hemistitching!" said he, after a speechless pause, much as another Missourian, standing upon Sandy Hook, might say, after impressive inspection, "So this is the Atlantic Ocean!—let me try to realize it."

Milly was as proud and pleased over this fraudful applause as if she had been the inventor of hemistitching and it was the one godlike art. Hugh took up an end of the work reverently and arranged it upon one of his broad palms for convenience of examination, and went on admiring and trying to think of another remark, while Milly experienced that exquisite and indescribable tingling of the scalp which has no name, but might fairly be called bliss, and which gives one the sense of being under a spell while it lasts—a spell which one longs to remain under, and dreads to see broken. Presently Hugh said—

"It's beautiful—beautiful. Very different from basting, I reckon."

"Basting! O, I should think so. Let me show you. Every one of these little three-cornered holes has to be made ever so carefully. O, ever so carefully!"

"No! is that so? I never should have thought it."

"But it's so—indeed it is. You have to pull out threads this way—and so—and so—and then you have to take your needle and—. Here, I'll make one, and you can see for yourself."

She began the marvel, and the two heads bent over it till they touched. Hugh watched every stitch with the profoundest interest, and when the miracle was finished he said—

"How *can* you do it!"

"O, it's easy after you know how. Why I do believe I could almost do it in the dark."

"No—but could you, though!" Then after a pause: "There was one part that I didn't exactly get the hang of. Won't you make another?"

She made another. Their hands touched occasionally, as well as their heads, now, and Hugh realized that there was a charm about hemistitching, under the right conditions, that amounted to fascination. The second lesson being finished, he sighed to think that he might not ask for another without risk of awaking suspicion. Presently he fumbled in his pocket and drew out a folded paper which he gave to Milly and said—

"I wrote it for you. It's only a little thing."

It was some wretched drivel, in verse, entitled "The Wail of a Wounded Heart."

Milly read the first stanza, and said with rapture—

"It is so lovely! O, I *don't* see how you can do it!"

"O, it's nothing. I can do it any time. There's nothing about poetry that's difficult but the end-words. It crowds you to make them rhyme, sometimes. But put it away.—Don't read it now."

Milly, beaming with happiness and with pride in her poet, tucked the precious rubbish into her bosom to keep company with some spools, a thimble and an assorted cargo of other odds and ends. Then she dexterously brought up from among these a something which she did not exhibit. Her heart increased its beat almost to a flutter, and she said, timidly, and watching Hugh's face wistfully—

"Do you like book-marks, Hugh?"

"O, what an idea!" laughed the burly youth. "A *man* don't care for such things. They're for girls and old women. A body might as well ask a man if he likes doll-babies. *Why?*"

The young girl's face was crimson, and her eyes were full of tears. Hugh exclaimed—

"Why Milly! What is the matter?"

She stepped quickly aside and turned away her head.—Hugh, filled with solicitude, stepped after her and seized her hand; but she snatched it from him and ran out of the room, with her face still averted. She flew to her bed chamber, locked the door, put the book-mark and "The Wail of a Wounded Heart" together in a piece of paper which she laid away with mournful tenderness in a very private and sacred corner of one of her drawers, and said with a quivering voice—

"When I am gone they will find them, and then they will know." (The "they" referred to surviving friends and relatives.)

Then she flung herself on the bed and fell to sobbing bitterly.

Hugh, in the parlor, stood petrified. He wondered, and continued to wonder, what could have brought about this catastrophe, but no solution suggested itself. He was feeling very uncomfortable. He grew more and more so. He expected Milly to come back; but as minute after minute dragged by and still no footfall was heard, this expectation began to die a slow and miserable death. Presently his heart gave one jubilant bound, but straightway retired, weighted again with woe, for it was Dexter who entered.

"All right now—I'm ready!"

But Hugh was not ready. He wanted to examine the pictures on the walls—and it was time, for although he had seen them many a time before, he had never in the least examined them. He kept an expectant ear open, and started hopefully at every slight noise, but it was all vain—she never came. Finally Dexter was tired waiting, and said—

"Why, you must have seen these pictures a hundred times; do you always freeze to them like this?"

The Broken-hearted blushed, and sadly said he was ready to go. Milly heard the front door close behind the cousins. She got up and watched them move away, concealing herself with the window curtain. She said, deeply hurt,—

"Yes, there he goes, sure enough. One would think he would at least have wanted to ask what it all was. But no, it is nothing to him; that is plain."

She returned to the bed and cried harder than ever.

The young men strolled up the river road and into the forest, and Dexter had but a dreary time of it. He tried, for a while, to covertly lead up to some general talk about Clara, but all he got was absent-minded monosyllables punctuated with sighs—seven sighs to a monosyllable. So he gave it up, and was silent for some time. Finally he said—

"Are you often taken this way?"

"Taken how?" said Hugh, fiercely.

"O, no matter, if you don't observe any peculiarity," said Dexter, with a pretense of unsarcastic simplicity which was not wholly successful.

"If you don't like me the way you find me—"

"Now look here!" exclaimed Dexter, cutting him off abruptly, "let's not have any nonsense!"

"Well, then, don't peck at me. Can't you let a fellow alone when you see he's in trouble?"

The anger went out of Dexter's face, and he said—

"There—I was heedless, and I'm sorry. Shake hands, and I'll be more considerate."

Hugh received and returned the shake, then said with emotion—

"May you never suffer the agonies *I* suffer!"

Dexter was nearly surprised into laughing, but saved himself in time.—He was silent after this, out of respect for Hugh's woes.

Hugh moved here and there in a corner of the wood trying to seek for wolf-signs, but his wits were on furlough and he discovered nothing. Finally Dexter said—

"Here—what is this?"

"Ah, those scoundrels have been at it again," said Hugh. "That's a piece of raw meat—but you see that yourself."

"Yes, and I understand it, too. I have heard of poisoning wolves before, to get the bounty."

"Yes, it's meaner than dirt. I wish I could catch them at it once. Old Si Wheeler's on the watch. He says he'll track out the villains that are spoiling all the sport this way. He has got clews, he says."

"This meat was put here last night, of course; so there was no wolf here this morning."

"No, they mighty seldom come. They're pretty scarce." He held up the meat and gazed at it absently for a while, then sighed deeply and said—

"It's full of strychnine. Ah, I wish it was cooked!"

He let it fall, with another sigh, and wiped away a tear. The more thoughtful Dexter turned a great stone over the meat, to save the wolf for the rifle. Then he reminded Hugh of the wild flowers, but the poor youth said, with a glassy eye—

"Flowers are a mockery. There is nothing real but the tomb."

He had the presence of mind to get out his note-book and set down this thought for future use in some peculiarly damnable poem.[26]

Dexter resolved to gather the flowers himself on the homeward stroll, and was not sorry to have the privilege. The moment the young men moved away from the tree they had been standing under, Captain Si Wheeler thrust his head out from behind it and watched them until they disappeared. Then he began to talk to himself—

" 'Tain't any use to follow them any more; I haven't got enough out of this tramp to make it pay. When they do come to a halt they

[26] A faint notation at the top of MS p. 140 reads: "Work in the glass eyes?" and beneath that: "Wheelers do it." Apparently Twain was thinking of a story similar to that of the one glass eye shared by Miss Jefferson and Miss Wagner in Jim Blaine's story, *Roughing It*, II, chap. 12.

don't seem to talk much.—But *that's* a sign, itself! When people don't talk, it's because they're thinking. Now, the idea is, what are they thinking about?" He paused a good while, with contracted brow and his finger on the side of his nose, deep in rumination. Then he said: "I've found out Dexter hasn't been to see old Humphrey, after all. Well, that's because he knows he's going to get the property anyway. So I'll let that drop. Now what did Hugh wish that that poisoned meat was cooked, for? There's something in that—there's something mighty deep and dark about that!" After another long and thoughtful pause, he said: "Look here! the more I throw the detective eye on that thing, the blacker it looks. Let me just set down here and put this and that together and see what comes of it." He sat down on a log, took a red bandanna handkerchief out of his poor old battered plug hat, wiped his red brow, put back the handkerchief, put the hat on the ground in front of him and said, "You set there—I can follow my clews better with something to talk to." He addressed himself to the hat, and began to talk, accompanying himself with impressive gestures. "Now give me your attention for a minute. This young man comes here, all the way from Kentucky. Very good. Does a man come all the way from Kentucky for nothing? No, says you; and you're right. What does he come for? To get that money, you'll say. Right again. He's got to wait a bit, for the old man to die. Very good; what's the natural thing for him to do while he's a-waiting? Stop with his aunt? Why, of course. What does his coming there remind his cousin Hugh of? O, you begin to see the point, do you? Well, to go on. Hugh gets to thinking, and don't talk. What's the natural thing for him to be thinking? This: if 'twarn't for Dexter, the money'd come to *me*. You're right again. What's his next thought? This: if Dexter was to die . . . the money'd come to me! Right again—go it! What does such thoughts lead to? Sourness and brooding, says you. You never said a truer word. Is Hugh sour and brooding to-day? I don't say a word—I leave it to your own candor and honesty if he ain't. Now we come to the loudest and awfulest clew of all. You heard him say, with your own ears, that *he wished that poisoned meat was cooked!* What was the inside meaning of that remark? Can you put *two* meanings on it? *No,* sir! What does it mean in plain English? Just this: if that poisoned meat had been cooked, he would 'a' made him eat it! Now there you are! Is it neatly done? Have I followed the clews as straight as a bee-line and never missed a trick? O, *I* ain't no detective! of *course* not! I'm only a blundering old fool that don't know anything. *Any*body'll tell you that. But mind you—just keep quiet about this thing. Just wait—don't get impatient—just lay low and keep dark—*I*'ll show 'em, one of these days. You'll see. Now look here; do we stop where we are, or do we look ahead? Don't I *always* look ahead—I ask you that? Don't I? Well, what do I see ahead, now? *Only* this—he's a dead man if he eats beefsteak in the Burnside house! That's all. That's exactly the size of it. 'George, but this is a black affair! And to think that this whole community looks upon that young Burnside as a kind of a sweet, giddy, poetical muggins that wouldn't even hurt his grandmother in cold blood! And I ain't a-going to deny it—so did *I,* till I run my eye over these clews and found him out. But blame his murderous skin, he little thinks that there's a pair of eyes on him that's got for a motto, '*We never sleep.*' " [27]

The old man put on his hat and moved slowly away, thinking. Soon he nodded his head with satisfaction and said: "Yes, that's the idea; it'll put him on his guard, and he'll never suspect who done it. And he won't mention it to anybody—he knows enough for that."

Half an hour later he was leaning lazily against the front of the post-office with his hand behind him. He was there some little time, apparently with no object but to yawn and enjoy his rest; but when he went away at last there was an envelop in the letter box addressed to "Mr. Hail Dexter"; with the addition, *"private and confidentiall."*

"There," said he, "that's the detective way of doing a little thing like that."

About this time Hugh and Dexter were drawing homeward. They met a gentleman whom Hugh bowed to and called "Major Barnes." Dexter thought, "Hang that note! I would give anything if I hadn't sent it. I've got to make this man's acquaintance pretty soon, and explain. And what shall I say? Tell him I was minded to

[27] The motto of the Pinkerton Detective Agency.

kill—. Well, if I ever get out of this hobble I'll never get into another one like it."

He went on bothering over the matter and getting himself into a state of irritation of a larger size than the thing required or justified. However, he judged that when he came to show Clara what wonders he had done in the flower-gathering way, she would say something or look something that would improve the state of his mind. He hoped she would do something to stop Hugh's intolerable sighings, too.

But it was all a miscalculation. A dead and empty silence reigned in the Burnside house—a silence which the melancholy droning of a bee in the honeysuckles only intensified. A servant was called; she said Mrs. Burnside was gone to help at the church where the fair was to be, and that Miss Clara was not feeling well and had lain down. Dexter threw his flowers on the table with an air that said, "The world is hollow and life is vain," and turned toward the door. Hugh said, in a sepulchral voice—

"Right. Leave me—this is no place for the gladsome and gay."

At supper that evening, Milly was subdued and silent, Dexter depressed and untalkative. Miss Martha Griswold could have talked about the church fair, but she preferred to think. The meal dragged solemnly to its close; then Miss Martha said—

"Ah, I forgot, Mr. Dexter—in truth I am always forgetting. Here is a letter for you which I got out of the office as I came along."—

Dexter carried the letter to his room. It read thus:

> "Dont eat Beefstake in the House wher you are stoping. Bewair.
> "From a frend."

"Well, this *is* a cheerful addition!" said Dexter. "I get up in the morning to murder a man; I am in hot water, first here, then there, all day; and at night a maniac warns me against the Griswolds and their beefsteak."

He puzzled over the wretched writing a while, then threw it on the floor, and fell to wondering if Clara Burnside got sick intentionally or only by accident. The gloomiest mood must wear itself out eventually. Dexter's began to thin a little in the middle and fringe off into spitefulness at the edges; an unreasoning spitefulness, which should have chosen him as its target, to be just;

but this mood is never just: witness how often it assaults innocent furniture or kicks a dog that is asleep. Still, this change was an improvement; for it was in the direction of good-humor, for the reason that when spitefulness follows heavy-heartedness, good-humor follows heavy-heartedness by a natural law. There was a knock at the door.

"Come in!" This with asperity.

Toby entered.

"Well, what do *you* want?"

Toby smiled widely and mollifyingly, bowed several times with embarrassed diffidence, and said—

"Mars. Hale, I come to ast if you wouldn't write a little letter for me, if it ain't too much trouble, sah."

"A letter! O, go along with you and don't bother me!"

Toby moved humbly toward the door, crushed, but still bowing, still smiling as well as he could. He said—

"Thank you, sah. I's very sorry, sah, but I didn't mean no harm."

Dexter felt a twinge of remorse. His mood, being in a transition state, was like a ship's empty sails when the vessel is "going about" but has not quite swung to the point where she will fill away on the other tack—bellied, first this way and then that, by every passing puff of wind. He said—

"Hold on. What can you want to write a letter for? Who is it for?"

"My ole mother, sah—'way down in Arkansas."

"O! That's a different matter. Of course I'll write it." Then with a burst of irritation—leveled at the wrong target, of course—"What the devil were you going away for? Did you suppose I wouldn't write it?"

"O, no, Mars. Hale. Please don't git mad, Mars. Hale, I know'd you'd write it if you said you'd do it."

"Well then, what the devil do you mean by—. Look here—can your mother read writing?"

"O, no, sah; but dey reads it to her—young Mars and Missis does—dey's good chillen. She very ole, now, an' I hain't seed her sence I was little. She like to git letters f'm me. Miss Milly she write 'em for me, every time I ast her; but she feelin' bad now, I reckon, so I wouldn't ast her."

This soft zephyr fanned the other side of the sail.

"Well, you come to me whenever you want to, Toby; I'll be your amanuensis."

"My . . . my which, Mars. Hale?"

"Amanuensis! Confound it, don't you know what an amanuensis is?"

"No, Mars. Hale, I's mighty ignorant, fo' my size, and I hain't never seed one—dat is, I don't 'member to."

"Well, *now* you see one. Now tell me what I'm to say, and . . . look here!" said Dexter, impetuously, rising and confronting Toby, "what ever possessed you to give that note to Major Barnes?—answer me that!"

"Please, Mars. Hale, don' look at me so turrible—I 'clah to goodness I didn't do it!"

"Say it again, and I'll hug you!"

"Please don't, Mars. Hale—I 'clah to goodness I didn't give it to him! I wisht I may never stir if I did!"

"Here—here's a quarter for the only speech I think I've heard today that didn't gall me. What did you do with the note?"

The negro hesitated, looked confused a moment, and then began to pour his words out in a zealous torrent—

"Well Mars Hale, I tell you jes' how it was. I was down dah in de parlor, and Miss Martha she was a-hurryin' me up, an' I says, s'I, 'I'm a-doin' my bes,' s'I, an' she say, 'Well, hurry up, hurry up, hurry up,' she say,—jes' so—an' s'I, 'Dey ain't no grass gwyne to grow under *my* hoof,' s'I, an' wid dat I heave' on a stick, an' it tore de letter out'n my han' an' 'fo' I could snatch it out she was burnt up. Dat's jes' de way it happen' Mars. Hale, I wisht I may die if—"

"O, rubbish! A fire in the parlor, in dead summer time?"

"What! did I say in de parlor, Mars. Hale? Well, if dat don' beat all! In de *parlor!* says I. Why 'twas in de kitchen, of course. Well, I 'clah to goodness if dis don'—"

"Well, never mind, it's all right, just so its burnt—I ain't particular where the fire was." Dexter sat down. His ship had made the turn, at last, and was filling away on the other tack with a wind that would stay. "Now I'm ready to begin, Toby. What shall I say to your mother?"

Toby swabbed the perspiration from his face with his sleeve, remarked to himself, " 'I jings, I never seed a nigger in no closter place 'n' what dat was!—I was mos' ketched, sure"—then produced a greasy little book. He wetted his thumb and began to flip the leaves over, pausing now and then to scan a page critically. At last he said in a gratified tone—

"Dah she is! 'I jings I 'gin to git afear'd she done gimme de slip. Dah, Mars. Hale, dat's de one."

"Do you mean to say you're not going to dictate the letter yourself, but are going to get it out of the book?"

"Dictate?" said Toby, scratching his head perplexedly; "Dic . . . Mars. Hale, please don' bust dem big words at me, I don't stan' no chance 'gin 'em. Yes, Mars. Hale, dat's a prime book; I gits de mos' o' my letters out'n dat book; dey ain't nuffin in de worl' but what dat book know 'bout it. I reckon Sol'mon writ dat book, but I don' know. But it *soun'* like Sol'mon, sometimes,—so de ole nigger preacher say,—and den it know so much, and say it so beautiful.—Mars. Hale, dah's *beautiful* words in dat book—great long beautiful words dat dey ain't *no* man kin understan'. My ole mother and my brother Jim is mons'us proud o' me on accounts o' dem letters dat I gits out'n dat book; dey ain't no mo' niggers roun' heah but me dat sends letters to anybody."

Dexter took the little open book, glanced at its back, and through the grime made out to decipher the title, "The People's Ready Letter-Writer." [28] Then he looked at the page indicated by Toby and burst into a laugh. Toby said—

"What is you laughin' 'bout, Mars. Hale?"

"Well—can you read, Toby?"

"Dat's a curus question to ast a po' nigger, Mars. Hale. 'Course I can't."

"That's the reason you've made a mistake. This is not the letter you were after, Toby."

"O yes 'tis, Mars. Hale; I knows it kase I marked it wid a piece o' fire-coal. You read it, Mars. Hale, you'll see."

---

[28] I have been unable to discover any actual volume of model letters with this title, but, of course, Twain's purpose is to burlesque with the various letters Hale copies for Toby the numerous books with similar titles circulated in large numbers during the latter half of the nineteenth century.

Dexter read aloud, as follows:

*From a Young Lady to a Suitor whom she greatly Esteems but feels obliged to reject because she cannot love him.*

ESTEEMED SIR: I have perused your honored epistle with deep gratitude, but with flowing tears. For while my esteem for your lofty character and manifold virtues is boundless, I am admonished by my heart that I can never feel for you that affectionate devotion of soul that the perfect marital relation requires. Therefore I am compelled to reject the noble offering which you have laid at my feet, and to utter the edict that we can never be to each other more than we are at present. Do not hope: for this is final. Yet do not despair; but seek in fairer fields a companion more worthy to adorn thy pure and beautiful life than she who feels herself compelled to indite these lines. Farewell: and may she whom thou shalt crown with the precious diadem of thy love's rich gold, be to thee a double and treble recompense for my poor loss; and as the river of Time glides to its unknown sea, may thy bark float calm and peaceful upon its troubled waters, unbuffeted by its storms, untossed by its tempests, and ride at last secure in that haven where moths do not corrupt nor thieves break through and steal. Farewell: and though we can be no more, to each other, I beg that we may still be friends.

"Dat's de one, Mars. Hale, dat's de one! Don't dem words taste good in you' mouf! don't dey 'mind you of suckin' a sugar-rag when you was little? an' don't dey *soun'* softy and goody! Don' dey blobber-blobber-blobber along like buttermilk googlin' out'n a jug! King Sol'mon he must 'a' writ dat, kase I reckon dey ain't nobody else dat kin bounce words aroun' like dat. O yes, dat's de right letter, Mars. Hale. I know'd dey warn't no mistake 'bout it."

"But here! Do you really want this letter sent to your *mother?*—and as coming from *you?*"

"Yes, dat's it, dat's it, Mars. Hale. You see, fust I got Miss Milly to write out dis letter and send it to my brother Jim, an' he—"

"To your brother Jim! This same letter?"

"Yes, Mars. Hale. You see Jim he's a fiel' han'; works in de cotton fiel'; so de white chillen dey read de letter to Jim, an' lots o' other niggers was dah, f'm de plantations aroun', kase it was a Sunday; an' dey tole everybody 'bout it, an' so every Sunday sence den de niggers comes dah to hear dat letter; some of 'em walks fifteen mile; an' dey all say *dey* ain't never hearn no sich letter as dat befo'. Dey keeps a-comin'—de same niggers an' new ones—to hear dat letter—dey don't ever seem to git enough of it. Well you see dat make Jim mighty proud. He tote de letter 'roun' all de time, an' dad fetch him he mos' too good to speak to anybody now, less'n it's seven-hund'd-dollar niggers and sich-like high flyers. Well, you see, my ole mother she don' like to see Jim a-havin' it all to hisself so; so she ast one o' de little missises for to write and ast me to write *her* dat letter, too. An' you bet she'll be powerful glad when she git it, Mars. Hale. She's a good ole 'oman, too, dat she is!"

So Dexter copied the absurd thing, addressed it to "Old Mammy Betsy, Care of Col. Whiting, Bayou Noir Plantation, Arkansas," and signed it "Your Loving Son, TOBY."

Toby's gratitude was outspoken, when Dexter handed him the letter complete and ready for the post-office.[29] But Toby had not been idle while the writing was going on. He had stolen an envelop, and also Capt. Wheeler's warning note, and concealed them about his person. On his way down stairs he got out the Wheeler note, also a soiled scrap of writing which he had found in the sheet, and lastly Judge Griswold's note to Major Barnes!—so this Phenix had thus early risen from its imaginary ashes.—He put his three treasures into his envelop and presently got Miss Martha to direct it to his brother Jim!—Apparently all was fish that came to Toby's correspondence-net.

Dexter was in quite a happy frame of mind, by this time. He no longer cared to moon in solitude. It was early yet, so he started down stairs with a definite purpose. As he was passing through the parlor, he noticed that Milly was sitting with her arms upon the piano and her face buried in them. She did not look up; was she feeling lonely? did she miss her parents? Dexter was ashamed of his selfishness in forgetting all sorrows but his own. He went to her and spoke her name softly. The little maid looked up wearily and made an effort to smile, but there was not much life in it. She had been thinking over her day, and now that the smart of the wound Hugh had given her had lost the most of its sharpness she was questioning if she had not been wrongfully abrupt with him. Dexter was gentle and persuasive, and presently beguiled her into talking; her depres-

[29] In the top margin of MS p. 169, Twain wrote, "7-up——" and beneath that, faintly, "corn shucking."

sion began to yield. Now Dexter proposed a walk; she was undecided, nearly indifferent, but asked whither. He hesitated, as if considering, then said suddenly, as if the thought had just that moment occurred to him—

"Suppose we saunter over and see the Burnsides."

"Very well!" said Milly, and looked so pleased that Dexter remarked to himself, "I begin to think I suspect something!"

The Burnside supper that evening had been no more cheery than the Griswold supper. Hugh was morose, all through the meal, Clara thoughtful. Hugh's thinkings about Milly took this shape: "I hadn't done anything, yet she could treat me so! I will never look upon her more!" Clara's thoughts dwelt upon Dexter—to this effect: "It was not gracious, or even civil, in him to prefer the woods and Hugh, to me; but I wonder if it was altogether right or kind to let him come back to an empty, unwelcoming house? Will he come to-night? I hope he will, for my conscience is not entirely easy."

Supper was finished; then came two striplings, timid undeclared suitors: Tom Hooker, reporter and maid-of-all-work to the *Torch of* [*Civilization*] [30] and Lem. Sackett, a clerk at Bagley's "Emporium." This invasion would have been tolerable to Clara at nearly any other time, but it irritated her now. The young chaps tried hard to be sprightly and agreeable, but Clara was gently sarcastic, and they began to grow uncomfortable. In time they very much wanted to go, but could find no way to launch themselves. Conversation ceased to pour, and began to drip, drearily. Clara sat near the window, and glanced nervously and anxiously out from time to time. Finally she said to herself, with a sigh, "No, he isn't coming." A moment or two later she said, with temper, "Very well, he needn't come if he doesn't want to." She left the window, took another seat, and shot poor Hooker through the heart with a venomous sarcasm. Even the sullen, world-hating Hugh was moved to say to himself, "Poor devil, *he* wasn't doing anything." The next moment, Dexter and Milly entered, the one casting a beaming glance upon Clara, and the other its mate upon Hugh. The great pouting cub got up without a word and marched coldly, sternly, out

[30] Originally Twain left a space for the name of the paper. During a revision of a much later date, he filled in *Torch of* but left the remainder blank.

of the room; the sister said, with a smile and an easy grace of manner that gave no sign of the vengeful spirit within—

"Why how pleasant!"

Introductions followed. "Good!" thought Dexter, "she's in an angelic mood; Toby has turned the luck."

Clara said—

"Why, my poor Milly, I thought you looked happy, a moment ago, but I see you are thinking of your father and mother. You shall be cheered up, you shall be comforted. Here is *my* mother, she will make you forget your loss. My cousin will help her."

She grouped the three together, began the comforting work herself, and when the conversation was well and happily under way, she rose and deserted,—to Dexter's crushing disappointment. She returned to her young fellows, and, to their grafteful surprise, began to pour out upon them an animated badinage which was full of charm and free from sarcasm. By and by things stood thus: Milly and Mrs. Burnside were chirping along, softly and contentedly, the young chaps and Clara were blithely chatting and laughing, and Dexter sat empty-mouthed and with a sense of being a pretty conspicuous cipher. He had given up trying to talk to his aunt and Milly, since he could keep neither his eyes nor his jealous mind from the other group. If his eyes tried to wander elsewhere they never got further than the table, where the flowers still lay which he had gathered with such elaborate pains that day.—Their withered forms insulted his self-love sorely. After a while Clara stole a furtive, triumphant glance in Dexter's direction; he was idly inspecting his hands, with the air of one who was very much at a loss for some way to put in the time. The girl was stricken with a sudden shame, and resolved that she would put an end at once to her inhospitable folly. She was about to rise, but young Hooker began a humorous anecdote and she halted, on nettles, for him to finish. A moment later she heard Dexter say—and the words filled her with a sort of vague dismay—

"No, the Judge's house is right on the way, and it will save steps if Hugh will come by for me, instead of my coming here. I will send Toby for my gun some time to-morrow, and be ready early next morning."

Clara sprang up, cutting short the Hooker anecdote, and was about to say something to Dexter, she hardly knew what, but he turned at that moment to answer some remark of his aunt's, and the opportunity passed. She stood where she was, undecided, and a moisture born of shame and of anger at herself came into her eyes. Dexter shook hands with his aunt, bowed pleasantly to Clara and the young men, and he and Milly went forth. For a moment or two Clara was half-conscious of wordy sounds at her ear, then wholly conscious of them—they formed the consumingly funny climax of the Hooker anecdote; then the jocund author paused, radiant, for the applause. The girl gazed into that shining face with vacant and mournful eyes; and in that moment the light of it was quenched, and the joke that had flamed out with such glorified promise lay a blasted and smouldering ruin there, with a blighted spirit and a blistered heart behind it.

In a little while the joker and his friend, blue and forlorn, were wending homeward, and Clara sat alone in the parlor seeking in her heart for some excuse, some crumb of palliation of her evening's behavior, and finding none.

Hugh entered, solemnly, and began to ransack the table for a pen. The flowers were in his way. He threw them petulantly into the empty fire-place.

"I loathe flowers!" said he.

"Then you needn't have gathered them."

"I didn't."

"You didn't?" said Clara with a quick interest; "who did, then?"

"*He* did."

Clara felt another remorseful pang, but there was a pleasurable something about it at the same time.

"Did he gather them for . . . for me?" she asked, with a hesitating diffidence.

"Of course. Who else? The cat?"

The dismal poet found pen and paper; sat down and wrote a line, then remained still, during fifteen minutes, gazing overhead, with the feather-end of his quill thrust into his nostril, trying to think of a rhyme for it.

Clara sat silent, thinking; at intervals breathing long sighs. She said to herself, "I am bad—bad all through—bone and fibre and tissue—bad at heart. It must be so." Presently she said, "The next time, I will not wound or . . . Folly! there will never be any next time!" [31]

During two sweltering hours the poet travailed, and then the birth-pains were over. The result was a ten-line deformity, christened "The Crushed Heart's Farewell," and leading off with this couplet,—by way of head and shoulders: [32]

Tho' ~~[illegible]~~ chill be the desert & ~~arid~~ bleak its ~~waste~~ aspect, ~~face~~

~~There the heart-broken outcast~~

~~Let the heart-weary~~ ~~sore~~ ~~blighted~~ ~~pilgrim its refuge embrace~~

~~The sore heart shall find there a kindlier~~ ~~sweeter~~ ~~solace~~

Far ~~better~~ kinder its ~~[illegible]~~ storms than this cold world's neglect.

~~[illegible]~~

[31] This paragraph was written over the following penciled notes:

Carries off flowers
poem
Hugh's heroic day dream
Dex and Milly at home
Absent from Clara 2 days

[32] On the top of MS p. 184, Twain wrote, "Private to the publisher: Do this in fac-simile."

The poet read his ten lines over and found them faultless, since they moved him to tears. They might have had the same effect upon Milly if he had carried them himself instead of entrusting them to Toby: as it was, they were greatly admired on the Arkansas plantation a week or ten days later.

Hugh turned, and looked surprised and touched—

"Clara! you here yet! Ah, I do not deserve such devotion!"—He came and kissed her tenderly, heaved a sigh, and said in a dead voice—

"There—remember that I loved you, when I am gone. Something tells me I am not long for this vale."

He dragged his sorrows wearily up stairs, and when Clara heard his door shut she took the forlorn flowers from the fire-place and carried them to her chamber. In a little while all the household were asleep but Hugh. He was abed, building a waking-dream wherein he saved Milly from a burning house, but at the cost of his own woe-worn young life; and when at last he dozed off to sleep, he left her weeping over the corpse.

Milly and Dexter were full of thought when they started homeward. So they walked slowly along without speaking. Dexter, thinking of Clara, said to himself, "She has a strong aversion for me—that is plain. I am a scorched moth, now; I must keep away from her, else I shall be a consumed one." Presently Milly sighed. Dexter smiled, and said this knowing thing to himself: "There—it is a hundred to one that this inexperienced little creature is taking the most glaring and palpable signs of Hugh's love for her to mean just the opposite. How blind a person can be at her age!"

As they passed a narrow alleyway, a bent and coarsely-clad old woman, with her jaws muffled in a red handkerchief, stepped out and hobbled along in their wake supporting herself with a cane. Shortly she muttered—

"Yes, they don't talk—they're in love. Sure sign. Well, good match; good stock, and both'll be rich."

She overtook the young people, bent her breast down upon her cane, held out her hand, and said in a reedy falsetto—

"A dime for the old gipsy and she'll read your palms and tell your fortune. A dime for the old woman, please."

Dexter paid, and said—

"Here is our opportunity, Milly; stretch out your palm."

She did so, and the old woman examined it attentively, then said—

"There's much trouble in store for you, and much joy. You will be very rich, by and by. You will marry a dark, handsome gentleman from another State, and be very happy—provided he keeps a sharp look-out on his enemies and gets the better of designs which they are hatching up now against his life. Your great grandchildren will come to great distinction, though you may not live to see it."

Milly was deeply impressed by these prophecies, and wondered how a mere human being could map out and foretell the future with such accuracy. The gipsy examined Dexter's hand and said with solemnity—

"You love a blonde lady that's only two-thirds your own age, and your love is returned. You are a-going to be rich and happy if you overcome the designs of your enemies. But don't be afeard—you have powerful friends about you: among them there's one that's a-watching always." Then in a whisper, at Dexter's ear, "Young man, beware of beefsteak! You turned a rock over one to-day to save the wolves—do the same for your *own* sake!"

The gipsy hobbled briskly around a corner and disappeared, muttering, "I've saved him from poison, anyway; and I'm the man that can save him from any job Hugh can put up on him. I bet I ain't going to let a man be murdered that chipped in and took a hand when I was in a close place—and played it like a major, too! If anybody thinks different, they don't know Si Wheeler the detective!"

Dexter went to bed much perplexed, that night. Said he—

"So there are *two* lunatics at large! One a man—by the handwriting—the other a woman. How in the world did this witch know I turned a rock over that beefsteak? I think I do need a sane guardian angel, but I am not going to discomfort myself over the absurdities of these mad ones."

He dismissed the subject from his mind. Straightway Clara

Burnside took its place. He dismissed her, too—reluctantly, but promptly. "There is no safety but in keeping her entirely out of my thoughts," said he.

As Dexter stepped out of the front door, the next morning he was troubled to perceive that his resolution to keep away from temptation had so weakened already that his steps were turning in her direction unconsciously—and not only that, but gladly. He put a stop to all that, at once. Now came Hugh briskly along, in high spirits, and hailed him with a proposition to go boating, riding, fishing, or roaming the woods and hills—anything that might be agreeable. So they struck for the woods.

Hugh's wind-mill was in fine working order to-day, its clack was incessant; one could hardly believe it was the same that so lagged and creaked and groaned the day before. Dexter found the simple and hearty fellow good company and his liking for him grew steadily. When at last the top of the highest bluff was reached and the two sat down to rest, Dexter said—

"Now tell me something. I'm a little puzzled. Have you seen Milly this morning?"

"No."

"Did you see her last night after she went home?"

"No."

"Then what has put you in such spirits to-day?"

"Why, what has she got to do with it?"

"Everything!"

"Well, that's an idea!"

"It's a sound idea.—You know very well you love her. Wait—don't deny it. You were just going to. Don't do it—because I know better."

"Well, then. . . . but look here, who could have told you that?"

"Nobody told me. I saw it myself. But never mind about that. That isn't the puzzle. The puzzle is your cheeriness to-day. I can't account for it."

"All right; if that's all, I'll account for it for you."

"Good—go on."

"I don't love her any more!"

"O, nonsense!"

"It isn't nonsense. I'm going to make a clean breast of it, Hale.—I did love her, and I thought she loved me—though I never told her so and she never told me so. Well, yesterday morning she treated me shabbily, and I thought it all over, all day, and I saw she didn't love me. I was so miserable! I was miserable all the evening. I couldn't go to bed till I'd written a poem to show how I felt. Then I went to sleep, but I woke up by and by, my sufferings and the mosquitoes distressed me so. I got up and dressed, and took that poem and hung around her house, perfectly miserable.—Finally I shoved the poetry under the kitchen door, because there was a light in the front of the house,[33] and then I said, 'What's the use? let her go; she don't care for me; I will tear her out of my heart though it kills me.' So I tore her out and it did nearly kill me, for a while; but I'm over it now, and I'll never go near her again. There, that's the whole thing, clean and straight. So I'm feeling good, to-day, you see."

Dexter was thoughtful a while; then he said—

"Just by signs I found out you loved her, didn't I?"

"Yes."

"Well, I know by signs that she loves you, Hugh."

"No. She don't."

"But she does."

Dexter tried hard to convince him, but Hugh's romantic mind was full of the charm that goes with blighted hopes and severed ties, and he was not to be persuaded. Dexter felt nearer to Hugh than ever, now that both their hearts were in a state of blight and both their minds bent upon a like resolve. He determined upon a confidence. He said—

"Hugh, I'll make a confession. I've been disappointed too. I've been singed, and have retired from the candle, so to speak, just as you have done."

"No! Is that so? Give me your hand! Let's be brothers in

[33] Apparently Twain forgot, when he wrote this, that a few pages earlier Hugh had entrusted the poem to Toby, who dispatched it to Arkansas.

misfortune. Now I like this. I didn't suppose I should, but I do. I like it better than the other way. Don't you?"

"Ye-s, I think so. O, yes."

"But you're in better luck than me, Hale. You're a way off here in Missouri where you *can't* see your girl; but look at me—I'm likely to run across mine any time. But I'm firm. You'll see."

As the friends wandered homeward late in the afternoon, still chatting, Hugh gathered a fine bouquet of wild flowers for his sister, but Dexter felt no disposition to help, after his late experience in that line. When they arrived in sight of the Burnside home, Dexter said—

"I'll turn off here. I'll expect you early in the morning."

"But ain't you coming home with me? They'll be expecting you."

But Dexter made his excuses and they parted. Hugh found his sister looking rather low-spirited, but when he gave her the flowers she brightened up and seemed about to ask a question, but she ended by keeping it to herself.—Hugh said—

"I noticed you had the others in water, this morning, so that reminded me not to forget, this time."

"That was good of you. They are very beautiful."

"Yes, I took a good deal of pains in selecting them."

Hugh went off about his affairs, and Clara laid the flowers down, absently, and took up her cheerless reflections again.

At the earliest dawn, next morning, the young men were in the woods with their guns, but they found no wolf. They found tracks, but not the animal. They practiced long at a mark and Hugh discovered that Dexter was an incurably bad marksman, with a rifle. He explained that he was only used to shot guns and feathered game, but believed he could hit a wolf if he should see one, because living game would bring up his powers more effectually tha[n] an inanimate target. Hugh differed with him there.

The friends were gay during the first half of the day, but their spirits calmed, after that, and they presently lost interest in everything but silence and thought. They were soon exquisitely unhappy.

Now followed two or three days of black solemnity. They were moping in the twilight on the river road about seven o'clock one evening. There had been a long silence.—Suddenly Hugh broke it. He said there must be a change; he could not live under this state of things. Said he—

"You're as dismal as I am, and I don't find anything better at home; Clara's as dreary as both of us put together. I can't understand it; it's not her way. I think she's in love."

Dexter winced, and said, with pretended indifference—

"Who is it?"

"O, I don't know. This morning she said that since you had come I was never around any more; said she was lonesome and wished Hooker or somebody would come."

Dexter said to himself, hotly: "I will end this boyish foolishness and be a man again. If being in love makes such a baby of me, I want no more experience of it. Since the spell has been on me I am so pitiful and silly that I am ashamed to be in my own company. I will go straight to her this very evening and tell her I have been absurd but am cured. I'll say, 'Now let us be plain sensible acquaintances, you to curb your prejudice against me as much as you can, I to make myself as endurable as possible—and go ahead on this basis; for while I am in the town we *must* be together more or less, we being cousins.' There—I feel healthier already!" Then aloud—

"Hugh, we are a couple of fools!"

Instantly the sunshine burst through the black misery of Hugh's face and he seized Dexter's hand with enthusiasm. Said he—

"Shake hands on it! They're the noblest words that were ever spoken! You're going to stop all this foolishness—I see it in your face."

"That is precisely what I'm going to do!"

"Me, too. Shake again! It's been in my mind two days; I hadn't the pluck to out with it. Hale, I feel a hundred years younger and a hundred tons lighter! Now—when to begin?"

"The quicker the better."

"That's the right word again! You'll go by our house and say a word to the folks; I take the shortest cut from here to the Judge's. Good-bye."

"Good-bye."

As Dexter approached the Burnside house he saw young Hooker leave it with a springy gait and a happy air. This spectacle smote him sharply, and he wished he had been spared it; for now he should have a chilly and awkward interview and make a failure. The door was open. He stepped within without knocking, and stood a moment undecided; for Clara sat before him, bent over some work and did not raise her head. He could not believe she did not know he was there, so she must be maliciously enjoying his embarrassment. He was sinking into a mire of humiliation; he wished he was out again, yet was ashamed to retreat. He hesitated a fraction of an instant, then stepped fearfully forward and stumbled against a footstool. The girl looked up, in a startled way, then she sprang to her feet with a face alive with pleasure, and seized both of the unfortunate's hands, exclaiming—

"I am so glad to see you!"

This sort of a reception was so entirely unlooked-for that Dexter's defeat was complete; he forgot his mission, he forgot his speech, his brain offered no suggestion, his mind was a blank. He could only hold the girl's hands and look stupidly and blissfully into her eloquent eyes and worship the enchanting beauty of her face.

Let us condense. At the end of a half hour there had been a good deal of conversation between these, and of a most agreeable and cheery kind. Then there was a knock at the door,—which had meantime been closed,—and young Hooker entered. What he saw seemed to disconcert him for a moment; then he said—

"I hope you have made up your mind favorably, Miss Clara; it is a lovely evening."

She said—

"I was very favorably inclined, but I am going to ask you to excuse me this time, Mr. Hooker."

"You said you thought you'd go," said Hooker, a little ruefully.

"Yes, that is true, but upon second thought I decided differently. —I hope you will not mind it."

When young Hooker was gone, Dexter said—

"What was it?—a ramble up the river road?"

"Yes."

"You changed your mind?"

"Yes."

"Why?"

A faint tinge of red showed in the girl's cheeks, and she said—

"Well, I—I don't care for walking—that is, not much—not generally, I mean. Walking is a dull matter."

The subject was changed, and the conversation wandered pleasantly afar in other channels. By and by Dexter said—

"Clara, shan't we go walking? It is a perfect night?"

The girl's face gave quick consent; then she looked up, hesitating, and said, as one who has been confronted with a doubt?

"Would it be right, after refusing him? What do you think?"

"Well, I don't know, exactly. Will you go tomorrow night?"

The girl answered, with simplicity untrammeled with doubt—

"O, yes—if you wish it."

By nine o'clock they were playing chess together—and both sitting on the same side of the table, which was too wide for any other arrangement—a thing which both spoke of with regret, but did not dwell upon. Occasionally the young girl heedlessly moved a knight into a wrong square. Instead of telling her so, the young man gently closed his hand over the hand that held the piece and lifted both to the proper square; and while she protested that she was right and he protested the contrary, her hand remained a prisoner, neither party seeming to think of that. These disputes grew more and more frequent and charming; the hand became so used to captivity, by custom, that it came to have a discontented look during its intervals of liberty, and presently got to drifting into imprisonment of its own accord, apparently. Things were progressing.

At eleven o'clock all was quiet everywhere—outside in the street, and in the house as well. The young man was sitting on the sofa with the young girl's head upon his breast and his arm around her waist. Conversation had ceased; words were not equal to the occasion.

Hugh burst suddenly into the room, with a jubilant "It's all right with *me!*" He paused, transfixed, while the couple before him unclasped themselves in confusion; then he added—to Dexter: "And it looks as if it is all right with you, too!"

"Indeed it is," said Dexter, smiling, and putting his arm, unforbidden, where it was before.

Hugh struggled with the situation, but could not seem to comprehend it entirely. Said he—

"Yes, it's all well enough, but look here! What you going to do about the Kentucky girl?"

"What Kentucky girl?" asked Dexter, amused at Hugh's perplexity.

Hugh leaned a hand upon the table, for bodily and mental support, stroked his troubled forehead with the other, and said—

"Maybe joy has joggled my mind off its balance a little, but as I understand it *I* was to make a final settlement one way or the other with my Milly to-night, who is the very perfection of her sex! and you were to clear out for Kentucky and make short work with *your* girl!"

"Well, I *have* made short work with 'my girl,' as you call her, as you can see for yourself—but I didn't say she was in Kentucky. That was your own deduction—but I thought I wouldn't meddle with it."

"Well, I'll be hanged if. . . . so you ain't going to Kentucky at all, then?"

"I can't say that, exactly—that is, I can't state the time. It will depend mainly upon this young lady," said Dexter, glancing at Clara.

Hugh said—

"Are you two engaged?"

"I hope to be able to tell you before long that that mere formality has been arrived at," said Dexter. "Indeed, if you hadn't interrupted, there's a possibility that—"

"Now you have asked questions enough, Hugh," said Clara, bridling a little and covered with blushes, "go along with you and harass yourself with some other matter."

"So you are not engaged! Good—I'm ahead at last!" shouted Hugh, "for I *am!*" He paused a moment, and said, "Honest, now, Hale, wasn't there any Kentucky girl at all?"

"No."

"Was it my sister all the time?"

"Yes, all the time."

"Then it's all right, and I'm glad, and we'll shake hands all around—for I *like* you, and when I say a thing like that, I mean it!"

After the nightmare the happy dream, the semi-lethargy of rapture. The days no longer went on crutches, now; they were winged, and flew. It was curious to see how naturally and with what easy facility the lovers cast off their accustomed reserves and took to themselves the ways that belonged to their new relationship. The matter was as speedy and simple as is the putting off one familiar garment and putting on another that is equally familiar, and even fits a trifle better. The very first morning after that most memorable evening of her life, Clara Burnside found herself making her toilet under wholly new conditions: without perceiving anything odd or strange about it, she was not concerning herself as to whether her adornments might please herself or her mother or the world, but whether "he" would like them. She would cast aside a well-beloved ribbon, without a pang, saying simply, "No, he would not prefer that." She sang low to herself all through the mystery of the toilet service, but was hardly aware of it, since it was her heart that sang, her mind being busy with dreams, pictures, that followed one upon the other with augmenting splendors, like the gaudy surprises of the kaleidoscope.

When she came down stairs she saw that her mother knew everything, and also that she was profoundly happy and content in the knowledge. Dexter came early: the day slipped by, in a lingering ecstasy; the four lovers rambled the river road in the evening; then the elder couple had the Burnside parlor to themselves till a late hour. Everything was changed; everything was new, but nothing strange. When the two first entered and the girl laid aside her hat, it seemed a natural thing for the young man to smoothe her deranged hair with his awkward but caressing hands, and equally natural for her to bend her head with naive docility and endure and enjoy it. When she observed that his cravat was out of line with the horizon, it seemed a natural procedure for her to tip-toe and re-tie it with her dainty fingers—and also natural for her to pull it out and tie and re-tie and tie it again, although both knew that the first effort was successful and that the later ones were nothing more; and it seemed equally natural for him to steady her with his broad hands upon her shoulders while she did her work, steal a kiss when she looked up for her thanks at its conclusion, and take her requiting love-box as a grace, although it was plainly intended as a punishment. When she threw off her shawl, he, with the manner of one having authority, commanded her to put it on again and not catch her death of cold; and she answered, with the manner of one who is under authority—

"Let me keep it off only a minute—I'm so warm."

"No, not a minute; it is the most imprudent thing you can do; put it on at once."

She, pleadingly—

"Do let me—only just the least little while."

He simply replied by taking the shawl and enveloping her in it with his own hands and hooping it to her form with his arm around her shoulders. She being obliged to endure these close quarters, did so, only saying, in the meek voice of the oppressed and helpless—

"Well, have it your own way—I can't prevent it."

All the history of the acquaintanceship was gone over that evening, and each precious detail of it lovingly dwelt upon. She charmed him by confessing that she had loved him at first sight, and he enchanted her with a confession that was the fellow to it. More than once, as the talk went on, he mentioned that it was late and perhaps he had better go, but she said it *could* not be as late as the clock pretended, and so detained him, he being very willing. Late passers in the street judged that there was sickness in the Burnside house, and they were not strictly wrong; but there was nothing dangerous about it.

Other intoxicating days followed. Once Clara said—

"Did you ever imagine what it was like, before?"

"No, not even dimly, vaguely, faintly! My conception of what true happiness must be, was crude to grotesqueness; it was a pauper's idea of wealth, a blind man's notion of the sun."

That suggests the state they were in. They could talk of nothing but their marvelous happiness; they did nothing but contemplate it, wonder at it, inspect it from different standpoints,—walk around it, (so to speak,) trying to get a realizing sense of its mighty proportions and its bewildering altitude; and they always ended with honestly believing that the loves which the world had seen before were but Brooklyn Heights and Ben Lomonds to their Chimborazo.

As for Hugh the romantic, there was one little lack, his bliss could not be absolutely perfect until that lack should be supplied. The time quickly came for the eradication of this single defect.[34] Upon the highest summit north of the village was a small cottage which Judge Griswold had built as a pleasure resort for his wife. She had long been in the habit of driving to this place in warm weather and spending a part of the day there. She took a few friends with her and a servant or two; a dinner cooked on the spot, the bracing air, the wide prospect, and the luxurious rest after the fatigues of the steep and toilsome drive, made up a sufficient bill of compensations for the trouble taken.

One day Miss Martha drove up to Mrs. Burnside's door in the family carriage, followed by a buggy and a light open wagon; the buggy contained Milly and Toby; the wagon was freighted with colored servants and provision. Mrs. Burnside, Clara, and Dexter were taken into the carriage, and the procession moved on. Hugh's chance to drive Milly to the Hill Cottage was lost, for he was absent

[34] The following episode is based upon an actual event which took place at Quarry Farm in August 1877. See Twain's letter to Howells, 25 August 1877 (*MTHL*, I, 194–199).

—so Toby retained his place. However, word was left for Hugh to follow, when he should come home.

The cavalcade prosecuted its slow and wearisome journey up the long hill, along a narrow, winding road bordered by a steep bank on one side and a precipice, "guarded" by a rotten fence, on the other, and finally halted on a sharp turn, five hundred yards below the Cottage, to give the horses a last rest. The view from this point was very fine, but Mrs. Burnside could not confine her thoughts to this feature. She said—

"Has there ever been a runaway here, Miss Martha?"

"No—God forbid!"

"We will suppose one, then. What would be the result?"

"A runaway horse might come from the Cottage down to this turn, alive, because the road is straight, and only tolerably steep; but neither horse, carriage nor driver could ever pass this turn and live."

"I should think that, myself."

"Think it! I *know* it! Destruction would be inevitable. If the horse kept straight on, there's the precipice. If he made this turn at full speed, the vehicle wouldn't make it, but would whirl instantly upside down and go crashing over the verge. Whoever tried to stop a running horse at this place would simply lose his own life and save nobody else's. There—you see, yourself, that a runaway here means death—nothing less."

Mrs. Burnside realized that all this was true. She shuddered, and proposed a change of subject.

The five hundred yards of straight road were soon traversed, and the fun began. Dexter and Clara wandered off together, the elderly ladies took post upon the front porch to talk and enjoy the superb view, and Milly found an isolated outlook and sat down in the shade of a tree, ostensibly to read, but her mind was elsewhere. Dinner was served in due time and the horn called the loiterers home. Two or three pleasant hours followed, and then, late in the afternoon, the horses were brought, for the return journey. Milly went outside the fence and got into her buggy, to wait for Toby, who had gone to the barn for something. The other white people were grouped upon the front porch, ready to step into the carriage, and three or four colored servants were gathered together on the lawn before the house observing the proceedings and waiting for their wagon. Clara said—

"Milly's impatient; she is starting without Toby."

Miss Martha glanced toward the road and said—

"That is very imprudent. The horse is young and not to be depended on."

Clara looked again, and said—

"Look at her—she doesn't know that she is driving too fast for a down grade."

At that moment Milly turned her head and cast toward the group an appealing glance for help that turned every heart to stone with dismay. The horse was breaking into a run! Dexter started down through the grounds, with the servants shrieking in his wake. The three ladies stood white and motionless upon the porch gazing down the road after the flying vehicle. At every second it struck an obstruction and bounded high in the air. It traversed three hundred yards of the straight road in this frightful way, then flashed past a grove of trees and vanished like a thought. All along the path of its flight rose a thick cloud of dust.

The coachman had started down the hill, now, with the empty family carriage. All the servants had gone, before. The three women still stood looking in the one direction, speechless, almost breathless. After all the noise and turmoil and movement, had succeeded a stillness and absence of life and motion that was like death. The same thought was in each mind: "How many seconds will it take to reach the turn?" When they knew that the necessary time had elapsed, they glanced at each other's faces—a look which said "All is over." They shuddered, but no one spoke, no one shed a tear. They began to softly and unconsciously wash their hands together—that dumb expression of a suffering that is beyond conveying in words.

The family carriage came into view, returning. It climbed the hill tediously and slow, the servants following after it. Dexter was riding with the driver. Twice he shouted, as he approached. His voice brought a sharp shock to the three women, though they only divined the meaning—they could not understand the words. The carriage drove in, with its curtains all closed, and stopped before the three women; and while they hesitated as to who should first uncover its awful secret, Milly stepped out, alive and unhurt!

What fright had failed to do, the sudden and supreme joy of this moment accomplished: it swept away the strength of the three watchers, and they sunk into their chairs helpless and drowned in tears.—Then followed a season of devouring the young girl with kisses and caresses, and Mrs. Burnside said—

"We were not prepared for this, and not expecting it. The revulsion from despair to joy was overwhelming."

Dexter said—

"I shouted to you that all was safe and nobody hurt."

Mrs. Burnside said—

"It is very strange.—I heard the words, but they made no impression. I could not realize that the child *could* be saved; I heard the words distinctly, and yet I no more grasped their true meaning than if they had been said in an unknown tongue."

This was found to have been the case with her companions, also. Miss Martha gathered Milly to her arms for the third time, and said—

"You are alive, child, but it will take days to realize it; one can only believe it, now, nothing more. If you had been lost it would have killed your father. But how were you saved? What miracle did it?—and who was the instrument?"

"Hugh!"

The history followed, as Dexter had received it from the hero's lips. Hugh was on his way to the Cottage, on foot. He stopped at the sharp turn to rest. A farmer's heavy two-horse wagon, upward bound, stood upon the turn. Suddenly the farmer sprung from his seat and sought a safe place, shouting, "Out of the road, young man!"

Hugh glanced up and saw a horse coming furiously down toward him, throwing his forefeet high in the air with every plunge, a buggy bounding aloft behind him, and a cloud of dust following after. His first impulse was to save himself, but just then he recognized Milly. He seized the farmer's horses and turned them across the roadway, so that the wagon formed a V-shaped angle with the fence; into this opening the runaway must come, there being nowhere else for him to go. Then he sprang into the opening himself, braced his big frame firmly, and as the horse plunged by, seized the bit and surged back upon him.

That was the whole story. On the face of it it was impossible, and yet it was done. Hugh was not conscious of having really taken thought—he had only acted; there was not time for thought. Dexter concluded with—

"I have told it you just as it happened.—You may go there and look at the ground, and you will say just what I say, 'It was absolutely impossible to do it, and yet it was done.' "

Hugh had remained behind, while a farmer's wife bandaged his cuts and bruises, but came in sight, now, driving Milly's horse. Very few heroes have ever received a more rapturous welcome than fell to his lot.

His bliss was perfect, now. The one lack which he had felt before, was supplied. That is to say, he had been conscious that his happiness could never be rounded and complete until he should save Milly's life in some splendid and blood-curdling way.

The adventure was a marvelous thing in the eyes of the servants. They discussed it, gilded it, and amplified it, with measureless satisfaction. Two of the elder ones were rabid and implacable religious disputants, and were always engaged in a holy war. "Aunt Hanner" was orthodox, "Uncle Jim" was a sort of free-thinker. The former was overheard to say, in a burst of triumph—

"Dah, now, Jim, I reckon dis settles it! I reckon dis'll shet you mouf fo' you! Don't tell *me* no mo' dat dey ain't no special prov'dences! Dey ain't no use tryin' to git aroun' it *dis* time: de Lord sent Mars. Hugh dah for to stop dat hoss—you kin see it you own self!"

"Den who sent de hoss dah in sich a shape?—dat's what *I* wants to know!"

The next day found Hugh a hero to the whole village. Many people climbed the hill to look at the spot where the impossible feat had been performed. The two village papers published accounts of the affair three days later. The accounts differed in several respects;

the facts suffered in both; neither account was a photograph of the matter, yet both bore a resemblance to it—that sort of remote likeness which protects the horses of amateur painters from being mistaken for alligators, or their storm pieces from being regarded as prairies on fire.—One of these accounts said—[35]

HEROIC ACHIEVEMENT.—On the 26th inst., as the fabily of Judge Griswold were decsending the long hill from the Hill Cottage, in the family carriage, consisting of Miss Matrha Griswold and Miss Milly, the other occupants being Mrs. and MisS Burnside and Mr. Hale Dexter, lately arrived from Kentucky, and two negro servants in front with the diver, the others following in another two horse wagon and a buggy, they ran off adn came plunging down the hill with frightful ra*p*idity and constantly accelerating spEed, and had just burst past the dang*e*rous turn and were in the act of plunging into space over the precipice into instant and inevitable death, all the occupants shrciking and giving themselves up for lost, when our valued townsmen and contributor to the Poet's Column of this journal over the signature "H" and the mom de plume "Alphonso," Mr. Hugh Burnside, and which has ben copied extensively an*d* greatly admired in this region, especially his shorter peeces and emanations of sentiment, sprang forward, he being fortu*n*ately on his way to the Hill Cottage at that moment, riding on the manure waggon of one of our oldest and most est*ee*med subscribers, Mr. Buck Farley, who had been ot town and was on his way home again this early in the day with his manure on account of his wife being sick, and siezed the off horse by the throat latch, with herculean &trength and threw him upon his hauncHes as he would a child, and held him ther, which checked the other's onward flight and saved the entire family including servants and coachman from a sickening and horrabel death too dreadful to conTemplate even in imagination, though he sustained some severe but not serious injuries *h*imself, through his noble self-sacrificing act, *m*ainly in his legs and adjacent portions of his head and body, though no bones borken, thanks be to Him who suffeReth not even a sparrow to fall to the ground u*n*noted, let alone people like teh Griswolds, whos position in this community is too well known by all to require en*d*orsement from us, and is now about the village again the recipie*n*t of praises and congratulations from high

[35] On MS p. 236, Twain wrote, "To Compositor—Please mis-spell a little, turn some letters and get in some wrong fonts. SLC."

and low, and the cynosure of al leyes, the observed of all observers, may his glory di*m*inish not and his shadow never be less! Will the lying slave of the *Torch of* [*Civilization*] [36] attempt to pervert the facts in *this* noble episo*d*e as in all others where he drags his slimy length athwart the fair fields of truth, leaving it bilstered and smouldering be*h*ind him with the corruption of his fetid utt*e*rance and the veno*m*ous blight of his crime-festered soul?

The history of the adventure, as given in the other paper, was as near the truth as this, and closed with a vigorous reflection upon the editor whom I have been quoting, the cracker on the end of it being a suggestion that his family of beggars had improved in raiment since he had been appointed to hand around the contribution-box in church, and yet were manifestly giving the neighboring clothes-lines a rest.

Milly wrote a glowing and grateful account of her peril and preservation to her parents, and gave it into the hands of Toby, who sent it to his mother in Arkansas. Miss Martha's account, with interesting additions about our four lovers, traveled the same road.

Dexter and Hugh had become pretty constant companions—at least during the earliest part of the mornings, before their dearer friends were up. Hugh had bagged one wolf with his gun, one had been poisoned by some bounty-seeking pelt-hunter, and Dexter had had one chance—but missed. Dexter was sorer about his marksmanship than he allowed to appear on the surface; for, to be a Kentuckian and a bad shot was to be unpleasantly conspicuous. It was a new thing in nature. The honor of his State was at stake in his person; so he resolved to achieve a triumph if perseverance could compass it. Every morning found him haunting the wolves' lurking place.

---

[36] Here again, Twain originally left a space for the name of the paper and later filled in *Torch of* but omitted *Civilization.*

Three weeks after the date of the beginning of this story, there came an unlucky day for Hugh Burnside. Everything went wrong with him. By nightfall he had reached a very advanced stage of irritation. Now appeared Clara with a copy of the [*Torch of Civilization*] [37] damp from the press, and assailed her brother in caustic terms about a poem in the paper entitled "Hail, Cupid's Holy Darlings!" and signed "Alphonzo." The verses were so frankly descriptive and significant, that there was no need to name names; it was plain to all that our four lovers were the darlings whom the poet exalted with his laudations and bedewed with his sentimental sap.—Hugh was astonished to find that Clara was not charmed and grateful. He said as much. Clara burst into tears of mortification, then flew into a rage and delivered herself of such a volley of sharp and lacerating words that the poor poet was hurt beyond help. A great and portentous calm settled down upon the soul which the day's ill luck had so tortured and bedeviled, and he rose up as one who is wounded in the house of his friends, and said in a voice choked with emotion—

"My mother has chidden me for another's fault, I have tried to do honor to my sister in my poor way and she tramples ruthless upon my heart for reward. I have tried to do right, but the unfortunate are ever at odds with fate. I have often felt that I was not wanted here, yet strove to blind myself to the bitter truth. But have your will. I go forth to wander friendless in the cold world—perhaps to die. So be it. And if you shall sometime chance to hear that the poor outcast is no more, say of him, 'His merit was small, his virtues few, but his true heart ceased not to beat for his own while life remained, even though they despised him all his days, and in the frail blossom of his helpless youth spurned him from the home of his fathers with loathing.' "

He stood upon the threshold, cast one agonized look around the house of his fathers, then solemnly departed.

---

[37] As in the previous two instances, Twain left a space in the manuscript to be filled in later with the name of the paper, although he never did so. Despite the fact that two weeklies are published in Guilford, the second unnamed, I have chosen *Torch of Civilization* because elsewhere in the manuscript Twain has consistently supplied that title.

Clara said—

"O, the huge intolerable baby! Now he will come back at midnight with the appetite of a menagerie, and then sit up till morning churning his clabber brains for buttery rhymes of woe and suffering—a pest take all poets, amen!" Then after a pause: "In his right mind he is so good and dear—it is only when he is inspired that one wants to kill him."

In due time the sufferer, staggering under the burden of his woe, entered the Griswold parlor, with tragic mien.—Milly was there alone, crying over his odious poem. She raised her wet face and exclaimed with anguish—

"O, go away, go away! I don't see how you can look anybody in the face!"

Hugh straightened himself up, folded his arms, then dropped his chin upon his breast. He said, with dismal resignation—

"This, then, is the fiat! Very well. So be it. Spurned with contumely by those allied to me by ties of blood, driven forth from the home of my fathers almost with blows, it is fitting that I be banished with ignominy, forever and without a hearing, by one whose slave I was and am and ever shall be, yet to whom I am nothing—nothing but despised dust, a hated viper! It is well. I go—and may heaven forgive you for what you have done, as I do. All is over. Here—take your book-mark,—imperishable symbol of a perishable love—"

"O, Hugh!"

"Take it. Return to me the tributes of affection which I have given you in happier hours, that no memento of my wronged heart's beguilement shall remain to mock my few remaining moments of existence in this troubled world."

"O, Hugh, what can you mean? Why do you—"

"Hear me, woman! When I am no more, say of me, 'He' "—

The frightened girl waited to hear no more, but flew from the room calling hysterically for her aunt, and the next moment Dexter entered from another door. Said he, furiously—

"You incredible ass! You deserve a hiding! What the mischief could have possessed you to—to—"

"Spare your reproaches, sir," said Hugh, with lofty dignity. "You have insulted me. Yesterday I would have taken your life for it. To-day I am a crushed and broken being, whose pride is gone, whose self-love is dead, who desires only to lay his ruined life in the grave and be at peace. That life will I sacrifice with my own hand. Seek me on the morrow and you shall find not me, but only my poor corse. Spend your fury upon that; dishonor my remains—what else shall they be good for?"

"Your remains will be good to feed worms with. That is what I will do with them."

Judge Griswold, dusty with travel, thrust his head in at the door just in time to hear this last remark, smiled grimly at Dexter, then drew back and closed the door softly. Dexter continued—

"Look here, Hugh, drop this calf-talk, and do drop writing poetry, too. If you must write it, write it about yourself, and leave other people alone."

"My end is near—I shall never write more."

"O, rubbish! There is no danger of your committing suicide, but there *is* danger of your wailing around and threatening it until you make yourself the laughing-stock of the village."

Hugh said with gloomy impressiveness—

"Rail on, if it pleases you—I am dead to affront. By this hand I die before the morrow's sun shall gild the eastern hills."

"What an idiot! Go home and take a pill!"

Hugh said, mournfully—

"You little imagine with what fatal fidelity I shall follow your mocking counsel." He put out his hand. "Farewell—do you forgive me?"

"For your infernal poem? Yes—and it's a good deal to do, too. Now take a dose of paregoric and go to bed."

They shook hands, and Hugh said, tearfully—

"When I am gone,—"

"O go and be hanged!" cried Dexter, cheerfully, and the stricken one moved solemnly away.

Dexter watched him a moment or two, musingly, then said—

"I shall have to go after the wolves betimes, in the morning, if I want to be ahead of him, for this mood will keep him grinding doggerel all night and give him an early start."

There was a knock at the door, and a servant ushered in four men, Captain Simon Wheeler at the head. He said a word was desired with Mr. Dexter. He introduced them as Mr. Baxter, Mr. Billings, and Mr. Bullet, and added—

"The most celebrated detectives in America—all belong to Inspector Flathead's celebrated St. Louis Detective Agency—Flathead that writes the wonderful detective tales, you know."

There was something contagious about the Captain's adoring admiration of the great personages. It infected Dexter somewhat.

"Sir," said the little red-headed, quick-motioned person, named as Baxter, speaking rapidly, "please to allow us to put a few questions to you in a professional way. You are aware that the desperado Jack Belford has broke jail again?"

"Yes—I saw the notice three days ago."

"Just so. Here it is—five hundred dollars reward, dead or alive. A great pity, very great pity—he was to be hung tomorrow. Large build—Had on when he escaped, prison uniform, and so-f'rth and so-f'rth and so-f'rth—no use to go into particulars if you've read it. You hunt in a certain part of the woods every morning, I understand."

"Yes."

"Seen any suspicious characters around?"

"No."

The short, slow, dull-looking man called Billings, lifted a fat finger, paused a moment, then said with weighty deliberation—

"That is, in prison uniform?"

"No."

Billings nodded his head slowly three times, and muttered "Um" each time.

Nobody spoke for a moment or two. Then the long lean man called Bullet, who had been sitting pondering, with the end of one of his talons pressed against his forehead, looked up, fixed his eyes upon Dexter and said—

"Tracks?"

"Do you mean have I seen any?"

"Yes."

"What sort?"

"Human."

"I remember none."

"Think."

Dexter thought—then said—

"No—I call to mind none but wolf tracks."

A look of intelligence passed between the several detectives. Bullet murmured—

"So?—in disguise!"

Billings murmured—

"Aha—just so—in disguise."

Baxter murmured—

"As one might expect—in disguise."

Capt. Wheeler slapped his thigh and murmured, admiringly—

"O, don't they know how to go about it, though! You bet your life!"

A considerable silence ensued. Then Billings raised his fat finger, paused a moment, and said—

"Were the tracks bare, or shod?"

Dexter looked a trifle surprised, then said—

"I would not know a wolf's track if the beast were shod."

Billings nodded his head slowly three times, and gravely muttered "Um" each time.

Baxter rattled off a sharp fire of questions about matters that seemed foreign to the subject, and appeared to value the enlightenment he got out of the answers. By and by the lean Bullet removed his reflective finger from his forehead and broke the silence—

"No other tracks?"

"Well—if it is worth mentioning—I've seen a cow's tracks there."

Another look of intelligence was exchanged between the detectives.—Bullet murmured—

"So?—another disguise!"

Billings murmured—

"Another disguise!"

Baxter muttered irritably—

"Confound it, this complicates it!"

Captain Wheeler muttered under his breath, and suffocating with admiration—[38]

"Dad blame 'em, nothing can't escape 'em—they're inspired!"

There was deep pondering, now, and a long silence. Then the fat finger came up impressively, there was a pause, and Billings said—

"Was the cow shod?"

Dexter stared a moment, then said—

"They don't shoe cows here."

Billings nodded and "Um'd" as gravely as before.

At the end of two hours the interview came to an end, and detective Baxter said—

"We are much obliged to you sir. You must excuse our intruding here the moment we reached the village, for ours is a profession that cannot wait and never rests. You perceive our motto."

The three men threw open their coats, and displayed, pinned to each vest, a big silver disk with a staring human eye engraved upon it, surrounded by the modest legend, "WE NEVER SLEEP."

They took their leave, and as Capt Wheeler passed out he whispered in Dexter's ear—

"You see what they are, hey? By George if he was disguised in a chipmunk's hide, let alone a cow's, they'd find him."

Dexter found that supper had been waiting some time; but the family were not visible.—Toby answered his call, and said—

"Ole missis sick. She didn't git no furder dan Drytown. I reckon she considable sick, too, kase ole Mars. he come an' make Miss Martha pack right up an' tuck her away a-boomin'."

"That is bad news. Did he leave any word for me?"

"Yes, sah. He gimme dis little note, an' he say he gwyne to bust my head if I fo'git to gim it to you."

The note read thus:

> "I had but a moment to stay. I had often wondered what could be delaying your mission, but I heard a sentence from your lips that showed me that its consummation is now close at hand; therefore I would not interrupt your conversation. I shall return with all possible speed to compass your escape, and shall be here as early as I can in

[38] In the top margin of MS p. 262, Twain wrote, "Follows Miss Sanning."

the morning. If you should need assistance before, apply promptly to Major Barnes, who will furnish fleet horses and everything necessary."

Dexter said to himself—

"This is odd. Either nobody has written him or else the letters have miscarried. He is not a brute, but a gentleman. If he knew that Hugh saved Milly's life, he would stand between Hugh and any man's bullet, instead of making himself an accessory to his murder. Very well; he will hear all about it before he gets to Drytown; and then in place of despising me for not killing Hugh he will be pretty sincerely grateful. It's a comical thing that he should have overheard about the only sentence in my whole talk with Hugh that *could* be misunderstood!"

Toby wanted a letter written to his old mother, after supper. He showed the one he preferred, in the Ready Letter-Writer, and Dexter sat down and copied it—to-wit:

*Form for a Letter of a Young Gentleman of Fortune to the Father of a Young Lady, requesting permission to pay his addresses to her.*

HONORED SIR: I am a young gentleman of position, education and independent means, of which [ma]tters you can satisfy yourself by applying to (*here insert name or names.*) I have observed with deep interest, the varied excellencies of your angel daughter, in whom I find rare and exquisite beauty, combined with the nobler charms of purity, truthfulness, a sensitive and poetical nature, a fine mind, equipped with elegant accomplishments, and that sweetest of feminine functions, the gift of song. Such a life-companion, to cast the oil of peace upon the troubled waters of the arid desert of my lonely life and bid its flowers spring anew adown its blighted, joy-tombed vistas, my heart has longed to call its own, all unworthy as I am, of such a Boon. With your permission, kind sir, I desire to lay the poor offering of self and fortune at the feet of Miss (*here insert name of party,*) with a view to ultimate matrimony, if my suit shall prosper and this the faint dim ray of my early hope expand into the rich and clustered fruit of perfected fruition.

With sentiments of Exalted esteem, I beg to sign myself,

(*Name.*)

It was duly signed "Your loving Son, TOBY," and forwarded to "Old Mammy Betsy" in Arkansas.[39]

## Chap. [5]

DURING THE tedious journey to Drytown, Judge Griswold sat absorbed in thought. He could not understand Dexter's long delay in so important a matter as the destruction of a fellow being for duty's sake. However, those words about feeding Hugh to the worms, meant that the delay was to cease now. That, at any rate, was satisfactory. Miss Martha's several efforts to start a conversation got small attention; so she finally gave up and went to sleep. Drytown was reached about midnight.

Mrs. Griswold said she was feeling better, and believed she should be able to go home in a day or two. Miss Martha said—

"I judged by brother's letter that you were only worn out with watching, and with grief for your great loss, and that a good rest would make you well again."

"Yes, watching and grief—and another matter that lay heavy upon my mind." Here she looked wistfully at her husband, but he gave no sign. He knew what she referred to. He found himself in an uneasy position; for he wanted to be hurrying toward Guilford, to be ready for the coming tragedy, yet did not know what excuse to make for going, since he did not wish to make any distressful revelations to his wife in her present circumstances. Mrs. Griswold boded no good from the Judge's silence. She was troubled and thoughtful a moment; then she said to Miss Martha—

"I was expecting mournful news from home. I still am."

"Then you may set your mind at rest, for there's none of that sort for you—very far from it."

Mrs. Griswold's face lighted with a surprised gladness, and she said—

[39] At the top of MS p. 270, Twain wrote, "Milly does not go to D. town."

"You have no bad news to tell? I can hardly credit it. Then what news have you?"

"Well, no news is good news, isn't it? There's nothing new since that which we told you in our letters, and surely that was good news."

"Your letters!—Whose letters?"

"Mine and Milly's."

"We have not had a line from either of you."

"Not a line from either of us? That is astonishing. Then you don't know that Milly escaped horrible mutilation and death by what was simply a miracle and nothing less?"

Mrs. Griswold's face blanched, and the sudden dismay paralyzed her tongue. The iron Judge, too, was stricken for once, and he betrayed that he was human. He showed strong excitement—an unusual thing for him; he even trembled like a girl. Evidently the hidden great deeps of his nature had been touched at last.

"Tell it!" he said; "tell the whole matter! We know nothing of it. —Go on, go on—why do you hesitate!"

His eye flamed upon his sister as if it would consume her. She began her story, with loving attention to detail and dramatic circumstance; and as she proceeded the fire in the Judge's eyes burned more and more eloquently, and few had seen him so stirred in all his long life. When the story was finished, he exclaimed—

"And we came so near losing her!—It was superbly done! Strength, courage, generalship—there are not two men in the State who could have done it. Now, no more dramatic concealments—who is this marvelous man?"

"You would not guess in an hour, brother."

"I do not wish to guess. I want to go and tell him he has saved our all and he can command our all!"

"He can command your all?"

"Yes—I have said it. Why?"

"He is young; he is a gentleman; he loves Milly, she loves him. *She* is the reward he will demand."

"Then he shall have her! Tell me his name."

"Hugh Burnside!"

The Judge was standing. This shot almost brought him to the

ground, so great was the unexpectedness of it. Mrs. Griswold sprang partly up in bed, turned an imploring look upon her husband, and fell back again, exhausted with terror, without speaking the words that were in her mind. The Judge strode swiftly to her side and bent down and whispered in her ear—

"Tell Martha nothing. I will be in the saddle in five minutes. I will save him. Never fear; I shall be in time. No harm shall come to him."

Mrs. Griswold looked her gratitude, and the next moment the Judge was gone. A few minutes later he was spurring toward Guilford with a long journey before him but a fleet horse under him.

Mrs. Griswold said to Miss Martha—

"There, now you may go to your bed, and tell me the rest of the news in the morning. I could bear no more to-night, good or bad. You little imagine the full importance of the tidings you have given us, nor how thankful we shall be, all our lives, that they came so timely.

## Chap. [6]

TOWARD THE middle of the same night of which we have just been speaking, two young druggist clerks, of Guilford, were on their way home.—They were laughing over something that had just happened. One said—

"O, there's no danger of it's hurting him. It will only make him sleep like a brazen image for a few hours and then he'll come out of it all right. *He* commit suicide, indeed! It will be the best joke on him we've ever had in the village. We'll never let him hear the last of it!"

"Good—so we will. But look here: suppose he just takes enough to make him stupid, and goes mooning around and tumbles into the river?"

The other thought a moment, then said—

"There's something in that. Somebody might have seen him buy the stuff, without our knowing it; or he might tell somebody he bought it."

"Yes; then we'd be in a pretty fix. If the bottle was never found, we couldn't prove it wasn't poison we sold him."

"It begins to look less and less funny to me, Jimmy."

"Dog'd if it don't to me, too, Bob. Now I'll tell you what we've got to do. We've got to keep perfectly mum about this business if anything happens to that fool—don't you know that?"

"You bet you I know it! Mum's the word. I ain't in as much of a hurry to run and tell about this thing as I was."

About this time Hugh Burnside was passing Mrs. Higgins's, the last house at the north end of the village. He moved on, with groping, uncertain steps, up the river road, some fifty-yards to a grassy open in the hazels. He said plaintively, and with a thick utterance—

"It has begun its fatal work! How drowsy I am! The sleep of death—the welcome sleep that the sore-hearted and the banished long for—is coming. Here, in this public spot, where the first passers will see my lonely form, I will lay me down and forget my trials forever. At last the hard hearts will soften, perchance. At last there will be some to pity the poor outcast who never did any harm and yet was ever repulsed and despised."

He sat down on a huge log, a favorite resting place for village promenaders, leaned his head upon his hand and began to breathe heavily. Gradually the drowsiness stole over him and he muttered as one does in sleep—

"Will she, the stony-hearted, recognize her cruel work and be smitten with remorse at last? Will she—will she—shed one little tear of pity over—over—"

He was nearly asleep. He was silent a little while, then muttered—

"This—then—is—is Death! . . . Awful thought! . . . I—I—took more—th—than I—intended to."

His voice sunk to incoherent mutterings, and he presently fell and lay stretched upon his face in front of the great log, torpid and motionless. The sympathetic moon, hidden until now, put her face to first one and then another ragged window in the drifting cloud-rack and peeped pathetically down upon her sorrow-worn calf.

Now came Captain Wheeler picking his stealthy way on tip-toe along the river path, stopping occasionally to listen. When he reached the grassy open, he halted, some six feet from where Hugh lay, and began to talk to himself—

"I wonder wher' he could 'a' went to." He scratched his head in a puzzled way, and continued. "I knew by the way he hung around in the shadows by the drug store that he was up to some murderous villainy or other—got the cold eye of a pirate, that poet. I see him slink away with that bottle. He thought he was playing his game pretty sharp, but he had the old detective's eye on him—unerring as fate. But rot him, I've lost track of him! Can't seem to start sight of him anywhers. Well, I'll take a minute's rest here and think it over. This moonlight ain't bright enough for detective work, hardly—that is, when a body hasn't got his clews arranged and decided on."

He sat down on Hugh's big frame, and leaned his back comfortably against the log. He put his hat on the ground in front of him and proceeded to talk to it—

"Now gimme your attention a minute. I've lost him, but my! it's only for a minute or so—when I get on a man's track, you understand, he might as well throw up the sponge. *You* know me well enough to know that, don't you? Very well; then you just bet all you're worth that he's my meat, sooner or later. There ain't no escaping me—I'm as bound to trace him out and get him as if he was a spectator at a riot and I was a random bullet. Ain't that so? Don't you forget it! There's something awful about being a detective. If you're a true detective, night's just the same as daylight to you—a whisper's just the same as a yell—nobody can't hide a secret from you *no* way.—Just give you a clew and that's all you want. Just an old glove's enough—or a foot-print from a ragged boot —or an old cigar-stub with the defendant's particular chew-mark on the end of it. If a detective's got three or four little clews like that, they just lead him as dead straight to his man as a train of powder would show fire the way to the magazine. Why, when that great mysterious murder was done yonder in Chicago, what sort of clews did the detectives have? Nothing in the world but a sledge-hammer, and one of the criminal's boots, and his handkercher with his name on it, and his ambrotype, and some other little traps of his'n. That's all the clews they had. They've got 'm yet. Do you reckon that that assassin 'll escape? Never! Not if he lives long enough. You bet your life, they'll get him . . . This log's mighty warm; mighty soft, too: rotten, I reckon. Sort of uncomfortable."

He got up, took his hat, and moved off a step or two, buried in reflection.—He stood musing awhile, then said—

"Now lemme see—how'll I go to work to track out this chap and find him? . . . Good! I've got it—got it sure! In five minutes I'll lay my hand on him! I'm as dead sure of him now as if I had him in my grip. In just five minutes by the clock, if I don't take him into camp, call me no detective!"

Then he hurried away toward the village.

The Captain was hardly gone before Tom Hooker, the reporter, came strolling along. He was talking to himself, after the manner of persons in a certain condition—no, uncertain condition is the better phrase. But for one thing, this trim and tidy youth would have looked as he always looked.—That one thing was, that he had his cap on wrong side before. Trivial as this variation was, it transformed the young fellow. It changed him from himself into an ingenious and artistic caricature of himself. It was as significant, too, as Ophelia's straws. Tom Hooker had been drinking. He had not drank enough to make him stagger, but enough to make him just a shade uncertain on his legs. A random hiccup afflicted him at intervals. He halted in Hugh's neighborhood and began to fumble in a thick-fingered way about his forehead. Presently he stopped, and looked puzzled. He thought awhile, shook his head, then fumbled again. Again he desisted, and said—

"Tha('k!) that's curious. Brim's gone. I thought I brought it with me."

He fumbled about his forehead again, without result, then took off the cap and examined it, following its circle around until he found the missing brim. He was greatly pleased. He said—

"Here 'tis! I must 'a' o('hk!) overlooked it before."

He put it on again—wrong side first, as formerly—then felt, to make sure all was right.

"Brim gone again! Something's mattter wi' this cap; I ca('k!) can't unstan' it."

He took it off, searched and found the brim once more, and was greatly surprised and puzzled. He stood thinking it over and inspecting the cap in silence. Finally he said—

"I see how 'tis. Somebody's played a j('k!) a j('k!) a j('k!)oke on me. They've turned the cap around and sewed the brim on the back side. Fix that easy enough,—get tailor to s('ic!) sew it on front side where it belongs."

He ripped the brim off, put it in his pocket, and put the rest of the cap on his head again, with a satisfied heart and a mind at peace.[40]

He took a couple of steps, stopped, and said—

"There—my legs are so weak. It is on account of love. That is, d(*uck!*)isappointed love. I wish Dexter hadn't come. I wish I'd never seen *her*. None know her but to see her, none lose her but to praise,—p('ic!) poet says." (Here he observed Hugh, and his spirits lifted at once.) "Hey? *Dead* man?—Noble item! O, *this* ain't any good find, I reckon! There hasn't been an item in six months that could begin with it. Suicide, I wonder? . . . 'S('k!)'Sassi*nation,* I hope! A suicide's a prime thing in its way, but it don't begin with 'n' assassination. You've got to be mighty reserved and respectful about a suicide, or you'll have the surviving relatives in your hair. You can't spread, you know—family won't stand it. You've got to cramp your item down to a short quarter of a column—and you've always got to say it's t('k!)emporary aber*ration.* Temporary aberration!—and half these suicides haven't got anything to aberrate!"

Still rattling cheerfully along, as if he were entertaining a company instead of himself, he sat comfortably down on Hugh's

---

[40] At the top of MS p. 297, Twain wrote, "Wheeler shall *play drunk* like Garrick." David Garrick had a gift for simulating drunkenness which made his portrayal of Sir John Brute in Vanbrugh's *Provok'd Wife* his favorite and most renowned comic role.

sturdy bulk, got out a pipe, cleaned it, knocked it on his palm, blew through it, then proceeded to load it.

"But you let a man be assassinated once, and you can string him out to five columns. More you say, more the family like it." (Scrapes a match on the "corpse"; forgets it, talks on; it burns out, scorching his fingers with its last gasp.) "Yes, a suicide's a kind of lean stuff for literature, but" (giving the "corpse" an approving slap,) "y(ic!) *you're* the right sort, m' fren'! I wish they'd gashed you up a little. You'd show up a nation sight gaudier in print. I wonder if it wouldn't be all fair in the way of business to gash him up a little myself . . . No, 'twouldn't be pleasant. I couldn't do it. But I regret exceedingly that it was o('k!) overlooked. Now half the time" (scraping another match on the "corpse"—without result, since he scraped the wrong end of the match—though he enclosed it carefully in the hollow of his hand and went on talking while he waited for it to burn,) "half the time, what you take for a suicide's only a drunk—that's all—only a drunk—and all of a sudden he comes alive on the inquest, and where's your item?—That's it—where's your item. G('k!) gone where the woodbine twineth! A bogus suicide's a painful object. It's discouraging to journalism. But" (slapping the "corpse" affectionately), "*you're* all right, you know. I'm proud of you; and you're worthy to be proud of, too. . . . I've got him all to myself, too! Won't the other paper feel sore when I fetch him out with thunder-and-lightning display-lines in the morning!"

Here a disturbing thought struck him, and he got up and stood pondering a while. Presently he said—

"No, there's no getting around it. It's after midnight; our paper's gone to press. Too late to get him into this week's issue! O, this is too bad. If he stays here, the other paper will get him too. Come, that won't do. I found him—he belongs to me. . . . Can't I hide him somewhere till next week, and then realize on him? . . . It's a g('k!) good idea. I'll take him home. If my room-mate objects, I'll flog him . . . Yes, I'll take him home and hide him under the bed till I want him. It's pretty warm weather but I reckon he'll. . . ."

The rest of the sentence died out in mutterings as he walked away. He traversed the fifty-yards between Hugh's grassy retreat and the widow Higgins's boarding house and presently returned with a wheelbarrow. With infinite trouble he finally managed to get his limp treasure across the barrow, and then proceeded toward Mrs. Higgins's, remarking—

"Noblest item of the age! Perfect m(ic!) mine of literature!"

His room was a back one on the ground floor. His room mate, Lem Sackett, had found his bed unendurable because of the heat, and was stretched upon the carpet, sound asleep. Hooker trundled his barrow softly in there, stumbled over something in the dark, and his freight slid ponderously out and rested, limp and massive, across Sackett's face. Sackett struggled from under it, half smothered, sprang up and came in contact with Hooker, whom he floored with a random blow, then lost his balance, and went down with him. But he immediately mounted his adversary's breast and began to pound him well. As soon as Hooker could get his breath, he exclaimed, in a guarded voice—

"Hold up, you fool!—it's nobody but me."

Sackett desisted, and said—

"You, is it? Well, what do you come sprawling over me for?"

"I didn't sprawl over you."

"You did. Somebody did."

"It wasn't me—it was the dead man."

"The what!"

"Dead man."

"What dead man?" asked Lem, with a shudder.

"The one I fetched here."

"Gracious! where is he?"

"He's around here somewhere. Feel for him."

"Feel for him yourself if you want him.—I don't. . . . Ugh! here he is!"

Sackett recoiled from the touch, then shrunk away, out of reach of the object. Said he—

"Did you kill him?"

"Me? No!"

"Who did?"

"I don't know."

"Well then, how does he come to be with you?"

"I found him."

"You found him, you idiot! You talk as if he was a valuable property."

"That's what I take him to be."

"Tom Hooker, have you lost your mind?"

"Why?"

"You find a dead man lying around, and you lug him home with you, as if it never occurred to you that he would be tracked here, and you and me be—"

"Good land, I never thought of that! I've been drinking, but I'm sober enough now to begin to feel sick about this business. What shall we do?"

"Do? Why we've got to get him out of this, in less than two minutes. Not a second to lose. Pretty soon it will be dawn."

"I tell you, Lem, I begin to feel scared. Where 'll we take him to?"

"Put him where you got him. Is it far?"

"No. Right up yonder at the Lover's Roost."

"Well, come!—don't fool away any time. I'm getting in an awful state."

They freighted the wheelbarrow with Hugh and trundled him softly away, with many a frightened glance over their shoulders. They deposited him where Tom had originally found him, and then retired to a safe distance and sat down on the river bank, tired, puffing and perspiring, to steal a moment's rest. The moon was hidden, there were no sounds, all nature lay in a boding gloom. Presently Lem said, in a low, dismal voice—

"It's a nice piece of business—that's what it is. We'll swing for this."

"Well, it's your own fault, Lem—to hop up and smash a friend's nose for nothing, that way. I never saw such a peppery devil."

"For nothing! Slam a clammy corpse across a man when he's sound asleep!—Call tha. nothing?"

"It was dark as pitch,—how could I help it?"

"Confound it, what did you want to bring the grisly thing there, for, anyhow?"

"Where else could I put him?—in the buttery?"

"No—leave him where you found him."

"Yes, it's all well enough to say that, *now*—anybody can tell what ought to have been done, *now*. But I was trying to save him for an item." Then he added, regretfully, "and he would have made the very sublimest item this poor little one-horse town ever saw, too! I had a monopoly; but now he's got to be divided with the other paper, of course. I can't ever seem to have any luck."

Lem said, gloomily—

"There's another item that's got to be divided, too—that's our hand in this business."

Tom said, with a shiver—

"Yes, that's so. And Lem, who knows but we've had more hand in the business than we think for?"

Lem started, with a vague apprehension—

"What do you mean, Tom?"

"I mean, suppose he wasn't dead, in the first place, but only stunned?"

"O, Tom, it's been in my mind a dozen times!"

"He was very limp, Lem. Maybe he wasn't dead—at first."

"It's awful, Tom! He tumbled out on me—"

"And when I fell, I fell on him—heavy, too! I thought I heard him groan! I *did* hear him! Seems to me I did, anyway."

"Tom, he was only stunned at first, sure as you live. *We* finished him, O my goodness!"

"No, *I* did, Lem. I tumbled him out—I fell on him. I wish I was dead!"

"No, it ain't any use mincing it—it was *us*. If I hadn't hit you, you wouldn't have fallen on him.—It was falling on him that finished him. No, we are brother murderers, Tom. And doomed!"

"Lemmy, I feel worse about it now, than I did before—ever so much."

"So do I, Tom—because before I didn't seem to be to blame. But now!—it don't make any difference if it *was* an accident, the very idea of killing a human being, even accidentally, is horrible. O, I kept thinking maybe he would come to."

"So did I, Lem. But he was good and dead when we got done with him."

"So he was, so he was, poor devil. Tom, shall you ever be able to sleep again? I know I shan't."

"Nor I. I'll always see him, night and day, as long as I live."

Now that fear had set their imaginations at work, there was no end to the horrors that were conjured up. They succeeded in convincing themselves, by the absurdest reasoning, that they had killed that man and could never hope for peace of mind again.

The young fellows went home and finished their conversation in their room, in the dark. Tom said—

"We must save our lives as long as we can. As soon as it is light we must straighten things up, here, and then go to bed and stay there all day. We must pretend to be sick, and say we were not out of the house in the night."

"What is the use, Tom?" said Lem, despondently, "didn't your nose bleed all over the body? and didn't it bleed all along the road? It's a track that a detective—"

"Don't you worry about detectives. The average detective couldn't see it, if it was pointed out to him; and he couldn't follow it if it was eleven foot wide. But other people will find us out. Maybe the other boarders—"

"No, it won't be them, I reckon, because they never hear anything and never see anything. But it's all one—somebody will find us out."

"Lem, let us be brothers from this out, and stand by each other, through thick and thin, till we go to the gallows."

"There is my hand on it, Tom—but don't speak that awful word any more. It kills me to hear it. Tom, we must never divulge."

"Never! Not even on the rack."

"The dawn is breaking—there will not be many more for us to see. Tom, we are so young to die!"

"I know it—and yet I feel old—so old and miserable!"

## Chap. [7]

As LEM had said, the dawn was breaking. The gray twilight stole gradually upon the still world, and the features of the soft summer landscape began to reveal themselves. Hugh Burnside stirred uneasily in his torpor; turned over; turned again, and presently sat up and looked about him wonderingly. He reflected awhile, then said to himself—

"No, it is not the other world. I am very glad of that. Plainly I didn't take enough. I am very glad of that, too. I have been a fool. Well, it is the last time I'll be one. I'll go home and be sensible."

He got up and stretched his stiff limbs and was about to start, when another thought struck him, and with violence, too—

"No! I should be a greater fool than ever to do that. Those drug clerks will make me the laughing-stock of the whole town. That won't answer. Now what shall I do? I think my cue is to mysteriously disappear for a while. That is the very thing to do. The drug clerks will keep still—no question about that. Mother will grieve over her injustice to me; Clara will grieve for having ordered me to never cross the threshold of my childhood's home again; and *she,* even she whose unexacting slave I was, may peradventure feel some touch of remorse for banishing me her father's house with threats and execrations when she comes to know the full extent of her awful work. The cruel public will pity me and will cease at last, when too late, to make jibes about me. Then be it so. I will mysteriously disappear from the haunts and the eyes of men. There is nothing in literature more romantic than such a fate. None is so mourned as such a victim, if he be young and persecuted by those who should have befriended him."

While he was still reveling in the bliss of limitless castle-building, an odd sound broke upon his ear. He listened; evidently it was approaching. He detected the long-drawn, wheezy agony of "The Last Rose of Summer"; somebody was grinding it out of a peculiarly execrable hand-organ—a reluctant hand-organ—a hand-organ that valued it, and wanted to keep it, and hated to give it up, and ought to have been humored in its whim. The musician presently arrived. He was a great, broad-shouldered tramp, arrayed in a fluttering chaos of rags, and otherwise adorned with blue goggles and false whiskers. He saluted Hugh, and asked an alms. Hugh said—

"I am not in a giving humor, but I am ready for a trade."

"Trade what?"

"Outfits."

"Well that's a rum go! Clothes, you mean?"

"Yes—everything. I want to have a bit of a lark."

The tramp hesitated. He thought, "Have I struck luck at last? This is the most dangerous disguise I could have." He said, aloud—

"I'm very poor, and I hope you ain't saying it just to make fun of me."

"No, I'm in earnest—I want to disguise myself and have some fun."

"All right, then, I'm ready to trade."

"Come into the woods, and we'll exchange; and mind, don't you go into the village—you might get into trouble on account of my clothes."

"Very well, I'll go some other direction—it's all one to me." He added to himself, "Belford, you are in luck, sure."

The exchange was soon made. The tramp, in Hugh's clothes, struck deeper into the woods, and Hugh, in the tramp's fantastic array, slung the hand-organ about his neck and returned to the "Lover's Roost" and sat down to lay out a plan for his future course.

The tramp had moved stealthily through the thick wood for a long distance, picking his way carefully, for there was a plentiful lack of light there, when a gunshot suddenly startled him and a bullet whizzed past his head. He dropped instantly on his face, muttering, "If it is an officer, I'm out of luck again; if it is a hunter, I'll play dead till he goes for assistance."

In another moment Hale Dexter was bending over him, exclaiming—

"Hugh! Hugh! Speak! answer me! O, he is dead, and I have killed him. What shall I do! what shall I do! To think that the one true-aimed shot of my life should have a result like this! Fool, fool, I might have known he would be here before me. Fool, to think every shadowy form that stirs in this place must needs be a wolf! . . . Not a sound, not a motion—poor boy, there is no hope; he is dead. . . . Ah, there was no crime in the intent, but my heedlessness was a crime—in my own eyes I shall be a murderer, always . . . Sh! was that a noise?"[41]

---

[41] In the margin beside the last portion of this speech, from "Ah, there was no crime" to the end, Twain wrote, "Describe this instead of talking him."

He broke away and fled through the wood. He ran some distance, then stopped in a thicket and listened, with a beating heart. He heard nothing. He began to commune with himself. He tried to map out a course of action, but his mind was a chaos of conflicting thoughts. At times he had the impulse to go and tell what he had done. But before he could take a step this thought always followed: "How can I ever bear to let his mother and his sister know it was I that did it!"

Presently he plunged away at random through the wood, not heeding the direction, his brain feverishly creating plan after plan, and adhering to none, and at last, to his great surprise, for he could hardly believe he had come so far, he found himself emerging upon the Drytown road. In the same moment Judge Griswold came flying by on a horse that was white with foam. The old gentleman came to an instant halt, threw himself from the saddle, and exclaimed—

"In time, thank God! Don't touch a hair of his head, for my sake!"

He came eagerly toward Dexter, holding out his hand. The young man stood silent, with his head down. Judge Griswold stopped and the gladness began to fade out of his face. There was a moment of painful suspense, then Dexter said, scarcely audibly—

"It is too late."

Neither spoke, for some seconds, then Judge Griswold said, mournfully— [42]

"I had rather it had been me. I was hoping I should be in time. But for the miscarrying mails . . . but no matter. We were fated not to know. I do not blame you—You only did your duty. But we must not be loitering here. Hide yourself till I bring horses."

"No, I am not going to fly the country."

"What do you mean?"—said the Judge, surprised.

"I was innocent of any intent to take his life. I did it by accident."

In view of the portentous remark which the Judge had heard Dexter make to Hugh, this assertion had a suspicious sound, but when he had listened to the young man's account of the tragedy,

---

[42] At the top of MS p. 331, Twain wrote, "Capt. tackles 2 drug clerks, Hale, Tom and Lem."

and learned of the new relation in which he stood toward Hugh's sister, there seemed to be no ground for doubting. At length the old gentleman said—

"You are right. There is no need to fly the country. There were no witnesses; you will never be suspected. You would be safe in giving yourself up, in the circumstances—that is, safe from any hurt at the hands of the law; but you would find that where one man believed your story, two would find more pleasure in doubting it,—these are about the proportions of generosity and malice in the world.[43] It would be hard enough for Mrs. Burnside and her daughter to know that you killed poor Hugh, although by accident; it would be hard for them to be haunted night and day with the thought that if you had not come here he would be alive yet; to add to these burdens the consciousness that more than half of the community held you under grave suspicion, would be to banish sunshine from their lives utterly, and make the misery complete. The day would soon come when you would have to part; you would only suffer in each other's presence."

"I know it," said Dexter, with dull despair in his voice; "the sight of me would become unendurable to them." Presently he added: "See how I am placed! I was to have removed to their house as soon as you and Mrs. Griswold came home. It is impossible—impossible! To look into their stricken faces hourly, see their tears flow, hear them lament, with that secret shut up in my breast—I could not endure it. I should lose my reason. What shall I say? How can I explain?"

Judge Griswold saw all the perplexity of the situation, but could offer no suggestion at the moment. He proposed that they go to his house and consider further. They forded the river and took the nearest way.

Meantime something had been happening in the forest where we left the escaped desperado, Jack Belford, personating the corpse of Hugh Burnside. The three St. Louis detectives arrived in that vicinity. Mr. Baxter said—

---

43 In the margin beside this and the following sentence, Twain wrote, "Break this up more."

"According to the description, this must be about the spot."

He bent down and began to search the ground critically. Billings and Bullet did likewise. Baxter picked up a stick, with which he flirted the fallen leaves aside as he proceeded, as boys do when they hunt chestnuts. Billings and Bullet got sticks and followed suit. Thus the three stooping men wandered about in procession, saying nothing. The only sound heard was that which the sticks and the leaves made.—At the end of ten minutes Baxter stopped and bent lower. His comrades ranged up to him, bent low and clustered their heads with his, all gazing intently at the ground, nobody saying anything. Baxter pointed to the ground with his finger, then looked into his friends' faces. Said he—

"Is it a cow-track?"

The two nodded a gratified assent. Baxter stuck a stick in the ground to mark the place, and the procession moved on. Presently another cow-track was found, and then another. These also were duly staked. Baxter got out a tape-line and measured the three tracks elaborately. His friends got out tape-lines, and each in his turn measured the tracks and set down the dimensions in their note-books. Baxter said—

"You see, they are the same."

"Exactly the same," said Billings, nodding his slow head two or three times, with gravity.

"The same man made all three," said Bullet, after a thoughtful pause.

"We will proceed to shadow him," said Baxter.

The procession formed again, and traced the cow-tracks here and there, some twenty yards; then the trail was lost at the foot of a tree. Baxter glanced significantly at his comrades and lifted his hand to impose silence. The other detectives nodded acquiescence. At this moment Jack Belford came stealing rapidly through the bushes, and his quick eye detected the detectives just in time to prevent his own discovery. He halted, under cover, within five steps of them and began to watch them anxiously.

The detectives went tip-toeing around the tree, gazing up into the thick foliage. Presently they grouped themselves together for counsel, almost at Belford's elbow. Baxter said, in a low voice—

"Well, to sum up: What do the cow-tracks mean?"

"They mean Jack Belford—in disguise," said the others, with muffled voice. The hidden scoundrel was within an ace of ruining himself with an explosion of laughter.

"The cow-tracks stop at the tree," said Baxter. "What does that mean, gentlemen?" said Baxter.

"It means that he's up the tree," said the others.

"Right," said Baxter. "Follow me—and be wary."

Baxter started to climb the tree; he was followed silently by the rest of the procession. They presently disappeared among the boughs and foliage.

The concealed malefactor remarked to himself—

"These are detectives. I am in luck again. It's a true saying that it's always darkest just before the dawn. Every time I get into a very close place Providence sends me a detective to get me out of it. Young hands buy them—but I am an old hand."

He crept away and took up a position twenty or thirty steps from the tree, and waited until he saw the detectives descend; then he approached and gave them good morning, and added—

"Gentlemen, have you seen any suspicious characters around here this morning?"

"No," said Baxter. "Why?"

"O, nothing, only I reckon I'm putting the thing up about right. He has slid for Illinois."

"Who has?"

"Well, a man I'm after. It wouldn't interest you—but it interests a detective."

The friends pricked up their ears.

"Are you a detective?" asked Baxter.

"Well, that's what they call me, up around Boggsville, there," said Belford, with an air of self-complacency. "I'm only a country detective, as you may say,—O, yes, only a mere *country* detective, that's all—but if you live in these parts I reckon maybe you've heard of Bob Tufts once or twice, or maybe even as much as three times. I see you know the name!"

The veterans smiled inwardly; then with a great show of having heard the name before, they exclaimed in one voice—

"No! Are you the famous Tufts?"

"Well that's about the size of it; and if I had authority to go to Illinois I'd make it lively for one Jack Belford pretty soon, and don't you make any mistake about it! And I'm not going to fool around these woods more than a day or two more, I can tell you. I mean to get that authority, somehow. Good-day, gentlemen."

"Good-day, Mr. Tufts," replied the detectives.

"Tufts" started away, and the detectives had just begun to laugh privately over the country detective, and congratulate themselves upon their easy riddance of his competition, when he turned, with a hail, and came toward them again. Said he—

"Do I look like a maniac?"

"Certainly not," said the veterans.

"Look at me good. *Do* I look like a maniac?"

"Very far from it," said Baxter.

"Well you'll think very differently in about a half a second. Do you see that tree yonder? Well, I've seen a cow climb that tree!"

"What!" cried the detectives with one voice; and at the same time a lightning-glance of pride and triumph passed between them.

"There, I said so," said Tufts. "Call me a maniac. It's all right. I don't ask you to believe it, but if I didn't see a cow climb that tree I wish I may never die. Good day again, gentlemen—and just chew that over at your leisure."

"Hold on, please," said Baxter, quietly. "This is a very strange thing. We should very much like if you would tell us more about it."

"There's nothing to it but this. I was watching here for my man yesterday evening, and just about dark I saw a cow climb that very tree there. First I thought it was strange; and the more I thought about it the stranger it seemed. So I hid in the bushes this morning, and while it was still dark I saw her come down and go away. Now you needn't believe that, but the proof of the thing is in the seeing. It's my opinion that that cow lives up in that tree. I haven't any doubt but it's a new kind of a cow. Now I'll tell you what I'm going to do. I'm going to be here tonight with a double-barreled shot gun loaded with slugs—and you listen to what I say: that cow'll never climb another tree. I don't ask you to believe my racket, but I wish you'd make it a point to be here and see for yourselves, gentlemen."

Baxter the nervous, could hardly keep his happy excitement from showing in his face. He said—

"The thing you have told us is marvelous. It is a great pity that our business is so urgent that we cannot be here this evening. Couldn't you put it off three or four days? If those are the cow's habits it will be safe, you know?"

"Certainly I'll do it, if it is any favor. Meantime I'll run over to Illinois."

The veterans exchanged gratified glances. But "Tufts" added—

"No, come to think, I can't run over to Illinois—that authority is wanting. I'll watch her a day or two, and put some corn at the foot of the tree to encourage her in her habits and let her know she's got friends, and when you are ready you come and I'll finish her."

The wary Baxter did not care to see his game scared away with corn; so he said as quietly as he could—

"I'll offer a better plan if I can. What sort of authority is it you refer to?"

"Authority to arrest that fellow in Illinois. It has to come from the governor, you know."

"Yes—or from detective head-quarters in St. Louis—of course you have heard of the new law?"

"O yes; O certainly; I had forgotten about the new law," said "Tufts" with the air of a man who is not in the habit of confessing ignorance on any point.

At a sign from Baxter, the three detectives opened their coats and displayed their staring silver badges with the diffident motto. The "country detective" was apparently overwhelmed with pride and gratification to find himself in such distinguished company. Introductions followed, and he exclaimed over each illustrious name as it fell upon his ear. He was soon furnished with a page torn from a note-book whereon was inscribed a writing vesting in him full authority from the St. Louis detective head-quarters to "prosecute official business in the State of Illinois," and recommending "detective Robert Tufts" to the "confidence and assistance of all officers of the law in the States of Missouri and Illinois."

The desperado took his leave, then, saying to himself, "No more night travel for Yours Truly; no more starvation; no more hunting beds under haystacks. I will eat with sheriffs, drink with constables, sleep with detectives, and borrow money from them all. I bid a long adieu to these regions. My hardships are over—I've got a soft thing."

The three city detectives had a consuming laugh over the simplicity of the "country detective," and then started townward, after planning to return at nightfall with lariats and lasso the eccentric cow.[44]

While the events which we have been describing were taking place, Capt. Wheeler was on his way to the Burnside home, accompanied by his wife, a simple-hearted creature who loved him for his native goodness and admired him for his detective talent. The captain said—

"You see, Jenny, this is the way I put it up. If he committed suicide at home, he's here yet.—If he committed suicide away from home, he ain't here. Now how would you go about finding out which it is?"

"Well, I would ask his mother where he committed suicide, Simon."

"Now that is the difference between the ordinary run of people and a detective, Jenny. A detective wouldn't say a word about suicide at all. He always keeps the main business in the dark."

"Then what would you ask, Simon?"

"*I* wouldn't ask anything, Jenny. Because if he has done it away from home, *my* asking them a question would scare them to death, I being a detective. *You* are to ask the questions while I keep out of the way. Then they won't be scared."

"I wouldn't have thought of that."

"Of course you wouldn't, Jenny, because you haven't been trained, and so you don't know the importance of these things."

The Captain then furnished his wife with half a dozen mysteri-

[44] Two notes appear in the top margin of MS p. 356: "He avoids taking up quarters at Mrs. B's" and "Clara has made his room fine."

ous questions, and stood aside in the dim gray twilight while she roused up the household and delivered herself of her mission. She found that Hugh had not been home, and that Clara and her mother were not alarmed about it; but by the time those ingenious questions were ended the very effect had been produced which the captain had framed them to prevent; that is to say, the mother and daughter were frightened out of their wits.

The detective and his wife moved on, and Clara and her mother dressed themselves hastily and were soon on their way to Judge Griswold's to make inquiries.

As the captain approached Mrs. Higgins's house, by and by, he said in a low voice—

"It was right along here that I lost him, Jenny. It is getting light enough for me to strike his track, now. I'll run him down before long."

Twenty or thirty steps beyond the house the captain was expatiating with effusion upon a "theory," about the suicide, which he was forming in his mind, when he fell over the wheelbarrow, which the youths had forgotten and left beside the path, at the spot where they had sat down to rest and talk. He got up rubbing his shin and said—

"There—anybody but a detective would 'a' gone by it without noticing it; but nothing escapes a detective's eye. Wait, Jenny—I'll examine it. It might be a clew. Just wait a minute—I'll shadow this wheelbarrow."

He examined it carefully, and then began to search the ground in its vicinity. Once or twice he picked up something. Then he stood under a tree and peered up through its foliage; plucked off a leaf and compared it with one which he had found half way between the tree and the wheelbarrow; broke off a twig and compared it with a twig which he had found near the leaf. Now he dropped his head on his breast in profound study, and remained so for perhaps a minute. Then he began to walk to and fro, telling off his cogitations on his fingers, nodding his head when they pleased him, shaking it when they perplexed him. Presently his face assumed a look of calm satisfaction and he came up to his wife and said—

"Jenny, prepare yourself for the worst."

"O, Simon!"

"He didn't commit suicide!"

"O, I am so glad, on his poor mother's account!"

"So am I, Jenny. He was murdered!"

"Gracious me! O, don't say that, Simon.—Ain't there some hope? —Some hope that there's a mistake?"

"There's some little, maybe, but not much.—I'm afraid not much, Jenny. The clews are too awfully straightfor'ard and outspoken."

"O, his poor mother!—and that sweet sister of his! They'll never, never get over it, Simon. And he was such a good young man. What a pity—and he so young. Tell me about it, Simon."

"Well, it was a dreadful thing. This is the way it happened. You see, he started out to commit suicide. That was his idea at first; because I saw him get that stuff at the drug store—poison, of course. But he changed his mind—I don't know why, because there's a clew missing, there; but it ain't important, anyway. Do you see these leaves?"

"Yes. Are they a clew?"

"That's what *I* call 'm. Same as the leaves on that tree there. Jenny, he clumb that tree."

"Laws, I never would have thought of that."

"Because you ain't a detective—that's the reason."

"What did he climb the tree for, Simon?"

"Well, there's a clew missing as to that; but my theory about it is this. He had concluded he wouldn't commit suicide, and here was his poison left on his hands. Would he throw it away? Of course he wouldn't. Could he sell it? There ain't any market for it. He clumb that tree to have a quiet place to study out what to do with that truck so as to get his money's worth out of it. What does he conclude to do? What's the most unnatural thing for him to conclude to do with it?"

"I don't know; but I should think the most *natural* thing would be to—"

"Hold up!" said the captain, interrupting. "There's the difference between the common herd and the trained detective again. The common herd always goes hunting after the *natural* thing for a man to do. The trained detective knows better; he always hunts after [the] *un*naturalest thing a man would do—and just there is the little point that makes him superior to the common herd.—Very well; what we want to know, now, is, what was the most unnatural thing for this poet to do to get his money back?"

"What should you say, Simon?"

"It's as plain as your nose on your face:—kill somebody else with it!"

"O!"

"That's it. Now what we want to think out, next, is, who was it most unnatural for him to conclude to kill with that stuff?"

Jenny thought deeply, a moment, while the captain contemplated her uneducated gropings with smiling complacency; then she looked up, hesitating, and timidly asked—

"Might it be the cat?"

"The cat! What an idea!" Then with deep impressiveness: "Prepare yourself Jenny."

"O, Simon, you make me shudder. Who was it he concluded to kill?"

"The author of his being—his mother!"

"O, the horrid creature! It takes my breath away!"

"But there's a Providence over us all. A higher power interposed to beat that villain. Let us proceed. What we come to now, is, what was the most unnatural thing for him to do while he was contriving to kill his own mother?"

"My poor head is all upside down with these awful things. I couldn't ever guess. You tell me, Simon."

"Very well. The most unnatural thing for him to do when he was contriving to kill his mother, was to go to sleep."

"Simon, it's perfectly wonderful! I never would have thought of that, but now as soon as you mention it, I can see myself that that *was* the most unnatural thing for him to do. Simon Wheeler, I do think you get to be more gifted every day you live."

"It's practice, Jenny, only practice. Practice can do anything. Very well, he went to sleep. Pretty soon a man came along here—a kind of a loafer—a thief—and he—"

"What makes you think he was that sort of a person, Simon?"

"Because he stole this wheelbarrow, which is Mrs. Higgins's, ain't it?"

"Yes, it is."

"She don't leave her wheelbarrow out nights, does she, this way?"

"No."

"Then it's as I say. That loafer stole it."

"Well why didn't he take it away?"

"You'll see, in a minute. He was a very powerful man—most unusually powerful man."

"Simon, it's wonderful! How *can* you tell?"

"You wait. He was a-sneaking along here, with the wheelbarrow, and just as he was passing under the tree, this inhuman poet went to turn over in his sleep, and of course down he comes! See this twig, broken off—that's how I know he fell down 'stead of climbing down. He takes this loafer exactly on top of the head and drives him part-way into the ground like he was a nail. Here's where he was, then—do you see this deep foot-track?"

"Yes. How marvelously you do trace things out. But there's only one deep foot-print, Simon. Was he a one-legged man?"

"My dear, does a man walk with both feet on the ground at the same time?"

"Of course not! How little I do know about detecting! Go on, Simon—it is as exciting as a tale."

"This loafer was in a perfect fury, of course. What does he do?—See this dent in the edge of the wheelbarrow? See this leaf? I found it by the barrow. What do these two clews say? Why, that loafing thief ups with the wheelbarrow and smashes Hugh in the head with it."

"O, my, does it say that, Simon?"

"Say it? It don't simply *say* it, it *yells* it! I've never run across louder clews in all my days. For dead moral certainty, a clew like that is better than to see the thing done. I said this fellow was powerful. Am I right? You try to lift that wheelbarrow once. There ain't a man in this camp can swing it round his head. Hugh Burnside himself couldn't do it, and he's a shade stronger than I am. That is, he *was*, poor devil, before this loafer laid him out."

"Poor boy! Simon, where do you reckon the body is?"

"Well, my theory is, that this vagabond wheeled it away off into the woods and robbed it and buried it, and got this far on his way to town, when he heard something or saw somebody, and dropped it and skipped into the woods again. Let others find poor Hugh; my business, from this out, is to hunt down this sin-seared, bloody-minded, left-handed loafer that murdered him! It's the biggest case I've ever had, Jenny—a heap the biggest. If I work it up right and make a strike on it, I wouldn't wonder if it was worth three or four hundred dollars to me."

"Simon, it would make us easy for life! [45] I do hope you'll get it, or even the half of it. But what makes you think he is left-handed?"

"Why Jenny, if you had read as many detective tales as I have, you would know that pretty much all the murders are done by left-handed people. In the stories, the detectives most always notice that the wound is made in a way that couldn't be made only by a left-handed man. Now keep quiet a minute—let me think . . . The parson—no, he's right-handed . . . The magistrate—no, he's right-handed, too . . . The butcher—right-handed. . . . Hello, yonder goes a man!—and he—yes,—no,—yes, it's so, thank heaven! —he's scratching his head with his left hand! Travel, Jenny!—home with you! I'll run this villain down!"

He flew through the brush and disappeared in the wood. His wife took her way homeward. Presently the captain returned, panting, and growling to himself—

"Hang him, he was right-handed, after all. Blast a right-handed man, you can't make no use of them in our business. 'Twasn't anybody but Crazy Hackett. It was well for him he wasn't left-handed—prowling around here this way when there's been a murder done."

The captain walked along the river road, cogitating. He approached Hugh's retreat. Hugh had been thinking diligently, but had found it impossible to contrive any satisfactory way of disposing of himself and his time during the week or two which he wished to devote to a mysterious disappearance. So he concluded to leave

---

[45] In parentheses at the top of MS p. 376, Twain wrote, "Detective library and wardrobe."

planning alone and trust to luck. Wherefore he rose up, in his fearful and wonderful disguise, with his hand-organ swung about his neck, and stood a moment pondering whether to go toward the town or toward the gorge. He had in his left hand the stick which was to support the organ whenever he should stop to entertain the public. At this moment Capt. Wheeler reached the grassy nook he stood in. Hugh was not aware of it. The detective eye was upon him; it glared with delight, too. The captain said to himself—

"There's the murderer, for a million! That's the assassin of the inhuman poet, the bloody-minded Burnside! Left-handed, too, by the holy poker!—Now would a true detective go and grab him and put him on his guard? No, sir, he'd worm his crime out of him with the innocentest-looking questions in the world—questions that an angel might ask."—He cleared his throat, to attract Hugh's attention, and said—

"Good morning, friend."

"Good morning sir," answered Hugh, who added, to himself, "I shall have to play deaf and dumb to everybody else, but old Wheeler will never recognize my voice, if I disguise it ever so little."

The captain bent a wary eye upon the dilapidated tramp and said—

"Have you seen anything of an old yellow tom-cat going along here with a blue velvet collar on?"

Hugh paused, wondering, and said to himself, "Nobody nor nothing is safe from this busy detective's suspicions: now what can he suspect that poor cat of?" The captain marked the hesitation—"guilty hesitation," he termed it in his own mind. Hugh spoke up and said—

"I believe I don't remember seeing the animal."

"Ah. I hoped you might have seen him—that is, if you'd been over yonder way." He indicated the direction with a nod.

"I *have* been over there—that is, around about there in a sort of a general way, but—"

"But what?"

"Nothing. I was only going to say that that was earlier. I have been in the *woods,* since then."

The captain almost betrayed his joy. He said to himself, "A

hundred to one he was there burying the body! What an evil eye he's got!" Then, although he was raging with interest, he asked with counterfeited indifference—

"Been in the woods long?"

"No, only long enough to attend to a little matter that fell in my way."

The captain shuddered. He said to himself, "He calls it a little matter; a body would suppose it was a dog he'd been burying, 'stead of a widow's only son, and him a poet made partially in the image of his maker." Then he asked, aloud—

"Been there alone?"

"Well-a—not entirely." Hugh added, to himself, "What can he be up to? Does he suspect me of being an accomplice of the cat?"

The captain's thought was, "Well I never saw simplicity and black heartedness mixed up the way they are in this hellion, before. He's walking right into the trap!" Then he said aloud, carelessly—

"*Friend* with you, perhaps?"

"Well, not exactly what you might call a bosom *friend*. We didn't shed any tears at parting."

The captain gazed with horror upon this abandoned villain who could come with light speech upon his lips from such hideous work. He considered a moment, then said—with trembling misgivings that the question might be too pointed—

"You-a—you left him there?"

Hugh answered cheerfully—

"O yes, I was done with him, and he won't have any more use for me."

The captain started, in spite of himself, and almost said aloud, "The heartless butcher!"

Hugh said to himself, "What ails the man? He started as if he had been shot. There is no question about it, now—I am implicated with the cat."

The captain was charmed with the progress he was making, and the neatness and ingenuity with which he was weaving the fatal toils about his victim. He summoned all his artfulness to the task of throwing the utmost indifference of manner and voice into his next question—

"You left him *comfortable*, I suppose?"

"Well, he didn't *say* he wasn't."

The captain said to himself, "Poor devil, I judge he didn't! O, this is a grisly scoundrel! This is the very worst face I've ever seen in all my detective experience. Now for a finisher! now for an entire broadside! If I don't make him jump clean out of his skin, call me no detective!" Then he fixed his eyes steadily upon Hugh's, wagged a punctuating finger before his face, and said in an impressive stage-whisper—

"My friend—there's been—a poet . . . MURDERED here, last night!" Then to himself, "Why, damn him, he looks pleased!"

For Hugh's instant thought was, "So they think I've been murdered! This is superb! It will be talked about, both papers will be full of it, I shall be a hero! My plan is fixed—I'll not turn up for a year! What a tremendous sensation it will make when I come back!"

The captain, utterly stupefied, stood watching the jubilant play of expression in Hugh Burnside's face, and muttering to himself, "Well, this stumps *me!*" It occurred to him, now, that if he could secure a monopoly of this tramp for a few weeks, and keep him always under his eye, he could so ply him with ingenious questions as to trap him into a confession at last. Therefore he presently said—

"Trampy, are you going to lay around this village long?"

Hugh said to himself, "Why I *am* a tramp!—I had almost forgotten it. Very well, I will play the character; and I will try to exaggerate it enough to get some private fun out of it." In answer to the captain's question he said, aloud, indolently—

"Maybe—if it pays."

"Well, you'll saw stove-wood stuff for grub, I reckon?"

"Yes. That's my line. Hot grub required."

"All right—I want to get you to saw a stick for me. Come along."

But Hugh did not move. He absorbed himself in making an imaginary calculation on his fingers, while saying to himself, "This is luck; his house is a safe out-of-the-way place; I must billet myself on him. He will stand it, for he has a deep purpose of some kind in view. Now I must keep up my tramp-character—and the more extravagantly the better." Meanwhile the captain was waiting and wondering. Hugh ceased from his arithmetical labors and calmly asked—

"How many times do you want that stick sawed in two?"

The captain exclaimed to himself, "*That* stick! Well that's good! But no matter." Then he said aloud—

"Three times."

Hugh said, reluctantly—

"It is a longer stick than I am accustomed to. How much of it shall you want done per day?"

"Whew! Why how much time would you like to have on such a job?"

"Well, more or less, according to size and hardness of the stick."

"All right, you fix it to suit yourself. There ain't no occasion to rush the job."

"What kind of timber is it?"

"There's several kinds. There's oak, there's hickory, there's—"

Hugh interrupted him with a protesting wave of the hand, and said with wounded dignity—

"Sir, I have done nothing to deserve this affront."

"Affront?"

"Sir, there are *grades* in tramps. I am not a hard-wood tramp."

"Good land! what *is* your line?"

"I do the delicate kindlings for the parlor stove."

The captain made a profound bow of mock humility, and said—

"I *beg* your pardon, Sire. Parlor kindlings is your line—"

"That is, when I am in adversity."

"O, I see! What is your line when you're in prosperity?"

"I uncurl shavings for the drawing-room stoves of the opulent."

The captain contemplated him a moment with stupefaction, then asked—

"At how much?"

Hugh, yawning—

"A shaving a meal."

Capt. Wheeler looked puzzled, and said to himself, "He's pretty high-priced—but I've got to have him, anyway." Then aloud—with deference, fearing to offend again—

"Are—are you in adversity *now?*"

"Alas, yes."

"Well," said the captain, charmed, "Would you be willing to tackle a *pine* stick—"

Hugh interrupting—

"*Kind* of pine, please?"

The captain, eagerly—

"White—thoroughly seasoned—soft as butter—"

Hugh interrupting—

"Thickness, please?"

"Just the thickness of a yard-stick—if anything, not so thick."

Hugh, pondering—

"To be sawed in two three times . . . To do it right, and make a tasteful and elegant job of it, I shall require a little time to make estimates, lay out the work properly, consult authorities—"

The captain, interrupting, "and select an overseer, appoint subordinates, get up working models, take out a license, bid good-bye to your family, make your will—O, take all the time you want. Time ain't any object, just so this job's done right. I don't want it for utility, I want to send it to the British Museum! . . . Well, ain't it all settled? Come along. What are you waiting for, *now?*"

Hugh yawned again, and asked—

"Is it far?"

"Far? No! 'Tain't over a mile, or a mile and a half."

Hugh—after pondering a while—

"Could you get a hack?"

The captain was obliged to support himself to keep from fainting. Then he said, pleadingly—

"O *don't* require that, Trampy. I'm poor—*I* can't afford such things, you know."

Hugh, mournfully, and shaking his head—

"I have conceived a great liking for you, sir; I would do much to accommodate you, but I must take care of my strength."

The captain started away, slowly, with his despondent head down, and breaking his heart over this great loss, this noble chance to achieve fortune and reputation when they seemed verily in his grasp. But suddenly a saving idea struck him, and he darted away and disappeared—just in time to prevent Hugh from yielding his point, for he perceived that for the sake of the fun he was carrying his fantastic requirements too far. In a twinkling Capt. Wheeler reappeared, beaming with delight, and exclaimed—

"Here you are, my boy! On with you!"

It was the Higgins wheelbarrow. In another moment Hugh had become for a second time its passenger; and as the captain went wheeling him off, up the lovely river road, now lighted by the earliest beams of the sun, the tourist awoke his lyre, so to speak, and added the wheezy anguish of The Last Rose of Summer to the ravishing music of the birds.

## Chap. [8]

JUDGE GRISWOLD and Dexter had but a brief conference at home.[46] Before any conclusion was reached, Mrs. and Miss Burnside arrived. They swept past the sleepy and marveling servant who admitted them and burst in upon the two gentlemen, unannounced. Dexter almost dropped from his chair; even the Judge was disconcerted; but both rose and advanced. There was a trying time, for a while, for both women had allowed Mrs. Wheeler's strange and dark questionings to work upon their imaginations until they were now thoroughly frightened. They had met one of the young drug clerks, on the way, and he had acted so strangely and looked so scared when Mrs. Burnside poured out her fears and inquiries upon him, that the poor lady exclaimed, "O dear! you look as if you know something has happened to him!" Whereupon the young fellow stammered out something about a frightful dream he had had concerning Hugh, and then got himself away as quickly as he could.

Clara was full of self-upbraidings for her conduct of the day before toward her brother, and eloquent with resolves to be kinder

---

[46] At the top of MS p. 400, Twain wrote, "Wolf poisoned Dr. calls bones human. Only 1 or 2 left—spinal column—can't account for tail."

to him in future if she should ever see him again. Her mother sat rocking herself to and fro in anguish, sobbing, and voicing her distress in moans and broken exclamations freighted with despair, with pathetic repetitions of Hugh's name, and supplications for divine help. This spectacle of suffering wrung the heart-strings of the men, and yet they were obliged to witness it almost in silence, since their tongues were tied by the secret that was hidden in their breasts. The few words of hope and comfort which they forced themselves to utter, grated upon their own ears, they were so false, so artificial, and seemed so like wanton trifling with the misery they were meant to assuage.

But at length the storm of grief and apprehension spent its force and the women began to dry their tears and take hope from the calmness of the gentlemen—for they could not know that it was a frozen and compulsory calm that came of the impossibility of saying any honest thing of a cheering nature. A revulsion followed the tempest, and Clara was the first to see how femininely "absurd" she and her mother had been. She said a stranger would suppose her brother was a child and had never been from home by night before, instead of a great stalwart creature able to protect himself from all harms. The more she examined the matter the more unwarrantable her late fears appeared and the more comical they became in their new and more rational aspect. She recounted the hour's events in this vein, exaggerated its mock terrors and laughed at them, and kept up her raillery until even her mother began to feel rather ashamed of her fright and her lavish exhibition of feeling.

The grief of the mother and daughter had been so hard for Dexter to bear, that he was grateful when it began to subside; but this gay and cheery badinage that had taken its place was a hundred times harder to bear. It made him shudder, it made his blood run cold; for the laughing girl's form was no plainer to his vision than was that other form which he still saw, in his mind's eye, lying out yonder in the wood. He thought of a time when Clara would know all and would recall this moment and this light talk and break her heart over the remembrance.

The topic changed, but it brought no comfort, for every unwitting sentence had some remote reference to Hugh as a person alive and well, and so brought its pang. Once Clara turned suddenly and said:

"Hale, do you know we are going to do you a great honor?"

"Me? When?"

"When you come to stay at our house."

"How?"

"You are to have Hugh's room, and we will make him sleep in narrower quarters."

That simple phrase almost wrung a groan from Dexter. He said to himself, "She little knows that half of her blank cartridges turn to bullets before they reach me." Another time she said—

"I am glad it all happened, although I suffered so; because I know, now, how much I love Hugh, and I didn't know before. It would kill me to lose him: now I could not have believed that, yesterday. We have always been lovers, but I supposed the feeling had limits. I am impatient to see him and tell him my discovery. If you should see him first, Hale, you are to say nothing—I want all the pleasure of telling him myself. He has become your rival, now, in my affections—think of that!"

Dexter was suffering. The thought crossed his mind, "I can hardly bear it *now*—it will break my heart to hear her when she knows the ghastly truth—I must fly the country!"

In the same moment Clara said, playfully—

"Do you know how to break the rivalry and make me value you above him? *You* must disappear, too! Loss so increases love.—You must disappear, in the most mysterious way—but only for a day; that will be long enough. There! that is Hugh's step, now! an hour ago I thought I should never hear it again! I'll go and tell him."

She ran into the hall, but came back in a moment and said it was only a servant.

After a little more conversation, in which the gentlemen did not shine very brightly, the ladies took their leave, fully restored in mind and heart. Clara's good-bye to Dexter was in a whisper—to this effect—

"There—do you see what you are to me? I come, harassed with bodings and terrors, and the mere sight of your face, with hardly a word spoken, banishes them and gives me peace. The mere sense of being near you is succor from all threatenings and impending harms. You are my refuge!"

The two men found themselves alone. Neither spoke for some moments. Then Dexter said in a voice which manifested a firm purpose—

"My course is plain."

"I think so."

"My mind is made up."

"Tell me your plan."

"Before their visit, all was confusion in my mind; now all is clear. I had thought of flight, confession, suicide—a hundred selfish, treacherous things. But all that is at an end. I realize, now, how they are going to suffer. It would be cowardly to desert."

"Their visit clarified my mind, also. I had been thinking far more of how to diminish your share of the siege of horrors that is to begin to-day than anything else; I perceive, now, that the higher and worthier consideration will be, how to diminish these bereaved women's share of it. You have chosen rightly, I feel sure.—But let us look the ground over and be perfectly certain."

"Very well. To begin: One's first thought is to confess publicly—but that door is barred."

"Yes. There would be a trial, acquittal, and lasting suspicion. It would end relations between you and the Burnsides—without prejudice or hard feeling, but still it would end them, eventually. That door is barred."

"One's next thought is private confession to the bereaved ones. But that door, also, is barred."

"Yes. You could never be happy in each other's society, for your presence would keep the memory of the fatal accident always alive—it would be a cloud that nothing could ever dissipate. That door is barred."

"One thinks next of flight. That door, likewise, is barred."

"Beyond all question. It would be confession, with disgrace added. Those women's lives would not be worth the living, afterward."

"And last, suicide suggests itself. It, too, is a barred door."

"Yes—for it is only flight in another form, with confession and disgrace. It would leave those women lonely and without a protector or any hope of further happiness in this life."

"Then it is as I believed. All doors are barred that seem to lead out of this trouble. I must remain. Is it not so?"

"It certainly is so. We have viewed the situation on all sides. It is a curiously complicated position. It is like one of those chess problems where the king seems to have plenty of exits at his disposal, but when one comes to examine the matter he finds that the king is only safe where he stands—to move is to be checkmated."

"Yes," said Dexter with a dreary sigh, "I stand upon my last square, and here I must remain."

"I wish the task before you were easier. But there is nothing easy about it; one knows that too well."

"I can begin it, and I will begin it—no man could be safe in promising to go through with it."

"I like better to hear you talk like that than to boast. Now let me suggest something. Do not tax your powers too far. Do not take Hugh's room."

"I would not sleep in it a night under any consideration. Every object in it would bring him before me—and not in life, but as I saw him last."

"And that would ill refresh you for next day's task in the mourning household. You must remain our guest for some days yet."

"I shall be grateful if that can be! The days will tax my fortitude to the utmost stretch; unless the nights brought respite and oblivion I should break down. But you know they expect me. What shall I say? Find me a way out."

"It is easy. It is well understood that you are not to go there until I and my wife can be here again. This dreadful news will retard Mrs. Griswold's recovery, and I shall be with her, of course. Now that is all settled."

"It is a great gain. It lightens my task."

"Now be of good courage. These first days are going to be the hardest. If you weather them it will be easier sailing afterward."

Dexter rose and walked the floor nervously, muttering—

"Ah, you have said it, indeed! These first days! The finding of the body! *I* must go and tell them! May some merciful gossip spare me that! The public excitement, the clamor of the village tongues! The inquest! I must be there and look upon my work! I must bear home the verdict! The funeral! I must support them there, I must be their solace, their comforter; I must soothe them with soft lies out of a guilty heart! O, one needs the shoulders of a Hercules to carry burdens like these, one needs the double-faced guile of the devil to play my part!" He calmed himself with a great effort, sat down, and said resignedly, "It is over, now—I am a fool—go on."

The Judge said—

"The days that follow will be easier. Mind, you will be often moved to confess. Be on your guard; to confess will be to destroy those poor people's happiness utterly. You can become more and more to them every day, if you keep your secret. You will be their stay and their comfort; having you, they will learn to bear the loss you have unintentionally caused them, and by and by they will cease to feel it. When the day arrives that you stand at the altar with Clara Burnside, nobody there will be unhappy, nobody there will be otherwise than joyous."

"Except me—for the secret will rise up against me there, once more, and accuse me."

"Of what? Of nothing. You will see that the keeping of that secret has made two people rich with happiness whom its betrayal would have burdened with misery for life. But if you shall still have any weak misgivings, no matter: You must suffer the penance of silence for the sake of those women. The secret *must* be kept."

The yellow glow of the tallow candles was paling in the fresh new light of the day, now; the household were astir; footsteps were growing frequent in the streets; the village was waking up. Dexter thanked the Judge for his wise counsel and his encouragement, and ascended to his room with a heavy heart. He sat down and wrote a brief letter to his mother in which he shared with her his fearful secret. He sealed and directed it, called Toby and told him to mail it.

Toby retired to a private place and unsealed it before the mucilage had had time to dry. Then he put it into a blank envelop and pocketed it, purposing to get it directed to Arkansas as soon as he could collect and add to it enough more manuscript to make a respectable letter of it—for Jim and his mother complained when his letters were brief.

Dexter tried to snatch an hour's sleep, but he found it impossible. As long as his eyes were open, he was drowsy; the moment he closed them he was broad awake, his brain a whirl of harassing thoughts and flitting images. At breakfast he was silent, absent-minded, and without appetite. He went out, and strolled down the street, dreamy, dreary, and feeling old and worn. But a change soon came. Rumor had begun to stir. He presently found himself accosted at every turn, by inquisitive villagers. When one goes to a strange city, the question "Is this your first visit to our city?" seems innocent enough; but it begins to madden him when it is an hour old and has been answered thirty or forty times. The question "Have you any idea what has become of Burnside?" became such a persecution to Dexter before he had walked half a mile, that he finally fled to the woods to get away from it. It smote him like an accusation. The horror of it had grown with every repetition, until he had come to believe that in a little while longer it would either drive him mad or to confession. It was noon before he could gather courage enough to go to Mrs. Burnside's.

But he had less to bear there than he had expected. Comforters were coming and going, all the time. That is, the visitors came disguised as comforters, but their real business was to inquire. Dexter mainly spent the afternoon apart with Clara. She was trying to believe that Hugh was only keeping up one of his "pets" a trifle longer than usual, but would presently be delivered of it and might be expected to step into the house at any moment. She was succeeding pretty well in her effort, though it had to be forced somewhat.

Dexter was at his post again in the evening, and new relays of comforters and inquirers were at theirs, also. Clara still kept up her spirits, but the forcing grew hourly more apparent. Her eyes, instead of wandering fitfully to the door with a pretense of having no particular object in doing it, got the habit of turning swiftly and anxiously to it, now, at every sound, and without any dissembling.

The ill disguised despondency in her face deepened with every added disappointment. Still she talked on with a fictitious cheeriness that went to Dexter's heart. But his miserable evening drew toward its close at last. The visitors were all gone; Mrs. Burnside kissed Clara good-night and shook hands with Dexter, but did not trust herself to speak, at the moment. She bent her gray head, as she moved away, and Dexter saw her put up her handerchief. When she reached the rear door, she turned and said in a voice that trembled a little—

"Leave the light burning, children—I will wait up for him, he will be tired and hungry, poor boy."

A sudden faintness went to Dexter's heart, and his pulse missed a beat. The moment the mother was gone, Clara turned a hopeless face upon him, and said—

"Something tells me he will never come again. . . . There—say nothing—not a word. I should break down. I must keep up, for my mother's sake. Talk of other things. Talk, talk, keep talking. Get me away from this formless, boding horror!"

As Dexter was wending homeward at midnight, he stopped in a dark angle to take a last compassionate glance in the direction of the twinkling light in the Burnside windows. Three men brushed past him, and one of them said in a voice which he recognized—

"My hands are cut to the bone, and I am all fagged out with lassoing the wrong cattle and hanging on to them. Maybe we'll fail, in this job, but if we do, there's another ready to our hand. If this young fellow stays disappeared another day, there'll be a reward for him."

A second voice said—

"And another for the party that helped him disappear. Both in our line."

Dexter shuddered, and said to himself, "Every chance remark refers to *him*.[47] I am never to get away from this awful business. And now ill fortune has sent these detectives, far from their beat, just in the nick of time, to hunt me down. There is no hope for a man so clothed in toils and fetters as I am."

---

[47] A note in the top margin of MS p. 433 reads: "Gillette's SS speech."

When he reached home he found Milly sitting solitary in the parlor, dry-eyed, white as marble, with her gaze fixed on vacancy. She was in a dead apathy of terror. On the floor near her lay a blurred little printed page, garnished with a moving array of fantastic display-lines—

EXTRA!
ALL ABOUT THE
SUDDEN AND MYSTERIOUS
DISAPPEARANCE
AND
PROBABLE BLOODY ASSASSINATION
OF THE LATE
Mr. Hugh Burnside,
OF THIS VILLAGE!

Dexter sighed, resignedly. He realized that his labors for the day, as a comforter, were not over yet.

## Chap. [9]

During the next four days Dexter suffered all the tortures that such a situation as his might naturally be expected to yield. He saw, too, that in one detail, he and the Judge had made a mistake. That was in the provision they had made for relieving Dexter of duty as a consoler for a part of each day by removing him from the presence of the Burnsides. A very great mistake—

it only provided double duty for him. When he had borne all he seemed able to bear at the Burnside homestead, he always found poor Milly sitting up, waiting for solace. He had to soothe her down for the night, with coaxings, comfortings and melancholy ballads, and shore her up in the morning to support the burden of the day.

His tortures never abated; they grew, constantly. Out of doors he could not walk a block without being questioned and commiserated. He saw the excitement of the village rise, and spread, and swell, hour by hour, until all other interests were swallowed up in it, buried out of sight. If ever by any chance, another subject was spoken of by any creature, Dexter never had the luck to hear the blessed words.

He had to go daily (to keep up appearances) and help the citizens beat the woods and drag the stream for the missing man—but there was one spot which he never searched, neither did he advise anybody else to search there. And after each search he had to go to the Burnside home and see two hopeless faces look the inquiry, "Is he found?"—an inquiry which he never had to answer in words. Every night he had to undergo the same ordeal with Milly.

Mrs. Burnside wished to offer, the third day, a reward of a thousand dollars for any information that would lead to the discovery of her son's . . . but there she broke down and cried bitterly. She finally sobbed out, to Dexter—

"You know what I mean—I cannot speak the dreadful word."

It was as dreadful a word to Dexter, to write. He tried hard to persuade her to let him advertise simply for her son, and stop at that; Clara pleaded with her also, but to no purpose; grief, fear, sleeplessness, the wear of racking thought, followed at last by the death of all hope, had brought her to an unnatural state, a sort of gloomy self-aggrandizement where she found a painful pleasure in fondling her woes and making the worst of them; so, lifted above the earth and its paltrinesses, she moved in a cloudland of sombre exaltation, and from this height would not see her son otherwise than dead, nor have the fact called by any modifying name.

It cost Dexter a pang to add to the advertisement the lacking word "remains," but he had to do it.

Why the body was not found, was a most perplexing mystery to Dexter. However, he always said to himself, "The finding it is only a question of time; I am too elaborately and painstakingly pursued by ill luck to hope to be spared such peculiarly lacerating tortures as the discovery, the inquest and the funeral."

The weight of his woes was growing heavier and heavier. A brooding melancholy settled down upon him which he found it almost impossible to shake off, even in the presence of the three mourners whom it was his business to cheer.—The deeper his dejection grew, the more it endeared him to these mourners and the more and more they lapped him in their hearts and poured out the riches of their affection upon him. So their very tenderness was a pain to him, since it came from such a grievous misunderstanding of the cause of his dejection. When they said, "Poor Hale, how you loved him, how you mourn him! how merciful of God to have sent you to us!" it wrung him with such anguish, and it made him so hate himself and loathe the shackles that bound him to his double-dealing office, that all his vigilance and all his strength of will were required to keep the devastating secret from leaping from his lips.

Late one night, after some such experience with the Burnsides—it was about the fifth or sixth day after Hugh's disappearance—Dexter said to himself as he dragged himself homeward, "If there is any comfort in knowing the whole extent of the program of torture I have got to endure, I have at least that comfort: my evil genius has reached her limit; she can invent nothing more."

But this was a mistake. He found Milly waiting, as usual; as usual, utterly smileless and miserable; but there was an added something about her look, now,—a hard, bitter, ungirlish something in the expression of her face, that attracted Dexter's instant attention. This soft young thing had cried away all her tears, and in the process a change had come over her. She had apparently changed into a woman—a woman with a purpose, too. Dexter perceived that she looked like her father, now, though she had never resembled anybody but her mother before. He sat down and took her hand. It was so cold it made him start. He said—

"Milly, you do not look like yourself; and you are cold. You must go to bed; you are not well."

"Never mind me," she said, "but listen. I have been thinking. I have made up my mind. You have tried hard to give me hopes, but there was something in your voice, something in your manner that —look me in the face and tell me whether you think he is dead or not!"

Dexter was surprised into confusion by this sudden and unexpected assault. He showed it, and his eye fell before the girl's steady gaze. She said, calmly—

"That is enough. You believe he is dead. So do I."

Dexter hastened to recover his lost ground with a lame speech, but she tranquilly interrupted it and went on—

"Yes, you believe it, and I believe it. *Say* you believe it. . . . Why do you hesitate? Do you think I cannot bear it? Look at me."

She said it almost as disdainfully as her father might have done. Dexter raised his eyes and met her steady gaze for a moment, and then said, in a reluctant voice—

"It is useless to dissemble any longer. I believe he is dead."

The girl's face did not change. A period of silence followed which seemed long to Dexter; then Milly's face began to cloud, and presently she shot forth the thought that was in her mind with startling suddenness—

"He was murdered!"

The words almost took Dexter's breath away. He wondered if they had brought a guilty look to his face. Milly continued, without any stop—

"He is dead. He was murdered. I have thought it all out. Now I come to what I was going to say to you. His murderer must be found. His murderer *shall* be found. He shall be hunted night and day—he shall not escape. Will you do me a favor?"

Dexter was in a cold perspiration by this time. But he made shift to promise the favor.

"Very well," said Milly. "I am going to do you an honor which you deserve, for you have shown yourself a dear and faithful friend to him and to his memory. You shall help me hunt down the miscreant that murdered him!"

Dexter tried to stammer out his thanks, but they choked him. Milly continued—

"I am rich in my own right. I want to offer a thousand dollars reward for the discovery of the assassin—more, if you think best. Now—"

"I will write your father about it at once," said Dexter, eagerly, being aware that Judge Griswold would promptly squelch this new danger.

"No, not a word to him!" said Milly. "He would take it all on his own shoulders. What satisfaction would that be to me? I want to hunt this wretch down *myself*. I shall be jealous of all rewards but my own. I will spend every penny I possess but I will have him. I do not want this to get to my father's ears and be spoiled; therefore my reward for the apprehension of the assassin who took away my poor Hugh's life must be published and signed with your name as coming from *you!*"

This most unexpected denouement shook Dexter to his foundations, and he said sadly to himself, "No, I was mistaken when I supposed the limit of invention had been reached, in the matter of devising tortures for me. I, the murderer, must sign an advertisment offering a reward for my own apprehension!" Then with a sigh, "No mere journeyman is conducting my case; it is Satan in person." His next thought brought a glimmer of cheer with it: "Well, at least she does not suspect *me*—I was afraid she did."

He promised to write, sign, print, and publish the advertisement, and then ventured to ask Milly if she suspected anybody in particular.

"Certainly I do. Crazy Hackett! Poor Hugh has lost his own life because he saved mine. Hugh did not save a weakling or a traitor in me. Crazy Hackett will know this, presently."

Dexter tried to make the girl understand that the law does not hold crazy people responsible for their acts, but this roused her to such a burst of illogical and indignant disbelief in such an unrighteous, idiotic and impossible thing, that he forebore to argue the case.

Dexter's instinct suggested to him that he was taking an unwise contract upon himself. The thought crossed his mind, "If I am ever found out I should die with shame to be confronted with this advertisement." So he set to work to dissuade Milly from her purpose. She listened gravely; he warmed to his subject, and sailed along with increasing zeal and pleasure in the progress he was making, but in an unlucky moment, he forgot himself and stupidly threw out an argument born of his secret knowledge—

"You see, Milly, it might have an odd look, coming from me, and might cause rem—"

He caught a grave, surprised look in Milly's eyes, and stopped, inwardly cursing his supernatural obtuseness. He said to himself, "It is a true saying, 'Leave the guilty alone to say the incautious thing.' " Milly regarded him a moment, then said—

"Odd? From you, his cousin, his nearest friend, in effect his brother-in-law?"

There was no answering that. Milly was inclined to pursue the matter, and things were growing uncomfortable for Dexter, when the lucky thought occurred to him of turning her attention to Crazy Hackett once more. This was effectual. While she unburdened her mind upon that text, Dexter re-gathered his composure, and so was able, when she had finished, to properly formulate a matter of importance that was in his mind. He told her she must allow him to reveal this matter to Clara, and to her mother, if necessary—and continued—

"Until the death is proven, it will be best for Clara to do everything she can to keep her hopes alive. I am helping her all I can in this direction. This advertisement puts me in the position of not only believing him dead but murdered. How shall I explain? You see how awkward it is."

Milly did see. She answered promptly, and said—

"O, let her hope as long as she can! She can never suffer supremely until hope is gone. You shall tell her that it is only I that believe him dead and that he was murdered. You shall tell her that I am weak and foolish through grief, and my vagaries will not brook control.—Beg her to avoid talking with me about them.—Then tell her you do not believe he was murdered, tell her you do not believe he is dead, and you will see her hopes revive and her confidence return. I wish I were in your position!"

Dexter gasped out a "Why?"

"Because for her sake I could so dissemble a mere belief in his death as to make my hopeful words sound honest and full of cheer. Ah, I would give the world to be in your place. Happy you, who only *believe* he is dead—it leaves a blessed gap of uncertainty, a little rift in the black cloud-rack that the sun can come through! But put yourself in my place and see the difference—for I seem to *know* he is dead!"

In time Dexter escaped from this trying interview and sought the refuge of his room. He sat down, wearied with the toils and distresses of the day, and leaned his head in his hands. His spirits were at a very low ebb. He said—

"The further I go, the deeper I sink into the mire of duplicity. Every hour seems to add a new and more diabolical requirement to the list of frauds I am appointed to perpetrate. I am the unhappiest soul that cumbers the earth—yet observe the unjustness of my situation: the guiltiest criminal may end his miseries by suicide and welcome; but I, who am innocent, am denied it!"

## Chap. [10]

Captain Simon Wheeler was a man who had tried various occupations in life, but had fallen just a trifle short of success in all of them. He was of a hopeful, cheerful, easygoing nature; therefore his partial successes encouraged him to expect an entire and colossal success some day, instead of being to him an accumulation of evidences that the thing to be more confidently looked for was a conspicuous and unmistakable failure in the fulness of time.

Among other experiments, he had tried the small country show business in various forms, and had come out about even on each experiment. He did not know he was too ignorant of business and of men to succeed as a showman. He merely believed that the reason he had not made a fortune and a name was that he had not happened to get hold of the right kind of a show. So his confidence in himself was in no degree impaired. Ten years before our story opens, his last show had demonstrated itself to be only a copper mine instead of the gold mine he had bought it for. He cheerfully boxed it up and stored it away at the homestead in Guilford, for he was near his native village at the time.

The homestead consisted of a log dwelling and three or four log farm buildings, scattered about a small farm. One of the buildings, which was separated from the dwelling house by a tobacco field, was called the "negro quarter," for grandeur. A family of slaves had inhabited it, formerly, but Wheeler set them all free as soon as his father was dead, for he was an advanced thinker, in his groping way, and always had opinions of his own.

The Captain had profound religious views, and their breadth equaled their profundity. He did not get his system from the pulpit, but thought it out for himself, after methods of his own. One may get an idea of it from a dream which he professed to have had once, and which he was very fond of telling about. Here it is, in *his* own language— [48]

"I dreampt I died. I s'posed, of course, I was going to lay quiet when the rattle went out of my throat, and not know any more than

---

[48] The following account of Wheeler's dream visit to heaven was probably based upon the 1872 or 1873 version of "Captain Stormfield's Visit to Heaven" which Twain described to Orion in a letter dated 23 March 1878 (*Mark Twain's Letters,* ed. Albert B. Paine [New York, 1917], I, 323). As this letter suggests, the Wheeler version led Twain to a reshaping of the Stormfield story which Twain outlined to Howells during Howells' visit to Hartford, 6–7, March 1878. It was probably this reshaping of the Stormfield story which resulted in the first surviving draft preserved in the Mark Twain Papers, a version in which the central character is named Captain Hurricane Jones. The name of the character suggests a relationship in time with "Some Rambling Notes of an Idle Excursion" in which the same character appears, and the paper (Crystal Lake Mills) and ink (violet) used for this draft fix the composition at some time between 1876 and 1880. According to Walter Blair's study, the violet ink was used at Hartford from late November 1876, to mid-June 1880, and sporadically in Europe in 1878–79; the paper was used from 1876 to 1880 ("When Was *Huckleberry Finn* Written?" *American Literature,* XXX [March 1958], 7, 9–10). Blair's study of inks and papers makes it clear that the "Hurricane Jones" version cannot be the 1872–73 version described to Orion, but must be the one described to Howells in March 1878.

if I was asleep. But it wasn't so.[49] As I hove out the last gurgle, 'stead of settling down quiet, it was just as if I was shot off!—shot out of a gun, you understand! I whizzed along, head first, through the air, and when I looked back, in about a second, this earth was like a big, shining, brass ball, with maps engraved on it. But did it stay so? No, sir! It shrunk together as fast as a soap bubble that is hanging to a pipe when you take your mouth away from the stem and let the air slip out. In another second it was nothing but a bright spark—and then it winked out! I went whizzing right along, millions of miles a minute. Dark? Dark ain't no name for it! There wasn't a thing to be seen. You can't imagine the awfulness of it. Says I to myself, 'Knowing what I know, now, no friend of mine shall die with useless flowers in his hand if I can raise enough to buy him a lantern.' And cold? Nobody down here has any idea what real cold is.

"Well, pretty soon a great wave of gladness and gratitude went all through me, because I glimpsed a little wee shiny speck away yonder in the blackness. But did it stay a speck? No, sir. It seemed to start straight for me, swelling as it came. In the time it took me to breathe three breaths it had swelled till it filled up the whole heavens and sent off prodigious red-hot wagon-wheel rays that stretched millions of miles beyond. And hot? People down here don't know what hot is. I shut my eyes—I couldn't stand the glare. Then I felt a great breath of wind and a sudden sound like *whoosh!* and I knew I'd passed her. I opened my eyes, and there she was, away yonder behind, withering up, paling down, cooling off—another second and she was a twinkling speck—one more instant, and she was gone! Black again—black as ink—and I a-plowing along.

"Well, sir, I run across no end of these big suns—as many as half a million of them, I judge, with oceans of blackness between them, which shows you what a big scale things are got up there on—and I saw little specks sometimes that I didn't come near to, and every now and then a comet with a tail that I was as much as ten seconds passing—one as much as fifteen or twenty, I reckon—which shows

---

[49] Along the margin Twain wrote, "Knock out" "[quotation] marks."

you that we hain't ever seen any comets down here but seedlings, as you may say—sprouts—mere little pup-comets, so to speak. *You* won't ever know anything about what He can do till you have seen one of them grand old comets that's been finished and got its growth —one of them old long-handled fellows that He sweeps the cobwebs out of the far corners of His universe with.

"In the course of time—I should say it was about seven years—not short of seven, I know, and I think it was upwards of it—my speed begun to slacken up, and I came in sight of a white speck away off yonder. As it grew and grew, and spread itself all over everywhere and took up all the room, it turned out to be the loveliest land you can imagine. The most beautiful trees and lakes and rivers—nothing down here like them—nothing that begins with them at all. And the soft air! and the fragrance! and the music that came from you couldn't tell where! Ah, that music!—you talk about music down here! It shows what you know about it.

"Well, I slacked up and slacked up, and by and by I landed. There was millions of people moving along—more different kinds of people, and more different kinds of clothes, and talking more different kinds of languages than I had ever heard of before. They were going toward a great high wall that you couldn't see the end of, away yonder in the plain. It was made of jewels, I reckon, because it dazzled you so you couldn't look steady at it. I joined in with these people and by and by we got to the wall. There was a glittering archway in it as much as a mile high, and under it was standing such a noble, beautiful Personage!—and with such a gentle face, when you could look at it. But you couldn't, much, because it shone so.

"I ranged up alongside the arch to watch and listen and find out what was agoing on, but I kept ruther shady, because I had old clothes on, but mainly because I was beginning to feel uneasy. Says I to myself, 'This is heaven, I judge, and what if I've been preparing myself on a wrong system all this time!' I listened, and my spirits begun to drop pretty fast.

"The people were filing in, all the time, mind you, and I a-watching with all my eyes. A mild-faced old man's turn came and he stepped forward. He had on a shad-belly coat. The Beautiful

Personage looked at him ever so kindly, and in a low voice that was the sweetest music you ever heard, he says to him—

" 'Name, please?'

" 'Abel Hopkins,' says the old man.

" 'Where from, please?'

" 'Philadelphia,' says the old man.

" 'Denomination, please?'

("That word made me shiver, I can tell you. I felt my religious system caving from under me.)

" 'Quaker,' says the old man.

" 'Papers, please?' says the Beautiful Personage.

("I felt some more of my system cave from under me, and my spirits went lower than ever.)

"The Beautiful Personage took the papers and run his eye over them, and then says to the old man—

" 'Correct. Do you see that band of people away in yonder, gathered together? Go there and spend a blissful eternity with them, for you have been a good servant, and great is your reward. But do not wander from that place, which has been set apart forever for your people.'

"The Quaker passed in and I glanced my eye in and saw millions and millions of human beings gathered in monstrous masses as far as I could see—each denomination in a bunch by itself.

"A wild-looking, black-skinned man stepped up next, with a striped robe on, and a turban. Says the Beautiful Personage—

" 'Name, please?'

" 'Hassan Ben Ali.'

" 'Where from, please?'

" 'The deserts of Arabia.'

" 'Denomination, please?'

" 'Mohammedan.'

" 'Papers, please?'

"He examined the papers, and says—

" 'Correct. Do you see that vast company of people under the palm trees away yonder? Join them and be happy forever. But do not wander from them and trespass upon the domains of the other redeemed.'

"Next an English Bishop got in; then a Chinaman that said he was Bhuddist; then a Catholic priest from Spain and a Freewill Baptist from New Jersey, and next a Persian Fire-eater and after him a Scotch Presbyterian. Their papers were all right, and they were distributed around, where they belonged, and entered into their eternal rest.

"Not a soul had gone in on my system, yet. I had been a-hoping and hoping, feebler and feebler, but my heart was clear down and my hopes all gone, at last. I was feeling so mean and ashamed and low-spirited that I couldn't bear to look on at those people's good luck any longer; and I begun to be afraid I might be noticed and hauled up, presently, if I laid around there much longer.—So I slunk back and ducked my head and was just going to sneak off behind the crowd, when I couldn't help glancing back to get one more little glimpse of the Beautiful Personage so as to keep it in my memory always and be to me in the place of heaven—but I'd made a mistake. His eye was on me. His finger was up. I stopped in my tracks, and my legs trembled under me.—I was caught in the act. He beckoned with his finger, and I went forward—you see there wasn't any other way. The Beautiful Personage looked on me, a-trembling there, a moment or two, and then he says, low and sweet, the same as ever—

" 'Name, please?'

" 'Simon Wheeler, your honor,' says I, and tried to bow, and dropped my hat.

" 'Where from?'—just and mild and gentle as ever.

" 'I—well, I ain't from any particular place, your honor—been knocked about a good deal, mostly in the show business, your honor—because, on account of hard luck I couldn't help it—but I am sorry, and if your honor will let me go, just this once, I—'

" 'Denomination, please?'

"He said it just as ca'm and sweet as ever, and I bowed—and bowed again—and tried to get my hat, but it rolled between my feet, and I says—scared most to death—I says—

" 'I didn't know any better, your honor, but I was ignorant and wicked, and I didn't know the right way, your honor, and I went a-blundering along and loving everybody just alike, niggers and

Injuns and Presbyterians and Irish, and taking to them more and more the further and further I went in my evil ways—and so . . . so . . . if your honor would *only* let me go back just this one time, I—'

" 'Papers?' says he, just as soft and gentle as ever.

"I had got my hat, but my fingers shook so I couldn't hold onto it and it dropped again. The perspiration was rolling down my face, and it didn't seem to me I could get breath enough together to live. When that awful question come, I just gave up everything, and dropped on my knees and says—

" 'Have pity on a poor ignorant foolish man, your honor, that has come in his wicked blindness without a denomination, without one scrap of a paper, without'—

" 'Rise up, Simon Wheeler! The gates of heaven stand wide to welcome you! Range its barred commonwealths as free as the angels, brother and comrade of all its nations and peoples,—for the whole broad realm of the blest is your home!' "

Captain Wheeler had a voice like a man-o'-warsman, and he always brought out that closing passage with the roar and crash of a thunder-peal.

As we were saying, Wheeler retired from the show business and set up as a small farmer on his little homestead; but he soon found that the cultivation of corn and tobacco was rather a monotonous occupation for one whose life had been so full of variety and activity as his. He began to grow restless, and presently fell to turning over new schemes in his mind. He looked upon it as a special providence that just at this unsettled time, when he was so certain to make a move soon, and so likely to make a wrong one, a book fell into his hands which showed him instantly and as clear as day what he was born for. He had a mission in this world—he had not a shadow of doubt about it—a great career was before him! He promptly banished all the crude schemes that were fermenting in his brain, and turned his whole attention to his "mission."

This book which located him securely and permanently when his anchors were dragging was entitled "Tales of a Detective." It became his Bible. He read and re-read it until he knew it by heart; he adopted its professional slang and buttered all his talk with it; he reverenced its shallow, windy hero as one who was inspired; he marveled over its cheap mysteries and trivial inventions and thought they were near to being miracles. Now this was all perfectly natural, for these reasons, to-wit: Captain Wheeler was a country-born and village-bred; all his goings to and fro had been among backwoodsmen and villagers; he was almost without education and real experience of men and life, and this gave him a confidence, a self-appreciation and a deep knowingness which nothing but ignorance can afford—ignorance carefully selected, and boiled down and compacted to pemmican; he was very brave, he was a manly man, and void of meannesses and implacabilities; but at the same time he was as gentle-hearted as a girl, as simple-minded as a little child, and as easily seen through as glass. The capstone to his character was a fervid and romantic imagination—and this naturally made him a hero-worshiper and kept his head filled with dreams of some day being a hero himself.

All this is as we see Simon Wheeler. How did he see himself? Like all other villagers, he was a professed "student of character"; he believed he could cast his practised eye on the most inscrutable of men and read him like a book; he believed he had a consummate knowledge of men and life; he was proud to believe himself as vengeful and implacable as an Indian, and his constant divergences from this character he regarded as mere experiments to show himself what a supreme mastery his will held over the dearest appetites of his nature; be believed he was very deep, very wary, very wily, and gifted with a cunning that was capable of deceiving the most sagacious intellect that could be enlisted against it.

Therefore, we repeat, it was natural for this kindly, simple-natured, transparent old infant to fall down and worship that detective rubbish and its poor little tuppenny hero.

Captain Wheeler was right in one thing—he was a born detective. He had every quality that goes to make up the average detective: not the "booky" one, that brilliant, sagacious, all-seeing, all-divining creation of the great modern novelists, but the real detective, the one that exists in actual life.

The Captain's appetite increased with what it fed on. He sent for every detective book he could hear of. He devoured all these tales with avidity and accepted them as gospel truth. To him these detective heroes were actualities; and in time their names and their performances came to be quoted and referred to by him with the facility and the loving faith with which scholars quote the great names and recal the great deeds of history. He was another Don Quixotte, and his library of illustrious shams as honored, as valued, and as faithfully studied and believed in as was the Don's.

He established this library in one of the ground-floor rooms of the house called the "nigger quarter." He did not call this apartment his library; far from it: he called it the "Chief's Office"; and he loved to sit there alone, in great state, at particular hours, and receive imaginary "reports" from imaginary "inspectors" and other subordinates, detail couples and groups of these for special secret service for the next watch, issue general orders to others, and appoint various book-renowned shadows to go and "shadow" sundry suspected villains whom he dug out of his own brain and furnished their villainies to them from the same source.

In a room which communicated with the "office," the captain kept a lot of old theatrical costumes, a melancholy relic of his old showing days. They began to gather value in his eyes as his detective mania grew; later, when he began to branch out as a detective himself and required disguises, they became his most precious possession. This room, the office, and one or two rooms on the upper floor, were sacred; the captain kept their mysteries under lock and key. Even his wife came no nearer to this holy building than was necessary to the delivery of messages—which was not very near, for she had a long-range voice when she chose to elevate it. Mrs. Jenny Wheeler was as child-like and simple-hearted as her husband, and had as full a faith in his detective abilities and his great future as himself. There was not a lazy bone in Wheeler's body. With all his detecting he never allowed his little farm to run behind; he made it furnish a good and sufficient support for himself and his wife; there was plenty to eat and plenty to wear; if there was little money, it was no matter, for little was needed. If Mrs. Wheeler wanted something done, and Simon said he was "on duty," or had to receive a "report" or "issue orders" to a relief-watch, or go and "shadow" a "crib" or a "fence," or a "crossman," or "pipe" somebody suspected of "shoving the queer," she waited patiently and without a word, for she felt that these great official duties were paramount.

Hugh was given a large ground-floor room in the "nigger-quarter" which had formerly been the kitchen. It had a great fire-place in it, a comfortable bed, several old chairs and a table. The captain charged his wife never to come in sight of this tramp, for he was a "deep one" and required lulling and sagacious treatment, else he would be sure to take the alarm and decamp. He charged Hugh to keep the tobacco field between himself and the house, because his wife "did not like the expense of hired men and would want him sent away"—an unnecessary warning, for Hugh had no mind to risk detection where he could avoid it. He had small fear of the captain's seeing through his disguise, but he judged that it would be best to get used to being a tramp, and easy in the costume of the character before displaying himself too freely.

The captain brought Hugh's meals to him at regular hours, and used these opportunities to study his man. He talked to Hugh apparently at random, but with a deep purpose. He usually got a brand new theory as to minor details, out of these conversations, but the big bottom belief that this tramp was the murderer of Hugh Burnside remained, fixed and unalterable in his mind. By practice, Hugh soon achieved a change of voice; he felt secure, now, from discovery by the captain, though he had had but slight misgivings in that matter before.

Hugh might have soon wearied of being a person who had mysteriously disappeared, romantic as the thing was; he might have soon wearied of his ragged disguise and the trifling drudgeries his character of a tramp required of him; he might have soon wearied of his monotonous life in and about the "nigger quarter"; all these things might have soon lost the charm of their novelty and moved him to bring his adventure to an end, but for a certain other and more powerfully restraining interest. This was a strong curiosity he felt to discover what the captain's suspicions about him were. The old man was watching him and pumping him—these things were certain. The door which opened from the kitchen into the office was kept locked; he detected slight sounds in the office at night. Was the captain spying through the keyhole?—Once or twice when Hugh was playing at wood-chopping he thought he heard a movement in the bushes near at hand. When Hugh had been in the nigger quarter a couple of days he thought he would explore the building. He was surprised to find that the office and another room on the main floor, and two rooms overhead, were locked. Here was a mystery which must be solved.

When he heard the captain leave the office by the outside door that evening, he dropped softly into his track. He saw him enter a little grove of peach trees a short distance away and seem to reach up and fumble about the trunk of one of them. It was not light enough for him to make out more than this, but he judged that the keys were being concealed.—He was not mistaken. The old man had dropped them into a shallow natural pocket in the crotch of the tree. It took Hugh some little time to find the right spot, but he succeeded at last, and carried off the prize. Five minutes later, he was in the office with a lighted candle.—He took a cursory glance at the books, and then a slate that hung against the wall over the desk caught his eye. At the top of it, rudely lettered in white paint, was this:

CHIEF'S HEDQUARTERS.

Underneath, written with a slate pencil, was this:

NIGHT-DUTY ORDERS.

*Chief will be absent in villadge on special duty from 9 till midgnight.*

*Inspector Adams will shadow Nobby Bill and report to Chief.*

*Detective Barker will pipe the Jew fence for prigged*[50] *thimbles,*[51] *props*[52] *and dummies.*[53]

*No change of duty for rest of force.*

*Reliefs rep't to Hedquarters at usual hours.*

WHEELER,

*Chief of Detective Dep't.*

The names used above were those of famous detectives who figured in the Captain's favorite books.

Hugh went to his own quarters, now, to wait until 9 o'clock; for

---

[50] Stolen [Twain's note].

[51] Watches [Twain's note].

[52] Breast-pins [Twain's note].

[53] Pocket-books [Twain's note].

he did not doubt that the "Chief" would obey his own orders and go on special duty in the "villadge" at that hour.

When the proper time arrived he invaded the Captain's mysteries, candle in hand. He found the room adjoining the office full of cheap old theatrical costumes, and among them various odds and ends likely to be held precious by a professional of the Captain's sort.—The costumes depended from pegs in the wall, and the first dim flicker which the candle threw upon them produced rather a startling effect, for it turned them into hanged people swaying to and fro in the last agony. But as it was only their shadows that swayed, this ceased as soon as Hugh and the candle-flame stood still.

Each costume bore a label. One was "An Old Saler"; another "A Hiwayman"; another "A Nigger"; another, "Irish-woman"—and so forth and so on. Hugh recognized some of the costumes; he had seen Wheeler about the village in them on imaginary detective duty.

Here and there were the valuable specimens of detective bric-a-brac just referred to. One was labeled "Peace of the skelp of the half-breed that killed Conklin's hired man"; another, "Peace of the rope that hung Whitlow"; another, "Huff of the jakass that kicked Johnny Tompson in the hed of which he died and whom I bought when he was shot to get the huff"; another, "Brickbat which busted Archibald Skidmore Nickerson deceas'd"; another, "Left Thum of a horse Theef"; another, "Part of second hand glove said to ben used by detective Larkin of St Louis as a clew to find out who rob'd the State Bank, but did not succeed, the burglar not wearing gloves that time"; another, "Shin of celebrated N.Y. detective"; another, "Bottle that had the asnic in it that Elizabeth Sapper took but was pumped out and nothing come of it"; "Part of a dog which bit deacon Hooker of which he died"; another, "Tooth out of a stranger supposed to ben murdered by hiwaymen." There were many more grisly gems in the collection, but we will leave the rest uncatalogued.

In one of the locked rooms upstairs Hugh found another museum like this one; when he unlocked its larger neighbor he came upon a spectacle which startled him for a moment. Through the flickering light and the dancing shadows he saw a swaying and bowing assemblage of pale and silent men and women, who were most gaudily and fantastically dressed. He stared, speechless, at these people a moment—then he perceived that they were only wax figures.

Hugh approached, and inspected the convention at his leisure. General Washington was there, duly labeled, stiff as a monument, and with ten years' dust on him. He imagined he was taking leave of his generals, no doubt, for his two hands were advanced suggestively; but as these two hands were now wire-bridged with cobwebs, ignorant persons would jump to the conclusion that he was holding yarn for Queen Elizabeth, who sat before him. The Duke of Wellington was there, with the stuffing sticking through his trousers where they were torn at the knee. Daniel Lambert was present, his mighty stomach a home for happy mice. Ajax was defying the lightning, and Lafayette had lost his props and was leaning against him, with a loose familiarity of attitude which hinted that he needed a lamp post and thought he had found one. Poor Louis XVI, in his tin crown, had fallen across the lap of the terrible Robespierre, who had a dagger in one hand, a horse pistol in the other, and an innocent caterpillar asleep on his chin. Around a coffin which had once been gaudy with cheap finery, stood some Romans holding imaginary handkerchiefs to their eyes, and in the coffin lay imperial Caesar, in dusty magnificence. Murderers and pirates abounded, and there was a couple of very passable devils with Benedict Arnold in charge.—

During a couple of hours Hugh amused himself with re-grouping these figures in all sorts of absurd ways, and then retired, promising himself further entertainment with them when other excitements ran low.

Shortly after midnight the captain arrived and paid him a visit. Hugh inquired what news was stirring.

"Well, there ain't anything stirring, these days, but the murder, of course, Trampy."

Hugh was interested. Said he,—

"What do they say about it?"

"All sorts of things.—They don't seem to know how to feel grieved enough about that poor young Burnside."

These were grateful tidings for Hugh. He hoped the subject would be enlarged upon.—The captain presently went on,—

"You see, his mother advertised for his remains, two or three days ago, and that warmed up the general distress considerable."

# *Working Notes for*
# "Simon Wheeler, Detective"

The thirteen sheets of working notes fall into three fairly distinct major groups which I have designated A, B, and C, although it should be understood that the grouping is entirely my own, inferred from the matter treated in each group.

## Group A

This group of notes is written in pencil on five half-sheets of Crystal Lake Mills paper numbered 1 through 5 by Twain. Because the notes concern "Charley" Dexter, not Hale, they obviously belong to the very earliest stage of the 1877–78 period of composition and are related to the first thirty or so pages of the manuscript, those pages written before Twain changed the name from Charley to Hale.

### A-1

Hugh 18 or 19 is only giddy—his mother and sister must never mourn in his presence.
Only his sweetheart
Let him ask himself—
*Do* they mourn? *Am* I doing wrong?

He must be in a romantic pet against his ma and s—they have said something that "hurt" him. He is *so* sensitive and chuckle-headed.

Mrs Hugh is Ma

Clara is Cl. Spaulding [54]

Mill is a sappy sweet creature of 14 or 15 with 2 long tails down her back

A-2

Wheeler plays maniac.—Charley plays keeper.

No, let Wheeler, *as* a sailor, tell wonderful sea-yarns to Tramp.

Were you ever on a canal? I was in a *storm* on one, once?

His life with the Tram—conversations, etc.—shall be the fun of the book.

Suppose Charley disguises and hides, and Cap'n tells *him* his plans and clews? Good! Charley sometimes sees Clara (who

A-3

is broken hearted) at a distance—drops mysterious hints?—hey? *No,* guess not.

Hugh and Charley, at different times, see Clara and Milly walking with the new young minister getting consolation, and mistake their grateful glances for love.

Spread out on the *real* grief of Mrs. Hugh—make her find more comfort in her daughter Clara's brave and loving ministrations than anywhere else.

A-4

3 villains in the piece—those detectives.

The old woman is a good old soul, whose boarders, Tom and Lem,

[54] Clara Spaulding, later Mrs. John B. Stanchfield, was Olivia Clemens' girlhood friend from Elmira. A frequent visitor both at Quarry Farm and at Hartford, she was also Mrs. Clemens' companion on the 1873 trip to England and the 1878–79 European tour.

lead her a tormented life. She misquotes Scripture, proverbs, and everything else.

Charley is 30, Hugh 18 or 19.

Wheeler is married, but his wife stays at her son-in-law's—sickness in the family.

Charley overhears Mrs. Hugh praying for the murderer or something like that.

## A-5

Capn comes his "You done it!" on Charley as first proposed.

Guilford

Mrs. Hugh and Clara attend the funeral, but are not around when Hugh is.

Hugh visits home by night and leaves mysterious signs—wants to reveal himself, but 2 things are stronger—enjoyment of the pity his death occasions, and fear of ridicule.

Put in these editors and give some personal editorials.

# Group B

This group consists of five half-sheets of Crystal Lake Mills paper, two of which contain matter on both sides of the sheet. Miscellaneous notes apparently written from time to time during the course of composition in 1877–78, the pages are unnumbered and therefore exhibit no clear evidence of sequence. The arrangement of the notes is entirely my own; the reasons for assigning each sheet to its particular place in the sequence are given in the separate headnotes.

## B-1 and 2

These two sheets are written in the same violet ink as the manuscript itself. The first sheet is unnumbered; Twain numbered the second one "2." At first glance the notes appear to be review notes similar to sheet

C-1 of the notes for *Huckleberry Finn* (see Bernard DeVoto, *Mark Twain at Work* [Cambridge, Mass., 1942], pp. 72–74), but such a conclusion is improbable because the list of characters culminates with several projected for a portion of the manuscript never written. The notes were probably made sometime during the composition of the first eighty or so pages, a conclusion suggested by a comparison of names on the list with revisions in the text.

B-2 is written on the reverse of what was apparently the beginning of p. 2 of a business letter. Also numbered 2, the reverse contains the words "ceive them from me as cash." About midway down the page under the Wheeler notes appears the numeral 78E, and under that 75.

## B-1

Jack Belford—$500 reward, dead or alive.
Hoxton
Old Humphrey, at Marley
Mrs. Mary Burnside
Mr. Edward Dexter (elder)
Boggsville, where jail is.
Maj. Hoskins, sheriff.
Guilford Torch of Civilization
Mrs. Ruth Griswold
Old Mammy Betsy, care Col. Whiting, Bayou Noir Planta$^{n}$ Ark.
Bagley's Emporium
Baxter, little red-headed quick motioned person, rapid speaker.
Billings, short, slow, dull looking man, lifts fat finger, pauses,—then?—nods head 3 times, saying "Um."
Bullet, long, lean man—ponders, with finger at face—then asks ?s of a single word.
Bob Tufts detec [written in left margin.]

## B-2

Crazy Hackett
Happy Winny

Sappy
Holy Jacobs.

## B-3

These notes are written in pencil on a half-sheet discarded from some other manuscript. Page 3 of the manuscript from which it came, it is half-filled with the following aphorisms written in the same violet ink as the *Simon Wheeler* manuscript:

> The offender never pardons.
> Praise a fair day at night.
> Take heed of an ox before, an ass behind, and a knave on all sides.
> Short reckonings make long friends, old reckonings breed new disputes.
> Nothing comes out of the sack but what was in it.

These sayings are similar to the one written in the margin of MS p. 116 (see p. 342) and possibly represent a collection of proverbs intended for the use of Mrs. Higgins (see second note, A-4).

The Wheeler notes are written across the bottom half of the sheet at right angles to the discarded text. They deal with events described in chapters 3 and 4, and, since they are obviously jottings made in haste, they probably represent notes made while Twain was composing that portion of the manuscript.

> Meet W
> Note to Barnes
> Letter fm mother
> Hugh's girl.
> Toby "loses" note to
> *Destroy* will?

---

> Here introduce Toby wanting a letter copied out of R. W. Toby sends to his mother the letter in wh Dex begs leave to come and explain, and does the same with Clara's letter to Dex in wh she says now or never. So next time they meet they don't speak. By and by they try writing once more with the same result.

## B-4 and 5

These notes are in pencil on both sides of a half-sheet on which Twain originally had written and then discarded seven lines of text for MS p. 203. The notes project events for the latter portion of chapter 4.

### B-4

Mrs. B's satisfaction
Toby says Hugh and Milly sick kit to hot brick Hale and Clara together increasingly—bliss perfect—endless lally-gagging—pictures and incidents—or talk of theirs of how poor and empty the world was before and how innocently they took this and that laughably absurd and insipid state of things for happiness—how inexperienced they were, indeed! They hunt for solitudinous places and he reads poetry while she gloats upon him, praises his reading and knits. Mrs. B. "now don't get your feet wet—or do be careful with the gun,

### B-5

for you have become very precious. Clara—now *do* be careful—and don't be gone long."

Button off—here Clara, sew it on.

Clara—There—you are *so* hard on your clothes—I just sewed that on a day or two ago—(love pat)—There, go 'long. (Heart sings for joy.) Laughs idiotically at the least trifle—joy bubbling always.

Toby gets him to copy letter beginning, "I think it better that we part, though it rends my heart to say it etc." to send to Mam in Ark—Hale gives him one for Clara of a different tenor, begging that next time they meet she show by her manner if she is willing to let him try to explain and make up. But the latter letter is on pretty paper and looks prettiest every way—so Toby exchanges and gives the *former* to Clara. Toby says he delivered it. That note makes permanent breach—especially as Clara's note asking if he really feels so, is sent to Ark.

H and Milly quarrel twice a day

## B-6

Written in violet ink on a half-sheet of Crystal Lake Mills paper, the same ink and paper as the manuscript itself and the other notes, these notes are therefore from the 1877–78 period of composition. Because they project events beyond the point where the manuscript breaks off, they were evidently made just before Twain abandoned the story, either just before sailing for Europe in 1878 or during his European tour of 1878–79.

Hugh burglarizes clothes.

Toby to give Mrs. Dexter's letter to Clara.

Dexter to explain offering[55] reward for Hugh and keep Clara believing he may not be dead.

Hugh to see that offer.

Detectives to shadow 3 women and scoff at Craz Haz being the one.

Hugh reads "ad" for remains—his mother's. It is 3 days before Milly's.

Milly goes secretly to detectives about Crazy—they don't believe. It confirms their belief in *her* guilt.

Hugh worried about his mother and sister, because of the ad. Inquires of Cap, who tells him who Hugh is, and that the mother and sister only sham distress.

# Group C

The notes of Group C are of a much later date than either the manuscript or the previous notes. Written in black ink on three sheets of paper numbered 1 through 3 by Twain, they contain Twain's last projection for the conclusion of the story. The paper on which they are

---

[55] Above "offering," Twain wrote "455."

written is a very light blue, medium-weight laid paper with horizontal chain lines. Although the sheets are similar in size, 5½ by 8⅞ inches, to the half-sheets of Crystal Lake Mills paper previously used, they are not half-sheets, i.e., full sheets torn in half; the edges are trimmed, and bits of gum clinging to a sample in the Mark Twain Papers indicate that they came in tablets.

## C-1

Wheeler has got the murderer in the person of Hugh the tramp, and is waiting for sufficient evidence, which comes by and by—for Hugh will find out the above and will confess to Wheeler—W. thinks the $1000 reward secure.

Hugh goes out when he chooses, leaving a dummy asleep to represent him.

To his own family and to Milly he is a deaf and dumb old woman.

Clara knows Dexter for the murderer by his confession to his mother, beginning, "Dearest, I have killed Hugh Burnside. Wait till I come and explain all. Pray for [56] Your miserable son, Hale.

She determines to not let on. If he is a true man he will tell her—as being her due—and will prove it was an accident, then she will stand by him against the world. She has to suffer dumb heart-break, for no hint brings him to confession.

Meantime he knows his letter has miscarried or he would hear from his mother—and meantime *she* is not worrying, knowing him to be in love and busy.

## C-2

Milly thinks Crazy Hackett is guilty.

Dexter pretends to be shadowing him. Reports to her.

The half-blind old woman comes and sits around eating her alms and overhearing her lamentings.

---

[56] At this point Twain inserted the word "over," but nothing appears on the reverse of the sheet.

Bullet thinks Dexter did it to get all of Humphrey's money. Half-blind woman heaves Robespierre in on top of Wash. Pumps Toby.

Baxter thinks Milly did it out of jealousy, she being his sweetheart. The half blind deaf and dumb old woman (Hugh) overhears him questioning Toby and thinks he suspects Toby—so Hugh fetches General Washington and throws him down unused well—Baxter can dimly descry it—heaves down a bucket of chloride of lime to make the body keep—heaves straw on top of that—and waits in confidence for further evidence, shadowing all the village girls (or old Miss Griswold) seeking for the Milly was jealous of.

Bucket [57] thinks Miss Griswold did it to supplant Milly. Pumps Toby. Heaves Julius Caesar in on top of Robespierre.

Hugh dumps Louis XVI down on top of Caesar and confesses to Wheeler that after concealing Hugh's body in the woods he went and got it at night and threw it in that well to cast suspicion upon Milly's father—who, this tramp had heard, was ferociously opposed to the match. Wheeler slips at night through the high weeds of that disused great garden with sparkle-lantern, lowers it with a string, as the others had done, gets chloride of lime—great trade in it of late—heaves it down, and weeds on top of it.

## C-3

Hugh, with hurdy-gurdy, and disguised out of all recognition; Judge Griswold; Milly; Dexter; and Miss Griswold are all arrested at the same time and brought with Sheriffs and all the village—with Clara and her mother—to the old well, and the bodies are fetched up, one by one—the detectives maintaining every time that the wax figures are mere blinds and the real corpse is down there yet—till at last, when Milly lets go some peculiarly strenuous wish that it was all a dream and she could die happy if she could but see him once more, Hugh theatrically sheds his disguise and plunges into her arms —then Dexter into Clara's.

I guess we had better go back and make the judge privately believe Dexter did it to carry out the feud and entirely against his desire and feeling and only from a lofty sense of duty. Which lifts D. to the

[57] Twain apparently forgot that the third detective is named Billings, or he had decided to change the name during this revision.

very summit of human perfection in the judge's eyes; and thinks him all the nobler for concealing the deed in order to save the women suffering, whereas a lower spirit would want to *include* them in the suffering to make the vengeance the more comprehensive.

At the end he is willing to be glad his daughter's Savior wasn't killed, and he still loves Dexter but does *not* revere him any longer.

Toby's letters must always *help* the confusion—even *cause* it.

# APPENDIXES

# APPENDIX A

# *Dates of Composition*

"A NOVEL: *Who Was He?*":

Although the draft of the *Alta California* letter for 12 January 1867, follows "A Novel: *Who Was He?*" in the holograph notebook with several intervening pages of notes, the sequence of dates for the various entries and the state of the notebook make it clear that in the course of drafting the letter Twain ran out of space in the back of the notebook and turned forward to a sequence of blank pages on which he wrote the burlesque as an intended conclusion. The burlesque is preceded by an entry for Sunday, 6 January, describing the approach to Key West. The next two entries read "Jan. 8. Chas Belmayne" and "Jan. 11. P. Peterson." The two names are those of men who died aboard ship on the passage from Key West to New York. The entries are numbered 7 and 8, indicating that they were to complete the list of dead in the cholera epidemic compiled on 5 January. A blank page intervenes between these entries and the beginning of the burlesque. Immediately following the burlesque the notebook entries resume with one headed "Sunday, Jan. 6 continued" and continue with daily entries (except for 9 January) to 12 January, the arrival in New York. The *Alta* letter begins with no break immediately after the 12 January entry and runs to the end of the notebook. If this reconstruction is correct, Twain left some ten to twelve pages blank after the first entry for 5 January. He must have done so intending later to give further details about the landing at Key West and, possibly, an explanation of how a ship with cholera aboard managed to get past quarantine. But it is quite possible that in a pessimistic mood he left this much space for a continuation of the list of dead with biographical information on each victim.

## "Cap'n Simon Wheeler":

Twain was being somewhat disingenuous in his reports to Howells. Most of the pages in the manuscript were renumbered once, a few two times. If these renumbered pages are arranged in a chart such as that below, they reveal that the work performed between 6 and 11 July was not simply a matter of correcting mispaging. It was instead a rather thorough rewriting and expansion. The page numbers appearing in column A reflect the method of composition by separate acts which Twain reported to Howells. Because he did not write the acts in sequence (but in the following order: second, first, fourth, then third) it is logical to assume that he started the page numbering from 1 in each act. The renumbering of the pages bears out the assumption. The numbering system represented in column B presumably reflects the state of the manuscript on 6 July, when Twain reported that his manuscript, "just a fraction under 250 MS pages," was completed. If this assumption is correct, column C, then, reflects the state of the manuscript on 11 July, the result of the work described in a later paragraph of the 11 July letter: "All day long, & every day, since I finished (in the rough), I have been diligently, altering, amending, rewriting, cutting down. I finished finally to-day."

Further evidence to support such an assumption comes from the working notes and several discarded pages (43–49) preserved with the manuscript. As the notes I have designated as notes for Plan I show, Twain originally conceived the character of Charles as that of a rascally cousin named John Hooker. The villain of the piece, John was to be the poet's rival for the affections of Mary (later renamed Millicent) and a somewhat underhanded contender for the inheritance. The discarded manuscript pages contain a scene between Millicent and the cousin in which the cousin reveals himself to be just such a scoundrel. Because these discarded pages fit into the pagination of the "B" manuscript, picking up without a break in the midst of a speech the first portion of which was deleted at the foot of "B" manuscript p. 42 (p. 74 of the "C" manuscript), it becomes fairly clear that the "A" manuscript and one version of the "B" manuscript were written in accordance with the Plan I notes. Twain revised this conception in

VARIANT PAGE NUMBERS IN SIMON WHEELER PLAY

| A | B | C |
|---|---|---|
| | | 1–28 |
| 1–3 | 10–12 | 29–31 |
| | 13–26 | 32–45 |
| | | 46 |
| | 28–39 | 47–58 |
| | | 59–67 |
| | 49 cont–49 cont | 68–71 |
| | 40–46[a] | 72–78 |
| | 50–57 | 79–86 |
| | | 86x1–86x7 |
| | 58–63 | 87–92 |
| | 64–78 | 93–107[b] |
| | 79–100 | 108–130 |
| 1–8 | | 131–139 |
| | 101–132 | 140–171 |
| | 133–137[c] | 172–176 |
| | 137–150x1 | 177–192 |
| 1–8 | 150x2–150x9 | 193–199 |
| | 151–203 | 200–253 |
| 1–20 | 204–223 | 254–273 |

[a] A note at the foot of p. 47 reads "run to p. 50."
[b] There has been some minor juggling of the page sequence in this area.
[c] In this page sequence there were two pages numbered 137.

accordance with the Plan II notes while still retaining substantially the same scheme of pagination to form that version of the "B" manuscript retained in the "C" manuscript. It was this work which Twain finished on 6 July. That the "C" manuscript was completed on 11 July is fairly clear not only from Twain's letter but also from the synopsis which Twain composed on 12 July as part of his copyright application. Although some of the dialogue quoted in the synopsis differs slightly from that of the play, the synopsis was obviously based upon the text reproduced here, the "C" manuscript completed on 11 July.

# APPENDIX B

## *Clemens' Political Affiliations Bearing on "L'Homme Qui Rit"*

"L'Homme Qui Rit" is Twain's most personal statement during this period about his attitudes toward the Civil War and Reconstruction. Discussing Twain's attitude toward the Southern cause focuses attention on his role as a volunteer in the Missouri (Confederate) militia, his abrupt departure for Nevada in 1861, and his silence from 1861 to 1865 on the issues of the war. There are other clues pointing toward a continuation of his loyalty to the South during Johnson's administration.

From November 1867 to March 1868, Clemens was in Washington, D.C., as free-lance newspaper correspondent and personal secretary to his old Nevada friend, William M. Stewart, senator from Nevada. This was the period during which the impeachment of Johnson was taking shape: the bill of impeachment was formally presented to the Senate on 13 March 1868. And William M. Stewart was a Radical Republican who consistently supported the Radical Republican commissioners (Benjamin Butler, Thaddeus Stevens, *et al.*) on the various procedural votes during the impeachment trial and who consistently voted guilty on the various articles of the impeachment. He had been swept into office in the Radical Republican landslide in Nevada in 1864 in the same election which saw Clemens' brother Orion defeated at the polls despite the fact that he was a Republican and an incumbent from the Territorial government.

During his stay in Washington, Clemens was attempting to secure an appointment for Orion and at least halfheartedly seeking one for himself. But he was not working through Stewart. When he learned that the postmastership in San Francisco was to be offered to a total stranger after he had withdrawn in favor of a friend, he wrote his mother and sister (6 February 1868):

> I hunted up all our Senators and representatives and found that [the stranger's] name was actually to come from the President early in the morning.
>
> Then Judge Field said if I wanted the place he could pledge me the President's appointment—and Senator Conness said he would *guarantee* me the Senate's confirmation.[1]

Stephen J. Field was a Buchanan Democrat who had resigned as Chief Justice of the California Supreme Court to accept Lincoln's appointment to the U.S. Supreme Court in 1863. Although a Union man, he had become highly suspect in the eyes of the Radical Republicans in Congress because of his concurrence in the unanimous decision (3 April 1866) affirming the appeal of Lamdin P. Milligan, a decision which, by extension, supported Johnson in the controversy with Congress over reconstruction.[2] The extent of Radical Republican animosity became clear during the impeachment move against Johnson in 1868. An anonymous newspaper report asserted that during a dinner party Justice Field had declared his belief that the Reconstruction Acts were unconstitutional. The Radical Republican majority in the House immediately shouted through a resolution forming a committee charged to investigate Field's pro-Southern sympathies and, if the evidence warranted, to draw up charges of impeachment. Clemens, who at this time was seeking political preferment through Field and booming him as the best Democratic candidate for president, defended him against the impeachment move in various newsletters, using arguments furnished by Field.[3] Louis J. Budd comments, "It is obvious that he

---

[1] MTL, I, 149.

[2] Milligan was an Indiana Copperhead whose activities in 1864 so outraged the military commandant of the District of Indiana that he was arrested on orders of the commandant, tried by a military commission, and sentenced to be hanged. The issue involved (Is the citizen of a state where no hostilities are in progress and where the normal civil legal structure is unimpaired subject to martial law?) struck at the heart of Radical Republican plans for reconstruction by martial law. The Court upheld Milligan.

[3] Louis J. Budd, *Mark Twain: Social Philospher* (Bloomington, 1962), pp. 30–31.

sacrificed little if any principle by defending Justice Field when the Republican Radicals accused him of softness toward the ex-Rebels."[4] But it is equally obvious that, in defending and supporting Field against a Congress dominated by Radical Republicans, Clemens was sacrificing his chances for political advancement. His other champion, Senator John Conness of California, was a much safer one for a man who hoped to pass the scrutiny of the Radicals. Conness was among the more vocal Radicals in the Senate who later consistently voted for Johnson's conviction on the various articles of impeachment. But Conness hardly swung enough weight in the Senate to offset the obloquy which would inevitably be heaped upon any nomination made by Johnson on the recommendation of Field. For that matter, such was the political climate of the period, we may turn the whole proposition about: there is every reason to doubt that Clemens, despite his championship of Field, could have secured Johnson's approval if it had been known that Conness would be his senatorial sponsor. Clemens himself was in the awkward position of the office seeker he described in his Washington letter of 5 February 1868, to the Virginia City *Territorial Enterprise:* "And he don't take into consideration that the moment he gets the President in his favor the Senate will be down on him for it, and that if he gains the Senate's affections first, the President will be down on him."

In other words, for a private secretary to William M. Stewart, Clemens was keeping rather strange political company in his efforts to secure an appointment. Although normally a candidate worked through the congressmen and other Washington officials from his home state (the pronoun "our" in Clemens' letter suggests that he considered California his home state), the political situation in Washington in February 1868, was such that to seek preferment in such a manner was to commit political suicide. That Clemens was aware of this fact is suggested by his letter to Orion, 21 February 1868, concerning Orion's bid for an appointment to the Patent Office:

> I am glad you do not want the clerkship, for that Patent Office is in such a muddle that there would be no security for the permanency of a place in it. The same remark will apply to all offices here, now, and no doubt will till the close of the present administration.
>
> Any man who holds a place here, now, stands prepared at all times to vacate it.[5]

---

[4] *Ibid.*, p. 35.

[5] *MTL,* I, 150.

Clemens' open support of Field at a time when, as he well knew, Radical Republican tempers were high suggests strongly that a hostility to the Radicals had emerged from his suppressed pro-Southern, pro-Democrat sympathies or had developed as a result of his political education in Washington. Such an inference lends significance to and gains some support from the rupture with Stewart in late February or early March 1868. In November 1867, the two men were close enough that Clemens became Stewart's private secretary and had a room in his house. By early March the two had separated angrily, and the record of the rupture hints that one or the other may have resorted to fisticuffs. Albert Bigelow Paine notes that in his memoirs Senator Stewart "refers unpleasantly to Mark Twain, and after relating several incidents that bear only strained relations to the truth, states that when the writer returned from the Holy Land he (Stewart) offered him a secretaryship as a sort of charity. He adds that Mark Twain's behavior on his premises was such that a threat of a thrashing was necessary." Paine goes on to ascribe Stewart's animosity to various supposed insults in *Roughing It:* an accusation of cheating, an unflattering picture, and an assertion that Twain had "given [Stewart] a sound thrashing." [6] Since the rupture occurred prior to the publication of *Roughing It,* there is a very strong possibility, in view of Clemens' political activities and associates, that it resulted from differences in political alignments.

Nevertheless, before one hastens to the conclusion that Clemens was a Johnson Democrat who came to threatened or actual blows with a Radical Republican, several other bits of evidence pointing in the opposite direction must be considered. Among these are the thumbnail sketches of congressmen jotted in his notebook during his stay in Washington. Although in most of these the unflattering comments and the compliments are distributed with impartiality among both Radical Republicans and Johnson Democrats, one contains a phrase which definitely points away from Democrat sympathies: "Eldridge of Wis.—leading and malignant copperhead." [7] "Copperhead" is in itself a term which a Democrat would probably not use to describe a fellow-Democrat, and the coupling with it of the word "malignant" makes it almost beyond cavil the phrase of a Republican (although not necessarily a Radical). A suggestion of radicalism creeps in when one considers the close friendships Clemens formed in the period from 1867

[6] *MTB,* I, 347 n. Only the statement about the picture is true.
about the picture is true.

[7] *Mark Twain's Notebook,* ed. Albert B. Paine (New York, 1935), p. 114.

to 1869. On the *Quaker City* excursion to the Holy Land he had met and formed a strong attachment to Mrs. Mary Mason Fairbanks, "Mother" Fairbanks, which grew stronger in the subsequent months and years. Mrs. Fairbanks' husband, Abel W. Fairbanks, was co-publisher and co-editor of the Cleveland *Herald,* next to Greeley's *Tribune* one of the most rabid Radical Republican, anti-Johnson sheets in the country. In 1869, Clemens seriously considered buying an interest in the Cleveland *Herald* and was prevented only by last-minute changes in the purchase price. If he were a Democrat, he seems in the negotiations to have felt no apprehensions about a possible rupture with Abel W. Fairbanks similar to the one with Stewart. A little later in the year, with the aid of Jervis Langdon, his prospective father-in-law, he purchased a share in the Buffalo *Express,* another Radical Republican paper, with the proviso, however, that he should have nothing to do with political news. Despite the proviso, almost immediately after entering upon his editorial duties, he wrote his allegory of Johnson's political career.

# APPENDIX C

# *Textual Notes*

No attempt has been made to preserve Clemens' numerous minor stylistic revisions or slips of the pen. Even longer revisions which represent a mere restatement in different words have been ignored. The only deletions and revisions preserved here are those indicative of a change in characterization or of direction in the plot. The notes are keyed to the text by page and line numbers, and the following symbols have been used:

| | |
|---|---|
| < > | deletion |
| ↑ ↓ | substitution for a deletion |
| <↑ ↓> | deleted substitution |
| ^ ^ | insertion |
| // . . . // | illegible word(s) |
| / | alternative reading |

"L'Homme Qui Rit":

43:25 A putrid <murderer> ↑carcass↓—with obscene ravens. . . .

43:26–29 decaying <convict> ↑party↓, this boy saw. . . .
He did not want the <convict> ↑corpse↓.

"Burlesque *Hamlet*":

56:19–29 chapter <upon 'Obsolete Methods of Digging Clams'—with accompanying illustrations."> ↑upon 'The Mythological Era of Denmark';— <and this one upon the old

vexed question> and to this one upon 'Denmark's High Place Among the Historical Empires of Antiquity'; and *most* particularly to this noble, and beautiful, and convincing dissertation upon the old, old vexed question, 'Inasmuch as Methuselah lived to the very building of the Ark and the very <beginning> day of the flood, how was it he got left?' ‸And also to this exquisite satirical description of old men: 'Old men have gray beards; their faces are wrinkled; their eyes purging thick amber and plum-tree gum, etc., etc. and so on"—O, it's just tip-top—lays over anything you ever saw.‸↓ Let me. . . .

70:21–29 if *they* can. <Now if I can get old Polonius to subscribe —<but> ↑and↓ here he comes—no, it's Bub and Sis. The old man can't be far—I'll go and hunt him up.

(*Exit,* L.>

↑Meantime my little benevolent . . . host of imaginary friends.

(*Exit.*↓

"1,002$^{d}$ Arabian Night":

127:33–34 contributed not were cut. (121)

<(*About six pages of presents.*)>

The day that the lovers. . . .

129:34–35 roar and crash thereof.

<(Describe Bridal Dress)>

During the extended. . . .

[MT later inserted the description of Fatima's bridal dress between 128:4 and 129:1]

"Autobiography of a Damned Fool":

140:25 <But I wander from my narrative.> <↑Mr. Bangs had no religion. He <was> had latterly even grown↓>

<↑At breakfast on Monday Mrs. Bangs said to me: "So you have got religion, they say."↓>

But I wander from my narrative.

153:23–26 Hank was <always playing jokes and making game of people in quiet way, anyhow, so I judged he was at something of the sort now, and I was not in a mood for jesting.> ↑always doing innocent, stupid things, with the best of intentions, and I never paid any attention to him when my mind was busy with weighty matters.↓

160:20 <When the proofs came back they were fairly riddled.>
By and by, the great man walked slowly in. . . .

"Hellfire Hotchkiss":

191:32–34 <the village might think of the matter.>
Part of what she was was born to her, the rest was due to environment and to her up-bringing. <The environment-detail was <a large feature> of a sort not common, and would necessarily produce results not of the usual ∧order.∧> She had had neither brothers nor sisters. . . . [The first paragraph of this chapter was inserted on two new sheets, the original one-page being discarded and the last line of the discarded text deleted from the top of MS p. 52 (renumbered 52 ½).]

194:8–9 She took her full share in all their sports, <except those of the swimming-hole. She had to deny herself in that matter, because bathing dresses were not worn. She was called tom-boy, of course; and she was the only tom-boy of respectable family in the village.> ∧and was a happy child.∧

196:15 [After a four-page insertion of new text and some discarding of old text, MT here returns to the original manuscript.] <lesson—far from it—but she made a large improvement. She still had her <phenomenal> tremendous outbursts of <wrath,> ↑passion,↓ but the intervals between them grew noticeably wider and wider.>
By the time she was ten. . . .

"Cap'n Simon Wheeler, The Amateur Detective":

221–24–25 *Barrel or something there.* <*Mrs. Swash sitting near wing, knitting peacefully.*>
*Chas. and Hugh discovered.*

221:29 imagines he's a detective, <is behind that barrel—I know his heels!> <is dodging and> ∧is∧ spying around

222:28–35 a *poor* poet! (*Lifting his hands.*) <Now *they* can live on moonshine—get fat on it. But our girl would starve on that sort of board.>

↑*Capt.* (∧*Yawning and stretching,*∧ *protruding head, with sacking thrown over it, to conceal face, from barrel.*) Hallo, have I been asleep? Well, it's the *first* time I ever forgot myself since I've been an amature detective. Hello, who's this? Old pap and mam Griswold. <Now what sort of devilment can they be up to? I'll lay for 'em>. (*Conceals himself again.*)↓

Mrs. G.—Well, well, I see your mind's

222:36–37 and she'll obey. ∧(*Sits down on barrel.*)∧

223:3–4 smacks of insubordination. ∧(*Punches Capt. in eye with his umbrella.*)∧

223:22–29 G.—Pah! you <old fool!> ∧talk too much!∧

<*Mrs. G.*—Pah, yourself, <you old ass!> <↑you impudent old thing!↓>

*Exit.*>

∧*Mrs. G.*—M'f! Don't *every*body that gets the best of an argument?

*Exit.*∧

∧*Capt.*—'Gad she had him there! These quarters are getting too warm. I guess I'll climb out and hide in a <better> ↑cooler↓ place. Hold on—somebody *else* <is> coming. (*Retires again.*)∧

*Enter Hugh and Millicent.*

224:3 barred from hoping!—<it is the cruelest situation! (*Starting up* ∧*furiously*∧). O, I see it all!> Give me one little

225:9 told Spence <Billings> Buckner, and Spence

225:16–17 *upon pa.*)∧ (*low voice*)—Pah! you *talk* too much!∧

229:3–4 together. <Last night I was worse than usual, Lem, because I was dreaming of sweethearts and rivals. And I may as well tell you that things have gone wrong with me and> ↑But a truce to trifles—↓ my soul is full of troubles.

231:3–14 <∧*Change. 1st Act—contin.*∧ 2d <*act.*> ↑SCENE.↓ *A street lamp. One house and a garden.*

*1* A.M.—*Moonlight.*
*Enter Poet and commits suicide*>
↑(*Change Scene.*
*First Act—continued.*
*Moonlight—time, after midnight.*
*Enter Hugh.* (*Slow music.*) . . . (*Seemingly dies.*)↓
*Enter Capt.* <*Swash*> ↑*Wheeler.*↓

231:19–20 unerring as fate. <'I-George, he wasn't more than out of the front door till I was <in> at the back one with my ear so wide open you could <a thrown> a hove a dog down it. And sure enough says one drug clerk to tother, "Much *he* wants to <poison> ↑pison↓ rats!—<Zippie Burton's> ↑Milly Grizld's↓ what's the matter with him." But <consarn it> ↑plague on him,↓ while I was hiving that information I've> ↑But rot him, I've↓ lost

233:21–22 [Following the reporter's exit, a scene between the two drug clerks has been deleted. Interleaved in the manuscript at this point is an unnumbered sheet bearing a notation relative to the scene. The note was cancelled along with the scene.]

*Mem.* The drug-clerk scene is also to account for the news not getting around that Hugh tried to buy poison. If the scene is better out, though, the Captain <will> can cover the ground in *his* speech, maybe.

*Enter 2 drug clerks.* ‸(To give time for Reporter to get home and back again.‸

*1st*—Well, you *have* done it!

2$^{d}$—I know it, I know it, but <curse> ↑confound↓ him I thought of course he'd go home to take it.

*1st*—What did they say there?

2$^{d}$—The black half-idiot that came to the door said he hadn't been <there> home to-night.

*1st*—Did you say what you wanted with him? Did you show you were scared?

2$^{d}$—I bet I didn't. Am I a fool?

*1st*—Well, <all right.> ↑never mind about that. That's a matter of *de*tail.↓ There wasn't any body in the drug store when he bought it. We must keep dark and never let on that he came there. How much did you give him?

2[d]—O, <I> gave him enough to make him sleep two or three hours. I most wish I'd sold him poison sure enough.

*1st*—Well *I* don't.—Come, don't worry; I reckon there won't any harm come to him.

2[d]—There *wouldn't* if he'd gone home and gone to bed, like a Christian; but to go drowsing around with that dose in him, why he's bound to fetch up in the river or somewhere. <O> Lordy, it ain't so funny <a joke>, now, as it *was.*

*1st*—Well, come along (*going*) let's hunt further, but ask no questions. No matter what happens to-night, the thing for *us* to do is to keep mum.

*Exit.*

233:31–32 when my <Joshua> ↑Goliah↓ disappeared

233:37 You pray, sister <Spaulding> ↑Burnside.↓

236:1–2 I wouldn't a lost this item. <Come, now,> Lem, we've washed it all off of him pretty much—<there ain't anything to be afraid of—please let's hide him.> do you believe they'll suspect us if he's ever found?

*Tel*—(*Starting up*) Didn't you hear something? Quick, let's throw him in the brush and cover him up! (*They do so.*)> And the thing that grinds

236:30–31 <*Tel.*> *Lem*—With sealed lips from this sacred hour.

<*Tom*—Standing by each other through grief and misfortune—

*Lem*—Through grief and misfortune—

*Tom*—Privation and suffering—

*Lem*—Privation and suffering—

*Tom*—Suspicion and calumny—

*Lem*—Suspicion and calumny—

*Tom*—Persecution, <danger> peril and impending death—

*Lem*—Persecution, peril and impending death—‸It's beautiful!‸>

*Tom*—So, breast to breast, heart welded to heart—

237:12–17 ‸*Hugh*—(*Solus*)‸—So I didn't <poison> ↑quite manage to↓ <kill myself> ↑take enough,↓ after all! I'm <exceedingly> ↑most honestly↓ glad *of* it. <But those drug clerks will tell on me and> ↑If I don't turn up, that druggist will keep mighty still. If I *do* turn up, he'll tell on me and↓ the <town> ↑village↓ will ring ‸with derision‸ at my expense. (*Thinking*) I've got to mysteriously disap*pear*. <That's the idea!> Ah, that will be romantic! <Alas, must let this ‸humiliating‸ thing have time to blow over.> Ah, heartless Millicent

237:20–28 *Enter <wooden-legged> ↑limping↓ beggar in a cloud of rags, blue goggles, ‸cane,‸ false whiskers, sign on his breast "Pity the Poor Old Soldier" ‸—playing hand-organ.‸—singing (or not, as is best.)*

<"There was a woman etc.">

<This fellow has killed somebody.> [in margin.]

<‸Tramp, tramp, tramp the tramps are marching,
Cheer up comrades we will swarm
Where the people are not mean and philanthropists are green,
*And* the loathsome tramp is welcome as the morn.‸>

‸*Tramp*—(*solus*)—(*Good-humoredly*) <Blame it,> What show's <a> ‸an escaped‸ desperado got *here!* And yet they call this a land of Bibles! - - - - - <Mf! I've swindled one *more* gallows - - - - - by the skin of my teeth. - - - - Thousand dollars on my head. - - - - Mighty inconvenient place to put it. - - - - Druther have it in my pocket, two to one.> - - - - (*Examining himself*) - - - - - Mighty conspicuous disguise - - - - <couldn't do no better, though.> (*Starts off, grinding his organ.*) Just my luck, to have a thousand dollars on my head—and not a *red* where I can get *at* it!

*Enter Hugh.*

238:2–4 <*Poet*> ↑*Hugh*↓—I *mean* it. <I used to be a beggar <↑tramp↓> myself. I'm out of business and I'm going at it again.> ‸<But> I want to have a lark. I'll swap outfits with you and give you a trifle to boot.‸

*B*—<Is that honest?> ‸Honest injun?—no joking?‸

238:5–8 <*Poet* <↑*Hugh*↓>—There's no trade like it for quick money and easily made. I found that out. Come—make a price—I'll buy you out in detail—<clothes> rags, ∧cane,∧ goggles, ∧hurdy-gurdy,∧ lying <bill> placard, wooden leg and ∧all your∧ imaginary campaigns and <invented> ↑bogus↓ sufferings.>

<*Hugh*—Honest injun. Come—would>

*Hugh*—Honest injun. Come—would twenty-five dollars boot—

<*Beg*—(*Charmed, with admiration*)—O, dern ∧you,∧ you've been thar!

<*Poet*> ↑*Hugh*↓—O but haven't I, though! Say—would twenty-five dollars ∧boot∧—

*B.*—(*delighted*)—∧No but∧ will you though! Shake! (*They shake hands.*)

<*Poet*> ↑*Hugh*↓—Now you're to go *on,* you know—<*home*—and die.> You're to leave here instanter.—<and never come again>↑so as not to spoil my fun.↓—Is that ↑it↓agreed?>

*B.*—It's a whiz! <If you'll> ↑Mind you're to↓ gimme <your outfit.> ↑all the clothes you've got on.↓

*Hugh*—To the <very> last rag!

238:15–16 found his hat here <with three fresh blood spots on it.>

239:27 What does <the three blood spots on> ↑the bruised place on↓ his hat say?

239:30 It hurt him, <it fetched blood> ↑it jolted his insides all up,↓

240:17 Let me <Now in the detective stories, murders are mostly committed by left-handed men.—Detectives ∧most always∧ notice that <it's> the wound is made in a way that couldn't be made, only by a left-handed man. Very well. My course is plain. Let me> see—the parson [The disjunction evident in the opening words of this deletion results from the fact that MT here returned to the text of a previous draft after inserting several new pages of manuscript.]

241:17 (*Flies into the thicket.*)

<Run back to 40 (Enter Millicent.>

<Poet <↑Hugh↓>—<These clothes?> To the very last rag! Come into the woods here, and we'll exchange. ∧All I require of you is that you give me time to get well away before you stir out of the wood again.∧

*Exit Both.*>

[As the deletion indicates, this text and the subsequent scene originally followed immediately after 238:6–7.]

242:4 [The remainder of this scene has been completely rewritten. Preserved with the working notes are seven pages of manuscript which continue after Milly's speech with an earlier version.]

*Enter the Cousin.*

*Cous.*—Found at last! O, Millicent, where have you been? All the house-hold are uneasy about you.

*Mill*—(*frigidly*) O, *are* they!

*Cous*—Ah, Millicent, do not look so at me. *I* cannot have done you any wrong. My love for you is my only offense. But it is an honest, earnest love, and if you would only—

*Mill*—Do not talk to me of love. I cannot hear it.

*Cous*—But your father says—

*Mill*—Father me no fathers! I will listen to no one.

*Cousin*—If you knew the undeserved pain you inflict—

*Mill*—(*Snatching paper and pointing*)—There! Now leave me to my grief—torture me no more.

*Cous*—(*Glances at paper—his face lights up.*) (*Aside.*) If he will but *stay* gone—I am the heir! (*Aloud.*) I grieve with you. Poor, poor lad—I—(*putting handkerchief to eyes*)—

*Mill*—(*Eagerly*)—Did you love him?

*Cous*—How can you ask it? Were we not inseparable?

*Mill*—Yes, yes, it is true. (*Change of expression.*) That is, until—until—

*Cous*—I know what you mean. Until his suit began to prosper and mine to fail. We *could* not be comrades then. But I never *loved* him the less.

*Mill*—(*taking his hand.*) I have wronged you. —This moment I was hating all the world—you with the rest. But my heart is

[In the top margin at this point is the note "Hat drops off while boys are hiding the body."]

so torn, so wrung. None of them loved him—not one. You will be my friend. ^You will comfort me.^ You will talk to me about him. You will stay my fainting hopes—you will tell me he is not lost.

*Cous*—O, Millicent, now you are your own kind self again. Trust me—lean on me (*going*)—believe in me. He is not lost. You shall see him again.

^(*Poet thrusts out his head in time to hear Mill say*—^

*Mill*—My whole heart thanks you for these words. ^(*with beaming, thankful look up into his face.*)^

*Exit both.*

^*Poet*—O, perfidious! So soon! So soon! (*Reels off, supports himself against wing*^

<46 follows 40> [note in top margin]

<*Enter Poet as Beggar.*

(*Looking off.*)—Ah - - - - I don't like <that> the look of that altogether. They're coming back.>

^*and remains looking off, mumbling and grieving.*) (*or exit.*)^

*Enter Capt.* (*Scanning ground.*) They ^say they^ found his hat here with three fresh blood-spots on it. Now lemme see. Lemme put the clews together and see what we arrive at. He bought the pison. What would a common man draw from that? Why, the most obvious conclusion—that he was going to commit suicide. What would a <deep> detective, that naturally looks deeper into things, draw from it? Why that he was going to pison somebody else. Who is that somebody else? An ordinary man jumps to the most obvious conclusion—he's going to pison an enemy. But a detective don't. You don't fool a detective that way. A detective knows human beings better; *he* knows he's going to pison the very last person a common man would think of. Very well, now. Who is the unlikeliest person for this poet to pison? Lem - - - me see—his mother! Shucks, when you once get your clews well in hand, a thing that looks like a mystery first off, unrolls as clean and clear as crystal; and there ain't any more mystery about it. Now comes the blood spots on his hat. *Per*fectly plain, you see: started out to murder his mother and got murdered himself! Plain as day! Talk about your fascinating businesses—there's nothing that beg*ins* with detectiving, when you're born with a natural gift for it. Now let's see. The next question is, who murdered him? <(*While he*> (*Stands thinking, scratching his head, nodding it, shaking it, in perplexity*) <enter>

<*Enter* ∧*the*∧ *Beggar.*

∧*Beg.*—∧ (*Mumbling and grieving, discovers Capt.*) There's the old Capt! This mystery is a windfall for him. He's in his glory, now. His head is a perfect chaos of crazy reasonings by this time. It's an even bet that his genius will fasten this murder on the very last man in America that could have committed it. —∧Well, I'm in no danger from *him.*∧ I've got to keep my tongue still before everybody but de->

243:15–25 [Hugh's speech ends the revised scene (see note above) and at this point MT returned to the text of the earlier manuscript with appropriate deletions and revisions to make a smooth joint and to adapt the old text to the new circumstances.]

<tectives. Anybody else would recognize my voice in a minute.— (*Forgets the Capt. and comes mumbling and groaning on, with head down.*)>

*Capt.*—(*fastening his eagle eye on him*—<*watches him a while, then stealthily steals behind him and cla*> *aside*)—There's the the murderer, for a *million!* He's got the mark of Cain all over him. ∧(*Hugh forgets all about the Capt. and flourishes his stick* ∧*left-handed*∧ *vengefully in the direction of the retreating couple*)—Left-handed, too, by the holy poker!∧ Now would a detective go and nab him and put him on his guard? O, no! (*smiling*). He'd ask him questions that <don't ↑are miles away from the *real* subject and don't↓ seem to mean anything in the world—but they're deep—deep as the sea! <If a ∧true∧ detective wanted to find out whether you was a professor of religion or not, would he come right out and ask you? O, no—excuse me. He would begin away off yonder

som'ers—he would ask you if your great grandmother on your father's side had ever had the small-pox.> (*Aloud.*) Ah - - - - I say, friend, have you seen anything ‸of an‸ old yellow tom cat going along here with a blue velvet collar on? (*Aside*) I've got my eye on him.

244:28–29 *murdered* here, last night! <(*Aside*)—My land, see him jump! O, I've nailed him, sure! This is the biggest job I ever done in my life. I'll be known all over America for this.> ↑(*Hugh gives a start but looks pleased*).↓

245:1 *Hugh*—<That's> O, yes. That's my line. <A faggot a meal.> ↑Hot grub required—and a napkin.↓

<*Capt.*—O, I don't want to wear you *out.* Half o' that'll be satisfactry. You come along—I'll show you my shanty. (*Going.*) ‸(*Aside.*)‸ O, this is a deep devil! Twon't do to hurry things with *him.* But I'll play him ‸a week or two‸ same as a cat plays a mouse, and first thing he knows I'll nail him!

(*Exit both.*)

(*Tramp grinding his organ exits before Capt.*)

CURTAIN>

247:10–23 *Enter Capt.* <*Swash*> ↑*Wheeler,*↓ ‸*followed by his wife, knitting.*‸ (*"disguised"*) *as a* ‸*pigtailed*‸ *old sailor* ‸*fashion of 18th cent. green patch over eye.*‸ *Goes through the same pantomime, with earnest solemnity. Exits the same way,* ‸*his wife following.*‸ *After a moment comes deeply musing back again,* ‸*his wife following.*‸<(*Solus*). I've had my eye on <him> <↑a certain person↓> <↑tramp↓> for 2 weeks, day and night, ‸Jenny,‸ in one disguise or another.> I'm a drawing the toils <around him> ↑closer and closer around that tramp, Jenny; it's been a pretty satisfactory 3 weeks' work.↓ Gimme a year and I've got him, sure. If I do it, it'll give me the biggest name in America. ‸It'll spread to England—it'll be put in books!‸

<*Mrs. S.*—<Couldn't you tell me who 'tis, just this once, Neddy?>

*Swash*—Twon't do, Nancy. —You know I always keep

these little things to myself. Women's made different from men. They can't seem to enter into detective business.

*Mrs. S.* <↑*W*↓>—I <reckon you're right, Neddy. Your mostly always right.> <↑always said you'd make a name, and you *will,* Gideon.<I> <↑Gideon, I do↓> <wish you was> <↑were↓> ↑Mrs. W.—Simon, I do wish you were↓ in a bigger place, where your talents could get a <show> <↑chance.↓>

*Capt.*—That'll come by and by, <Nancy> ↑Jenny↓, you rest easy about that.

*Mrs. S.*—I ain't a bit uneasy about it, <Neddy> ↑Gideon.↓ <Be ‸sure and‸ careful and don't make any mistake this time.>

‸*Mrs. W.*—That's good.‸ You feel pretty sure about this fellow, <don't you?> I reckon?

*Capt.*—More and more sure everyday, honey! It's pretty tough <to England—it'll be put in books.> It's pretty tough to be pitted agin the. . . .

248:24–26 *knocks half the matches out of his box—passes one.*)

<*Simon*—Thanks, shipmet, thanks—and good-day to you.

*Char*—Good-day. (*Going.*) <Exit> (*Aside.*) I am faint and sick!

*Exit exhibiting it.*

*Capt.*—(*Solus*). (*After a thoughtful pause.*) He startles too *natural. He* ain't the murderer.>

<↑*Simon*—Thanks, shipmet. Goin' a fishin'?

*Chas.*—No. Going up here . . . to . . . They say there's been a . . . *body* found.

*Capt.*—<(*interested*)>—*Dead* one?

*Chas.*—I suppose so. (*Going.*) Everybody's flocking there. (*Aside.*)—What a sickening shock he gave me!

*Exit.*

*Capt.*—(*Solus.*)—‸*He* startles too natural—he ain't the murderer.‸ *Body* found. (*Stands deeply pondering.*) M'f! Who's lost a *body?*↓>

*Simon W.*—Thanks, shipmet. Goin' a fishin'?

249:8–12 [The brief encounter with Lem originally followed the long conversation with Tom (see below). During revision, it was shifted to this point in the manuscript. To make a smooth joint, the following passage was deleted at the top of the sheet containing the Lem encounter.]

*Tom*—O lordy!—O I just *knew* it!

*Exit staggering.*

[Compare 252:32–34]

249:13–14 that's the skip/spring of *innocence.* <*He* ain't the murderer. —It's that *tramp*—I'm nearly dead sure of it, now. I'll go and hunt him up and bullyrag him a bit.

*Exit.*>

∧*He* ain't the murderer.∧

[See also 249:26–27]

249:26–27 *He* ain't the murderer. <(*Aloud.*) Get up!> ∧It's that *tramp.* I'm nearly dead *sure* of it, now. (*Aloud.*)—Get up!∧

251:5–6 4. Can't bear the sight of his hat <with the blood on it> —when Billings. . . .

251:22–24 5. She won't go near the spot where the <blood stained> hat was found. ∧6th and ∧ blackest sign of all, she has taken a ∧class in∧ Sunday school <class>. <Bullet's comment, in his own words, is, "Formerly she always shook the Sunday School.">

252:23 thoroughly worked out. <He told me this much, though: They've always had a hymn book—a Plymouth Collection—at Mr. Griswold's, and lately it has mysteriously disappeared. There's *one* thing I know—all the churches in town are out of hymn-books, but *Bullet* ain't.>

252:35–253:4 *Enter Mrs. Higgins followed by the Griswolds, Millicent, Clara and her mother, ∧Chas, Lem,∧ <and> the 3 detectives ∧and the tramp.∧ Mrs. H. out of breath. ∧The crowd crowd around her.∧*

*Mrs. H* (*Sitting down.*) <O, I'm clean out of breath!> ∧I'll tell you in a minute.∧ I've run every jump of the way. <Just let me breathe a minute.>

*Griswold*—<What is it, Mrs. Higgins?>—What *is* this important news?

<*Mrs. Higgins*—Give me just a minute—prepare yourselves.

*Mrs. G.*—O dreadful! Is it bad news?

(*Enter Charley* <*and Tom*> *and Lem,* ∧*hurriedly,*∧ *but not in company—just as they reach the group*)—

*Enter Capt.* ∧(*Still as a sailor?*)∧>

*Mrs. H.*—∧O dear, Mrs. Burnside,∧ <prepare yourself.>∧—They've found the body!

253:22–23 *Tramp*—(*Aside.*) ∧It's *delicious*∧ <This is delicious! How could I ever have expected> to be <such a hero and be> grieved for like this. <I wouldn't swap places with a king on his throne. I tell you. It even makes my eyes moist.> (*Touches eyes with a rag.*)

253:32–33 appreciated what I was! <But *she,* she hasn't a word of kindness for the poor heart she coldly drove to <his> death.>

254:11 *in crying now.*)

<*Clara*—(*Goes to Chas.*) (*Coldly and accusingly*)>

<↑*Chas.*—(*to Clara who is passing near him*)—O, Clara, won't you speak to me?↓>

[See 254:30–31.]

255:21 had escaped and <probably came this way, and begged you to have the country scoured for him>—

255:26 *Char.*—<(*Aside.*)—Thank God for that!> ↑Have some pity!↓

255:28–29 indifferent like you? <Would he have deserted me in my misfortune? Would he have sung suspicion to sleep and opened wide the road for the assassin's escape? No—he would have roused this whole region! he would have been my constant stay, my support, I should have found hope and peace in the generous shelter of his love; he would have *closed* the gates <upon> before the escaping <assassin> ↑miscreant,↓ not opened them to him and paralyzed pursuit—> ∧No∧—for (*scornfully*) there. . . .

258:15–18 [See note below, 259:37. The intervening scene with the newsboy, Capt. Wheeler, and Policeman Long was added during the final revision.]

*Exit officer.*

259:37 <News boy extra. <Tom> Lem—tother paper's got it!> [Cancelled note in top margin.]

<*Billings*—<(*Aside.*)> ∧*to Bullet*∧—Going to be a fight!

*Bullet*—Looks like it!

*Exit both, quick.*>

267:19–21 *pass close to Chas.*

<*Mr. Gris*>

<*Mill*—<Poor> Ah, Charley, <you look worn and sad enough.> this is a heavy day for us all! ∧You are going?∧

*Chas*—None feels that more than I do, I am sure.

*Mr. Gris*—(Significantly)—There is slender reason to doubt *that.*

*Mrs. Gris*—(*low voice*) For shame, Horace!

*Mill*—Yes, Charley loved him like a brother and always treated him like one.

*Mr. G.*—(*low voice*)—Cain, for instance! (*Aloud.*) The funeral is preparing. (*Significantly.*) I suppose you'll go.>

∧*Mr. G.*—(*low voice*)—You are going?∧

267:25–26 *Mrs. G.*—(*low voice*) Horace, you are <brutal!> ↑*cruel!*↓

<*Mr. G.*—Thanks. I (*low voice*) like to see the rascal <squirm!> ↑wince!↓> (*They turn aside. . . .*

281:26 *Tr*—I'm ∧Jack∧ Belford <*Brothers,* of Toronto!> ∧the fugitive desperado!∧

<*Cap*—Gimme>

282:1 <↑*Cap*—∧(*Aside*)∧ I'm glad he's so willing—there's a thousand dollars reward on↓>

↑*Cap*—Gimme your hand—you're the whitest↓

282:5 once suspected it. —<Why there's a thousand dollars reward on his head. ∧(*Aloud.*) I wish you'd confessed a day or two ago.

*Tramp*—Why?

*Cap*—Because then you'd a told me where to look for poor Burnside's body and I'd a got the reward.

*Tramp*—I'm sorry I didn't. Who *did* get the money?

*Cap*—A rich old miser here, named Tupper, *will* get it—he found the body. Do you know he was a going to go right straight to that poor broken-hearted woman and collect, but the boys told him if he didn't wait a week for decency's sake they'd hang him. - - - - By George, old fellow this is a big day for me! You're sure you don't repent?∧>

282:7 Look here, <Brothers,> ↑Belford,↓

282:16 Give us your hand, <Brothers!> ↑Jack!↓

285:26–27 (*Sensation—murmurs.*)

<Mrs. Griswold—*What,* my child! O! (*Running to her.*)

*Mr. Gris*—This is stupendous>

<No, they run in just as Chas confesses.>

*Mrs. Hig*—What a wooden *fool!*

287:17–23 backing you agin the field! ∧*I,* detective <Swash!> ↑Wheeler!↓ (*Stripping off dress etc.*) Your claims lays over 'em *all!* And who do you reckon he *is?* (*looking around*). Stand by for a surge!—stay in your clothes if you can!—It's the bloody desperado ∧Jack∧ Belford <Brothers>! (*Tremendous sensation—people crowd away from him.*) <The> It's the black-souled <Canadian> pirate him*self!*—disguised like an honest man! *He* done it! ∧Judge he done it.

288:24 the desperado ∧<Brothers> ↑Belford↓∧,

"Simon Wheeler, Detective":

312:18–19 [Between this and the next paragraph, the following paragraph has been deleted.]

It was a Saturday afternoon in summer, and the sun was sinking fast. The villagers were out in force; the weather was too fine to be wasted. Groups and couples, in the lightest of summer raiment, were distributed along the <eastern> bank of the stream, from the village all the way up into the gorge, a mile and a half away—for this was the favorite promenade. Some sat in the shade of the rocks and trees, some walked. Some gossiped, some courted, some romped, some dozed or knitted or mused, according to age, sex or disposition.

314:34–35 [Between this and the next paragraph, the following passage has been deleted.]

For a month there had been a guest in the house—Charley Dexter, aged twenty-four or twenty-five; dark, <han> compact, muscular, manly, a spirited fellow, intelligent and educated. <He was from a Missouri town some fifty m> ↑His home was in Kentucky,↓ <but he was latterly from> ↑but for some months had been↓ visiting various families of relatives and old friends of his parents in several parts of Missouri. He had spent more than two months in Guilford, with his aunt the widow Burnside, before extending his visit to the Griswolds, where he was to remain as long. He was not related to the Griswolds, but Mrs. Griswold and his mother had been school mates in girlhood and devoted friends and neighbors in early married life. During the three months and upwards which he had now spent in Guilford, Mrs. Griswold had grown to be as fond of him as if he had been her son, and to treat him accordingly.

315:28 <"It is young Charley D> "It is Mrs. Burnside's nephew—young <Charley> ∧Hale∧ Dexter."

316:15 of <Charley> ∧Hale∧ Dexter's father

316:26–27 drink nor sleep till I have <killed> ∧warned∧ my sister's husband ∧and called him out and killed him.'∧

318:32–34 friends <waylaid> ∧met∧ me ∧unexpectedly∧ on the road, once, when I was twenty-five. ∧I drew—they did the same.∧ Dexter came

319:16 fortune will make <Charles> ↑Hale↓ very rich."

319:25 waiting for <Charles> ↑Hale↓ to die.

319:26 When is <young Charles> ∧Hale∧ coming here?"

320:7 except that <Charles> ∧Hale∧ mentions,

336:26–27 [Between this and the next paragraph the following passage has been deleted.]

<"I have formed none."

"You will give him a full and equal chance with yourself?"

"Sir!"

<"There—you must pardon it. It expressed more than I meant.>

"Good. You *are* a Dexter. I know it now. Don't be offended. I had only the merest shade of a misgiving—it is gone, now."

"What gave it you?"

"A sentence in>

338:25 of arranging the matter. <Toby is shrewd and reliable. He shall serve in my place.> I have a friend

372:12–14 As for Hugh ‸the romantic,‸ there was one little lack, his bliss could not be absolutely perfect until <he should save Milly's life in some blood-curdling way. His opportunity came presently, when he was least expecting it.> ↑that lack should be supplied. The time quickly came for the eradication of this single defect.↓

401:19–21 "I know it," said Dexter, with dull despair in his voice; "the sight of me would become unendurable to them."

<"Therefore, remain where you are. Make yourself a comfort to them."

"I? I cannot go near them. <They would> I, comfort them? I, talk with them about this awful thing, with this grisly secret in my heart? They would speak of his 'assassin'—that is the word they would use. They would wonder to see me labor in my talk; they would marvel to see me always struggling to get away from the subject. I should go mad! Put yourself in my place."

Judge Griswold had to confess that the case was more difficult than it had seemed before. Presently Dexter said, with something like a groan—> ↑Presently he added: "See how I am placed!↓ I was to have removed

411:32 Hugh had <matured his plans for a romantic, mysterious disappearance> been thinking diligently

417:18 rose and advanced. <Mrs. Burnside began in a> There was a trying

419:30–31 [From this point to 420:14, the text has been adapted by means of much deletion from an earlier state of the manuscript.]
a servant.
<It was well for Dexter that the candle light was dim; none saw the effect of this speech upon him. He stammered out his thanks <and an> and a protest against dislodging Hugh, but Mrs. Burnside said—
"No, Hugh will not mind it, it will gratify him. Besides, it is all settled and we won't have it any other way.">
After a little more conversation
[Compare 419:3–8.]

420:4 Then Dexter <turned> <turned a lusterless eye upon the Judge, and said, with a heavy sigh—
"You have seen, you have heard. Their restored> said in a voice

420:12 But all that is <at an end. You see how they are going to suffer. Shall they bear the whole burden of a calamity which nothing but my criminal heedlessness has brought upon them? I will not desert, but stand my ground, do my best to help them, and live through these horrors that will begin for me to-day if I can.> at an end.

422:12 Mind, <only generalized your course?">
<These first days are going to be the hardest. The finding of the body, the public excitement, the inquest, the funeral,—if you can endure these first days all is safe; those that follow will grow gradually easier. <By and by they> Mind,> you will be often
[This deletion results from the insertion at this point in the text of three pages from an earlier state of the manuscript. Apparently, in revision, MT decided to attribute to Dexter the sentiments expressed in this deleted passage; compare 422:1–10.]

speak the dreadful word."
426:25 <So <Dexter> he added to the advertisement the word>

426:35– [See next note.]

427:1 by any modifying name.

<"remains." Clara sat by watching, but said nothing. That is, aloud—though to herself she said: "This is the death of hope; he made no protest against that word. His good generous heart has made him say his hopeful things out of pity for us. But now I know that he, too, believes the poor boy is dead. I will be silent, for he is suffering much for our sakes, poor Hale!">

^It cost Dexter a pang to add to the advertisement the lacking word "remains," but he had to do it.^

<Yes, much more than she imagined.>

Why the body was not found

[Above this deletion, at the top of MS p. 439, renumbered 439½, MT wrote the note "No, he protests vigorously." In revision, he cancelled two lines at the bottom of MS p. 438 (see note 426:25), inserted a new p. 439 to provide the vigorous protest, and deleted the above passage.]

429:34–36 to argue the case.

<When Judge Griswold saw Dexter's advertisement, he wrote—

"It will help to throw the dogs of the law off the scent. It was a bold and ingenious conception, but I am not glad you have done it. In>

Dexter's instinct suggested